DANGEROUS PASSION

"Please don't make me do this," she pleaded. "I — I'm afraid. I've never been with a man."

"Well, I hope not. Because if you have, you're not a virgin, and your virginity is what you offered, isn't it?"

"Oh, please, Captain. . . ." The blood was pounding in her head, making her feel faint and shivery.

"Ty . . . call me Tiger. Captain is much too formal a title to use in bed. . . . Better yet, call me sweetheart . . . darling . . . beloved . . . whatever best expresses your tender feelings."

"Bastard!" she blurted out.

He infuriated her by laughing. "Do you always say what you think, Mouse? Your honesty would be refreshing if it weren't so damaging to my ego. Come here. This doesn't have to be a terrible experience, you know."

Enough starlight spilled through the windows to illuminate his strong, masculine, powerful, and very naked body. This was how she had imagined him, stripped to the skin, but the reality frightened her as much it caused her heart to flutter wildly.

Dear God, could she really go through with this?

Stormswept

Katharine Kincaid

ZEBRA BOOKS
KENSINGTON PUBLISHING CORP.

For my grandmother,
Catherine Muenz,
With thanks for so many happy memories

ZEBRA BOOKS

are published by

Kensington Publishing Corp.
475 Park Avenue South
New York, NY 10016

Also by Katharine Kincaid:

Prologue

Boston, 1843

As Tiffin Adam Xavier Carrington exited the massive red brick school building, he saw the boys waiting for him in the school yard. There were eight of them, all bigger and older. The leader was half a head taller, dumb as an ox, and mean as a polecat, with fists the size of smoked hams.

Jules's quick intake of breath sounded loud behind him. "Dey's waitin' for us," Jules said in a low, scared voice, and Tiffin knew that his friend's eyes would be as round as dinner plates in his ebony-black face. "We's in for a whuppin' now, Marse Tif."

"They won't touch you, Jules," Tiffin assured his friend, hoping it was true. "You're the reason they're waitin'. They think I beat you mornin' and night, and while I eat roast beef, you only get gruel."

"I wish we was home right now eatin' gruel." Jules clung to Tiffin's coattail, his breath hot on his friend's neck.

"So do I," Tiffin agreed, only he meant Cypress Hall in Wilmington, North Carolina, not the Boston home of his spinster Aunt Clara.

He had never wanted to come north for his schooling, but his mother had insisted. After the death of his father—kind, portly Adam Xavier Carrington—Tiffin's mother, known throughout the Carolinas as Lady Tiffin, the English Camellia, had wanted to get rid of him as soon as possible. "Li'l Tif's such a nuisance," she would often complain with a languid sigh. "Why, jus' by livin' an' breathin', he's proof positive that ah'm growin' old. How'm ah evah gonna find another husband if everyone far an' wide knows ah'm old enough to have a nine-year-old son?"

The mere idea of anyone thinking his mother was old astounded Tiffin; Lady Tiffin had long white-blond hair and enormous fringed eyes the color of violets in the springtime. It was the same unusual coloring he had, only on him the effect was startling. People were always looking twice to see if he was a girl, then thought it a pity he wasn't. They said they couldn't believe his mother had borne a child already; she herself looked barely out of the schoolroom. Even before Tiffin's father had been killed jumping a stone wall on his favorite English hunter, men were always flocking around his beautiful, young mother. Papa had been the one who was old; his hair had been the color of pewter, but he had been gentle, wise, and affectionate, and Tiffin missed him terribly—never more than right this minute. If his father were still alive, he would not be in this predicament.

"Mama, I hate you for sendin' me north," Tiffin muttered under his breath. Balling his fists, he reluctantly approached the waiting gang, knowing he must fight, as he always had to do to prove he was no sissy—and no slaver, either.

"Where'd you git them yellah-white curls?" one of his tormentors taunted. "I ain't never seen no boy with hair that color before."

"Lookit how he's got his nigger slave followin' right

8

on his heels. Don't you know it's a sin to keep slaves, boy?"

"What kind of a name is *Tiffin?* Why'd your ma give you a girl's name?"

"She give it to him 'cause he not only looks like a girl, he talks like one. How're you doin' this fine day, Marse Tiffin?"

Tiffin ignored the insults. He'd heard them all before. But he'd never had to fight so many boys at one time—or boys so much older and bigger. Spying a rock on the cobblestones of the school yard, he bent and picked it up. With his hand curled tightly around the rock, he felt better. At least, he now had a weapon, even if he was still outnumbered eight to one.

"Don't be scared, Jules," he whispered. "They're jus' poor white trash. I'll thrash 'em good, and we'll be outta here in no time."

"Who you callin' trash?" the biggest boy demanded.

Tiffin looked him over carefully. The ham-fisted boy had reddish-colored hair, freckles, crude features, and a coat that showed two inches of wrist. Knowing he was better dressed, better schooled, better bred, and hopefully, a better fighter, Tiffin tilted his head and looked down his nose at the ringleader.

"Ah'm callin' *you* trash, cracker," he goaded in his softly slurred Carolina accent. "You can't even take me alone; you had to bring all your friends along to help."

"You got your nigger," the big boy said, nodding at Jules.

"It's my job to protect him, not the other way around," Tiffin coolly informed him.

"Don't rile 'im. Oh, please don't rile him, Marse Tif," Jules pleaded into Tiffin's shirt collar.

"Hey, lookit that black boy beg!"

"You leave him out of it," Tiffin said. "He's nothin'

9

to you."

"Damn right he ain't. You're the one we want. Tiffin A. Carrington, the stuck-up Carolina slaver who thinks he's better than anybody else."

"I'm not a slaver. We don't keep slaves at Cypress Hall."

"Then how's come you got that colored boy trailin' after you wherever you go?"

Tiffin didn't answer. These tough Irish Bostonians, sons of common laborers, or "potato eaters" as Aunt Clara called them, would never understand the concept of a Southern gentleman's manservant, much less accept the fact that Jules was his dearest, closest friend — his *only* friend in all of Boston, if the truth be known.

"Spread out, lads, so he can't get past us," the big boy directed.

The other boys did, encircling Tiffin and Jules in a tight ring from which there was no escape. Tiffin looked through the wrought iron gates but saw no one on the street outside. He glanced back at the school. The big red building stood still and silent in the waning, gray afternoon. Teachers and students had all gone home. He and Jules had been lucky not to have been locked inside — or maybe unlucky. Tiffin had been reading a book about sailing ships in the deserted Reading Room and had forgotten about the time. Besides, the longer he stayed away from Aunt Clara's, the happier the old lady was.

Now, there was no hope for it; he was going to have to fight, and he'd probably get beaten to a pulp again. Whatever happened, he'd fight like a tiger. He'd seen a tiger once, confined to a cage in a traveling show. How fierce and defiant it had looked, all tawny, rippling muscles and flashing claws, spitting fury at the onlookers. If he had his way, that's what people would call him, Tiger Carrington, and no one would dare pick a fight with him. He held the image of the tiger in his mind, and it gave him courage, blotting out his fear.

"Here, Jules," he hissed under his breath, furtively reaching one hand behind his back. "Take my rock. You might need it."

"Oh, Lawdy," Jules half sobbed, accepting it with trembling hands. "We ain't nevah gonna see No'th Carolina a'gin."

"Yes, we will. I'll go after the biggest one—the red-head. I'll make him wish he never came after us. First chance you get, run home an' tell Aunt Clara."

"She ain't gonna like dis. She don't like us nohow."

"Jus' run. Run an' get help."

"Oh, Lawd, have mercy!" Jules whimpered.

The next moment, the gang attacked.

On the other side of Boston, in a shabby row house, a young woman knew nothing of a small boy's desperate fight to save his honor, his life, and his Negro man-servant. She was too involved in her own frantic struggle to bring a child into the world. Her husband, a tall, gaunt minister in patched and faded frock coat, bent over her, exhorting her not to give up.

"Push, Agnes, push! If you don't try harder, you'll never birth this young 'un."

The frail, wan figure on the bed merely moaned. "I can't push no more, Augustus. . . . I'm plumb tuckered out. It don't do no good anyhow. The babe must be turned wrong, or it would already've been born."

"Then I'll go fetch the midwife, if you're sure you can't do it on your own."

"Don't go. . . ." the young woman pleaded in a cracked whisper. "No tellin' if I'll still be here by the

11

time you get back. Sit here and talk to me instead. Tell me 'bout The Cause; your talkin' always could ease my mind and make me forget my aches and pains. Maybe it'll help now."

The minister sat down on the edge of the cornhusk mattress and ran long, bony fingers through his thinning brown hair. He did not know what to do. He had no money to pay a midwife or a doctor. Every penny of the meager income he gained from preaching went to benefit The Cause. He doubted a midwife could even help his precious Agnes. She had been laboring for over twenty-four hours, and all that had come out was blood. Despite his devotion, despite their many sacrifices, God had forsaken them. Never had such dark despair pressed so close on every side.

"The Cause, Augustus . . ." his wife reminded, her lips twitching in agony. "Tell me 'bout The Cause."

" 'Tis a dream I have, Agnes, a wonderful dream. The good Lord put it into my head ere I was just a lad, and I've been chasin' it ever since. . . . You see, He put me here for a grand and noble purpose, to help free the darkies enslaved in the South. In my dream, all God's children, black-skinned and white, are livin' an' workin' t'gether as equals, side by side, goin' to schools t'gether, plantin' crops, worshippin' in the same fine churches. . . ."

"An Eden, a paradise on earth . . ." Agnes prompted dreamily. A moment later, she clawed the sheets and cried out, her swollen abdomen arching on the blood-drenched bed.

Augustus grabbed her hand and held it to his sunken chest. "Yes, an Eden! Where the lion lies down with the lamb and the shepherd need not fear for his sheep. A land of freedom—like it says in the cawnstitution—only this freedom applies to all."

"God help me, it's comin'! I think it's comin' at long

last! Keep talkin', Augustus. . . . Oh, please keep talkin'!"

So Augustus gripped his wife's hand and talked their baby into the world. It was the best sermon he'd ever given, and if all the wicked slave-masters in the South could have heard it, they would have freed their poor captives from bondage that very afternoon. The baby was a girl, slicked with her mother's blood, and as he cleaned and bathed her, Augustus continued preaching, introducing his offspring to The Cause.

"There now," he said when the job was done. "Isn't she pretty, Agnes? When she's grown, she'll be pretty as you, I'll wager."

He lifted the child from the washstand, wrapped her in a tattered piece of quilt, and carried her back to the bed. Agnes's eyes were closed. She appeared to be sleeping. Relief flooded Augustus; he thanked God his wife's pain had ended. When the blood was mopped up from the floor, the bed linens changed, and Agnes herself washed, the dreadful, long ordeal would be over.

Holding out the baby so Agnes could see it, he studied his wife's pale face. She was calm now, relaxed, her features still graced with that rare, fine beauty that had once made men pause on the street to gaze at her in wonder. Their daughter possessed the same fragile bone structure, the same silky brown hair, the rosebud mouth, the tender air of innocence.

"I think we should call her Freedom," he murmured, peering at Agnes for approval. "Freedom Walker. 'Tis a fitting name; she, too, will be one of God's messengers, an instrument working for The Cause. Our daughter will be a force against evil, a light glowing in the darkness, a true handmaiden of the Lord. . . . Doesn't that excite you, Agnes? Think of it! We've created another brave soldier for God's

13

holy war on wickedness!"

Augustus reached down and lifted his wife's curled hand. It was cool and damp. When he let go, the hand fell limply upon the bloody sheets. "Agnes? . . . Agnes!"

His anguished cries startled the infant and she began to bawl lustily, belying her fragile appearance. Freedom Walker screwed up her tiny features, waved her tiny arms, and howled as if she knew her mother had deserted her barely moments after her first-drawn breath. With tears spilling down his cheeks, Augustus sought to comfort the child, but rocking and crooning did not work. Finally, he did what he had always done to comfort her mother; he told her about The Cause. As soon as he began to speak, the baby's cries abruptly ceased. Her dazed eyes blinked. She listened to her father, enraptured, and The Cause claimed her for its own.

Chapter One

Wilmington, North Carolina
April, 1863

"G'bye, Marse Ty. Go wid God."

"Good-bye, Jules. Take care of things at Cypress Hall. . . . Oh, and don't forget to give Mama those gloves and that fan I picked up for her yesterday. Tell her I'm sorry to miss her birthday, but if I don't make it past the blockade tonight, it might be next month before there's another moonless night."

"Ah'll tell 'er, Marse Ty. Ah'm sure she understan'."

"Don't bet on it, Jules. . . . Somehow, Mama's managed to ignore the fact there's a war going on. If it weren't for the loss of her little luxuries, she'd pretend everything was just as it's always been."

Knowing he might never see his friend again, Tiger Carrington shook Jules's big hand and smiled into his dark, worried eyes. Ty was a head taller than Jules, but Jules was built like a barn door and had finally learned to use his awesome strength to good advantage, just as Ty had learned to fight like a tiger, earning the sobriquet everyone had called him for so many years now that scarcely anyone even remembered his real name anymore. Ty gave thanks everyday for hav-

15

ing someone as loyal, strong, and dependable as Jules to oversee his affairs at Cypress Hall. Otherwise, he could never go off and leave his estate in his mother's hands; she couldn't manage getting her own breakfast, much less worrying about someone else's.

"If something happens and I don't make it back, move Mama into Wilmington, Jules. Close up the big house until this insanity is over. She's got friends in town who'll look after her. Encourage the household staff and field hands to seek work at other plantations. Without Mama to worry about, you, Elvira, and whoever else is left ought to be able to keep body and soul together."

"Won't none of the staff or field hands want to leave Cypress Hall, Marse Ty. You knows dat. Dey's ready to work foh nothin', if need be, b'fore dis war is ovah. . . ."

"Well, I hope it won't come to that. . . . If I can get the rest of my cotton through the blockade tonight, I can hang on a while longer."

"Dis be your last run, Marse Ty?"

"No, Jules . . . It's only my last run carrying Cypress Hall cotton — at least 'til next crop. After this, I'll carry whatever cargo I can get that will enable me to keep bringing back food, medicine, weapons, and ammunition. Just because I turned down a commission in the Confederate Navy doesn't mean I'm willing to let our people go hungry or Carolina boys die from lack of quinine. I'll run that damn blockade however many times I have to until the Rebels beat the damn Yanks."

"Don't you worry none 'bout Cypress Hall or Lady Tiffin, den. . . . Elvira and me'll look after 'em both and keep 'em safe 'til you comes home ag'in."

Tiger clapped his friend's broad shoulder. "With you in charge, I never worry, Jules . . . not even about

16

Mama. Why, Elvira handles Mama better than any-body. I swear that wife of yours could handle anyone ánd anything; it was a lucky day when you married her, my friend."

Jules's round black face split into a wide grin. "Dat's what *you* need, Marse Ty—a wife whut's good at handlin' thin's. Maybe after dis war be ovah, you can find time to court Miss Stephanie ag'in."

Ty jerked his head in denial. "If I find time to go courting again, it won't be Miss Stephanie, Jules. I've already told you. That's over and done with. Miss Stephanie and I have gone our separate ways."

Jules's smile disappeared. He shook his head disap-provingly. "Still don't understan' dat. . . . 'Peared to me you an' Miss Stephanie be made for each other."

"Appearances can be deceiving, Jules." Tiger clamped his jaws tightly together, unwilling to discuss the painful subject any further.

He had told no one, not even Jules, why he and Stephanie Clairmont had never married despite a long, passionate courtship. He'd caught her in a com-promising position with a dashing young lieutenant en route to defend Richmond. Though she'd wept and pled and sworn it didn't mean a thing, he had finally realized that flirtatious, beautiful Stephanie was cut from the same bolt of cloth as his mother. He'd never be able to trust her; she'd always be flirting with other men—or worse, and he'd wind up exactly like his fa-ther, drowning his sorrows in French cognac and tak-ing needless risks on his blooded horses.

"I've got to go," he said to Jules. "I want to reach Smithville while it's still light enough to see what the Federal guard dogs are doing out in the Cape. Too bad you can't stomach the sea; playing hare and hounds with the Yanks isn't all work, you know. It has its brighter moments. When I give 'em the slip, I feel as

17

good as I did when we were lads escaping the bullies."

" 'Cept we didn't always git away," Jules reminded him, grinning. "Good thing we learned to use our fists, or we wouldn't be aroun' to jaw about it. Naw, ah'm happy to be stayin' here on dry land. . . . You jus' hurry back, Marse Ty."

Tiger saluted Jules, then jumped onto the gangplank linking the shore with his ship, the *Sea Whisper,* a long, lean vessel painted gray and sporting two rakish funnels and two short, stubby masts. "Stoke her up down there!" he called below to the chief engineer. "The rest of you boys grab the lines and weigh anchor."

Only a dozen men leaped to follow his orders; that was all the crew Ty needed, for he was his own pilot, and if everyone did his job properly, the *Sea Whisper* responded beautifully. Shallow of draft, with a length eight times her beam, she had a hull so low it rose only a few feet out of the water, even when she wasn't loaded down with cotton. This gave her speed and maneuverability, so she could elude the deeper-draft Federal vessels waiting to pounce on her as she edged out of the Cape Fear River and nosed into the Atlantic, headed for Nassau in the Bahamas.

Ty had anchored slightly downstream of Wilmington, which occupied the east bank of the Cape Fear River twenty miles from where it flowed into the Atlantic at Cape Fear. He'd had business to attend to in town before making this run; otherwise, he would have stayed anchored farther upstream at Cypress Hall, which overlooked the river halfway between Wilmington and Fayetteville, in Bladen County.

Tiger loved Cypress Hall, and when he wasn't running the Federal blockade at Wilmington, he preferred to spend all his time there. His father and grandfather had built the initially modest holding into a thriving plantation, first by harvesting the tall pines and cypresses from which Cypress Hall took its name, then later by planting cotton. Despite his time in the North, which had all but eradicated his Southern drawl, Ty had kept his heart firmly entrenched in North Carolina. When he finally came home to Cypress Hall, he had promised himself never to leave it again. His mother had not remarried and in his absence, had almost driven the plantation into bankruptcy.

Were it not for Old Moses, the Negro overseer who had been a friend to Ty's father in much the same way that Jules was a friend to Ty, Tiger might have lost Cypress Hall to his mother's creditors. Lady Tiffin had no notion of what things cost, and even less notion of how to run a cotton plantation where the laborers were paid employees instead of slaves. As long as she could occupy her days with frivolous entertainments and visiting friends all over the Carolinas, she hadn't cared a fig what Moses did at home, so the old black man had faithfully run the plantation and held on as best he could until Tiger was ready to take over the responsibility.

Six long, hard years had passed before Ty had been able to pay off his mother's debts and make Cypress Hall profitable, then along had come the war to threaten everything once more. He dared not leave his mother to squander it all away again, so he had opted to do what he could for the Confederacy by becoming a blockade-runner. His first step had been to sell the serviceable little steamer, the *Cypress Queen,* which had plied the river with Cypress Hall cotton for years and years. Then he had invested in the sleek *Sea Whisper*, so he could outrun the Federalist gunboats and dart into coves and inlets where bigger ships could not follow. The *Whisper* had been built in Liverpool, England, and Ty had taken possession of her in Nassau.

There, British buyers eagerly awaited every cargo of cotton that arrived safely in port. The cotton mills in Lancashire were hungry for Southern cotton, and great fortunes could also be made on the goods brought back from Nassau.

But to Tiger, it never seemed enough. The *Whisper* had cost plenty, and his expenses at Cypress Hall were enormous compared to other plantations. Long before the war, his father had allowed Cypress Hall slaves to work off their purchase prices through periods of indentured labor, after which they were granted freedom and offered modestly paying jobs at the plantation. Usually, the workers remained, and virtually all were now receiving wages — an expense other plantations did not have and one which had made Ty's father and now Ty himself an object of local gossip and ridicule. Of course, no one dared say anything directly to his face, but he knew what people were thinking. They viewed him as an outsider or at the very least as an eccentric, to the point where in recent years many Carolina belles had actually shunned Ty as a potential husband.

Unbeknownst to everyone but Jules, Tiger nonetheless contributed heavily to the Confederate cause, for he sincerely believed in states' rights and saw no conflict between his abolitionist leanings and his loyalty to the South. If he himself wasn't willing to fight, he was at least willing to help finance the war effort and considered it his patriotic duty.

Every time he went out on a run, Ty brooded over how much depended upon his success. Iron, coal, textiles, medicines, and other necessities could no longer be bought and shipped overland from the North, and the North Atlantic Blockade Squadron was trying its damnedest to shut down the Southern sea routes through which such items could still be obtained.

Slowly but surely, the South was being squeezed to death; if it wasn't beaten on the battlefields, it would eventually die of starvation.

Thinking about what awaited him later that night made Ty perspire heavily, though the day was cool and pleasant. As the *Whisper* chugged down the river, he stood on deck and watched the pine-studded riverbanks glide past. The river was gradually widening from six hundred feet at Wilmington to over two miles at its mouth. Upon reaching Smithville, he had to decide which of two channels to use for the passage into the Cape. Smith Island divided the Cape Fear River into New Inlet on the north, protected by the guns of Fort Fisher, and Old Inlet on the south, guarded by the smaller Fort Caswell.

Both channels were watched by patrolling Federalists and rendered additionally hazardous by sandbars. Deciding which was the safest bet was always a gamble. Already, the slanted gold light on the river told Ty it was late afternoon. It would be twilight by the time he reached Smithville. With a curt nod at his helmsman, Pete Gambol, he ducked into the wheelhouse, retrieved his precious telescope, then called down the hatchway to his chief engineer, Stoker Harris.

"Don't forget, Stoker . . . I want to use the last of our anthracite for the run past the blockade. Once we're safely past it, we can switch to that god-awful bituminous that makes so damn much smoke. . . ."

"Aye, aye, sir," Stoker called up to him. "Sure hope we can pick up some good Welsh hard coal when we reach Nassau, or else we'll never make it past the blockade on the homeward run. . . . They'll spot our smoke for sure."

"Don't worry . . . If we make it to Nassau, we'll get the Welsh," Tiger assured him.

Coal was just one more thing he had to worry

about, one more reason why the South was at such a disadvantage in its war with the North. Clean-burning anthracite came only from the North, as did nearly everything else the South needed to wage a proper war. The South produced only soft, bituminous coal, whose smoke clogged engine parts and sometimes shut down engines entirely. Once, when his fuel was running low, he'd been reduced to using turpentine-soaked cotton in order to escape a pursuing Federal gunboat. The whole vessel had almost gone up in flame and smoke, but the ploy had produced a burst of steam that enabled the *Whisper* to escape. The episode made for good conversation over drinks in Nassau with his fellow blockade-runners, but it had scared Ty half to death, and now he practically counted his coal, lump by lump, to make certain he had what he needed.

Telescope in hand, he returned to the main deck and sat down on a bale of cotton in lieu of pacing, in which he couldn't indulge because the huge bales took up every inch of available space. While he sat, he planned what he would do in every conceivable circumstance he might encounter later on that night. It was impossible to prepare for all eventualities, but he had learned that a little forethought went a long way. Running the blockade was like playing chess; he must plan in advance how to counter each of his opponents' possible moves. Such moments of quiet introspection, when it appeared he was merely daydreaming, had more than once saved the skins of his crew members; they had thus learned to leave him alone when he was deep in thought. No one dared interrupt unless it was absolutely necessary, and on this pleasant April afternoon, not a single thing aboard the *Sea Whisper* proved worthy of Ty's immediate attention.

* * *

Not ten feet from Tiger, two pairs of eyes anxiously watched his every move. Two human beings, one a slender white female and the other a tall, muscular Negro, crouched in miserable, shared discomfort. Wedged so tightly between bales of cotton that they could hardly breathe, the stowaways could only communicate with their eyes. Freedom Walker thought she had never seen eyes as terrified as Omoroh's. Once, the big Negro had been a proud African ruler, but now he was a runaway slave, wanted for the murder of his white Georgian master. He was a fugitive from justice and so was Freedom, for helping him escape.

For Omoroh's sake, Freedom forced her stiff lips into an encouraging smile. In a few short hours, if everything went according to plan, she and Omoroh would be safe aboard a U.S. naval vessel bound for Boston, home at long last for her and safety for Omoroh, the last stop on his quest for freedom via the nearly defunct Underground Railroad. Assuring herself that everything would go according to plan, Freedom firmly clutched the small lantern, which she intended to use to signal the Federal fleet as soon as the *Sea Whisper* reached its vicinity.

While the captain and crew of the vessel concentrated on slipping past the sentinels guarding the entrance to the sea, Freedom intended to light her small lantern and dangle it over the side, alerting the Federal gunboats to the presence of the heavily laden blockade-runner. Once the Federalists spotted the *Whisper*, they'd be after her like a flash of lightning. Loaded down as she was with valuable cotton, the *Sea Whisper* didn't stand a chance. Freedom had resided long enough in Wilmington to learn about the fate of blockade-runners discovered too soon by the United States Navy.

For three years she had been living a lie, working at Hattie Draper's Fine Fashion Emporium, posing as a trimmer of bonnets and other ladies' sundries, while in reality she was a conductor on the Underground Railroad. Caught far from home at the outbreak of the war, she had been trapped in Wilmington. Her father had died four years before in the midst of a fiery sermon, but Freedom was nevertheless desperate to get out of the South. Omoroh's appearance one dark night had prompted her to concoct this wild scheme to rescue him, while at the same time attaining her own desire.

Because all the usual Northern routes were closed and had been since the war's outbreak, Freedom had been forced to consider the only transportation available, the blockade-runners bound for Nassau in the Bahamas or St. George in Bermuda. She had no idea where the *Sea Whisper* was headed; the striking blond-haired captain had never mentioned his destination when he visited Mrs. Draper's shop the day before. His purpose had been to buy a pair of gloves and a fancy lace fan. While there, he had met an acquaintance purchasing a vial of outrageously expensive perfume. The two men had stood together in the shop discussing the business of blockade-running and completely ignoring her and Mrs. Draper, as if two females could have no interest whatever in such clandestine activities. But Freedom had been all ears, recognizing at once that this was her and Omoroh's opportunity.

Later that night, she had discussed it with Mrs. Draper, whose frequent ill health prevented her from being as active a participant in the Underground Railroad as she might otherwise have been. Indeed, Mrs. Draper's ill health was the reason Freedom had come to Wilmington in the first place. After her father's sudden death, Freedom had been at loose ends, wanting more involvement in The Cause than she had thus far been permitted. Her father had occasionally helped fugitive slaves to find safe haven in Canada, but this had only been a sideline to his main work of preaching and publishing inflammatory tracts against slavery. Freedom had long wanted something more challenging, fulfilling, personal, and direct.

When she heard about poor Mrs. Draper down in North Carolina, who could not always properly assist the escaped slaves taking refuge in her cellar, Freedom had immediately volunteered to go to the old widow's aid. Despite her tender years—or perhaps because of them—the secret society to which her father belonged had decided that yes, Freedom Walker, then only seventeen years old, could assist Mrs. Draper at the Wilmington station of the Underground Railroad. During the last two years, however, few slaves had found their way to Mrs. Draper's cellar, and Freedom had spent most of her time trimming hats for Southern ladies.

She had grown increasingly frustrated and disappointed—and then Omoroh had shown up, a prime example of the tragedy and horror of slavery. Mrs. Draper hadn't wanted Freedom to stow away aboard the *Sea Whisper* with the tall, regal-looking Negro. Despite his tattered shirt, trousers, and rope sandals, Omoroh did indeed resemble a prince of Africa, and the old woman was certain both would be discovered before they ever got out of Wilmington. But sneaking aboard the vessel and hiding amongst the cotton bales had been easy, even fun. This was the sort of thing Freedom had dreamed about all of her young life. She was finally rescuing a slave—one who'd been beaten, tortured, and forced to watch his wife being raped by a cruel, lecherous master, an act that had incited him to kill the monster with his bare hands. Helping Omoroh

25

escape was adventure aplenty, but Freedom wasn't stopping there; no, she was also going to deliver a rare prize into the possession of the United States Navy. She was striking a blow for the Federalists and actually helping win the war . . . provided she didn't get caught, of course.

The minutes passed like hours as Freedom maintained her cramped position, not daring to move a muscle lest she catch the captain's eye. She stared at his rugged profile, silhouetted against the backdrop of a cotton bale, and admired his handsomeness. He had the most unusual coloring for a man — white-blond, curly hair, tawny, sun-bronzed skin, and startling violet-hued eyes, all of which she had noticed the day before and steadfastly ignored. But she couldn't ignore it now. Coloring like his belonged on a woman; she herself had always longed to be a fragile blonde, but there was nothing fragile or feminine about this man. If anything, he exuded raw strength and power, combined with a wholly male but feline, predatory grace.

The size of his muscles suggested that he hefted cotton bales all day long. His biceps fairly bulged, and his corded thighs stretched the fabric of his nankeen trousers almost obscenely. His tall, brown planter's boots must have been cut extra wide at the calf, for muscles abounded there also. The only narrow thing about him was his waist. He tapered in at the middle and his hips were correspondingly narrow, but otherwise, he gave the impression of bursting masculinity.

She shivered as she watched him stretch out one leg and study it as if a map were drawn upon his knee. What could he be thinking about? For a man about to take his life in his hands, he seemed remarkably calm and composed. But then he was a "Southern gentleman," a planter and a slaver, who made his living out of the sweat of other people's brows. Undoubtedly, he was accustomed to violence, if not personal danger. The cotton piled high on this vessel had come from a plantation somewhere upriver called Cypress Hall, or maybe it was Cypress Hill. She couldn't remember. She only knew that he was running the blockade tonight with his cotton and planning to bring back gunpowder so that Confederate soldiers could shoot Unionists and preserve the terrible institution of slavery in the South.

Suddenly, she hated him, hated all he stood for in his arrogant strength and startling beauty. Men like him were the reason men like Omoroh were forced to run, kill, starve, be beaten, and turned into hunted animals. If she had anything to say about it, the handsome captain of the *Sea Whisper* would sit out the rest of this war in a Federal prison. Why did President Lincoln want men like him to remain citizens of the United States, anyway? Southern planters would never change their minds about slavery; they'd always promote it because it suited their greedy, financial interests.

During her three years in Wilmington, Freedom had softened in her attitude toward Southerners. After all, Hattie Draper was a Southerner, born and bred, and *she* didn't believe in slavery. Nor did most of the women who came into the shop seem cruel or evil, though most of them *did* own slaves. Like women everywhere, the women of Wilmington were primarily concerned with domestic matters—running their households, looking after their menfolk and children. . . . Nowadays, they mostly talked about sons, husbands, brothers, and nephews dying in far-off battlefields, and how high the cost of a new bonnet had risen. Prices for everything were outrageous, and Freedom had even begun to feel sympathy for the beleaguered citizens of Wilmington.

But Omoroh's tragic story had reminded her anew how very much she despised the sort of lifestyle white Southerners led. This virile, blond blockade-runner was Omoroh's enemy and therefore *her* enemy; he was the vile instrument of the devil about whom her saintly father had ranted and raved. She remembered her father referring to big plantation owners as "whited sepulchers." This man, more than most, was indeed beautiful on the outside but surely rotten to the core on the inside. She couldn't wait to see his face when he learned he'd been betrayed by a Northern abolitionist — and a female, at that.

Leaning her head against the fluffy white cotton, Freedom stifled a large yawn. The heat of the sun and the close confinement were making her sleepy. She tried to stay awake, but her eyelids drooped, her shoulders slumped, and the next thing she knew, Omoroh's huge hand was on her shoulder, gently shaking her. She opened her eyes to utter darkness and the quiet clank of an anchor chain.

Then she heard the captain's low voice: "Are you ready, boys? It's time we made a run for it. . . . Remember, no lights and no sound . . . Snug that hood down over the binnacle, and make sure the tarpaulin is stretched tight over the fire hatch. . . . Good. Let's go, Pete. Ease her down the channel, and let's hope the hounds are looking the other way tonight."

Chapter Two

This was the moment of reckoning, and now that it had arrived, Tiger actually relished the danger and anticipation. At twilight, shortly after their arrival at Smithville, he'd been able to observe the dark, menacing shapes of the Federal cordon through his telescope. Some twenty ships were lying in wait on either side of Frying Pan Shoals; fortunately, they couldn't all come after him at once, even if they spotted him. The shoals prevented it. He had made the decision to depart the river under the guns of Fort Fisher, and because he was so heavily laden, he'd delayed until the tide rose. He wanted no difficulty getting over the bar that guarded the channel entrance.

The tide would be at its highest at eleven o'clock, and assuming the *Whisper* made it out safely, they'd be in the thick of the blockaders about five minutes after they crossed the bar. One last time, Ty checked his preparations: All lights were doused or concealed. Trustworthy leadsmen were stationed at the port and starboard chains, ready to take soundings he could rely upon, and his helmsman was at the wheel, awaiting whispered instructions. Ty did not adhere to the usual policy of dispensing immediate death to anyone who so much as lit a match aboard his vessel, but his crew members all understood the necessity of a complete and total blackout.

The only sound was the dull throbbing of the engines and the soft slap-slap of the paddle blades, which sounded deafening to Ty but were probably lost against the rush of surf breaking on the nearby beach. Cautiously, the *Sea Whisper* slid out into the channel. Shortly thereafter, she broached the bar, and Ty held his breath as the sounders signaled limited clearance. There was a slight bump and a scraping sound. For a moment, he thought they were hung up, but the chief engineer stoked the fire higher, and the extra push of steam drove the ship over the bar. As the *Whisper* settled into deeper water, Ty's straining ears picked up the collective sigh of relief from his crew.

He himself wanted to cheer as she started cutting through the white-flecked foam. Then he saw two long black shapes on the starboard bow and three others on the port. The *Sea Whisper* would have to thread her way between the waiting ships and skirt Frying Pan Shoals to reach the open sea. He had hoped to hug the shoreline for some distance but now realized that the hounds were anticipating such a plan on this moonless night; it might therefore be better to cut boldly through the center of the fleet and hope they never saw him. In vain, he searched for the single light identifying the vessel of the squadron's most senior officer.

In the earliest days of the blockade, the Federalists had guarded the coast with their lights blazing, making it an easy matter to slip past them undetected. Realizing the error, they had then taken to cruising and anchoring in darkness, like the runners, except for a lantern marking the vessel in authority. Thereafter, the runners had used that telltale light as a marker to get their bearings, but the Federalists must have discovered what they were doing, because the last time Ty was in the Bahamas, he had heard of a runner being lured onto a shoal by the soft glow of a lantern.

Tonight, he saw no lights anywhere. He knew the blockaders were out there, but he could only see the closest ones. He inhaled deeply of the salt-scented air, fancying he could detect the Federalists by smell or instinct. Sometimes, instinct was all he had to go by, and tonight seemed one of those nights. The *Sea Whisper* glided past the first dark shape. Straining to listen, Ty heard no sound of engine, except his own. He grinned with satisfaction. If they were spotted, it would take time for the big ships to get under way to pursue them.

As the *Whisper* approached another dark shape, an alien odor tickled his nostrils — sulfur, from a newly lit match! Tiger's first thought was that someone aboard the nearest blockader was lighting a cigar in defiance of orders; his second thought sent him leaping in the direction of the barest flicker of light visible between the stacked bales of cotton. Toppling bales helter-skelter, he came upon a scene he could hardly believe: two figures crouched over a lantern, one of them in the act of lighting it.

As he dove for the first figure, his helmsman dove for the second. His leadsmen dropped their chains and ran to assist. He and Pete tussled with the intruders, backing them against the heavy bales in a desperate effort to subdue them. One of the intruders was huge, taller than Ty, but Pete and the two leadsmen lost no time in wrestling him to the deck and holding him facedown so he couldn't sound the alarm. Ty's quarry was surprisingly small and lightweight; when Ty's fist glanced off his jaw, the figure slammed into a cotton bale and collapsed like a rag doll at Tiger's feet.

Before Ty could drag him up again and aim his blows more carefully, a rocket exploded overhead. "They've spotted us!" he cried. "All men to stations!

31

Pour on the steam and sail! Let's get the hell out of here!"

For the next hour and a half, Ty could spare no time for the Judas betrayers who'd tried to light a lantern to signal the Federal fleet—and succeeded. He was far too busy trying to elude twenty determined Union gunboats. The flare had come from a small, swift schooner; she continued to shoot off flares to tell her comrades which way Ty was running. Ty would have given anything for a few flares of his own, which he could have used to confuse the squadron.

The *Sea Whisper*'s single advantage was that she was already under full power, both steam and sail, while the pursuing gunboats had been lying at anchor—except for the little spotter with the cursed flares. He pushed the *Sea Whisper* to her limits, until she was cutting through the water at nearly fifteen knots, her top speed. The schooner began to fall behind, eliciting a storm of cheers from Tiger's crew.

When he had pulled far enough ahead as to be almost invisible to his pursuers, Ty abruptly cut his engines, hauled down his sails, and issued orders for total silence. His crew members sat on the stowaways to keep them quiet, and everyone waited breathlessly to see what the little spotter would do. She pounded past them, engines huffing, sails snapping in the stiff ocean breeze. Incredibly, when she was well ahead, she again shot off a flare, indicating to the rest of the fleet that they should follow her into open sea.

Ty did nothing until he was certain the hounds had raced by on their futile pursuit, while he saved his precious fuel for the long run to the Bahamas. Then he quietly restarted his engines, hoisted his auxiliary sails, and made for the shoreline, where the sound of his passage would be drowned out by the roar of the surf. Only when the *Sea Whisper* was out of danger did he give thought to the stowaways who had come so close to causing grave disaster.

"Bring them below, Pete. . . . Let's see who they are before we dump them overboard."

"Aye, aye, sir," Pete responded, relinquishing the wheel to an underling. "Go on, you two, git! Before ah dump y'all overboard mahself."

Freedom was near tears, sure the furious sea captain *was* going to callously kill them. For herself, she didn't care. Her body hurt in a dozen places and her jaw felt broken, but the worst injury had been done to her heart. She had failed to rescue Omoroh. And there was no telling what these slavers might do when they learned he was a runaway. One of them had to have seen the circular making the rounds in Wilmington; it contained a description of the big African, as well as a crude likeness—and, of course, a recitation of his heinous crimes. The noose had dropped around poor Omoroh's neck, and all that was needed was to tighten it.

The man called Pete forced them below deck into a cramped room and kicked shut the door before lighting a lantern. Freedom blinked against the flare of light, but didn't flinch or shy away from it. She'd face these two devils with every ounce of courage she possessed—and plead with them, too. For Omoroh's sake, not her own.

"Hell's bells, you're a woman!" the captain cried, holding up the lantern and shining it into her face. "Or I should say, a girl . . ."

"F—Freedom Walker," Freedom hesitantly introduced herself. "And my companion's name is—is Samson. You'll have to ask me your questions, because Samson is incapable of speech. His master cut out his tongue when he refused to learn the English language."

The captain's violet eyes widened, then he frowned suspiciously, as if he didn't believe her. "What language did he speak?"

"I'm not sure. Arabic, I think . . . Before he was caught by the slave-catchers and forced to come to North America, he was a prince in his own country."

"I'll bet," the captain drawled sarcastically.

"He was taken to Virginia, from whence he recently escaped," Freedom lied. "Yes, I'm sure it was someplace in Virginia."

"So, of course, he fled south, instead of north. . . . Cut the crap, Miss Walker. I'm plain not interested in the lies you're spouting. I know why he's aboard; this isn't the first time a fugitive slave has sneaked aboard a blockade-runner. What I want to know is why you're here. Usually, conductors on the Underground Railroad don't accompany their freight aboard outward-bound ships."

Freedom's jaw dropped open. "Then you know about the Railroad and the Wilmington station?"

The blond captain clicked his tongue with impatience. She wondered how she could ever have thought him handsome. In the flickering light of the lantern, he resembled the devil she was sure he was. "I'll ask the questions, Miss Walker. Why are you here? Why did you betray us to the Federal blockaders?"

To steady her nerves, Freedom drew herself up stiffly, but her head only came to the top of the captain's broad shoulder. He towered over her and was even bigger close up than he had been from afar. "I should think that would be obvious from my Northern accent. I'm a conductor who wants to go home, Captain, to Boston where I belong. Once we reach the North, I can easily send . . . Samson . . . to safety in

34

Canada — or he could stay in Boston, if he wants. The Fugitive Slave Law is no longer in force. It's gone the way of the Railroad, which means I no longer have a reason for remaining in Wilmington."

The captain narrowed his remarkable eyes. "You expected the Federal squadron to drop everything to escort you home? I find that a little incredible; nobody is *that* naive. . . . My guess is you're a Union spy. You only brought Samson along to pose as your cover. . . . Open your mouth, Samson, and let's see if you've really lost your tongue as she claims."

"Don't you dare humiliate him like that!" Freedom stepped between the big Negro and the two men in front of her, ready to defend Omoroh with her life, if necessary. "Hasn't he endured enough? How would you like to be beaten, enslaved, and have your tongue torn out? He's a human being, not a dumb animal, so keep your filthy hands off him!"

"Are you finished with your bleeding-heart tirade, Miss Walker? If so, get out of my way. I'm not going to hurt the man; I just want him to open his mouth. . . . That-a-boy, Samson. At least one of you knows how to behave sensibly."

Freedom whirled to see Omoroh obediently opening his mouth. Tears sprang to her eyes. How it galled her to witness this gentle aristocrat, whose veins bore the blood of kings, submitting to these arrogant, base-born Southerners, as if they actually were his betters! "Oh, you are despicable!" she hissed at the captain.

Completely ignoring her, the captain took a good long look before clapping Omoroh on the shoulder. "Good boy. You can close it now." He drew back and regarded Freedom with a suspicious flaring of his finely chiseled nostrils. "Well, you're right, Miss Walker. . . . He hasn't got a tongue. But that doesn't mean I buy the rest of what you're selling."

"I'm not a spy! That's a ridiculous accusation. You of all people should know exactly who I am and what I do—did—for a living. Yesterday, I sold you a pair of gloves and a lace fan at Hattie Draper's Fine Fashion Emporium."

For the first time, the tall captain showed recognition. "I thought you looked familiar, but I couldn't think where I might have met you. You have a very common face, Miss Walker. You're quite forgettable, actually."

His careless words stung worse than a lash. Freedom very well knew that her dark brown hair and matching eyes tended toward the plain, but to hear this blatantly handsome man confirm her deepest, darkest suspicions about herself again brought tears to her eyes. "Not all of us were granted physical beauty, Captain, but you may rest assured Our Creator does not judge us by our appearances, but by what is in our hearts. . . . His eyes see all of us as equals."

"A perfect abolitionist response, Miss Walker. You play your part well. But I still think only a fool would expect free passage to safety for herself and a runaway slave, just because she hailed the U.S. Navy from the deck of a blockade-runner."

"We might have received free passage in gratitude for having caught such a prize as you would have made!" Freedom exploded. "Why do you persist in believing me to be a spy?"

"Because frankly you *look* like one, Miss Walker—so young and innocent, so unassuming. You're exactly the sort of little brown mouse I'd choose to do my dirty work. No one but me would ever suspect evil things from you."

"Then . . . what do you plan to do with us?" Freedom asked, hating her voice for quivering. "If you take us back to Wilmington, Samson is—is as good as

36

dead. His master's brother—I mean, his master—has sworn to kill him if he ever catches him." She bit her lip in consternation at having almost revealed Omoroh's true situation. In point of fact, the brother of Omoroh's dead master was the one offering the reward for Omoroh's capture.

"Oh, we're not going back to Wilmington just yet, Miss Walker—if Walker is indeed your name. First, we're going to Nassau to sell my cotton. . . . Frankly, what happens to Samson doesn't in the least concern me. He can stay in Nassau for all I care; a man with no tongue isn't much use as an informant, and if he can't speak English, I doubt he can write it. Very few Negroes can write, anyway. . . . But you, Miss Walker, are another story."

"If you let Samson go free, I don't care what you do with me!" Freedom blurted out without thinking. Mentally, she kicked herself. He'd already said he'd let Omoroh stay in the Bahamas. Offering to sacrifice herself was a foolish, unnecessary gesture. "I mean . . . I hope you let me go free, too, but if you're only going to release one of us, I'd rather it be Samson."

To her astonishment, the blond sea captain lifted his hands and applauded her. "How noble of you, Miss Walker! And how cunning. You're obviously much brighter than you look. You say all the right things to avert my suspicions. Now, I'm convinced you're a clever Union spy. What information do you have that's so important you were willing to risk your life to pass it to the United States Navy?"

"I—I—" Freedom sputtered, at a loss as to how to defend herself.

"Clap her in chains, Pete, and lock her in my cabin. As for this poor dupe of a runaway who thinks he's an Arabian prince, put him to work stoking coal. If he does a good enough job, I will let him go in Nassau.

37

I'm not in the business of slave-catching for men who abuse their own property. Whoever this big fellow is, he deserves to go free."

"But, sir!" Freedom protested. "You've got to believe me! I'm no more a spy than—than you are. All I wanted was to go home to Boston and take Samson with me. And the only way I could think of to leave Wilmington was your ship. I never would have signaled those gunboats if I'd thought you'd let us go when we reach Nassau. . . ."

"I'm not letting *you* go, Miss Walker, I'm only letting Samson go . . . provided he stokes coal as if the devils in hell are after him."

Omoroh came to life then and, with a wide grin, made shoveling motions to show he would indeed stoke coal very fast. Freedom felt like screaming. "Then if I alone am to be your prisoner, will you at least tell me your name? I only heard the name and location of your vessel yesterday in that shop."

The blond sea captain bowed low from the waist. "Tiffin Adam Xavier Carrington, Miss Walker . . . but everyone calls me Ty, for Tiger, which rather aptly describes my character, if I do say so myself. I'm a man who'll stop at nothing to find out who you are and what you were *really* doing tonight. I'll even go so far as to tear you apart with my long, sharp claws, if that's what it takes to get at the truth."

"I wasn't doing anything but what I said! And you got away! You came to no harm. I don't see why you're so angry and suspicious."

The violet-colored eyes swept her coldly up and down. "I'm a Southerner, Miss Walker. By your own admission, you're a Northerner. And in case you haven't heard, we're at war with each other."

At that, Freedom fell silent. There was no reasoning with this detestable cotton planter/slaver turned sea

38

captain/blockade-runner. Meekly, she held out her wrists for the man called Pete to wrap a length of chain around them. And then it occurred to her: She was a woman alone on a shipful of men. The arrogant captain might think her plain, but he might not be above raping her, just for the sport of it. With a name like Tiger, she wouldn't put it past him.

"Will I be safe aboard this ship, Captain Carrington?"

"Safe?" he questioned. "What do you mean by safe?"

"I mean, are you a gentleman? Need I fear for my virtue?"

Once again, his eyes flicked over her from head to toe. "I don't see anything that interests me; how about you, Pete? . . . Of course, I intend to strip and search you thoroughly before we get to Nassau. Other than that, I see no reason for you to be fearful."

"Strip and—and search me!" Struck with horror, Freedom glanced from one man to the other. Pete, a sandy-haired, freckled-faced young man, blushed a deep rose-red.

"No, sir," he said. "Ah don't see anythin' to interest me, either."

"Well, then, Miss Walker, I guess you can consider yourself safe—from ravishment, anyway. Get her out of here, Pete, before I change my mind and decide to eat her for dinner."

Chapter Three

"What do you think, gentlemen? Is the little brown mouse a spy?"

The question hung in the stuffy wardroom like a whiff of rotten garbage. Tiger looked at the faces of his helmsman, chief engineer, and first mate, who were all silently considering the question as they sat over coffee, brandy, and biscuits, late-night refreshments to keep them going till morning.

"She don't look to me like a spy," Pete Gambol finally said. "If anything, she looks like somebody's kid sister. Fact is, she reminds me of mah own."

"Don't let your brotherly instincts get in the way of your best judgment," Ty cautioned. "We can't afford to make a mistake. What if she's got information about important troop movements or battle plans? She said that big Negro came from Virginia. . . . Maybe she's been spying on General Lee. It's no secret that the North wants Richmond, and if Lee and Jackson don't hold it, the war's all over. She may be trying to get word of what she's seen in Virginia to the commanding officer of the Union Army of the Potomac."

Matt Berringer, the first mate, set down his mug with a thud on the polished pine table. "How could that little slip of a gal know anythin' about Confederate troop movements? She's no older than eighteen or nineteen, at the most."

"How could she be a conductor on the Underground Railroad?" Ty countered. "Yet she claims she is. Who sent her South in the first place? Even before the war broke out, the atmosphere between North and South was hardly conducive to social visits."

"We don't know exactly when she came South, do we?" asked Stoker Harris, the chief engineer. "Lots of No'the'ne's got caught in the South when Fort Sumter fell, and vice versa. . . . That ain't so unusual. Nor is it so strange for her to be helpin' runaways. From what ah've heard, it ain't only men who work on the Railroad; women, children, young, and old alike have helped slaves reach safety in Canada."

"I'd say there's plenty we don't know about Miss Walker. That's the problem." Ty growled. "Well, lads, what do I do with her? If I set her loose in Nassau, the rowdies'll have her skirts up before she knows what's happening, and if I turn her over to the authorities in Wilmington, she'll be in worse trouble. I'll have to turn in the big slave, along with her. He'll be sent back to Virginia to a man who cut out his tongue, and the way sentiments are running against abolitionists, the girl will get tarred and feathered, if not hung."

"If you really think she's a spy," Pete said, "you oughta hand her over to the Confederate Army."

"To rot in prison, get shot, or have the truth beaten out of her?" Ty scoffed. "What the hell do we do with spies, anyhow?"

41

"We're Southe'n gen'lemen, and she's a woman," Pete insisted, looking affronted. "Ah doubt the army would harm a female. Maybe they'd just keep her under house arrest or something."

"Even that's unfair punishment if she's not a spy. What about her family—if she's got one—up North? They must be worried sick about her." Ty banged the tabletop with his fist. "Damn! Why did she have to pick my ship? Why couldn't she have picked someone else's?"

Silence greeted his questions. Ty finally realized he couldn't decide what to do with Miss Freedom Walker until he knew more about her. If he could satisfy himself that she really was a spy, he could keep her prisoner until he returned to Wilmington, then hand her over to the Confederacy without a single qualm of conscience. But if she was a conductor on the Underground Railroad, he didn't know what he should do with her. . . . Perhaps just set her free back in Wilmington to keep working where she'd been working. Then a new thought occurred to him: What was Hattie Draper's role in all of this? Was she, too, a spy, working to undermine the South?

Hattie Draper's Fine Fashion Emporium had stood for years on Third Street in Wilmington. Everyone knew where it was, though Ty himself had only rarely passed through its doors. It was a perfect setup from which to operate a spy ring—or a way station for runaway slaves. If Hattie Draper was indeed a secret abolitionist, the safest place to hide a runaway was probably right under the very noses of the slave-catchers occasionally roaming the streets looking for fugitives. The more Ty thought about it, the more convinced he became that whatever mischief involved Miss Walker also involved

Hattie Draper. And until he determined what that mischief was, he dared not let the girl go free. Helping escaped slaves gain freedom was something he could overlook, never having approved of the South's "peculiar institution," as Southerners were fond of calling it. Most of his crew members felt the same way. He wouldn't have been able to work in such close quarters with them if their attitudes toward slavery violently disagreed with his own. . . . But spying was something else.

He and his men were risking their lives for the sake of the Confederacy. A filthy, traitorous spy deserved severe punishment—male *or* female. Pushing back his chair, he rose to his feet. "It'll take us three days to reach Nassau," he said. "That's more than enough time for me find out more about Miss Walker. Don't interfere if you hear her screaming or sobbing, gentlemen. It might take some powerful persuasion on my part to convince her to talk. I won't hurt her, but I *will* get the truth out of her."

No one said a word, and Tiger knew he had his men's tacit approval to use whatever means were necessary to force Freedom Walker's confession. Every man in the room had the typical Southerner's inherent respect toward women, but none could forget that the girl had almost cost them their lives and their freedom. If the fleet had caught up with them tonight, they'd either be dead by now or headed for Union prisons.

With a curt nod, Ty left the wardroom, headed straight for his cabin, and entered it without knocking. A single sperm-oil lantern hung from a peg over his bunk, illuminating the spartan but crowded furnishings: built-in cupboards, shelves, and desk; a comfortable, padded haircloth-covered chair; stacks of books and spare nautical instruments; a closed, masked porthole; his locked portmanteau; and the single bunk that was longer and wider than normal, to accommodate his height.

Freedom Walker lay asleep on the bunk. Walking over to her, Ty saw that Pete had removed the chains from her wrists but had shackled one slim ankle to the bunk, leaving a long length of chain so the girl could move freely about the cabin, attending to her personal needs. He paused a moment, looking down at her slender form. His first impression had been correct: She was quite forgettable, especially dressed in simple brown twill of unfashionable cut, with no hoops or crinoline, and minimal petticoats. Her coloring was plain, and she dressed so unbecomingly that he had scarcely noticed her in Mrs. Draper's shop. Like the little brown mouse she resembled, she blended in perfectly with her surroundings. . . . Maybe that was her intent, Ty thought, to draw no notice to herself.

Bending over her, he studied her more closely. If one really looked, her face was actually passably pretty. She had high cheekbones, a straight, tip-tilted nose, a sweet, tender mouth, and long, gold-tipped lashes. Her skin resembled the finest, fragile porcelain, so transparent one could almost see through it, but she had no color. She was as pale as the white sheet below her head. Her only beauty seemed to be her hair, which was a rich, burnished brown, glistening with amber highlights. She wore it in a fashion he recognized as being currently popular: Madonna-style, with a center part, then drawn back and fastened into a chignon or codogon, as it was sometimes called, at the back of the neck. The hairstyle flattered her more than the plain, caped gown, accentuating the perfection of her even features and fine skin.

Of her body, he could tell little, except that her waist was tiny as a child's, and her hands were also childlike and delicate. They lay folded one atop the other on her slight breast and, unlike his mother's or Stephanie's, bore evidence of labor. Her nails were chipped, and he suspected she had roughened palms and fingertips. He had the oddest urge to trace his finger along the curve of her cheek to see if her skin felt as soft as it looked . . . but he resisted it. This child-woman did possess a certain charm—maybe it was her air of innocence—but he had no desire to get to know her better, other than to determine whether or not she was dangerous.

He cleared his throat. "Miss Walker, wake up, please. . . . It's time for our little talk."

Immediately, her head turned in his direction and her eyes flew open. For the first time, he really saw her eyes, and was startled by their brilliance and clarity. Her eyes were so large they almost filled her face. They were velvet-brown and flecked with gold. He had never thought brown eyes beautiful, but hers were. Stunned, he took a step back. Where was the little brown mouse he had first thought her to be?

For a moment, she stared at him, unable to get her bearings. Then, with a rattle and clank of chain, she leaped off the bunk so quickly she almost knocked down the lantern overhead. He caught her by the arm. "Careful . . . You got up too fast, and now you're probably dizzy. Go easy, or you might fall down."

"I'm quite all right!" she snapped, nevertheless grabbing for the side of the chair pulled up to the desk. "You startled me, is all. I'm not used to waking up and finding a man leaning over me."

"Settle down, Miss Walker. There's no need to go

45

into a panic. I just want to ask you some questions."

She gripped the back of the chair with both hands. "All right, ask . . . I'm listening."

He sat down on the bunk she had just vacated, leaned against the wall, casually crossed his legs at the ankles, and folded his arms across his chest. He, at least, intended to be comfortable. "Miss Walker, it's almost morning, and we're well on our way to the Bahamas. By the time we get there, I intend to know everything there is to know about you . . . so you might as well start explaining."

"Explaining what? You already know what I was trying to do."

Tiger sighed. He could see she was going to be difficult. "Where were you born? Let's start with that. How old are you?"

She lifted her chin. "I'm twenty, and I was born in Boston. How old are you?"

"I'm twenty-nine, and we're not playing games here. You'll answer my questions, and you'll answer them properly, without any sass. . . . Now, where are your parents?"

She looked away from him. "Both dead . . . my mother when I was born and my father three years ago. I have no other family, if that's your next question. My entire life evolves around The Cause."

"What cause, Miss Walker?"

"*The* Cause, Captain Carrington—at least, the only cause that counts. I refer, of course, to the abolition of slavery."

"And how far are you willing to go to bring about an end to slavery?"

She eyed him defiantly, her brown eyes glowing like golden coals. "As far as I have to . . . I'd do anything to rid the world of slavery. It's an abomination in the sight of God and man."

"Then I presume, since you feel so strongly, you'd not be averse to spying for the Union."

"I might not," she answered evenly. "But the truth is, no one's asked me to spy. I never thought of it and wouldn't know how to go about it, in any case."

Oh, she's a cool one, Ty thought, growing steadily more convinced that she was dangerous. He could imagine only one way to shatter her self-confidence and force her to admit how far she had actually gone to free her precious slaves.

"I think it's time you stripped, Miss Walker," he said brutally, keeping his face impassive. "At least you can prove to me that you don't have maps, battle plans, or other valuable documents hidden about your person."

Her face flooded with sudden color. In that moment, she was transformed from little brown mouse to ravishing beauty. Color stained her cheekbones and gilded her lips. Her eyes sparkled in the lamplight. Tiger dreaded having to be rough with her, but if she refused, he'd have to. She seemed to read his thoughts.

"What will you do if I don't?"

"I think we both know the answer to that question, Miss Walker. If you don't want the feel of my hands upon you, you'll do as I say, and you'll do it now."

Her lips quivered, but her hands groped for the front fastenings of her dress. "I thought Southern gentlemen were supposed to be chivalrous and protective of white women. I thought they only forced slave women to strip in front of them."

Tiger felt the heated stirrings of anger; she knew nothing whatever about him, yet assumed the worst.

"I assure you, Miss Walker, I've never had to force a woman to remove her clothes for me. In the past, they've always done it willingly."

"I have never been less willing to do anything for anyone," she pronounced in a ragged whisper.

"Hurry up, Miss Walker. I have other things to do before this night is over; you're keeping me from my duties."

Without another word, she peeled off the layers of clothing, taking them off over her head to avoid the chain and not stopping until she was down to her linen chemise and underdrawers. All the while, her brown eyes remained fastened on his, but when she finally stood before him half naked, she glanced away, her body trembling with embarrassment and outrage.

He snatched her dress and petticoats and examined them closely, hoping to find what he was looking for without having to force her to strip to the skin. In a deep side pocket, he found a wedge of cheese and a hunk of bread wrapped in a kerchief. He shook the garments, and an ivory comb fell out.

"Is this all you came away with?" he demanded, astonished at her lack of preparation.

"I—I didn't want to be hampered by carrying things."

"Or else the Federalists were already expecting you, and you knew all your needs would be met. Remove the rest, please, Miss Walker. I won't believe you're not hiding something until I can see for myself. . . . Wait a minute. I'll take off that leg shackle to make it easier."

A single tear trembled on the tip of her lashes, then slid down her cheek. To her credit, she did not break down and weep. Tiger almost relented but, remembering her treachery, resolutely hardened his heart. Quickly, he removed the chain and stepped back. "I'm waiting, Miss Walker. . . . If that's the only chemise you have, it would be a shame to tear it to bits, but I'll do it . . . and your underdrawers, too."

She moved rapidly then, and he himself was so embarrassed by his cruelty that he strove mightily not to glance at her body. But he couldn't help himself — especially when she finally straightened and lifted her shimmering eyes to his. As she handed him her most intimate garments, her eyes burned his soul. He took them without looking at them, so mesmerizing was the sight of her lovely, radiant nudity.

She had the same white, translucent skin all over her body that she had above the neck. It was the whitest, softest-looking skin he had ever seen, just like a pale magnolia. Her small, delicate breasts reminded him of magnolia blossoms, too, blushing rose at their centers. Her collarbones, knees and elbows, dainty hips, tiny hands and feet, all spoke of fragility and feminine grace. She was reed-slender but gently rounded everywhere it counted. He felt a crushing desire to touch her softness, to explore her tender curves, and he could hardly catch his breath.

"Let down your hair," he commanded in a hoarse whisper.

"There's nothing hidden in my hair," she protested.

"Let it down; I want to see for myself."

Her slim fingers plucked at pins, and her brown hair tumbled around her shoulders like silken ribbons. He longed to discover the texture of the shiny strands and knew they would feel as silky as they looked. Without realizing what he was doing, he compared the color of the hair on her head to the

49

color of the hair at the juncture of her milky-white thighs. She saw where he was looking, blushed furiously, and covered herself with her hands.

"No, don't!" he cried. "Don't be ashamed. . . . You're the most beautiful thing I've ever seen."

"You mean I'm not . . . *forgettable?*" she whispered, hurling his own insult back at him.

Suddenly, he realized what he was doing . . . lusting after a prisoner under his protection. He was degrading and humiliating her. Not answering, he shook out her chemise and undergarments, and finding nothing there, Ty threw them at her.

"Get dressed. I'll wait outside until you're finished."

He departed the cabin in three long strides, closed the door behind himself, and leaned against it. His head was pounding, his heart hammering, the pressure between his legs almost unbearable. Every nerve and muscle shrieked for him to go back into his cabin and take what he wanted . . . what she couldn't deny. No one would know; even if his crew members found out, they'd scarcely blame him. No cautious, virtuous woman would take the chances Freedom Walker had taken; if she roused a man to rape, she had no one but herself to blame . . . and to whom could she protest?

He pictured himself crushing her fragile bones, burying his nose in her burnished hair, touching and tasting her tender skin . . . and the images made him groan in frustration. For too long he had gone without a woman. Stephanie no longer interested him, and he couldn't bring himself to take advantage of the females who toiled on his land, though a few had given him encouragement. Up until now, the whores and prostitutes in Nassau had held scant appeal, but he promised himself to find

50

the prettiest one and slake his overheated passions as soon as he reached the Bahamas.

Freedom Walker was not for him. She was a riddle still to be solved, not some tasty tidbit to feed an old goat's lust. She made him feel old, soiled, and ashamed of himself. He had thought to break her down and destroy her aplomb, but instead, he was the one who felt shattered. . . . And what had he learned? Not a damn thing. If she was indeed a spy, she at least had enough sense not to hide evidence of it in her clothing.

He debated whether or not to continue questioning her tonight, then decided against it. He still didn't trust himself. Moreover, he was suddenly exhausted. In the morning, his head would be clearer. And the next time he confronted her, he'd make sure someone else was present. The *last* thing he needed was to fall under the spell of a Union spy.

Chapter Four

After a half hour of effort, Freedom finally succeeded in opening the masked, locked, and jammed-shut porthole in Tiger Carrington's cabin. The rush of fresh air into the tiny chamber felt heavenly and eased her queasy stomach; she had been unable to eat any of the breakfast or lunch brought to her by a silent seaman, and if she couldn't eat supper, she feared she would be sick, indeed.

Sometime during the previous night, the ocean swells had grown larger; the ship was now rising and falling with a steady regularity that provoked nausea. Peering through the small porthole, Freedom was relieved to see the sun shining on sparkling, blue-green water; this then must be the normal motion of the ship, not some dread precursor of a coming storm. If it was merely the normal motion, she hoped never to be aboard during a wild tempest.

Breathing deeply, she sat down in the captain's big, comfortable chair and wondered why he hadn't yet returned to finish questioning her or replace the

shackle on her ankle — not that it made any difference, since the door was kept locked, anyway. After
the highly embarrassing scene of last night, she had
sat up until dawn, afraid to go to sleep lest she
awaken to find him once again bending over her,
gazing at her with those penetrating, violet-hued
eyes. His eyes seemed to see everything — even when
she was fully clothed. Enduring his scrutiny while
naked had been the worst experience of her entire
life. She doubted she would ever forget the look on
his face as he shamelessly examined what no man
before him had ever seen — or wanted to see. Her
skin had actually burned from his intent perusal;
flames had licked wherever he gazed. His eyes had
darkened to the shade of banked thunderclouds as
they roamed her most private parts. . . . And those
very same parts now ached with a dull throbbing at
the memory.

She had never known such primitive fear of a
man yet couldn't deny the fascination he held for
her. He was so big, so virile, so handsome in his
dangerous, tigerish way. What would she have done
if he had reached out suddenly and dragged her
naked body into his powerful, muscular arms? The
very thought of it made her knees tremble. Why
had he not returned last night? What was he planning to do with her?

Now that she knew Omoroh was safe — thank
God, the captain didn't want to be bothered with
returning someone else's property — her fears had
turned inward. Despite her brave words, she was
terrified of what might happen, being totally and
completely at the mercy of a heartless Southern
slaver. Only her white skin had protected her thus
far; had she a single drop of Negro blood in her,

53

she had no doubt that Captain Carrington would have forced her complete and total submission.

She shuddered and fought down the ripple of excitement such an idea engendered. In all her twenty years, no man had ever made her feel as shivery and nervous as the tall, blond captain of the *Sea Whisper*. Long ago, she had given herself—heart, soul, and body—to The Cause. Not for her the normal feminine aspirations: marriage, home, and family. Until slavery was eradicated from the land, both North *and* South, she would hold herself aloof from all other emotional entanglements. . . . But her body, she now knew, was capable of betraying her. All the while she had been undressing in front of the captain, she had not been able to keep from wondering what it would be like if their situations were reversed. . . . What did *his* body look like?

Staring idly out of the porthole, she imagined the captain removing first his waistcoat, then his shirt and trousers . . . and his brown planter's boots. Was the hair on the rest of his body the same unusual color as the hair on his head? How much hair did he have? What texture was it? Lost in thought, she never heard the door open, until a man decisively cleared his throat.

"Ahem . . . Well, Pete, it looks like our little brown mouse has decided she needs a breath of fresh air."

Freedom jumped up and turned to face the two men coming into the cabin. One was the pleasant-faced, sandy-haired young man from the night before, and the other was . . . the captain whom she had just been undressing in her mind. A hot wave of shame flooded her; she was sure she was red from the top of her head to the soles of her feet.

"Can't you knock, Captain, and give me some warning? I was always taught it's polite to knock before intruding upon someone else's privacy."

Tiger Carrington entered the cabin as if he owned it — which he did. *"You* are the one who's intruding upon *my* privacy, Little Miss Mouse. Need I remind you this cabin belongs to me, and I'll enter it whenever I damn well please?"

His reference to her as a mouse finally caught her attention. So that was how he regarded her — as an ugly, loathsome rodent. In her vast inexperience with men, she had misinterpreted what she had seen on his face and in his eyes last night. He wasn't attracted to her; he was repulsed! The discovery took the wind out of her sails, and she meekly backed away.

"I — I'm sorry about the porthole. . . . But it was so stuffy in here, so hot. I couldn't breathe."

"Apparently, you can't eat, either," the captain said, leaning negligently against the doorjamb. "Tell me, Mouse, is it your intention to starve yourself before we get to the Bahamas? You're already as skinny as a flagpole; it wouldn't take much to reduce you to a matchstick."

So he thought she was skinny and unappealing. He had seen everything she possessed and considered it defective! "I — I couldn't eat. I felt sick," she said, feeling sicker by the minute.

"Haven't found your sealegs, yet, eh? . . . Pete, go see if we have anything in the medicine chest to dose a weak stomach. We can't have our stowaway starving to death on us."

"Aye, aye, sir . . . Ah'm sure we've got something."

Looking relieved to be sent on an errand, young Pete hastened to exit the cabin. Then the captain did a curious thing: Straightening, he looked after his crewman, as if he hadn't meant for him to leave right this moment. Was it possible he might be as embarrassed about last night as she was? The idea strengthened her flagging confidence.

"What are your plans for me, Captain? I demand to know what you intend to do with me."

He turned back to her, self-confident as ever. "*Do* with you, Mouse? Why, I don't know yet. That depends upon you. Are you ready to talk this morning?"

She tossed her head in exasperation. "I've already told you everything there is to tell. I can't help it if it isn't what you want to hear. Obviously, you won't be satisfied until I say I'm a spy."

The captain resumed leaning on the doorjamb. "You're wrong, Mouse. I won't be satisfied until you admit the truth. . . . The truth is the only thing I want from you."

"You've already heard it," she huffed. "And *seen* it. You know I'm not carrying any secret documents."

The violet eyes imprisoned her. "I don't know what's hidden inside your head, Mouse, only what's inside your dress."

Again, a strange burning sensation shot through her. She couldn't think of a thing to say and merely stood there, blushing, wishing she were somewhere else. Brute that he was, he took advantage of her confusion. Stretching out one hand, he took hold of her chin and tilted it toward the light spilling through the porthole. His incredible eyes examined her closely.

"What makes a little brown mouse involve herself in such dangerous activities as the Underground Railroad — or spying for the Union? Weren't you loved, sheltered, and protected as a child? Weren't you taught that a young lady isn't supposed to risk her life, not to mention her virtue, for a cause that ultimately she can do little about?"

Freedom felt the impact of his touch like a hot branding iron searing her flesh. "But I *can* make a difference," she insisted in a raw whisper. "If I work hard enough, long enough, and don't count the sacrifices . . ."

"But don't you want to live a normal life — fall in love, marry, and dangle fat babies on your knee?"

Freedom had always thought those things held no appeal for her. But at this moment, with Ty Carrington holding her chin and gazing deeply into her eyes, she was not so sure. She thought of the kind of babies he would be likely to sire — violet-eyed cherubs with tousled, white-blond curls. Then she thought of the act of siring them . . . and shivers ran down her spine.

"Are you immune to men, Little Mouse? Or is it that you've just never met one who's ignited your virginal passion?" He drew her closer, never losing his hold on her chin. She followed like a sleepwalker. His hand left her chin and fastened itself around the back of her head, just above her chignon. "I wonder if you would love as fanatically, as wholeheartedly as you embrace whatever cause holds you now in its thrall."

"I — I don't know. I've never been in love. . . . I — I don't *want* to fall in love," Freedom stammered, terrified.

"What, Mouse? Is your heart made of stone?"

57

His free hand came up and cupped her left breast. "It doesn't feel like it," he murmured, holding her immobile with the strength of his gaze. "Your heart's thumping like a captured sparrow's."

His thumb flicked across her nipple, nubbing it through the fabric of her dress. "Such a sweet, tender fullness . . . the very essence of femininity . . ."

Mesmerized, enervated, unable to help herself, Freedom leaned into his hand. No one had ever done to her what he was doing; never had she been touched so intimately. She knew it was wrong, knew she should scream, push him away, slap his hand, if not his face. . . . But his violet eyes compelled her meek subjection, even as his caressing thumb produced wondrous sensations. She feared she might swoon and fall down at his feet. She worried that if he insisted she undress again, she would do so gladly, willingly, obediently . . . if only he would keep touching her and gazing into her eyes. . . .

Suddenly, a voice sounded in the companionway. "Cap'n, ah couldn't find no medicine for an upset stomach, but ah did make tea for the lady. . . ."

At the first sound of Pete's approach, Tiger Carrington dropped both hands and moved away from Freedom. By the time the young man came through the doorway, the tall, blond sea captain was looking perfectly normal, even bored. To her horror, Freedom suspected that everything she had been thinking—and feeling—was written plainly upon her face. When Pete handed her a small tray, she almost dropped it, but he, thankfully, seemed not to notice anything amiss.

"Here, ah'll put it on the desk," he said solicitously. "A cup of tea should soon settle yore insides. . . . Don't worry. You'll soon get used to the motion of the ship. Here, sit down and have some. . . ."

The young man's kindness almost made Freedom weep. While the captain seemed bent on shattering her, the helmsman treated her with a sympathy she had known only fleetingly in her life. Her own father had cared little for her physical comfort; he had raised her to count her needs as insignificant when compared to the consuming needs of The Cause.

"Thank you, Mr. . . . Mr. . . ."

"Jus' call me, Pete, Miss. . . . There's sugar, but no milk for your tea. Sorry, but we don't keep milk or cream aboard."

The young man's polite manners produced a deep scowl on Ty Carrington's handsome face. "If you've finished clucking over her like a mother hen, you can go back to your duties, Pete. I doubt the Unionists would be half so kind to you, were you their prisoner, as you're being to her."

"But you said to fetch somethin' to soothe her upset stomach, Cap'n," the young man protested.

"Yes, but I didn't say you were to fawn over her as if she were an honored guest aboard this ship. She may be an enemy spy, for God's sake."

"Yes, sir . . . ah mean, no sir. Ah'll jus' be about mah duties then, sir."

The young man departed the cabin with a reddened face, and Freedom hated the arrogant captain for treating a subordinate with such contempt. Instead of drinking the tea, whose steam was curling up from the little teapot on the tray, she wanted to fling the contents of the entire tray into Ty Carrington's face.

"What do I have to do to convince you I'm not a spy?" she asked quietly, subduing her rash impulse with a determined effort of will.

He said nothing for a moment, then uttered a deep sigh. "I don't suppose there's anything you *can* do, Miss Walker. I certainly can't accept your word for it. . . . Therefore, the only course of action open to me is to keep you prisoner until I return to Wilmington, then to turn you over to the Confederate authorities. They'll have to decide for themselves whether or not you're a spy."

At the thought of remaining locked in the tiny cabin for days, maybe even weeks, Freedom sank down in the chair. "Must I be kept locked up all the time? Will you keep me chained to my bunk until we return to Wilmington?"

"I'm afraid so, Miss Walker. . . . I can't take the chance you might escape and get into more mischief. Perhaps, during this period of confinement, you will use your time profitably to meditate upon the error of your ways."

"You mean, to meditate upon your cruelty!" she shot back, again leaping to her feet. "My conscience is completely clear, Captain. I only want to help people with darker skins than my own to live in freedom, as you and I prefer to live. . . . I wasn't named Freedom for nothing. My name symbolizes the most precious possession a human being can possess. If I must suffer, lose my life even, to give the gift of freedom to others, at least I'll have lived a meaningful life and died a worthy death. . . . But what purpose will *your* life have served? You can't take your precious cotton to the grave with you. When you stand defenseless before Your Creator on Judgment Day, I sincerely doubt

60

He will accept your excuses and rationalizations for why you've lived the way you have. . . . So go ahead, and keep me chained, Captain Carrington. What I will do in my confinement is pray for you . . . pray that you and all your like-minded friends and acquaintances will one day open your eyes and see the light. . . ."

"Are you quite finished, Miss Walker?" The captain's expression gave Freedom pause. His face was livid. His eyes shot thunderbolts, and his teeth were clenched. A muscle twitched spasmodically in his lower jaw.

"Yes, Captain . . . I believe I've said all I have to say."

"Then I suggest you drink your tea before it gets cold . . . and before I do something we'll both regret."

Kicking her skirts out of the way, Freedom sat down. "As you wish, Captain . . ." She was intensely gratified when he stalked out of the cabin and slammed the door behind him, but he returned barely a moment later.

"Thank you for reminding me about that chain," he said, grinning evilly. "Would you prefer to be chained by your right ankle or your left?"

Two days later, Tiger stood on deck in the hot sunshine as the *Sea Whisper* nosed into Nassau's crowded, bustling harbor. Since the outbreak of war, sleepy little Nassau had turned into a boom town, and the traffic in her harbor rivaled that of any of the great American or European seaports. Everywhere Ty looked, there were ships: fat merchant vessels sporting the British flag; long, lean, lead-colored steamers with the short masts, convex forecastle decks, and Confederate flags designating them as blockade-runners; lovely, tall-masted schooners; flat-bottomed barges; and quick-moving lighters for transferring cotton from the runners to the overseas vessels.

A handful of small, wooded islands sheltered the main harbor and Nassau itself. Tiger knew the city was swarming with Southern refugees, the captains and crews of the runners, cotton-brokers, rum sellers, British captains and crews, prostitutes of every description, Jews, Gentiles, and Negroes, rich and poor, men of both high and low degree. King Cotton dominated everything. It was piled high on the decks of incoming and outgoing ships, stored tier upon tier on the docks, and weighed down the busy little lighters struggling to transport it from ship to ship, ship to shore, and shore to ship.

The odor of money permeated the air. Cotton could be bought for six cents a pound in the South and, by the time it reached England, brought more than sixty cents per pound. Ty had six hundred and fifty bales of cotton wedged in the hold and strapped to the deck, a small cargo compared to the larger runners, but one that ought to bring a walloping profit and enable him to turn around and buy other ridiculously high-priced things.

In Nassau could be found all of the goods he wished to purchase, as well as goods about which he cared nothing. In addition to the gunpowder, weapons, bolts of gray cloth, boots, Confederate buttons, sabers, medicines, and other supplies desired by the military, there were all the luxury items still coveted by wealthy civilians. Cigars, soap, pepper, fine Madeira wine, French cognac, coffee, sherry, hams, bonnet frames, corsets, cheeses, candles, tea, and wire frames for hoop skirts were all available. It was said that a man could buy anything in Nassau—for the right price.

A man could also come away from Nassau with things he did *not* want, such as yellow fever and the pox. Ty had learned to approach cautiously and to inquire from other ships whether or not any epidemics were running rampant in Nassau. Every time he arrived in port, he feared anew that the ghostly phantom of fatal illness might sneak aboard, stowing away like Samson, the slave, and Freedom Walker, the abolitionist/spy, whose presence he might only learn about when it was too late to do anything.

Twice, he hailed passing vessels and exchanged news. No one mentioned fever, but that did not ease his mind. An air of reckless jubilation prevailed in Nassau; men regularly played toss-penny on the veranda of the Royal Victoria Hotel with golden eagles and danced drunken reels on street corners to the tune of hornpipes. Ty had seen entire ships' crews stagger from groggery to groggery, never once attaining sobriety until it was time to weigh anchor. In such an atmosphere, few paid heed to the threat of sickness. Facing death on every run, the crews of blockade-runners eagerly embraced all the island had to offer during the brief time they were in port.

Tiger had to anchor some distance out in the harbor, but he did not worry about how he would get to shore. Already, lighters were heading in his direction, anxious to transport his cotton or do whatever else he wanted. He would have to leave a skeletal crew aboard to guard his vessel and Freedom, but the rest could all go ashore as soon as the first lighter reached them. Ty intended to waste no time conducting business and departing; the sooner he could head home the better, even if it meant he had to stay out to sea until a cloudy night or the next cycle of the moon permitted him to slip into Wilmington undetected.

He turned away from the rail to shout orders and found three of his crewmen already standing there—Pete, Matt, and Stoker. They looked as if they had something on their minds, but Pete was the one who mustered his courage and spoke.

"Cap'n, we been thinkin' 'bout Miss Walker. We know you plan to leave her locked in your cabin while we're in port, but we . . . the three of us . . . well, we were kind of wonderin' . . . that is, we thought . . ."

"Spit it out, Pete. What were you three gallant gentlemen wondering?"

"It's damn hot in your cabin, Cap'n!" Stoker Harris exploded, and Ty found it hard not to laugh outright.

Stoker, the chief engineer, was a huge bear of a man with a black-stubbled face, black shaggy hair, a massive chest and belly, and no social graces to speak of. He was hardly the type to worry about a lady's comfort, especially when he himself regularly endured temperatures capable of frying the brains of lesser men.

"You can't leave that bit of skirt chained inside your hot, stuffy cabin while we're in port, sir, or you'll bring the fever on her for certain."

"Is that so?" Ty coolly inquired. "What do you propose I do with her? I asked all of you for suggestions that first night, and none of you had a single one to make. As yet, I've heard nothing from anyone to convince me she's not a spy. And I'm certainly not going to allow her the opportunity to escape, just because it gets warm in my cabin."

Tall, redheaded Matt Berringer now spoke up. "Cap'n, beggin' yore pardon, but you know yoreself that cabin turns into an oven when we're in port. The breeze ain't stiff enough to blow through the porthole. With the sun beatin' on the metal plating overhead, that gal will die in there . . . or like Pete says, she'll sicken. Why, I've seen chickens in open crates on deck weaken and fall over from the power of the sun in these waters."

"Shall I put her in a crate then, gentlemen? Would that make you feel better? . . . At least, in my cabin, she won't get a sunburn."

"Sir," Pete interrupted. "Why couldn't you take her ashore with you an' lock her in your room at the Royal Victoria? She'd eat better there, and she could have a bath and clean up some. . . . She *is* a female, after all, sir, and this voyage has left her rather peaked."

Hands on hips, Ty scrutinized the three die-hard North Carolinian gentlemen. "You don't think the hotel staff will find it odd that I keep an obviously unwilling female locked up in my room?"

Pete grinned sheepishly. "Nobody would have to know she's unwillin', Cap'n. 'Course, ah ain't never stayed at the Royal Victoria mahself, but from what ah've heard, females often spend the night in gen'lemen's rooms at the Victoria. Probably, nobody'd think a thing of it."

"The idea's crazy," Ty snorted. "First chance she got, she'd try and escape."

"Not if you told her we won't let Samson go 'til she's safely back aboard, sir. . . ."

"That bit of blackmail might work, but how will you keep Samson from escaping? Do you intend to chain *him* in my cabin?"

"No, sir . . . we'll jus' tell him that if he jumps ship, it's pore Miss Walker who'll pay the price. We'll threaten to take her back to Wilmington and see she's punished for helpin' a runaway slave to escape."

Tiger thought a moment, then grinned, amused by his helmsman's inventiveness, if not by the plan itself. "You haven't lost sleep over this, have you, Pete? If you have, your effort's been wasted. I hardly want to spend my free time in Nassau playing nursemaid to Miss Walker. . . . Do you envision my sleeping in the same bed with her? Dressing and undressing in front of her? Entertaining my lady friends in the same room—or perhaps, entertaining *her?*"

Pete flushed to the roots of his hair. "You bein' a gen'leman an' all, sir, ah never spared a moment worryin' about Miss Walker's virtue. . . . We jus' thought she'd be a heap more comfortable at the hotel than stayin' aboard ship, chained to your bunk."

Stoker Harris folded his bulging, muscular arms across his huge chest. "Ah'll tell you straight out, Cap'n. Ah don't hold with that chainin' business, nohow. The chit may be a spy, but she's still a female an' no older than a kid. Seems to me if you was to talk things over with her and tell her where she's gone wrong, you could make her change her ways. . . . A man as persuasive as you, Cap'n, is more'n a match for a little skirt with more brass than brains."

"Gentlemen, it's obvious you know nothing about that little skirt! I've tried talking to her and gotten nowhere. Believe me, the safest spot for her is aboard this ship. . . . Now, let's get ready to go ashore, shall we? Except for you, Matt. I want you to stand the first watch. In a day or two, I'll send someone else out to spell you."

His three frowning crew members did not budge an inch—highly unusual for men who'd never before dared question an order. Their stubborn glares made Ty realize how serious the issue had become. It was true what experienced seamen claimed about women jinxing a ship; in three short days, Freedom Walker had totally destroyed discipline and set him at odds with his faithful, loyal crew!

"If you leave her with me, Cap'n, ah'm at least gonna unchain her and let her come on deck to get some air," Matt challenged.

"You do, and I'll leave you here in Nassau when we return to Wilmington!"

"Then you can leave me in Nassau, too, Cap'n," Stoker Harris growled. "Ah couldn't face me old mother knowin' ah'd treated a little lass so poorly—no matter what wrong she done."

"Me, too, Cap'n," Pete hastened to add. "Ah couldn't face my sister."

"Hell's bells! Did *she* put you up to this? Was this her idea or yours?"

"Ours, Cap'n," Pete insisted, though Ty doubted the claim. "You oughta take a look at her before you make up your mind, sir. Then you'd know why we're so concerned. . . . Why, she's fadin' away before our eyes."

"Fading away! Why wasn't I told of this? Hasn't

67

she been eating properly since I saw her two days ago?"

"She drinks tea, sir. Lots of tea, but that's about it. Clarence told me this morning that her trays come back untouched."

Clarence was the Negro freedman who did the cooking and kept the galley. He was polite and trustworthy, but not the sort to complain to his boss if someone didn't finish a meal. If Freedom Walker had fallen ill, Ty couldn't blame Clarence— or Pete, Matt, or Stoker. *He* should have looked in on her and made certain she had recovered from her initial bout of seasickness. The trouble was, he hadn't trusted himself. Every time he was alone with her, he behaved like a randy, old goat. . . . Damn! If she was sick, maybe he better not leave her on the ship. He'd *have* to take her to the hotel; it was the only place on the entire island suitable to lodge a young female. And he'd have to find a doctor who didn't ask many questions. . . . In naughty Nassau, that part, at least, shouldn't be difficult. Nor would it be all that difficult to keep her chained to a bed at the hotel. All he had to do was say he wanted no maid service, and his privacy would be assured.

"Allright, gentlemen. You win. I'll go down to my cabin and see if Miss Walker feels she can manage a ride in a lighter. You three just better make sure Samson sticks around until we're ready to leave Nassau."

"Too bad we can't convince him to work for you, Cap'n," Stoker Harris said. "He's a prime hand at shovelin' coal. . . . Only bad thing about him is his not bein' able to talk. Makes me feel like ah'm always talkin' to mahself."

"You want to offer him a job, go ahead," Ty said. "Between runs on the *Sea Whisper*, I could use him at Cypress Hall. The slave catchers won't bother him there. Tell him that, then give him a choice — a job or his freedom here in Nassau. Only he doesn't get his freedom until after Miss Walker returns aboard."

Ty's three crewmen were all grins. "Yes, sir, Cap'n . . . Aye, aye . . . We knew you'd see our side of it, sir."

"Hah! Then why did you all gang up on me? Next time it happens, I'll be looking for three new crewmen. . . . You can count on it."

On that somber note, Ty went below to fetch Freedom Walker.

Chapter Five

As soon as Freedom's feet touched solid land, she felt better. She was still weak and shaky, but the broth the captain had insisted she eat before leaving the *Sea Whisper* had settled her stomach and given her new energy. She knew now that she would survive. Once she recovered from the blinding glare of sunlight on water, she was eager to see Nassau and the hotel in which Captain Carrington intended to confine her while he saw to business. Any place had to be better than his hot, airless, cramped cabin.

The lighter had deposited them on a long wharf piled high with bales of cotton. Walking down it beside the captain, Freedom had a tempting glimpse of wide streets, handsome Georgian colonial-style wooden buildings, limestone-walled churches, and dozens of shops. Then Tiger hustled her into a horse-drawn carriage and heaved his portmanteau beside the driver, a congenial black man who tipped his hat at Freedom as she sat down on the tufted, worn velvet seat. She saw a street sign that said Bay Street and thought it must be the main thoroughfare. People, carriages, and horses jammed it, and it was lined with commercial establishments. The horse clopped down a side street and took them past some official-looking buildings, and they were suddenly on a spacious avenue leading to a beautiful four-storied building, lined all around with balconies. A front-facing veranda overlooked a grove of palm trees and flowers.

Beautifully gowned women and fashionably garbed men moved about the grounds and balconies, making Freedom conscious of how inelegantly she was dressed. "Won't you be ashamed to be seen with me in such a fancy place?" she asked her silent escort as the carriage drew up in front of the hotel entrance.

"Not really," the captain said. "You're going immediately to my room, and you're not coming out until we leave here. . . . So I'll neither be ashamed nor pleased by your appearance, because in fact, I *won't* be seen with you the entire time we're here."

Freedom sat rigidly in the carriage. "What do you mean, I'm going to *your* room? I thought I'd have a room of my own."

"I never promised that. We'll be lucky to get one room, much less two. The Royal Victoria is a veritable haven for blockade-runners, expatriate Southern planters, and British emissaries; everyone who's anyone stays here. It's always crowded and noisy, so even if you scream, no one will hear you . . . not that you'll have anything to scream about. Don't worry, I won't bother you. As long as you don't try to escape, you've nothing to fear from me."

"I'll hardly be thinking about escape, when I know poor Samson will pay for any such foolishness on my part. Your nasty threats have assured I'll be meek as a lamb."

"Nevertheless, I slipped your chain and shackle into my portmanteau. Whenever I'm out—which will be most of the time—you'll be chained to the bedstead. . . . So come along, Mouse, and see your new cage."

Freedom followed the odious blond captain out of the carriage and into the elegant hotel, where nothing had been spared to create the ambiance of a fine, old Southern mansion, though the building itself looked quite new. Inside, she waited in a corner near a huge pot of crimson flowers while Tiger Carrington secured a room, then she accompanied him up a wide, polished staircase to the third floor. There, he quickly ushered her inside a lovely furnished bedchamber, with a canopied bed and tall windows overlooking the balcony and a distant view of the harbor.

Freedom strolled about the room, touching gleaming wood surfaces, bending to sniff the luscious pink blooms in a vase on a small round table, and catching sight of herself in a full-length mirror near a decorative dressing screen. She was unaccustomed to such luxury—and also nervous about where she would sleep. The large bed was certainly big enough for two, but she'd never consent to share it with Ty Carrington.

While she examined the room and its contents, the captain engaged in conversation with the Negro servant—slave?—who had shown them the way upstairs. "Please see if you can locate a chaise longue in the hotel and bring it to our room. My companion is often ill, and reclining on a chaise longue seems to be the only thing that helps her."

"Yassah, Marster . . . I see dat one be brought by and by."

So that was how he intended to solve the sleeping problem, Freedom thought. She had never in her life reclined on a chaise longue and only knew what it was because she'd seen one in the front parlor of a high-ranking Presbyterian minister of her father's acquaintance. Her father had declared the French piece of furniture decadent and highly improper for gracing the parlor of a man of God. But the minister had defended his choice of furnishings on the grounds that his wife often needed to lie down during the day and could not manage the steps upstairs to the bedchamber more than once a day.

She wondered who would be relegated to sleeping on the chaise longue—she or the captain. After the servant had departed, the captain stalked to the tall windows overlooking the balcony and threw them open, admitting both the scent of flowers and the sound of men's voices wafting up from the balcony below.

"Will this be enough fresh air for you, Mouse?" he inquired with his back to her.

Silhouetted against the tall windows, he was a formidably striking figure in his fashionable fawn trousers, dark chocolate morning coat, and tall Wellington boots. The clothing emphasized his well-proportioned physique more than anything he had thus far worn—and also delineated the difference in their social status. Compared to him, she really was a drab mouse. His elegant appearance demanded the sort of lady who would have been wearing the airiest of muslins or silks over numerous petticoats and the huge hoop crinolines so popular among the upper class.

"I'm sure it will be more than adequate," she said in a small voice.

He turned to face her. "Good, then I shall leave the windows open, but only if you swear not to step out on the balcony at any time during your stay here. When I'm gone, of course, the length of the chain will prevent it, but even when I'm in the room with you, I prefer that you be discreet and call no attention to yourself whatsoever."

"I doubt anyone would notice me, anyway," she sniffed. "I'm hardly gowned to attract notice. However, I do plan to keep well back from the windows. When I'm by myself, I'd like to be able to rest at leisure in my undergarments, if that's all right with you. This gown"—she nodded at her caped brown traveling dress—"is exceedingly warm, but I've naught else to wear. So if you will consent to knock before entering, I can occasionally remove it."

His violet-hued eyes swept the garment under discussion. "That is a ridiculous dress for this climate. In truth, I can't say I'd like it if it was winter. I shall see to it that you get some clothing more suitable to Nassau's weather. As soon as my portmanteau is sent up, I'll be leaving; while I'm gone, I'll take care of that little matter."

Before he had finished speaking, a knock sounded on the door. The captain answered it, and two servants carried in his portmanteau and deposited it behind the dressing screen. Two more servants followed at their heels, lugging a chaise longue upholstered in green and gold brocade. The captain waved his hand toward the center of the room.

"Set it down there, gentlemen. . . . Yes, that will do fine." He slipped each of the four servants a coin, and they departed the room grinning happily.

How benevolent he was, how generous! But then, Freedom reminded herself, he could afford to be.

When the servants had gone, Tiger Carrington immediately stepped behind the screen, and she heard him opening his heavy portmanteau. A moment later, the chain rattled, and he reappeared with it coiled in his hand.

"Sit down on the bed, Mouse, and let's get this over with. I'll leave you plenty of slack so you can reach the washbasin and the . . . ah . . . other things you might wish to use behind that screen."

He was referring, of course, to the commode or chamber pot, but Freedom decided to pretend ignorance and embarrass this proud peacock, if possible. Just because she couldn't do anything about her predicament for fear of causing harm to Omoroh didn't mean she would make her captivity an easy chore for Ty Carrington.

"What shall I do if I have to relieve myself, Captain?" she boldly inquired.

His brows shot up at her frankness. "Why, the same thing you did aboard ship, Miss Walker, and also, come to think of it, in Wilmington. . . . Take advantage of the vessel provided." A wry grin played about his full mouth. "Taking advantage is something you do well and often, isn't it? I doubt you'll have any problems here in the hotel."

It took her a moment to realize he was making a pun and not crudely alluding to the frequency with which she emptied her bladder. "Then if you anticipate no problems with my personal comfort, what about the matter of bathing?" she pursued. "After three days locked up in your stuffy cabin, I should very much appreciate a bath."

"No doubt you would," he smoothly parried. "And so would I. But for modesty's sake, we'll both have to be satisfied with the ablutions made possible by a china basin and a pitcher of water. . . . Come now, Mouse. Sit down and stick out your ankle. Much as I enjoy matching wits with you, it's time I went about my business."

Seething with annoyance, Freedom plunked down on the bed, stuck out her foot, and nearly kicked him in the face as he knelt down with the chain. Unperturbed, he caught her ankle.

"Be glad I didn't leave you in my cabin, Mouse. . . . But I warn you: If you give me any trouble, that's where you're returning. There, now . . ." He locked the shackle, wrapped the end of the chain around the leg of the bed, and padlocked it in place. "You're safely secured in clean, pleasant, relatively cool surroundings. I'll be back in several hours, and when I return, I'll have dinner sent up for you."

She tossed her head and glared at him. "Won't you be eating with me?"

He grinned his charming, handsome grin. "No, Mouse . . . Sorry to disappoint you, but after you've eaten, I'm going down to the dining room to take my supper. Half the people in this hotel are friends, acquaintances, or business contacts; they'd think something was amiss if I didn't share dinner and a brandy with them during my first night in port."

"I'll die of boredom!" she cried, grabbing hold of his coat sleeve as he started to rise. "I nearly died of it in your cabin. At least there, you had books I could read. What do you expect me to do here?"

Gently, he removed her hand from his sleeve. "Rest . . . relax and regain your strength. Frankly, Mouse, you look terrible. Three days of not eating has made you pale and thin—thinner than you were on the night I made you undress in front of me. I can't promise you'll be provided with such excellent accommodations when the Confederate authorities assume charge of you. So I suggest you take advantage of the soft bed you've got. If I can, I'll bring you some books or newspapers to pass the time . . . now that I know you can read."

"Of course, I can read! What did you think . . . that I was illiterate? I received an excellent education. My father saw to it that I read all the classics and delved deeply into philosophy, science, and mathematics. He himself had no time for intellectual pursuits, but he always encouraged me to improve my mind."

"My congratulations to your father. It seems I've misjudged him. I thought the only thing he taught you was a pack of lies and half-truths about Southerners. Or did you come by your opinions of our wickedness all by yourself?"

"I came by it through personal observation; I

looked in Omoroh's—I mean, Samson's—mouth!" She snapped her own mouth closed, hoping he hadn't caught her slip of the tongue, but his expression revealed he had.

"Omoroh's?" Frowning, the captain rose slowly to his feet. "Is that his real name, then? I should have known—I *did* know—you were lying. And if you lied about his name, you lied about other things as well. When I return to Wilmington, I'll likely find out he's a freedman from the North, and you're in this spy thing together."

"I'm not a spy!" Freedom cried, jumping off the bed to meet him eye to eye. "I only lied about his name because I didn't want you to know his real one. There are circulars out about him in Wilmington, offering a reward for his capture. Such a reward would probably mean nothing to a rich man like yourself, but it might be quite attractive to your crew members. . . . *Please* don't say anything to them about it. Let them think his name really is Samson."

The blond sea captain eyed her coldly. "Rewards are usually only offered for the most valuable or most dangerous slaves, those who have harmed their masters or fomented rebellion. Is that what Omoroh is? One of John Brown's rabid followers? Has he murdered innocent white women and children in their beds?"

"No! No, I swear he hasn't. He's not that kind of man at all!"

"You said he came from Virginia. . . . That's where Brown led that slave uprising in '59. They caught Brown and hung him, but never could be sure they'd caught all the slaves he led on his blood-thirsty rampage."

"Omoroh didn't come from Virginia," Freedom admitted. "I — I lied about that, too. You see, I didn't want you to connect him at all with the slave described in the circular."

Tiger Carrington's hands seized her upper arms. His fingers dug into her flesh. "Then where did he come from? Damn it, I want the truth, and I want it now! What's in that circular that you're so afraid I'll find out?"

"I — I can't tell you! I *won't* tell you! If you know what he's done, you'll never let him go!" Freedom bit down so hard she almost severed her tongue; she was aghast at her clumsy revelations. How had she arrived at this point, anyway? One minute they'd been arguing about her attitude toward Southerners, and the next she was ruining Omoroh's chances for freedom.

"You're right about one thing," the captain grated. "Now I won't let him go. When I get back to Wilmington, I'll turn both of you over to the authorities and let them unravel the truth. . . . You're so stubborn and argumentative you've botched everything you've ever tried. If you are a Union spy, you're a damn poor excuse for one. And I pity the Underground Railroad if you're the best they could come up with for a conductor in Wilmington."

His stinging criticism was kinder than what she herself was thinking; Freedom burst into tears and began sobbing into her hands. "Oh, I hate myself! I have ruined everything. All I wanted was to get that poor man to safety, but I failed to alert the fleet in time and now I've destroyed all chance of freedom for him. I can't believe I told you his name . . . then said what I did about him."

Ty Carrington narrowed his tigerish, violet-colored eyes. "I'll know the truth about that circular by the time I get back tonight. You see, my little nitwit, all circulars about runaway slaves are posted not only in Wilmington, but also in the ports frequented by Southerners."

Not sure if he was telling the truth, Freedom blinked at him through her tears. "They are?"

"Many of the Negroes on this island are probably runaway slaves. Because of British disapproval, slave catchers aren't permitted to harass them, but circulars still make their way here. Wherever Southern planters congregate, they want to know what's happening in other areas of the South. Information is the most important commodity exchanged here. . .and I'm sure someone will have heard of an Arabian slave prince named Omoroh."

Freedom didn't know what to do, but as she sniffed and swallowed her tears, it became apparent. She must tell Ty Carrington the whole story and somehow convince him to let the big Negro go. If she didn't, Omoroh was lost. The captain would take him back to North Carolina, where the slave catchers would soon have him in their clutches. However, if she told the captain the truth, begged and pleaded with him . . . offered him anything he wanted in exchange for Omoroh's freedom . . . the poor man might still have a chance.

"Omoroh didn't come from Virginia," she blurted out. "He came from Georgia, and he's wanted for murder. But it's not what you think. He only killed his white master because the man

80

raped his—Omoroh's—young wife, right in front of him. Afterwards, Omoroh fled with the girl. But she couldn't stand the rigors of the journey. She died in his arms in the middle of a swamp, and Omoroh then made his way to Wilmington, dodging slave catchers and their dogs, eating garbage, sleeping on the bare ground. . . . I'm sure you can imagine the horrors he endured. The brother of the man he killed has been searching for him ever since. He's wanted, dead or alive, and the reward is five hundred dollars—in gold, not Confederate script."

Ty Carrington let go of Freedom's arms and stood staring at her with his remarkable eyes. "It says all that on the circular?"

"Not all of it, no. The circular only says he's a dangerous, deranged killer who massacred his master in cold blood."

"Then how did you find out the rest, since Omoroh can't talk?" Doubt and suspicion underlaced the captain's tone.

"Partially from a handwritten note that someone on the Underground Railroad in Georgia wrote for him and partially from Omoroh himself. He does an excellent job of expressing himself with his hands."

"So Omoroh's timing was perfect for you to take advantage of his situation and use him as an excuse for hailing the Union fleet."

"I didn't use him as an excuse for hailing the fleet! How many times must I tell you? I only wanted to go home and saw no reason why we couldn't both escape to the North."

The captain's expression didn't alter. Freedom doubted he believed anything she had said. In view of the lies she'd told in the beginning, she could hardly blame him.

"Miss Walker, you are either the most naive, foolish, scatterbrained, courageous girl in the entire Confederacy, or you are the most accomplished liar, the most sly, underhanded female it has ever been my misfortune to meet."

"I *swear* to you I'm not a spy."

"That, Miss Walker, remains to be proved. As for the rest of what you claim, I will at least attempt to verify it before I decide what to do with Omoroh."

Freedom lost all caution and flung her arms around the captain's neck. "Captain Carrington, I beg of you, please let Omoroh go! I know that what he did was wrong; murder is *never* justified. But he had provocation! He couldn't help himself. Surely, you don't condone the cruelty of Omoroh's master. For the love of God, show some compassion, sir! . . . Oh, please, I *beg* you! I'll do anything you ask . . . *anything,* I swear it!"

Ty Carrington's face registered a variety of emotions—so many she couldn't sort them out. Only one was clearly recognizable: anger, or perhaps, contempt. With callous deliberation, he removed her arms from around his neck.

"Your self-righteousness is exceeded only by your impetuosity, Miss Walker. . . . Take care lest I take you up on your offer. You certainly owe me something for all the trouble you've caused. . . . But would you actually hike your skirts for such a monster as you perceive me to be? You'd let me touch you, fondle you, get you with child? . . . You are incredible. Had Simon

82

Legree met such as you, I've no doubt he'd have called off his bloodhounds and contented himself with the pleasures of a well-warmed bed."

"You've read Harriet Beecher Stowe's novel?" she asked, astonished.

"Hasn't everyone?" he inquired cryptically. "Is the Stowe woman responsible for your misconceptions about all Southerners?"

"She only wrote the truth, as she saw it and knew it to be."

"No, she only wrote what she *supposed* was the truth, without ever having really lived the life of a Southern planter. We are not all like Simon Legree—or Omoroh's master. You insult me everytime you open your mouth."

"Then why don't you *prove* to me you're different from all the rest? . . . Let Omoroh go. I meant what I said. I have no money to give you. All I have is my—my virginity. I surrender it willingly. Just let Omoroh go."

His violet eyes darkened to a steely purple. "And what if I don't want your damn virginity?"

Tears spilled down her cheeks; she felt utterly bereft and humiliated. "B—but you must. I haven't anything else of value to offer. . . . You are a man. I am a woman. I thought men placed a great value on a woman's maidenhead."

"Oh, they do," Ty Carrington sneered. "But a man also places value on a woman's tenderness, her love and devotion . . . her loyalty and faith in him. At least, I do. . . . Above all else, I want a woman I can trust, Miss Walker . . . and in that regard, you fail miserably."

So saying, he spun on his heel and left, closing the door behind him and locking it from the outside. Freedom collapsed, sobbing, on the bed. Never in her life had she felt so miserable, and the worst of it was she didn't know why. Was it because she'd sunk to the depths of bargaining with her body? Or was it because the handsome captain hadn't jumped at her offer and quite obviously didn't want her?

Chapter Six

When Ty left the hotel, he wasn't sure where he
was going—back to the ship to confront Omoroh,
or simply down to the wharf to do what he'd
planned on doing in the first place . . . make arrangements for his cotton to be brought ashore. He
wished there were somewhere he could find one of
those damn circulars, but since slave catching was
not permitted in Nassau, no one bothered to distribute circulars, or else they were destroyed as
soon as they were posted. He had lied to Freedom
in hopes of forcing her to tell the truth—and he
still couldn't be sure she had told it.

She made him so angry he couldn't think
straight. Stalking down the street, he ignored the
traffic and the shouted greetings from one or two
acquaintances. The first thing he needed was a
good stiff drink, but had he sought one on the hotel veranda, he'd have been inundated by people
who knew him. The safest bet was to head for the
waterfront, where grogshops abounded.

As he strode along, he noticed several shops
where sailors could purchase feminine fripperies to

soften the hearts of even the most hard-hearted prostitutes. On impulse, he ducked inside one and shouted at the startled proprietress, a buxom woman with a pockmarked face and startlingly red lips. "Do you have any female clothing, ready-made?"

"Why, o' course, lovie . . ." the women answered in a coarse cockney accent. "What with machines doin' the work of seamstresses, most all the clothin' shops carry ready-mades nowadays. What sort o' garments do ye have in mind, and what size and height is the lady ye're plannin' on givin' 'em to?"

Despite her appearance and manner of speech, the woman seemed to know her business, causing Ty to study her more closely. "She's thinner than you but about your same height. Her waist is extremely narrow." He held up his hands to indicate the span of Freedom Walker's waist. "And she has small hands and feet, almost like a child's. She doesn't fill her bodice as well as you do, but she isn't flat by any means."

Not the least offended by his blunt speech, the woman thrust out her bosom and preened in front of him. "What a keen eye ye got, sir! . . . Is this clothin' to be for the bedchamber, or is it for the lady to go out in public?"

Tiger thought a moment. If he wanted, he could indeed purchase clothing suitable for the bedchamber, garments he himself would enjoy seeing on Freedom's slender but nubile form. After all, if she wanted to lose her virginity so badly, he should be happy to oblige her. Why not dress her like the whore she aspired to become?

"I want clothes suitable for both," he finally said. "But even the clothes the lady might wear to go out in public should pay homage to her female charms. . . . She's a most unusual young woman, and I delight in . . . ah . . . showing off her assets."

The woman's black eyes gleamed. She grinned knowingly, as if she outfitted mistresses every day of the week. "I kin furnish ye with an entire wardrobe, sir, one that will make all your gen'lemen friends drool with envy, and ye yerself, sir, won't be able to tek yer eyes from the lass."

"Make it a half-dozen gowns in total," Tiger said recklessly. "With all the appropriate underthings, including those enormous hoops ladies are so fond of now. Deliver the lot of them to the Royal Victoria in care of Ty Carrington. You'll be paid at the front desk."

"What about joolry, sir? I got some prime pieces I don't normally show to me customers, but then they ain't usually so discriminatin' an' generous. . . . Might ye be interested in diamond earbobs guaranteed to win a lass's heart?"

"It isn't her heart I'm interested in," Tiger snapped, suddenly irritated. "No diamonds . . . the clothing alone should suffice."

"There's one other thing b'fore ye go, sir. . . . What color is the lady's hair? I gotta know what flatters her if I'm to choose the right colors and fabrics."

"Think of a little brown mouse, madam, with brown hair and brown eyes . . . and skin pale as magnolias. Give me no dark colors or heavy fabrics. She needs light, airy things—muslins and silks. But I don't want gaudy, cheap colors . . . no reds or purples. See if you can make her elegant, as well as alluring." He leaned over the wooden counter, the better to emphasize his instructions. "I want her to look like the very essence of . . . a Southern belle. Spare no effort to garb her in finery that would melt any woman's heart — and delight any gentleman's eye."

"I un'erstand perfectly, sir. Believe me, I kin supply exactly what ye desire. I'll even include a bottle o' rare French perfume — Essence of Magnolias, sir, a heady scent, indeed."

"How can that be? Magnolias aren't known for their fragrance."

"Ah, but sir, this is how they *would* smell, if they *were* knowed for it."

"Make it Essence of Gardenias, and I'll purchase *two* bottles."

"Very good, sir. The clothin'll be delivered to yer hotel t'morrow mornin'."

"Not tomorrow morning — *tonight*. Or you can forget the whole thing."

The women's eyes widened. "But, sir, this is a big order!"

"Make it tonight, or not at all," Ty insisted. Then, feeling much better, he left the shop and headed toward the wharf.

Omoroh sat on the deck of the *Sea Whisper*, rested his head against the wall of the wheelhouse, and closed his eyes, as if he were dozing. To the handful of men still aboard ship, it would appear he was stealing a brief nap before the work of unloading cotton began. Everyone was waiting for the captain to make arrangements for the disposal of the *Sea Whisper*'s cargo. As soon as lighters came alongside, the unloading would begin, but until that moment, Omoroh had time to sit in the hot sun and think.

He had been offered a job working for Captain Carrington, not only a sea captain but also a planter who had promised actual wages and protection from slave catchers. Or if he preferred, Omoroh could stay in Nassau and make a new life for himself among the Negroes the island already held. By the time Captain Carrington returned to the ship with Miss Walker, Omoroh must make up his mind. These choices were difficult enough, but the thing that was really bothering him and making his decision impossible was what the captain intended to do with Miss Walker when they got back to North Carolina.

Captain Carrington thought Miss Walker was a Union spy. Whether or not this was true, Omoroh could not say; he had only met the girl when he'd made his way to the cellar of Hattie Draper's shop, forced his way inside by breaking the lock on the cellar door, and hidden in the damp darkness until Miss Walker had discovered him the next morning. The instructions he had received at the last station of the Underground Railroad had included no information regarding Hattie Draper or Freedom Walker; he had only been told that he must find the shop, break into the cellar, and wait there until he was discovered by someone who regularly checked it for runaway slaves.

At each station along the route of the Underground Railroad, the conductor had to decide how to get the fugitives to safety at the next stop along the line. Miss Walker had told him that there no longer was a stop after Wilmington. Moving slaves had become too dangerous. There was no way to get him further North, even if a way could be found to bypass the next few stations. All routes North had been closed by the war.

Omoroh had thought he was doomed to spend the rest of his life in Hattie Draper's cellar . . . until brave, plucky Miss Walker decided to sneak aboard the *Sea Whisper*. Her plan to alert the Federal fleet had gone awry, but Omoroh's dream had apparently come true; one way or another, he was soon to become a free man!

His only problem now was what he should—or could—do to help Miss Walker. She had helped him, and he felt obliged to repay her, no matter the danger to himself. Whether she had actually committed a crime or not hardly mattered. He wasn't even certain what a spy was or did, or why they were considered so dangerous. He himself had done something judged wicked and evil in this country, though in the country of his birth, it would be understood—even expected. Here, people did not act or think the same as they did in Africa. They worshipped different gods and pretended to be civilized, yet treated dark-skinned people as less than human.

Unable to understand it, Omoroh had finally concluded that white people, for the most part, were simply heathen barbarians. The young woman with the brown hair and eyes was one exception. She had fed him, treated him with kindness, and risked her life to help him escape. He admired her brave spirit and, were their situations reversed, would gladly have adopted her into the Foulah tribe that he had once ruled over as a prince.

But it did no good to think about his old life on the distant shores of the Senegal River; his old life was gone forever. No longer was he the tall, proud son of a king—well-educated, a follower of Muhammad, a pious man who knew the Koran by heart and could recite it word for word. Allah had forsaken him, and he had only survived this long because something inside him refused to die or admit defeat. In vain, he had tried to infuse his Mandingo wife with this same passion for living, but her spirit had been weak, and she could not endure what she must for the sake of gaining freedom. He had had to bury her in the muck of a swamp and abandon all thought of building a new life together somewhere safe and free. . . . Could he also turn his back on the young woman who had helped him get this far?

The old Omoroh would never have hesitated; he'd have defended the girl with his very life. But the new Omoroh bowed his head in the sunshine and debated the high cost of honor. His tribal beliefs demanded that he rescue the girl and adopt her enemies as his own, but selfishness demanded that he accept what her enemies offered and forget about her. He felt torn in two. Was spying a crime punishable by death in this country? Or would she be beaten instead? He only knew the penalties for disobeying, sassing the master or mistress, or refusing, as he had done, to speak the language of his captors, which he had learned far more rapidly than even they had realized.

If only he had had time to master reading and writing English before he fled that Georgian plantation! His former master had sought to train him as a majordomo, but when he refused to display the proper submissive attitude, he had been assigned to serve the young master of the household. The boy delighted in having someone as big, strong, and proud as Omoroh at his beck and call. Omoroh often had to wait for hours outside the door of the study while the boy was with his tutor. Always keen-minded, Omoroh eavesdropped and absorbed knowledge like a sponge, thereafter stealing books from the plantation library in an effort to teach himself the symbols whereby white men communicated.

Had time not run out on him, he would now be able to write down his questions and take them to the big man who ran the engines that powered the ship. Stoker Harris had treated him well during the last three days, having at times even shared the filthy task of shoveling coal into the hot furnace. The other men aboard also seemed kind in comparison to those he had known in Georgia. It was the first time since his arrival in America that Omoroh had worked side by side with white men, sweating to accomplish the same difficult task.

How he longed to ask one of them what was going to happen to Miss Walker! Omoroh stretched, yawned, and shook his head. It was useless to attempt sleep in the face of indecision and worry; he might as well get up and see if he could help the Mandingo freedman in the galley, who kept trying to assure him that working for Captain Carrington would be nothing like being a slave under his old master. According to Clarence, the blond-haired captain neither owned slaves nor treated his workers cruelly, and Clarence himself would far rather work for the captain than take his chances on surviving in Nassau.

There was no lack of work on the island, but many workers were homeless and had to sleep on cotton bales on the wharf, Clarence had told him. They wasted their wages on drink and women, lost it gambling among their fellows, or had it stolen out of their pockets while they slept. Using his hands to make himself understood, Omoroh had managed to ask if anyone farmed on the island, or grew tobacco or cotton, to which Clarence had replied with a shake of his woolly head: "Naw, not many. De soil be poor, an' mos' especially poor in de parts where de freedmen has got to live. Dey's no big planters like we gots back home an' no big plantations. . . . If'n it weren't foh de blockade runners, dis be a very poor place . . . easy on de eyes, but poor jus' de same."

Largely because of Clarence, Omoroh thought he might enjoy working for Captain Carrington. Perpetually hungry, he knew that if he stayed with the captain, he'd at least be decently fed. With no tools, money, or clothing, without even the ability to talk, he was more likely to be ridiculed in Nassau than given a job. . . . Yet how could he work for a man who intended harm to little Miss Walker?

No closer to an answer now than he'd been when he sat down, Omoroh rose to his feet and was startled to see the very man he'd just been thinking about approaching the ship in a small lighter. Spotting him at the rail, Captain Carrington called out, "Omoroh! You're just the man I want to see. . . . Catch this rope, I'm coming aboard."

As Tiger boarded the *Sea Whisper*, he thought Omoroh did not seem particularly happy to see him. The tall Negro's patrician features were twisted in a scowl, which disappeared as soon as he realized Ty was looking at him. Omoroh gave Ty his hand and helped him vault over the railing. For a split second, Tiger felt as if he were intruding upon the other man's domain. Despite the slave's tattered clothing, his air of calm dignity did remind one of a king, Ty thought, and he had the oddest sensation that Omoroh owned the ship and he himself was a mere trespasser.

Before he could say anything, Matt came forward, a look of concern on his freckled features. "What's wrong, Cap'n? Did you bring that lighter to start unloadin' cotton? Ah thought you'd send out a couple boats, but ah didn't expect to see you personally; ah can handle the unloadin' just fine."

"I'm sure you can, Matt, but to tell the truth, I haven't yet contracted with anybody to start transporting the cotton. I only hired the lighter to run me out to the ship, but I'm sure her captain wouldn't mind taking back a full cargo. . . . Go and ask him about it, would you? I want a moment alone with Omoroh."

"Omoroh, Cap'n? You mean Samson?"

"Yes, Matt. It seems his *real* name is Omoroh." As he said this, Ty watched the slave's face.

Omoroh's dark eyes flickered, but his expression remained impassive and remote. Suddenly, Ty could understand how Omoroh must have infuriated his former master. Most planters considered themselves superior to Negroes, slaves or otherwise. Faced with the intelligence and physical strength of a man like Omoroh, many would feel compelled to prove themselves better than he. This might well lead to cruelty and efforts to humiliate.

Tiger's eyes dropped to Omoroh's hands; his fingers were long and slender, every gesture graceful and elegant. It was hard to believe that these smooth, gentle hands had killed a man. Had he throttled his victim? Struck him over the head? Knifed or bludgeoned him? Ty wanted answers—honest ones, at long last. He couldn't trust anything Freedom said, but he had a feeling Omoroh wouldn't lie to him. All the man had to do was nod his head in affirmation or shake it in denial in response to Ty's questions.

"Come along, Omoroh. . . . Let's go down to my cabin where no one will hear us. I want to ask you about yourself and Miss Walker." Omoroh nodded, as if he already knew what Ty wanted to ask. On a hunch, Ty added, "You don't, by any chance, know how to write, do you?"

Omoroh looked startled but didn't deny it.

"Somehow I knew it," Tiger said. "This might turn out to be a hell of a lot easier than I thought."

An hour later, Ty's curiosity about Omoroh was greater than ever. Omoroh had taken the writing materials Ty had supplied and produced four entire pages of flowing script, the likes of which Ty had never before seen and could not understand. Ty tried reading the papers upside down, but no matter which way he held them, he could make no sense of the writing.

"You *must* be a prince of a foreign country," he said. "I've known few Africans able to read or write in any language, let alone one that looks like hen scratches. I can't make heads or tails of this. . . . Where in God's name did you come from, and how did the slavers get hold of you?"

Omoroh pointed to the papers, and Ty knew that the explanation was there, if he could just find someone to translate it. "Look, Omoroh . . . I understand your frustration with not being able to talk and my not being able to read this. I'm as frustrated as you are, and I promise you, I'll try and find someone who can read what you've written here. I know a man in Nassau everyone calls The Professor; it may be that he can translate this, or at least tell me what language it's written in. . . . In the meantime, if you could clarify what you know about Miss Walker . . ."

Omoroh raised his hands in a futile gesture.

"Do you mean you won't tell me?"

Omoroh shook his head, but not belligerently. He sincerely seemed to be trying but couldn't find a way to express his thoughts.

"All right, just nod your head yes or no. I'll try to keep my questions simple. Are Miss Walker and Hattie Draper friends?"

Omoroh nodded.

"Did Mrs. Draper know that you and Miss Walker were going to hide aboard my ship?"

Another nod.

"Did she approve?"

A vehement denial.

"Did Mrs. Draper seem supportive of Union efforts to blockade the harbor?"

Omoroh hesitated, and Tiger tried to think of a way to rephrase the question. What he wanted to know was whether Hattie Draper had expressed pro-Union or pro-Southern sympathies. "Whose side did she seem to be on—the North or the South?"

Ty held up both hands, indicating that his left represented the North and his right the South, then repeated the question. Omoroh frowned harder, then helplessly shrugged his shoulders.

"You don't know which side she was on?"

A slow shake of the head.

"What about Miss Walker?"

Another slow shake.

"Omoroh, I already know that Miss Walker hates Southerners. What I'm trying to find out is whether or not she was spying on them. . . . Do you know what *spying* is? It means she's collecting information to be used against us. She's selling our secrets to the enemy. Do you understand? She may have been using you as an excuse for signaling the Federal fleet. . . . She nearly got us captured or killed. Did she do it for *your* sake—or some other reason?"

Omoroh clapped both hands on his chest, as if to say "She did it for me," but Ty had no such certainty. If Hattie Draper knew about Freedom's plan and disapproved, why had the girl gone ahead and done it, anyway? She had to have another motive—such as passing valuable information to the Unionists. As for Hattie herself, why hadn't the woman been outraged at Freedom's intention to sabotage a blockade-runner? Hattie's own survival—the success of her shop—depended upon blockade-runners. Maybe the old woman's disapproval centered on the possibility of Freedom getting caught and losing the opportunity to pass important information to the Unionists.

The more Tiger thought about it all, the more perplexed and frustrated he became. He supposed he should not expect Omoroh to admit anything damaging about Freedom Walker. When told he must remain aboard ship to guarantee Freedom's return, Omoroh had been more than willing; he'd been downright eager. The man's protective barriers could not be penetrated by simple questions that could be answered yes or no.

Tiger sighed and looked down at the papers in his hand. If he could find someone to translate Omoroh's writing, he might be able to quiz him at greater length. It was certainly worth a try, and reading the details of the man's past promised to be interesting in its own right. Tomorrow, he'd take the papers to The Professor, if he was still in town, and find out as much as possible. As for today—or what was left of it—he'd see that the big job of unloading his cotton was begun, then return to the hotel. Suddenly, he couldn't wait to discover Freedom's reaction to her new clothes and to see them on her.

"Thanks for trying to be helpful, Omoroh," he said to the regal Negro. "But unless someone can tell me what you've written here, I'm afraid further discussions are fruitless. . . . Too bad you don't know how to write English."

To his surprise, Omoroh snatched pen and paper and beseechingly held it out to him. "You mean you want me to teach you?" Ty asked disbelievingly.

Tears sprang to Omoroh's eyes. Compounding Tiger's astonishment, the big man dropped to his knees in front of Ty, all the while holding up the pen and paper in a silent but eloquent plea.

"Good God! I don't know what my friends would do to me, were I to teach you, a runaway slave, to read and write English. If I wanted to, I wouldn't know how to go about it. . . . Jules, my friend and overseer, is literate because he always accompanied me to school, but he never flaunts it. My mother isn't even aware of it. You have to understand, Omoroh. I don't keep slaves, but that doesn't mean I stir up trouble. Neither my family nor my friends see a need for the education of Negroes beyond ordinary household tasks and field labor. It simply isn't done . . . or it's done very rarely."

The disappointment in Omoroh's eyes made Tiger glance away in embarrassment. It had never worried or bothered him about Jules being literate, but Jules had been born and raised in the South and understood its sensitivities. He was unlikely to try and rise above his station. This man, however, was a mysterious, possibly dangerous renegade, ready and able to make trouble. He possessed intimidating skills and knowledge, wrote in a language Ty couldn't identify, and understood yet another.

Maybe the reason Southerners enslaved Negroes

was because they feared what these strong, industrious, resourceful people might accomplish on their own if given half a chance, Ty thought. His own mixed feelings deeply disturbed him. He recalled Stephanie once complaining that a Southern woman always had to live her life surrounded by "a horde of filthy Africans, for whom she was responsible from the cradle to the grave."

The comment had irritated Tiger; his own servants made as good use of soap and water as anyone, and he had answered tartly, "Maybe if they were treated more like humans and less like animals, they wouldn't smell like pigs in a wallow, Stephanie."

Stephanie hadn't spoken to him for days, and he'd finally had to apologize. Stephanie would have hated Omoroh on sight; uppity Negroes had annoyed her even more than dirty ones. Standing in his cabin, trying to ignore Omoroh's disappointment, Tiger couldn't help comparing Stephanie's attitudes to Freedom's. It gave him no comfort that his own attitudes more closely paralleled the former's than the latter's. Freedom, he knew instinctively, would have dropped everything in order to teach Omoroh how to read and write. But, then, Freedom Walker was an amazing young woman . . . just how amazing he had yet to discover.

Chapter Seven

Freedom lay on the chaise longue in the darkness and strained to hear the conversation drifting up from the balcony below. There was nothing else to do but eavesdrop, and she was tired of lying on the bed; the chaise longue offered a comfortable vantage point close enough to the open windows to enable her to follow the discussion going on below between two gentlemen.

"If this keeps up, we'll be rich as British lords, Malcolm. . . . Could you ever have conceived of such profits before the war?"

"Hardly, old man, hardly . . . And it'll surely get better before it gets worse. Why, ah made a fortune on that last crate of quinine I got through to Charleston. Bought it here at ten dollars an ounce and sold it there at four hundred dollars for the same damn ounce. Can you believe it?"

"That's nothin', Malcolm. Ah disposed of one thousand corsets on my last trip to our beloved Confederacy. The ladies couldn't buy 'em fast enough. They'd rather have corsets than cloth for uniforms; no matter if there's a war going on,

101

Southern belles have got to be fashionable."

"Oh, everyone knows the aristocrats ain't about to suffer in order to clothe the army—or to feed 'em, either, though food will probably assume more importance the longer this altercation lasts."

"No doubt . . . But so long as Charleston and Wilmington stay open, the Confederacy should survive. . . Let's drink a toast to wartime and the wonderful prosperity it generates!"

"All right . . . Have you heard the toast they're raisin' their glasses to in all the taverns? . . . Here's to the Confederates that produce the cotton; to the Yankees that maintain the blockade and keep up the price of cotton; and to the Britishers who buy the cotton and pay the high price for it. Three cheers to a long continuance of the war, and success to all blockade-runners!"

There was a short silence while the men presumably drank. Freedom clenched her fists in anger and wished her chain reached far enough to shut the windows; she had heard all she could endure. The only thing these men cared about was making money. They affected to be Southern sympathizers, but in reality they were vultures, preying on the vanity of deprived housewives, while gray-clad soldiers fought and died.

The names of blood-drenched battlefields rose in her mind: Bull Run Creek; York Peninsula; Fredericksburg, Virginia; Shiloh, Tennessee; Chancellorville, Virginia . . . Casualty lists of the men who had died at these places were posted in Wilmington as soon as they became available. The townspeople then rushed to study them, searching for familiar names. How dare anyone make light of a war that was taking young men's lives and causing so much suffering and deprivation!

Freedom was outraged that anyone could toast a war and pray for its continuance. She had not personally experienced grief, but she did know firsthand of the shortages caused by the war. Hattie Draper's shop had once served not only the fashion needs of the wealthy but also the poorer woman; now only the wealthy could afford to shop there, and then the selection was greatly limited. Even when stock was available, Hattie could not always pay the going price for pretty hair ribbons or bits of lace. She bought only what she knew with certainty would be sold, paid outrageous sums for it, and had to pass the increases along to her customers. Both Hattie and Freedom had felt sorry for the women who looked longingly at the expensive merchandise but went away without buying anything. Freedom knew exactly how they felt. Hattie could no longer pay wages, and Freedom was working for room and board alone—another reason why she had been so anxious to return to the North.

The sound of a key turning in the lock of the outside door catapulted Freedom off the chaise longue, and she hurriedly straightened her dress and smoothed back her hair with her fingers. Tiger's voice preceded him into the room.

"Are you decent, Mouse? I'm having a few things delivered. . . . Why are you sitting here in the dark? I can't see a damn thing."

Ty's tall figure strode into the bedchamber, and a moment later, a light flared in an oil lamp set on a small round table. Seeing that she was dressed, Ty

103

motioned to someone standing outside the door. Two mulatto women came into the room, practically staggering under the weight of six large boxes and numerous packages wrapped in thin paper and tied with gaily colored ribbons. Freedom sucked in her breath. Using ribbon to tie packages during this time of deprivation was a shameless waste. Whatever could be inside all those boxes and bundles? she wondered.

"You may put everything on the bed. . . . Is that all of it?" Tiger asked. One woman nodded, and he flipped her a coin and tossed another to her companion. "Very good . . . You may leave us alone now — unless the lady desires your assistance." He turned to Freedom. "Are you capable of dressing yourself, Mouse, or do you require the aid of an extra pair of female hands?"

"I'm quite capable of dressing myself," Freedom haughtily replied.

"You heard her," Ty said. "Scat! Be gone with you."

Giggling together, the two servants left the room, and Ty turned to Freedom with a grand sweep of his hand. "Well, there you are, Mouse, a wardrobe suitable to the climate of Nassau. While I see to having our dinner sent up, why don't you change into something more comfortable? I'm going down to the dining room; I need to locate a certain gentleman whom I've been told has been spending his evenings here lately, but I'll rejoin you shortly."

"I thought I'd be dining alone," Freedom reminded him, not wanting to have him staring at her while she ate. "I thought you had business associates expecting you to share a meal and brandy with them."

"I do . . . but I've changed my mind about doing business tonight. What I really want is a quiet evening alone with you—not dressed as a church mouse, however. Please open the boxes and choose something to wear. . . . You must be eager to change out of that awful hot gown."

Freedom eyed the boxes and packages heaped high on the bed. "I'm not sure I should, Captain. I—I can't repay your generosity—at least, not yet, and maybe not ever. I know what things cost, you see, and right now I could not afford even the ribbons used to tie those packages."

Tiger Carrington surveyed her incredulously. "I'm not *asking* you to change, Mouse, I'm *telling* you. Either you find something to wear among all those things I bought today, or I'll find something. Frankly, if it's up to me, you won't be wearing much at all."

"You are no gentleman, sir!" Freedom flared, momentarily forgetting her earlier offer of going to bed with him in exchange for Omoroh's freedom. "Never in my life have I met anyone as despicable as you. I suppose if I don't wear these new clothes, you'll threaten to do something awful to Omoroh."

"There's always that possibility," Ty conceded. "But I'm sure you won't drive me to it—not over a little thing like clothing."

Freedom turned her back on him and flounced over to the bed, waiting until she heard the door again being locked, before she would touch a single package. When she was sure she was alone, she picked up a large box tied with a precious scarlet ribbon. Her hands shook as she carefully untied it.

105

Despite her disapproval, she could not quell the anticipation bubbling up in her. Her father had not been much of a gift-giver; when she longed for a pretty bonnet or a new pair of stockings, he was far more apt to give her a book, usually one that was old and dog-eared. She had received a well-worn copy of *Uncle Tom's Cabin* for her tenth birthday and a yellowed issue of *The Liberator* newspaper for her twelfth.

Of course, she had appreciated these gifts, but her childish heart still longed for . . . scarlet ribbons. She removed the lid from the box and stared down at its contents—an apricot-colored muslin gown with a scalloped neckline and white organdy sleeves. Lifting it, she shook out the skirt and gasped in wonderment. The hem of the skirt must measure at least ten yards in circumference, Freedom realized; she'd need a steel corset, a crinoline, and five or six petticoats to wear under it!

Examining the gown closely, she discovered tiny tight stitches—too uniform to have been done by hand. The dress was machine-made, probably from the textile mills in England, New York, or Boston. It was the first entirely machine-stitched garment she had ever seen; most of what was sold in Hattie Draper's shop was either entirely or partially hand-sewn, for the wives of North Carolina planters frowned upon manufactured clothing, regarding it as suitable only for slaves or soldiers. But this gown was beautiful, Freedom thought, caressing the soft fabric with her fingers.

She tore open the next package, and three petticoats and two pantalets of lace-edged white dimity fell out. Another package held the necessary crinoline and corset, and a third contained satin apricot slippers to match the gown and a pair of high-button shoes in black patent leather. Curiosity got the better of her then, and Freedom ripped through the remaining boxes and packages like a greedy, spoiled child. They yielded a wealth of finery that took her breath away: day dresses in mint-green, buttercup-yellow, rose-pink, and robin's-egg-blue, a beautiful taffeta evening gown shot through with gold threads on an amber background, another evening gown in ivory muslin trimmed with rosebuds, lace-edged silky lingerie and chemises, fine lisle stockings, two stylish hats accompanied by the requisite long hat pins, a gold hair net, a lacy shawl, airy fichus, and many other things, including two bottles of a rather harsh-smelling perfume faintly reminiscent of gardenias.

The mint-green gown appeared to have been taken in at the waist and bosom. Though the work was hand-done, it was clumsy and never would have passed muster at Hattie Draper's. Freedom found other small flaws in workmanship, but on the whole, she was enchanted—until she tried on the first dress she'd opened, the apricot muslin. Without assistance, she was unable to tighten the corset and so relinquished it and slipped the dress over the crinoline and petticoats alone. It settled to the floor with a swish, she did up the fastenings, then peered into the mirror. . . . Blessed saints in heaven! Half her bosom and all of her shoulders were revealed!

She reminded herself that many Southern belles displayed themselves thus, but she herself had never worn anything so daring. Examining each gown in turn, she discovered that not a one of them covered her decently, not even the day dresses, and the nightwear was far worse! Made of sheer, silky fabrics, laces, and ribbons, they were designed with only one thought in mind: to reveal more than they concealed. She ought to have known! Obviously, Tiger Carrington did intend to help himself to her virginity!

Furious, she threw a wispy undergarment across the room. A gust of wind picked it up, and it sailed out the open windows, skimmed the balcony railing, and plunged out of sight into the darkness. So he would force her to dress like a whore, would he? Well, she'd show him what she thought of his nasty mind and ulterior motives. Scooping up an armful of clothing, she stalked to the open windows as far as the chain would allow and commenced tossing the rest of the finery over the balcony railing. Some of the garments fell short, but most of them cleared the distance, billowed in the light breeze, and sailed out of sight.

She grinned with grim pleasure when she heard a voice on the balcony below cry out, "Mah word, Malcolm! Look at that, will you? . . . Ah think ah just saw a lady's chemise drift by."

"You've had too much to drink, old boy . . . Ah didn't see anything. . . . Oh, wait! There goes a gown! We've *both* had too much to drink. . . . No more toasts; we'd better quit this minute, or we're apt to see the lady herself fly by!"

Seated near the railing on the hotel veranda, Tiger poured another brandy for the short, stocky old man called The Professor, then sat back and waited for him to render an opinion on Omoroh's handwriting. "Well, Professor, do you recognize the language?"

"Now, now, Captain Carrington . . . This takes time," The Professor said, holding the papers closer to the candle flickering inside a glass on the table between them. He pushed his spectacles further up on his bulbous nose and frowned.

"You translate things everyday, don't you?" Ty inquired. "Bills of lading, foreign cargo lists, contracts . . . or so I was told."

"Yes, of course, Captain . . . I speak four languages and understand three more. That's what I am . . . a linguist. But that doesn't mean I can give my opinion on a moment's notice."

"Do you understand it or not?" Ty was growing impatient. "If it's money you want, I'll gladly pay you. . . . Just name your price."

"Hush, sir . . . We'll attend to details later. . . . I'm trying to make out some of these words. . . . Ah, yes, that one means the Sudan, I'm sure of it. And this next one is the Senegal River."

"Then you *do* understand it. Wonderful! What does it say?"

"Tut, tut . . . I understand a few isolated words, but a complete translation will take a great deal of time and effort. Even then, I can't guarantee perfection."

"Can you at least tell me the language it's written in?"

"Arabic, I think . . . or something remarkably similar." The Professor lowered the papers and grimaced. "I once set myself the horrendous task of translating the Koran—the Muhammadan Bible—into English. I spent years on it, working in my spare time, certain that if I could accomplish such a grand task, I'd be rich and famous. Then I discovered it had already been done. English translations of the Koran are available from a publisher in New York."

"I don't care about the Koran," Ty burst out. "Will you eventually be able to tell me the contents of those documents or not?"

"I think so . . . eventually. I don't remember much Arabic, unfortunately . . . haven't had much call to use it. But I do have English and Arabic translations of the Koran, and between the two, I may be able to make out what the man who wrote this is trying to say."

"Then go ahead and translate it. . . . I'll be in Nassau for several days unloading cotton and making my purchases for the homeward run to Wilmington. Before I leave, I'll consult with you and see if you've managed to finish it."

"Several days . . . That isn't much time, Captain, and I have other commitments."

"Make time, Professor. I'll pay you well."

"I promise you I'll do my best. . . . Gracious, what's *that?*" The Professor pointed to something white floating down from the sky.

Tiger saw it at almost the same time The Professor did. As they both watched, the object snagged itself on a nearby bush. The thing was within his reach, so Ty leaned over the railing, grabbed it, and held it up for inspection. It was a lady's delicate, lacy white chemise. Ty stared at it a moment, then burst out laughing. "Good Lord! I wonder where

110

this came from."

The Professor also began to laugh. "From upstairs on one of the balconies, most likely. Perhaps it was hung out to dry and fell off the railing by accident. . . . Oh, look! There's something else!"

The second object was unmistakably a pair of lady's underdrawers, and as Ty watched in mounting amusement, other garments rained down from the night sky—a gown with a huge, full skirt, a pair of satin slippers, a filmy fichu, a second gown. Other people on the veranda—mostly men—noticed the unusual shower and began talking in loud, excited voices.

"What is it? . . . What's happening?"

Several men ran out to catch the objects, and one man was struck on the temple with a steel corset. "Hey!" he shouted, suddenly enraged. "Who's doing that up there? What do you mean by pelting people with dangerous objects?"

"It isn't us!" a man shouted from the balcony overhead. "It's someone on the next floor up."

An awful truth began to dawn on Tiger. His room and Freedom's was almost directly above the veranda, on the third floor.

"Excuse me," Ty said to The Professor. "I just remembered a most pressing engagement. . . . In a day or two, I'll contact you again. In the meantime, do start work."

"Must you leave so soon?" The Professor rose to his feet. "Oh, my . . . There goes another gown!"

Tiger looked where The Professor was looking and saw a beautiful ivory-colored muslin dress being caught by a man who held it up with a delighted bellow. "Why, this might fit my wife!" the

111

man exclaimed. "Here, now . . . toss down another! I've a daughter at home, too!"

"And a whore down on the docks!" a voice added from the veranda. "who will you really give it to, William—your wife or your whore?"

Ty vaulted over the railing and snatched the gown from the man's hands. "Give me that!" he snarled. "I know exactly who's doing this and why. . . . The rest of you gentlemen hand over that clothing, or be prepared to defend your thievery with a pistol or saber, instead of lame excuses."

"This belongs to *you?*" the startled man inquired, eyeing Tiger with a trace of belligerence.

"It belongs to my mistress," he ground out. "She's bored and rebellious because I don't spend enough time with her. As soon as I gather up these gifts I just bought her, I'll see to it that she finds better ways to keep herself occupied."

"Ah, mistresses . . ." the other man commiserated. "They can be such nuisances. Here, let me help you. . . . You shouldn't buy the bitch another present until she comes to her senses and learns her place. Why, I once had a female throw a flowerpot at my head! Can you imagine it . . . a flowerpot! Damn near killed me!"

A jocular mood prevailed as men retrieved the fallen garments and heaped them in Tiger's arms, all the while relating their own experiences with tempestuous, moody women. A passing servant had to be pressed into service, because Ty couldn't hold everything and wound up with a bonnet perched upon his head and the ribbons dangling in his eyes.

"Is that you, Ty Carrington?" a man called out.

With a sinking feeling in the pit of his stomach, Ty recognized the voice of his friend, John Wilkinson, a fellow blockade-runner and an officer in the Confederate Navy. Now that John had discovered him in this ludicrous predicament, he'd never hear the end of it.

"Of course, it's me," he gruffly responded. "Surely, you didn't take me for someone's old maid aunt."

"Actually, I rather thought you resembled my grandmother. Guess I'll have to call you Granny from now on."

A whoop of laughter followed this exchange, spurring Ty to hasten his getaway. Oh, but Freedom Walker was going to pay for this! Not only had she subjected him to needless ridicule, but the clothes she had callously tossed away cost more than he cared to think about. He should have used the money to buy uniforms for Confederate soldiers, but instead, in a moment of weakness, he'd spent it on a little Union spy who wouldn't know fashion if it bit her on the nose. Since she obviously scorned his gifts, from now on she could go naked. But before he told her that, he'd take her over his knee and wallop some manners into her! The spoiled little brat deserved to be spanked unmercifully!

Chapter Eight

Freedom felt a pang of regret as she hurled the last of the booty over the balcony railing: the two bottles of perfume. She'd never worn perfume; her father had regarded it as an instrument of the devil, and it was beyond her modest means, anyway, even when Hattie had been paying her wages. She regretted the loss of the gowns, too, but mostly she mourned the ribbons. They symbolized all the sacrifices she had made for the sake of The Cause.

Sitting down on the corner of the bed and folding her hands in her lap, she took comfort in the fact she had done the right thing — removed temptation before it was too late and she succumbed to it. Of course, the gowns could have been altered so they would not be so objectionable, or she could have arranged a fichu around her shoulders and bosom to protect her modesty, but neither of these two choices removed the main stumbling block: If she accepted Tiger Carrington's charity, she would owe him something, and the only thing worth surrendering her virginity for was Omoroh's freedom, not a bunch of gowns. Captain Carrington mustn't get the idea that he could buy his way into her bed.

A scuffling noise outside the door alerted her to the

arrival of her captor. Straightening her shoulders, she remained where she was and calmly waited for him to enter . . . and waited . . . and waited. All she heard was his furious voice.

"Damn it, I can't reach my key . . . in my pocket, there. No, not that pocket, you featherbrained idiot! God deliver me from stupid, vexatious women! . . . Yes, that one. Go on, open the damn door!"

The door swung open, and one of the mulatto women scurried inside, looking cowed and frightened. Her arms were full of the clothing Freedom had just disposed of, and she dumped it on the chaise longue and scurried out again, without saying a word or waiting for payment. Ty himself staggered into the room — at least, Freedom assumed it was Tiger beneath the flower and ribbon-bedecked hat, his arms overflowing with muslin, his hands clutching shoes and slippers. She couldn't help herself; she started to giggle.

"What in hell are you laughing at?" he roared. "Get yourself over here and take some of this before I drop it!"

"I — I can't!" she sputtered, consumed with glee. "My chain won't stretch that far."

"By God, if you don't stop laughing, I'll flay you alive!" he thundered, advancing toward the bed.

She almost twisted an ankle jumping up to get out of his way. As he strode past the full-length mirror, Ty caught sight of himself, stopped in his tracks, and stared. Then he blew the ribbons out of his eyes and turned a murderous glance on her. "I really think," he said in all seriousness, "that you deserve to die for this, Mouse."

"You must admit the bonnet becomes you, Captain," she goaded before she thought.

A reluctant grin tugged at the corners of his mouth.

"Yes, it does, doesn't it? The only problem is that it wasn't meant for me; it was meant for you." The grin abruptly disappeared. "And you're damn well going to wear it!"

"Never," she said, putting the bed between them. "I'll never wear anything you bought. Don't think I'll play the whore for you just because you gave me a whore's clothing."

"But you do plan to play the whore, don't you?" He came as far as the bed and dumped everything in his arms upon it. "I believe you offered me your virginity if I would free Omoroh."

Freedom's throat constricted. "Yes, I did . . . but— but I certainly don't intend to dress the part just to please your—your base desires."

He took off the hat and threw it, too, down on the bed. "I wasn't dressing you like a whore; I was dressing you like a Southern belle."

"I can't say I see the difference."

"All right . . . Let's forget about the clothes. . . ." He swept everything from the bed with one swipe of a powerful arm. "We've more important things to discuss. Let me see if I've got this straight: You won't go to bed with me because you find me attractive, or because I give you gifts, or because there's any sort of feeling between us. The only permissible reason is the altruistic one of 'laying down your life'—spreading your legs would be more accurate—'for your fellow man. . . .' "

"If that's what I have to do, then I'll do it!" Freedom shouted. "I don't expect you to understand my motives, because you're blinded by who and what you are!"

"And just exactly what might that be, Mouse?" Ty's tone was deadly quiet, like a tiger's before it pounced.

116

"A slaver!" she hissed. "A man who risks his life and that of others to perpetuate an institution of evil and wickedness."

"How arrogant you are!" he hissed back. "How arrogant, blind, and self-righteous . . . What if I told you I *wasn't* a slaver, that I've never owned a slave in my entire life, much less beaten or mistreated one?"

"I wouldn't believe you," Freedom scoffed. "Who picked all that cotton you brought to Nassau? Who planted and tended it? . . . Don't lie to me, Ty Carrington. I know exactly the sort of man you are. All the denials in the world won't convince me otherwise; I'm not such a naive fool as that. . . . You have the haughty arrogance of a slaver. You have the look of one. Indeed, you have the very stink of one!"

Ty's glance was murderous. For a moment, he said nothing, leading her to believe he'd gone speechless with rage. Then he finally found his tongue, and his voice sent shivers up her spine. "Since you persist in thinking me such a monster, Mouse, I might as well act like one. . . . Take off that god-awful dress. If you want Omoroh to go free, then you can buy his freedom here and now."

Freedom flinched and backed away. Now that he really meant to accept her offer, she wasn't sure she could go through with it. "Do you . . . swear you'll really let him go?"

Ty's hands were busy removing his coat and shirt. "I swear to you the choice will be his. . . . But I warn you, he may not want to leave me."

"No man willingly remains a slave if he has a choice!"

"I've already given him a choice," Tiger said. "I told him he can come work for me, or he can stay here in Nassau."

117

"I don't believe that either! You're trying to trick him into going back to Wilmington with you, so you can collect the reward being offered for him."

"Whether you believe me or not doesn't interest me. I'll not defend myself to the likes of you—a devious little liar in your own right. You've made a bargain; I accepted it. You deliver on your end, and I'll deliver on mine."

Freedom was terrified. She was also . . . excited. Ty Carrington had bared his chest and now was working on his boots and trousers. His chest was beautiful, covered with gold, curly hair that spread like a rug across his pectoral muscles, then tapered to a V-shape low on his abdomen before disappearing into his waistband. Fascinated and intrigued, she could not look away from his emerging nudity. But when he dropped his pants suddenly, she closed her eyes and nervously clasped her hands together.

"Please don't make me do this," she pleaded. "I—I'm afraid. I've never been with a man."

"Well, I hope not. . . . Because if you have, you're not a virgin, and your virginity is what you offered, isn't it?"

"Oh, please . . ." she whispered, scrunching her eyelids to keep them shut. The blood was pounding in her head; she felt faint and shivery.

"Believe me, Mouse, I'm not going to make you do anything. This was your idea, remember? You're supposed to be a willing participant . . . not some damn shrinking violet. Open your eyes and look at me. Or are you afraid you might see something you like?"

"Can't you at least turn out the light?" she begged. "And close the windows?" She heard him moving about but didn't dare open her eyes.

"There, the light's out. But I've only closed one window. It's already too hot in here. The last thing you need to worry about is catching cold."

"That's not what worries me. I — I don't want anyone to hear us."

He sighed impatiently. "I'll try to stifle my moans of passion. If I get too noisy, you can stuff a pillow in my mouth."

Freedom wished she could smother him with a pillow. She opened one eye and saw that he had indeed turned out the light. But enough starlight was spilling through the windows to illuminate and outline his body — his strong, masculine, powerful, and very naked body. He stood on the other side of the bed from her and held out his arms.

"Come here, Mouse. . . . If you won't take off that dreadful gown, I guess I'll have to take it off for you."

She took another step backward, her chain clanking loudly. "Captain . . . I think I've changed my mind. I need more time to think about this. Maybe I was too hasty."

"Ty . . . call me Tiger. Captain is much too formal a title to use in bed. . . . Better yet, call me sweetheart . . . darling . . . beloved . . . whatever best expresses your tender feelings."

"Bastard!" she blurted out.

He infuriated her by laughing. "Do you always say what you think, Mouse? Your honesty would be refreshing if it weren't so damaging to my ego. Come here. . . . This doesn't have to be a terrible experience, you know. The women I've bedded in the past have always said they enjoyed my lovemaking."

"Did you chain them to the bedstead, too? Would they have run away if they could have?"

"Most definitely not . . . Here, let me remove that chain. Then maybe you'll be able to relax and feel

119

comfortable."

She turned her head away as he came across the bed toward her. This was how she had imagined him, stripped to the skin, but the reality frightened her as much as it caused her heart to flutter wildly. Dear God, could she really go through with this? Could she actually lie down on the bed, and . . . and spread her legs for him?

He knelt on the floor in front of her and fumbled with the chain, while she tried hard not to glance down at him. But she was acutely conscious that his tousled blond head came to the exact height of her breasts. When he raised his head to look at her, he accidentally brushed her left breast, and her nipple budded in response.

"There, Mouse . . . The chain is gone, now." He wrapped his arms around her hips and held her imprisoned, while he nuzzled first one breast and then the other. "God, but you're soft . . ." he murmured. "Soft and full . . . I had in mind spanking you, but now . . ."

His hands moved to her shoulders and began to rub up and down her arms, as if he were able to feel the texture of her skin through the fabric of her sleeves. When he spoke again, his voice was a throaty growl. "I want you, Mouse. I want you more than I've ever wanted any woman. God alone knows why. I don't think for a minute that you're as innocent as you pretend. . . . Damn, you've bewitched me! . . . Every time I look at you, you twist my insides . . . wrench me apart. . . ."

Rising to his feet, he rubbed his tall body along the length of hers, striking sparks, igniting a fire of anticipation deep in her belly. When he was eye to eye with her, he imprisoned her chin in one hand and captured her mouth with his. Greedily, he devoured her lips. His tongue forayed between them and dueled with her tongue, while his free hand found its way inside her bodice and caressed her breast. He tilted her backward onto the bed and expertly removed her clothing, all the while pressing kisses to her lips, temples, eyelids, and throat.

Frantically, she tried to hold onto her chemise and pantalets, but he relentlessly stripped them away, exposing her to his mouth and hands, which explored her shamelessly, never giving her the chance to pull away.

"I can't get enough of you, Mouse. I just can't get enough." He slid a hand beneath her buttocks and lifted her to meet him as he lowered himself on top of her. His mouth homed in on her right breast. He licked and laved it, then took the nipple in his mouth and suckled. Freedom whimpered and squirmed, helpless to evade him or deny the sensations rioting throughout her body. He paid court to her other breast, teasing the nipple until it stood to attention. He commanded all of her body, making her sigh, moan, gasp, and buck beneath him.

His assaults became increasingly intimate. His fingers discovered places of which she herself was hardly aware. Whatever and wherever he touched, he made his own. The more he kissed, petted, licked, and caressed, the more conscious she became of a mounting pressure, coiling and uncoiling in the pit of her stomach. Expectation sizzled along her nerve endings.

"Please!" she begged, not quite knowing what she wanted but realizing only he could give it to her.

He parted her thighs. As his gaze avidly ravished her, she found the courage to look at that part of him she had felt but not yet seen. Astonished at the size of him, she gasped, wondering how he would ever fit in-

121

side her. As he saw where she was looking, he chuckled deep in his throat.

"What is it, Mouse? Do I scare you? This is what you wanted, isn't it?"

If she'd had a response, which she didn't, the words would have stuck in her throat.

"Don't be afraid," he purred. "I'll try not to hurt you. We were made to fit together. . . . You'll see. Everything will be fine."

With a gentleness of which she had not thought him capable, he probed between her legs, his hardness pressing against her. The intrusion did not hurt. Rather, it felt wonderful, and she wriggled a little, savoring the friction. He surprised her by groaning, as if he were the one in pain. Then he began to kiss her again, deep, swollen kisses that made her arch against him in mounting urgency. She wrapped her arms and legs around him, drowning in his kisses. He pushed inside her, but not deep enough to satisfy her cravings. She tilted her hips to grant him easier access, and he rose up on his elbows.

"Mouse, I want you so badly."

"It's all right. . . . I—I think I'm ready, Ty."

His first name slipped out of her mouth as if she'd been thinking of him that way for a long time, without being conscious of it. With a swift, sure movement, he penetrated her fully. The pain was searing; she stiffened and cried out, certain he had torn some vital part of her.

He poised above her, his breathing ragged. "It will never hurt like this again. I promise you, Mouse. The worst is over. . . ."

"Are you finished then?" She hoped he was, though she herself had a sense of frustration and incompletion.

"I've barely begun."

Fear seized her. She tried to pull back from him and disengage their bodies. "You've taken my virginity; now please leave me alone!"

He resisted her struggles and held her pinioned beneath him. "Mouse, no . . . It gets better, I promise."

He started to kiss her again, to touch and fondle her, but she hardened her heart against him and lay stiff as a board, panting with fright and the effort not to respond. If they loved each other, if he cared for her and she for him . . . If they were husband and wife, it would be different. She could no longer give her future husband her virginity, but at least she could give him her ultimate surrender. She could hold back an essential part of herself and not waste it on a man who despised her.

At last, when she didn't move or speak, Tiger rolled away to the side, breathing heavily. His departure left her feeling chilled — both inside and out. Goose bumps prickled her flesh, and she waited anxiously to see what he would do next.

"Cover yourself, Miss Walker. . . ." His voice was brittle and icy as winter. "I'm sorry I hurt you. . . . I won't do it again. For the brief time we're in Nassau, I'll sleep elsewhere. Keep the clothes or burn them, I don't care which. Do whatever you want."

His tone of voice stunned her; he sounded as if *he* had been hurt and humiliated.

"What about Omoroh?" she forced herself to ask, remembering their bargain. Maybe he wouldn't keep it after the way she'd denied him and herself.

"I've already told you; as soon as I get you back to my ship, he's free."

"Then you still intend to return me to Wilmington and hand me over to the Confederate authorities?"

"You still haven't convinced me you're not a spy. Why should I take your word for anything? What this little episode has taught me is that you're a cold, calculating little bitch, Miss Walker. . . . For a while, there, I thought you might be as sweet and tenderhearted as you look. But you proved tonight that you haven't an ounce of softness or tenderness in you. You threw my gifts back in my face, coldly held to your agreement, and when you had fulfilled it, cast me aside. You're worse than any whore. At least, a whore would have faked some enjoyment of my attentions, so I'd feel I'd gotten my money's worth."

He got up from the bed and began rummaging around on the floor.

Freedom didn't know what to say. She *had* enjoyed his attentions — far more than she had ever thought possible, at least until the pain began. Even now, she was longing for him to come back into the bed, take her in his arms again, and finish what they'd started.

"What . . . are . . . you . . . looking for?" she finally managed to get out past the lump in her throat.

"My clothes. And your chain. I'll have your meals sent up, but other than that, you won't see me again until it's time to leave."

She turned over on her stomach and buried her face in the quilt. And she didn't — couldn't — move from the spot even after he left the room a short time later.

Chapter Nine

Tiger ushered Omoroh into the cramped office of The Professor, then banged on the desktop to get someone's attention. From a back room came The Professor's voice: "I'll be out in a minute! Whoever you are, sit down and make yourself comfortable."

Ty pointed to the only chair available on his side of the overflowing desk. "You heard the man. Sit down, Omoroh. . . . I hope I didn't bring you along on a wild-goose chase. The Professor may not have been able to translate what you wrote. If he didn't, don't be too disappointed. We'll just have to keep looking until we find someone who understands Arabic."

Omoroh nodded, his face impassive, but hope was shining in the big Negro's eyes. Not for the first time, Ty wondered what it must be like not to be able to speak or make oneself understood. The more he saw of Omoroh, the more convinced he was of the man's intelligence and refinement. That a man such as this should have been forced to serve a cruel master was a crying shame — but probably no worse than the entire system of slavery. Ty was growing weary of always having to defend the institution. He himself had never approved of it, yet Freedom made him feel guilty, as if he were personally responsible. He did disagree with her on one very important point: What other men did on their own property, *with* their own property, was not his business.

The entire economic system of the South depended upon slavery. To topple the system was to topple the South—and what right did the North have to tell the South how it should run its business, anyway? Ty firmly believed that in time the Confederacy would find some other way to get its fields planted and its cotton picked. Like Ty himself, many Southerners already looked down upon men who abused their slaves, but they would defend a man's right to keep slaves and live life on his own terms with all the resources they had available. They would defend a *white* man's rights, Ty silently amended. A black man, of course, had no rights.

He smiled at Omoroh to set him at ease. "As soon as we finish here, Omoroh, I'm going to the hotel to get Miss Walker. I want to leave for Wilmington tonight. Now that my cotton's been sold and my new cargo's loaded, there's no sense sitting around Nassau, twiddling our thumbs, waiting for the moon to wane. It isn't even full yet, so it would take too long. If we're lucky, we might be in for a spell of cloudy weather. Clouds are banking to the north, I noticed. I hope it doesn't storm, but I wouldn't mind a nice gentle rain and a dark night for our run past the Federal blockade."

Omoroh nodded, then glanced past Ty's shoulder. Ty turned to see The Professor entering the room through the doorway behind the desk. "Captain Carrington! How nice to see you again . . . and who's this fellow you brought along with you? Dare I hope it's the man who wrote the documents you gave me?"

"This is the fellow. His name is Omoroh," Tiger

confirmed, as Omoroh respectfully rose to his feet. "I thought he should come with me in case you were successful. That way he can write down answers to additional questions I'd like to ask him."

The Professor slowly looked Omoroh up and down. "Let me introduce myself, Omoroh — or perhaps I should address you as Your Majesty. Everyone calls me The Professor. I have another name, but like many here in Nassau, I choose not to divulge it."

"I take it you were able to translate what Omoroh wrote," Ty interjected, ignoring The Professor's reference to a mysterious past.

The Professor grinned. "Of course! Most of it, anyway. There are words here and there that I could not make out, because I don't have an Arabic dictionary. So please don't ask Omoroh to write anything additional. These papers took me long enough." The Professor rummaged around on his desktop and produced the original four sheets of paper, plus two extras on which were scrawled his notes. "Here they are, Captain. I wrote a brief summary of what I translated. That's probably what you'll want to read."

Tiger took the papers and scanned the summary. It confirmed what he already knew and added additional, intriguing information. Omoroh was an Afro-Arabian prince of the Foulah tribe. He had been born along the banks of the Senegal River in Western Africa, and his tribe encompassed many nations, including some in the Sudan region. Omoroh himself was descended from the Berbers and had traveled extensively before being captured by other Negroes and sold to a white trader. Omoroh adhered to the teachings of Muhammad and claimed to know the Koran, parts of which he had written down as proof that he was who he claimed to be.

"Didn't he say anything about what happened to him when he got to this country?" Ty asked, rifling through the papers in search of that information.

"There, on the second page of my translation . . ." The Professor said. "He almost died on the voyage here, was apparently brought to Charleston, and sold to a fat white man who took him home to his plantation in Georgia."

"The fat man is the one you . . . ah . . . escaped?" Ty was careful not to mention the word *murdered* in front of The Professor.

Before Omoroh could nod yes or no, The Professor clarified. "Yes, that's the man. Omoroh says his master fell down a flight of stairs and died of a broken neck, for which Omoroh was blamed. That's why Omoroh ran away, taking with him his young wife whom the master had abused in a shameless manner. She, poor thing, succumbed to the rigors of the journey."

Ty stared into Omoroh's black eyes. "You're saying you *didn't* kill your master . . . he died in a fall?"

Omoroh slowly nodded his head.

"Why doesn't Miss Walker know about this?" Ty probed. "She thinks you killed the man with your bare hands."

Omoroh held up his hands and made a shoving motion.

"You pushed him then. Is that it?"

Omoroh nodded. The Professor laughed. "No wonder the big fellow ran away. Pushing a man down the stairs is the same as murdering him."

"Not quite," Ty said. "Did you push him deliberately, Omoroh, intending to harm him?"

Omoroh stared straight into Tiger's eyes and nodded. At least, he's honest, Ty thought. And if I'd found someone raping *my* wife, I'd have done a hell of a lot worse to him than pushing him down the stairs.

"Did he write down the name of his master, or the name of the plantation?" Ty asked The Professor.

"I think he tried to, but I couldn't make out the words." The Professor held out his hand. "Give that back to me, and I'll show you."

Ty handed over the papers.

"See here?" The Professor pointed to a line of script."

"I've no idea what these words mean. . . . But here is the word for farm. And this word means hill or mountain. This one refers to a flower of some sort, but I don't know what kind."

Ty stepped back and allowed Omoroh to see what he had written.

"Omoroh, do these words stand for the name of the plantation you fled in Georgia?"

Again, the brief nod.

"A flower . . ." Ty mused. "A magnolia, a camellia, an iris . . . a rose?"

Omoroh excitedly nodded.

"Which one, Omoroh? The camellia . . . the rose?"

At the mention of the latter, Omoroh grinned.

"The rose," Ty repeated, sure of part of the name now. "The name of the plantation has something to do with roses, and hills or mountains."

Omoroh clapped his hands in delighted affirmation.

"Let's see. . . . Rose Hill . . . Rose Mountain?"

Omoroh kept shaking his head no.

"Well, I'll think about it, and maybe it'll come to me. . . . What I really want to find out is more about Miss Walker."

"Is Miss Walker the lady who tossed her garments over the railing of the hotel?" The Professor asked, grinning, and Tiger again regretted that embarrassing episode.

"Did Omoroh mention anything about her in those papers?" he asked.

"He only said that a young woman found him in a place of darkness and led him to a place of light."

"That's all he said?" Ty was disappointed.

"That's all, Captain. . . . What else did you want to know?"

"Never mind . . . Apparently, I'm not going to find it in those papers. How about if I ask Omoroh a few questions, he writes down the answers, and you translate them?"

The Professor sighed. "I've already said no to that, Captain. It's taken me days to translate this much. I lost the Arabic dictionary I once owned, so I had to go through the Koran hunting for words, one by one, until I recognized them. The work was incredibly tedious and painstaking . . . I can't spend any more time on this, and when I tell you how much you owe me, you won't *want* me to spend the time."

"That copy of the Koran . . ." Tiger noted Omoroh's excitement whenever the book was mentioned. "Could I buy it from you?"

"Oh, I don't know, Captain. It's the only thing I've got in Arabic. By comparing it to that English translation I told you about—the book I ordered from New York—I was able to make out words and phrases. That's how I translated what you gave me. Who knows? I might need it again someday."

"I'll buy both the English and the Arabic versions," Ty said. "And I'll pay you twice what they're worth. However, you must include in the bargain your solemn promise never to tell anyone about Omoroh or where he came from."

"Done!" The Professor exclaimed. "Who in Nassau asks such questions, anyway? We all have our secrets. Do you think I'd be wasting my talents in Nassau if I could go home again? Not likely, Captain. Wait here, and I'll fetch both books."

As The Professor retreated into the back room again, Ty caught sight of Omoroh's face. The big Negro's eyes were following The Professor as if the man were suddenly going to produce a miracle. Even when The Professor disappeared, Omoroh's eyes remained riveted to the doorway. It was the books, Ty knew. Omoroh could not believe he was actually going to see the Koran again, which for him must be as precious as Ty might regard a Bible.

When The Professor returned, Ty took both books from the man's hands and placed them in Omoroh's. "These are for you," he said gruffly. "I certainly can't read Arabic. Of course, you can't read English, but maybe you can learn now that you have a copy of the Koran in both languages."

Trembling from head to foot, Omoroh hugged the books to his chest. His obvious happiness needed no words to translate. Tears streamed down his cheeks. Ty had to look away in embarrassment. Not for a minute did he regret buying the books, no matter what they cost. He couldn't say why he had done it; it was an impulsive thing. Perhaps he had bought them because he felt guilty over refusing to teach Omoroh to read and write. Or perhaps he had done it because Freedom's fanaticism was somehow rubbing off on him.

"How much do I owe you?" Ty asked The Professor, who was staring at the weeping Negro.

"Um . . . for the translation, six gold sovereigns. I don't take Confederate script. For the books . . . ah . . . um . . ." The Professor could not seem to take his eyes from Omoroh, who was now caressing the leather bindings of the books and turning them over and over in his hands. "One gold sovereign."

"*One?*" Ty could not believe his ears.

"They were old books," The Professor said defensively. "I didn't realize how old and worthless until I really looked at them. What do I need with them, anyway? I'll probably never be called upon to translate anything in Arabic again. In any case, I've got hundreds of books in my back room . . . more books than I can read in a lifetime."

"I'll pay you six for the books, too," Ty said, reaching for his money. "Just because *I'm* a damn fool doesn't mean you should be."

Freedom sat on the bunk in Tiger Carrington's stuffy cabin and once again wrestled with seasickness. She was doing better this time than last, but only because she kept her thoughts focused on her hatred for Ty rather than on her physical discomfort. He was treating her abominably, and what had been mere dislike and revulsion before had coagulated into something far stronger: real, actual hate. She hated who and what he was; most of all, she hated what he'd done—was doing—to her.

First, he'd kept her captive in the Royal Victoria for almost a week, with nothing to occupy her time except a stack of old newspapers, and then he'd taken her back aboard the *Sea Whisper* and again chained her to the bunk by her ankle. They had been two days at sea already, and during all that time she had seen

132

him only once—when he brought her aboard. He saw to it that she was fed, provided with water for drinking and bathing, and had plenty of clothes to wear—the things he'd bought in Nassau—but other than that, he had totally ignored her. After that disastrous night when she had lost her virginity, Tiger had not bothered her again, nor slept in the same room, nor taken any meals with her, nor indeed spoken two words to her. The two mulatto women at the hotel had seen to all her needs there, and a nameless seaman had served her aboard ship.

She knew Omoroh was on the *Whisper* because the big Negro had accompanied Captain Carrington in the lighter taking her out to the ship, but she had not been able to speak with him privately. Something had happened to make Omoroh the captain's devoted servant. What it was she didn't know, and not knowing was very difficult. How quickly the big black man had seemed to forget all she had done for him! Did Omoroh care that Ty intended to hand her over as a spy? Did he even know what *spying* was? Probably not. Nor did he seem aware of what could happen to *him* when they arrived back in Wilmington.

Omoroh had made a terrible choice, agreeing to work for Ty Carrington. Had she had a chance to speak with him she would have told him so. In Wilmington, no matter what care he took to avoid discovery, Omoroh stood an excellent chance of being apprehended by the slave catchers, and there was also the possibility that one of Ty's own crewmen would see a circular and turn him in for the reward. Unfortunately, there was no way Freedom could warn Omoroh of these things. All that she had done, including sacrificing her virginity, had been for naught; in the end, Omoroh had swallowed Ty Carrington's

133

lies and *chosen* to return to Wilmington.

Bereft of her virginity and self-respect, she herself was en route to imprisonment. There might also be a trial by a jury eager to "make an example" of a Northerner, whether or not she could be proved guilty of spying. If Omoroh's future looked bleak, hers looked even bleaker, and what made it all so unbearable was her continuing attraction to the very man she hated above all others! Whenever she thought about what had happened between her and Ty Carrington—the kisses and caresses, the shocking intimacies—she could not stop her heart from pounding or her knees from going weak. For the first time in her life, she was helpless to control her body's responses. Every time she was in his company, she felt irresistibly drawn to him. Her flesh tingled at his nearness, and her senses came joltingly alive.

He had awakened something inside her that would *not* be ordered asleep again. She kept remembering the brimming excitement his kisses had engendered, the glorious anticipation and straining toward some long-sought goal. What the goal was she wasn't sure. No one had ever told her what to expect in such a situation; the only thing she knew about sex was that it was something men did to women that made the female pregnant . . . and pregnancy was something else she now had to worry about. The thought that she might bear a child, might be pregnant at this very moment, terrified her; if they hung her for being a spy, would they wait until after the baby was born, or would they kill them both together? Would her baby die before it had a chance to live? And if it did live, who would take care of it? Not Ty Carrington, surely. Nor would she *want* her child raised to be a slaver.

With such grim thoughts to occupy her mind, the

nauseating motion of the ship scarcely seemed to matter. Gradually, however, it began to intrude more and more upon her awareness. When the ship suddenly tilted in one direction, seemed to rise under her, then fell away abruptly, pitching her off the bunk, she could no longer ignore it; something strange was happening. No ordinary motion this, the waves were growing big as mountains, with deep valleys in between.

Clutching the side of the bunk, Freedom rose to her feet, then almost fell down again as the cabin rocked violently. She glanced at the lantern swinging wildly on its hook, going first one direction, then the other, and a wave of nausea washed over her. It was better not to watch the lantern, she decided. Bracing herself against the wall, she gingerly made her way to the door and banged her fists upon it.

"Help! Can anyone hear me? What is happening?"

The only sound was the monotonous creaking of the ship's timbers and a muffled roar that seemed to be coming from beyond the boards of the cabin walls. Could the roaring be the wind howling about the ship? Freedom listened intently and deciphered the thud of running feet and the cry of voices raised in alarm. They were surely in the midst of a storm. A crack of thunder shook the entire ship and confirmed her deductions. The loud crack was followed by the slash of rain against the closed porthole.

No one would be thinking about her at this moment, nor would they be able to hear her cries. With a deep sigh, she stumbled back to the bunk and sat down upon it, maintaining her hold on a nearby shelf to keep from losing her balance and being tossed on the floor again. Strangely enough, she felt no fear; if anyone could manage the *Sea Whisper* during a storm, it was Ty Carrington. She had no doubt whatever that Ty would keep them safe.

How close were they to Wilmington? she wondered. Tiger wouldn't try to take them past the blockade in the middle of a storm, would he? That thought did raise a prickle of fear; as ignorant as she was about seamanship, she did know that shoals and sandbars dotted the entrance to both channels of the Cape Fear River. How could Ty see them in the dark and rain . . . or avoid them in a heavy sea?

While she was pondering the question, the door suddenly opened and Ty himself stood in the entranceway. Dripping wet and holding a lantern, he resembled a drowning victim risen from the dead. His soaked shirt and trousers clung to his magnificent physique like a second skin, outlining every ripple of muscle and sinew, so that she could not stop herself from devouring the contours with her eyes. For a moment he simply stood there, returning her avid gaze, then he shook the moisture from his hair and entered the cabin.

"I just came to check on you and tell you to douse the light in your lantern. The way the ship is heaving, the lantern might crash to the floor and cause a fire."

"I'll do it right away," she responded, moving to get up.

"I also came to unchain you." He hung his own lantern on a handy hook, then bent down to grasp her chain. "If anything happens to the ship, you know where to find a dinghy, don't you? . . . Don't leave this cabin unless it's absolutely necessary, but if it is, get inside a dinghy and wait there until I or someone else comes to help you."

"The storm isn't that bad, is it? I thought the *Sea Whisper* was built to withstand storms; you've always

136

seemed quite proud of her."

Tiger unlocked the padlock and threw the chain aside. "I am proud of her. I should be; I designed her myself. In the normal course of events, she could easily outride a bad blow, but tonight isn't normal. I'm going to take her past the blockade, and in this storm, anything could happen."

"Isn't that dangerous?" Freedom gasped. "Wouldn't it be better to wait until a calmer night?"

Tiger straightened and held her gaze with his own. "Running the blockade is always dangerous, Mouse. Your Federalist friends have made it so. At least tonight I won't have to worry about you alerting them to my presence. You'd never get a lantern lit in this downpour, and if you did, they probably wouldn't spot it. . . . Considering the odds against me, tonight is a nearly *perfect* night for running the blockade."

An ominous foreboding caught Freedom in its icy grip. Clutching at his wet shirtsleeves, she voiced her rising panic. "Don't do it tonight, Ty! Please, I beg you, don't do it!"

"My, my . . . Is this a change of heart on your part? Are you actually worried about me? Or are you merely anxious to protect your own soft, tender skin?"

She clung to him in an agony of fear. "Ty, I can't explain it, but I suddenly have this terrible feeling that something bad is about to happen! It's so strong . . . so powerful. I just *know* we won't make it if you try to run the blockade tonight."

"We'll make it. And when we do, you'll soon be on your way to a Confederate prison. That's what's really worrying you."

"Oh, Ty, listen to me! It's not myself I'm worried about. It's *you*—and the ship, your men, and

Omoroh. I just have this feeling I've never had before. . . ." Another crack of thunder drowned out her words.

Ty coldly set her away from him. "I've got to go. . . . Stay in your cabin and put out the light. If you want to do something to help, then pray. Pray we don't run aground on a sandbar or be dashed to pieces against the wreckage of some other blockade-runner who didn't get through. Pray that the Union gunboats don't blow us away. If it goes too much against your grain to do that, then pray for Omoroh's safety. He's the only one for whom you're capable of feeling any compassion."

"That's not true!" she cried. "I have compassion for many people."

"For Southerners? Can you look me in the eye and honestly claim you have compassion for any white man, woman, or child born south of the Mason-Dixon line?"

"Oh, stop it! What has any of this to do with my feeling that something awful is going to happen if you run the blockade tonight?"

His eyes were blacker than the storm bearing down upon the ship. "It has everything to do with it, Mouse. Don't you remember? *I can't trust you.* Which means I can't trust your intuition or feelings. We aren't on the same side, and we never will be! We're enemies. So keep your damn warnings to yourself and let me get about my business!"

Freedom choked back sobs. Was there nothing she could say to dissuade him? Did he really hate her that much? Only moments ago, she had been thinking how much she hated him; but if she did hate him, why was she so afraid for him, and why did the knowledge of his contempt wound her so deeply?

He snatched his lantern from the hook and glared at her. "Don't forget to put out your light. Never mind . . . I'll do it myself before I leave."

When he had done so, he departed the cabin, closing the door behind. A thick, smothering darkness engulfed her, the deepest dark she had ever known. There was no light anywhere, not in her present, not in her past, not in her future. Tiger Carrington — bold, blond, and beautiful — represented the only promise of pleasure and excitement she had ever known. His kisses and caresses, his gifts of perfume, pretty clothes, and hair ribbons, his ability to charge the air with expectation, all combined to make her ill with wanting him. If something happened to him this night, she couldn't bear it. She'd want to die. Incredible as it seemed, somehow, someway, she was losing her heart to a man she despised.

Chapter Ten

Wishing he hadn't stopped to check on Freedom, Ty slung an oilskin across his shoulders before going out again into the storm. He had meant to reassure his captive but had only succeeded in badly frightening her. To make matters worse, his own demons had stirred awake when he saw her. He wanted desperately to return to the cabin, take Freedom in his arms, and kiss away her irrational fears, replacing them with the fire of desire. Avoiding her had not achieved the results for which he had hoped; the more he tried to stay away, the more he wanted her when he finally did see her.

Another moment alone with her and he might have said to hell with it; he'd wait out the storm where he was and run the blockade some other night. . . . Cold logic insisted there would never be a better night than this, but at the moment, he scarcely cared. Returning to the rain-battered deck, he lifted his face to the chilling downpour and let it wash away his temptations. At all costs, he must keep in mind that Freedom Walker could never be his. Even if she was innocent of spying, she lived and breathed in a different world; he hadn't been able to breach her defenses in the one place where he had always excelled at wooing a female — in bed. In the past, it had usually been easy to soothe a woman's fears, dissolve her hesitancies, and make her respond to him on a physical level, if not always mentally or emotionally, but Freedom had shut him out entirely. She scorned his lovemaking, his gifts, his politics, and his very heritage, so why couldn't he put her out of his mind and do what he must with no regrets or self-recrimination?

If they got through the blockade tonight, tomorrow he'd have to take her to the commanding officer at the Confederate Army Post in Wilmington. There was no use entertaining second thoughts about it; it was his duty as a Southern patriot. He couldn't back out now. Still . . . he wished he didn't have to do it. He wished he had more time to learn the truth about her and, yes, to seduce her properly. He wished he could make love to her again and teach her how wonderful it could be, how pleasurable. He wished . . .

"Cap'n? Is that you? . . . Why're you standin' out here in the rain, sir?" Pete was peering at him from the depths of an oil slicker.

With a start, Tiger muttered an oath. "I'm just checking the wind gauge," he alibied.

"I think the storm's gettin' worse, sir. . . ." Pete grabbed for something to hold on to as the ship tilted into a trough between two big waves.

Ty maintained his balance by instinct and force of habit. "The seas do seem to be getting heavier, but the thunder and lightning has lessened somewhat. Send a lookout back up to the crosstrees. Tell him he gets a dollar for every vessel he spots, but if I see it first, his pay gets docked five dollars. . . . What was our position the last time

141

you took it?"

Pete told him, and Ty did some rapid mental calculations. "That means it'll be daybreak when we reach Fort Fisher. . . . I had hoped we'd have several hours lead time, but this storm has prevented us from setting any new records for speed."

"How you plan on goin' in, Cap'n? Which route will we take—New or Old Inlet?"

"We'll do the usual," Tiger responded. "I hate to go ten or fifteen miles out of our way, especially when we're short of time, but I think it's safer in a heavy sea. We'll go north of the fort as far as we have to in order to round the northernmost blockaders, then we'll creep south again close to the shoreline and pray the surf isn't strong enough to drive us onto the shoals near the river's mouth."

"Wouldn't it be easier an' quicker to cut straight through the middle of the blockaders, Cap'n? They won't be lookin' for any runners tonight."

"No, they won't, but if the lightning reveals our position, we're as good as dead. In these seas, we've lost not only our speed but our maneuverability. . . . No, hugging the shore is a safer bet. Once we're in range of the fort's guns, we can turn our attention to avoiding shoals, and we should be able to negotiate the entrance without too much of a problem. . . . You'll see, it'll be simple."

"Don't sound too simple to me, Cap'n, but then you're the one callin' the shots. . . . If you didn't know this shoreline like you do, ah'd be in danger of peein' in my pants from fear of runnin' aground on a sandbar. But you've brought us through some tight spots b'fore, so ah'm sure you can do it this time."

"Don't worry, Pete, I can do it. Now go get that

lookout, and send up a leadsman, too."

"Aye, aye, Cap'n."

As Pete obeyed, Ty made his way to the bridge. From now until they steamed up the Cape Fear River, he must be ever alert and watchful, ready to make decisions that could mean life or death for every man—and woman—aboard. In a few moments, the leadsman arrived and took his position near the forechains, awaiting the order to cast the lead. Ty muttered a command down the engine room tube to Stoker Harris, and the *Sea Whisper* ceased plowing through the huge waves and came to a shuddering stop.

She was promptly buffeted sideways. Water crashed over her bow, drenching the leadsman, but he cast his lead anyway. His shouted report was almost lost in the boom of wind and waves. "Sixteen fathoms . . . sandy bottom."

It wasn't the report Ty had been expecting. He had calculated it was time to head toward the coast, but the *Sea Whisper* was still too far south. She was making worse time than he'd thought. "Port two points and let's go a little farther," he instructed Matt, who was relieving Pete as helmsman.

A sudden loud blast of steam as the ship got under way again made Tiger grit his teeth. The noise couldn't be helped, but still, this close to Wilmington, he wanted nothing to draw the attention of patrolling Federalists. On a clear night, such a chance blast could be seen and heard for miles; hopefully, the storm would mask it.

An hour later, he ordered another sounding taken; this time, the report revealed the depth he had expected the first time. "Port another two points. . . . Take it slow and easy. We're heading in, boys."

They went only a short distance before word raced back to Ty via Pete: A cruiser had been sighted on the starboard bow. Ty scanned the utter blackness of sea and sky. In the lightning's fitful glare, he finally spotted the enemy. The regular beat of the *Whisper*'s paddle floats penetrated the storm's roar, but Ty quelled his anxiety with the sure knowledge that although he could hear the ship's progress, those aboard the cruiser probably could not.

"Starboard again, Cap'n," Matt whispered hoarsely. "Look to starboard."

Tiger did, and he saw a second long, low object rising and falling with the waves. Straight ahead, there was yet another, and he glimpsed a fourth on the port side of the bow. Had he steamed right into the middle of the Federal fleet?

"Damn!" he muttered. "I've made a false reckoning somewhere. We should be well to the north of the blockaders by now."

"What should we do, Cap'n?" Matt's voice remained calm, with only a slight tremor.

Ty spoke into the engine tube. "Ease her down, Stoker. But stand ready. . . ." To Matt, he said, "Pass between them, Matt. To port or starboard won't make much difference, since they're flanking us on either side."

Ty held his breath and prayed for a momentary abatement of lightning; a flash at this critical moment could mean disaster. No one spoke, and the rain seemed to drum louder than ever. Ty wondered if flares would work in this wet weather. In Nassau, he'd been able to purchase some calcium rockets, called Drummond lights, which he intended to use to confuse the Federalists, should rockets be employed to reveal his location. Never having lit one, he did not know if they would fire properly when damp. . . . They might, if he lit them before they got wet.

Just as they were passing under the guns of the biggest cruiser, lightning did indeed flash, immediately followed by a peal of thunder that rolled from one end of the sky to the other. Ty barked down the engine tube, "Give Omoroh a shovel and tell him to go to work. We've probably been spotted."

Barely had the words left his mouth, when bright explosions ripped through the night and foam boiled behind the stern. The lookout started shouting, and the rest of the crew abandoned all pretense of silence and rushed to raise sails before Ty could give the order. Still uncertain of his position, Ty scanned the horizon with mounting desperation. It was still too dark to glimpse the shoreline. He could be anywhere along it — past the river entrance or before it. Even on a clear night it wasn't easy to pinpoint the mouth of the river; the flat coastline ran for miles with only one distinguishing feature: Big Hill, a small hillock about as high as an oak tree. One had to be almost on top of it in order to spot it. Once seen, it meant that Fort Fisher wasn't far away.

Tiger reckoned that his only hope was to run north a little longer, as he had originally planned, then turn sharply toward land and race back south, by which time he would hopefully know their position. The biggest blockaders could not follow him into the shallow coastal waters, though the smaller ones could. But in the storm, they'd be hesitant; they didn't know the shoreline as well as he ... didn't know the locations of all the shoals, shipwrecks, and sandbars. Once he spotted Big Hill he could tell precisely where he was. The same lightning that had betrayed him would eventually reveal the tiny landmark he alone might recognize.

"Starboard two points, and pour on the steam," he called.

Soon the *Sea Whisper* was lunging through the waves like a race horse running with the bit in its teeth. Behind her, a string of vessels struggled to get under way. Tiger took advantage of his precious lead by trying to put as much distance as possible between the *Whisper* and her pursuers. The huge swells prevented running in a straight line, but he cut a zigzag course due north and tried to ignore the shots peppering the water off the stern. A half hour crept by, then another. He could see nothing on his stern, and his hopes soared. For a few brief moments, he courted the thought that he might have outrun them after all.

Then, after the next lightning flash, the lookout shouted down the message that at least a half-dozen vessels were now hot on their tail. Bucking the heavy seas, the *Whisper* fought to outdistance them. Ty dared not stop to cast another lead, and he still could not see the coastline. He held to a northerly course until he was certain he'd gone far enough, then turned hard aport and ran before the wind toward landfall. He got out his telescope, but neither he nor his lookout could find the shoreline. The first indication that they were nearing it was a flash of distant white—surf breaking over a shoal.

Ty slowed the *Whisper* and again took her hard

146

aport. Not yet realizing what he was doing, some of the pursuing gunboats continued racing north. As the steady flickers of lightning persisted, the hounds doubled back. Ty had his rockets readied, in case he got caught in the midst of the blockaders. Keeping a close watch for the streaks of white that indicated surf, he moved daringly close to shore. Running south was easier than running north, but as yet he saw nothing to indicate where he was, and three of the smaller vessels seemed to be catching up. Just as his throat was closing in near panic, Pete appeared at his side.

"Cap'n, the lookout can see the beach now. The line of surf is runnin' straight in both directions, but there ain't no landmarks visible yet."

"Take over the bridge, Pete. I'm going on deck."

"Aye, aye, Cap'n."

The deck was slick with rain and brine. An icy gust of wind tore at Tiger's slicker, and he couldn't help shivering. His nerves screamed for release from the strain and pressure; he'd have given his soul for a cup of hot tea or coffee. But the night's adventure was far from over; he couldn't relax for a single minute. Had he gone too far north? If he had, they wouldn't reach the fort before daybreak, then every vessel in the Federal fleet would be able to see them.

He stumbled to the rail and stared at the shoreline until he thought he'd go blind with the effort. Only the faint line of white revealed where it was. As Pete had already told him, no lights or landmarks were visible. The rain lashed his face. He had a leaden taste in his mouth. His pursuers were clearly visible off the stern, sure enough of ultimate victory to have lit lanterns but also prudent enough to stay well offshore. They were letting him lead them in, smug in the knowledge that he would be first to run aground if an obstacle blocked the path. They probably thought he knew exactly where he was going, and they could catch him or drive him onto a shoal before he got there. Well, they might, if he didn't spot a landmark soon.

"White surf to port, Cap'n," Pete hollered down from the bridge. "You see it, sir?"

Tiger ran to the other side of the deck. "I see it!" he hollered back.

Sizing up the situation, Ty knew he'd have to pass between the shoal and the shore and hope the water was deep enough. If he tried to go around, the Federal ships would catch up and box him in, forcing him onto the shoal itself. Once again he scanned the shoreline, searching for the slight hump that indicated Big Hill. Where in hell was it? Something else farther down the coast caught his eye. . . . A light? A beacon? Could it possibly be Fort Fisher?

Sometimes on rainy, dark nights, Colonel Lamb, the fort's commander, flashed an occasional light to alert any possible blockade-runners to the location of the fort. It was never a constant signal, because identifying the fort too accurately would help the enemy as well as the runners. If it was the fort, this was the North Breaker Shoal, and the *Sea Whisper* could not possibly pass between the shoal and the shore; it was far too shallow. They must go around it, then head in toward the river mouth. Could he do it and still outrun the hounds? He'd have to, Ty realized; he had no choice.

"Hard to port! Full steam ahead!" he cried, dashing for the bridge.

The *Sea Whisper* wallowed sluggishly in the waves before she came about. Reaching the bridge, Tiger focused his telescope on the surf boiling around the shoal. They were dangerously close to it, and he heard and felt a rough scraping sound as something rubbed along the ship's bottom.

"Hold her steady," he cautioned Matt.

"Ah'm doin' my best, Cap'n," Matt said. "But ah sure wouldn't mind if Pete took over now."

"Keep both hands on that wheel until we reach deeper waters," Ty cautioned. "Thank God for the light. If I hadn't seen it, we'd be run aground by now. Remind me to send a case of champagne to Colonel Lamb when we get ashore, will you?"

"Yes, sir."

If we get to shore, Ty added silently. They still had a long way to go. The river entrance was tricky, and high waves were still crashing over the bow. Tiger thought of Freedom in his cabin below deck. If anything happened, he must make sure she got out. He couldn't depend upon her judgment to know when to seek a lifeboat; she might not realize soon enough that the ship was in danger of sinking.

Another long scrape on the bottom of the hull set his nerves on edge; the North Breaker Shoal was treacherous, and they were coming at it from a different direction entirely than the one he usually took. Had he been able to spot Big Hill, he'd have known exactly where to cut out to sea to avoid the shoal—if, indeed, this *was* the North Breaker Shoal.

The scraping abruptly ceased, but just as Ty was breathing a sigh of relief, there was a loud thump and a splintering sound. He was thrown off his feet, and his head struck a hard surface. His thoughts spun; the vessel had hit something! For a moment she hung there, her engines laboring loud but fruitlessly. Ignoring the shards of pain in his temples, he rolled over and got to his feet.

"Decrease steam!" he gasped. "Decrease steam immediately!"

Several moments of chaos followed. Ty helped Matt to his feet and the two men clung together a moment, breathing heavily and trying to gather their scattered wits. Until he knew how much damage had been done there wasn't much Ty could do. He shouted down the engine tube. "Stoker! Are you all right down there? What's happening below deck?"

A minute passed before Stoker answered. "We're not hurt, Cap'n, just banged up a bit. . . . Our biggest problem is the water pourin' in. Whatever we hit either ripped a hole in our bottom or cracked our hull. We'll try to find out which and see what can be done to stop the water, then ah'll get back to you."

"Never mind. I'm coming down. . . . Wait here, Matt. I'll shout instructions up through the tube to you. Before we do anything, I have to know if we've got a chance of saving the ship. If not, I'll send everybody ashore; we can't be too far from the fort."

"What about the gunboats, Cap'n? We're a sittin' duck for 'em now."

"Once they see we're in trouble, they may fire at us, but I doubt they'll chance coming any closer. Most of them need deeper water than we do; they won't risk the same thing happening to them."

Twenty minutes later, Tiger knew the hull was

cracked from stem to stern—or nearly so. He, Omoroh, Stoker Harris, and three other men tried to stanch the water flowing through the long, jagged gap, but they couldn't do it fast enough or securely enough. No sooner did they patch one section, when water broke through another—a place they had already patched. With the waves pounding the helpless vessel, no amount of patching could withstand the strain.

"It's hopeless," Ty finally admitted.

Stoker Harris stared at him morosely in the gloom of the ship's hold. Here, the damage was the worst. Water was already up to their thighs. Bolts of fabric and barrels of ruined gunpowder bobbed on either side of the men.

"If we could keep the engines runnin', we could turn her into the waves and maybe wait it out 'til mornin'. . . . When mornin' comes, the soldiers at the fort'll spot us and give us a helpin' hand. If they send out boats, which ah'm sure they will, we might still be able to save some of the cargo."

"That's a risky idea—especially since I can't be absolutely certain that we *are* near the fort. What if we're not?"

"Well, we do know we're near shore, an' we know the Federalists ain't about to come any closer, seein' what's happened to us. We'd still have time to jump ship."

"No . . ." Ty shook his head. "I'm not risking the lives of everyone aboard to save this cargo. Valuable as it is, it's not worth that much."

"Then just send some of us to shore—the ones who want to go—and the rest of us'll stay here 'til mornin'."

"No, I'm sending you all to shore. . . . The only

151

one who's staying is me. I'll keep a dinghy—the smallest one—in case I need it. Don't worry; if the ship goes down before then, I'll get off in time. But if she remains afloat, at least I'll be here to tell the soldiers what to take off first. Only one man is necessary for that job; as captain, I'm the one who should do it."

"It's your right, Cap'n, but ah sure as hell don't like the idea of leavin' you out here alone."

"Your staying wouldn't help me, Stoker, but I appreciate the offer. . . . Come on. Let's get out of here and tell the men my plan. Rather, you can tell them while I fetch our little stowaway. I'm sure she's green with fear by now, wondering what's happened."

"Does she swim, Cap'n?"

"How in hell should I know? If she doesn't, it's too late to learn."

Chapter Eleven

On her hands and knees in the dark, Freedom groped for the side of the bunk and, finding it, crawled into it. Her ears were ringing and her neck hurt. Her head had snapped back when the ship struck something, and she'd been thrown from the bunk. She felt dizzy and sick to her stomach. Fear, nausea, and the tension of the last few hours had all taken their toll; if the ship was sinking as a result of the recent impact, she wasn't sure she could make it up on deck to safety.

Pull yourself together, Freedom, she lectured herself. Don't expect Ty Carrington to save you. He'd probably be glad if you went down with the ship.

Taking several deep breaths, she tried to calm her racing heart and think what to do next. The obvious thing was to leave the cabin and locate one of the dinghies, as Ty had advised, but first she wanted to find Omoroh and make certain he, too, got off the ship safely. She doubted he could swim; like her, he might never have had the opportunity to learn.

It took an absurdly long time for her head to

stop spinning, but when it did, she stood and groped her way across the cabin to the door. Before she got there, the door suddenly opened. The blaze of a lantern light momentarily blinded her, but she immediately recognized the intruder's voice.

"Are you all right?" Tiger growled without preamble or explanation.

"Yes," she answered shakily. "What happened?"

"We ran aground on a shoal. Our hull is cracked, and we're taking on water. I came to get you. You'll be going ashore with the rest of the crew."

"And Omoroh? I'm so worried about him. I don't think he can swim."

"Do you think I'd leave him here to die? Of course, Omoroh is going, too. . . . What about you? Can you swim?"

"No, but I'm not afraid to try. I just need someone to tell me what to do."

"Swimming is not a skill you can learn on a moment's notice," Ty said dryly, tossing his blond head "Especially in ten-foot waves . . . However, your courage is most impressive."

He was mocking her, Freedom thought, thoroughly annoyed. But he *had* come to get her. Maybe he didn't hate her as much as he pretended.

"Thank you for not leaving me to die," she retorted.

"Take the lantern and get up on deck. I'll fetch Omoroh, and the two of you can leave in the same boat. If he can row as well as he can shovel, you'll soon make it to shore." He handed her the lantern, then started to remove his slicker. "Here, take this as well. It'll keep you from getting soaked."

"But you need it!" she protested.

"I'm already wet," he said. "Besides, I want to protect my investment in that dress you're wearing."

He glanced down the front of her mint-green day dress; her cheeks colored beneath his intent perusal. She had tucked a fichu into the low neckline to protect her modesty, but whenever he looked at her as he was doing now, his violet eyes glowing in their depths, she felt half undressed.

"I'll repay you someday for the clothes," she stiffly informed him. "Even though they aren't to my taste."

"Too bad you don't like them, since they're so becoming on you. . . . Of course, anything is better than that drab brown rag you were wearing when I first saw you."

"There was nothing wrong with that dress!" she flared. "At least, it didn't make me look like a . . . a fallen woman."

"Ah, but you *are* a fallen woman, aren't you, Mouse? Too bad you still haven't tasted the joys of your new position."

His goading infuriated her, momentarily pushing the storm and its resultant dangers to the back of her mind.

"I hope never to experience those joys until I can share them with a man I love and one who loves me!" she snapped. "Since you are not that man and never will be, I suggest we drop the subject entirely."

"Yes, we do have more important things to think about, don't we? . . . Take my oilskin. I insist. I wouldn't want you to catch a chill."

"Why ever not, Captain Carrington? Then you wouldn't have to go to the trouble of turning me over to the Confederate authorities. With the

155

slightest bit of luck, I might die of lung congestion."

"Take the damn oilskin!" He flung it over her shoulders. "Now, get moving. Pete will show you which dinghy to use . . . and Omoroh will be along shortly."

Realizing she was wasting precious time, Freedom clutched the ends of the oilskin together and fled past him.

Tiger was vastly relieved when the last lifeboat was lowered and the last dinghy pushed off into the sea, bobbing at the end of its tether on the big ocean swells. The *Sea Whisper* carried two fair-sized boats and three small dinghies; his crew fit perfectly inside the boats. Pete and Matt were in one dinghy, and Freedom and Omoroh occupied the second, leaving him the third. It was only fair, he thought, that the two stowaways should have to depend upon each other, though neither could swim. Several of his crew members were also non-swimmers, and in pairing Freedom and Omoroh, he had at least put together two people who cared deeply about each other's welfare.

By now, the fog-shrouded shoreline—only a mile or two distant—was revealed in the gray light of dawn. Ty could also make out Big Hill, the river mouth, and the location of the fort, all reassuringly close. The rain had not slackened nor the heavy seas abated, but soon the soldiers at the fort should be able to spot the foundering vessel. Most encouraging of all, the Federal gunboats had retreated. From a safe distance, they were now waiting to learn the fate of the *Whisper* through telescopes and spyglasses. Ty began to feel quite hopeful. If the soldiers came to his aid, he might indeed be able to rescue some of his cargo.

One by one, he cast off the lines connecting the smaller vessels to the slowly sinking *Sea Whisper*. As he freed the last dinghy containing Freedom and Omoroh, Freedom astounded him by standing up in the tiny boat and calling his name.

"Ty, wait! Aren't you coming, too?"

"No," he shouted back. "Sit down before you tip over! I'm staying here."

"But the ship is sinking! You'll drown if you stay!"

"Don't be ridiculous. . . . I've still got the other dinghy."

"What dinghy? Do you mean that one way over there?"

Freedom pointed past him to the other side of the ship, where the empty dinghy he had reserved for himself was floating topsy-turvy on the huge swells. He reached for the little boat's mooring line, tugged on it, and discovered that it had come undone; he *was* stranded on the sinking *Whisper*.

"Damn!" he muttered, realizing he'd have to swim out to the dinghy and catch it before it floated completely out of reach or was swamped in the waves.

"Ty, there's room in our boat," Freedom persisted. "We'll row over to you, and you can come aboard at once."

"No, I said I'm staying with the ship. When the soldiers see it, they'll come to my rescue. If we can lighten her in time, we may be able to float her off whatever's snagged her."

"But, Ty, there may not be time! With every

wave, she's settling deeper."

As if to prove Freedom's point, the *Whisper* tilted in the next big wave. Timbers creaked protestingly, and water flooded the deck, tossing up an angry spume. As it receded, it took crates and barrels with it. Tiger had to cling to a mast to keep from being washed overboard.

"Ty!" Freedom screamed. "Oh, Ty, hang on! We're coming to get you!"

"Damn it, get back! I'm fine. . . ."

But even as he said it, he knew it wasn't true. The next wave lifted the ship three feet into the air, then dropped it back down onto the reef. Wood splintered in the ship's bowels, and more water scoured the deck. Everything that wasn't tied down rolled overboard. A big crate struck Tiger's shoulder as it careened past and dropped over the side into the boiling sea. He felt himself falling but managed to catch a rope dangling from the mast. Hand over hand, Ty pulled himself up, until he could again clutch the mast. Now the ship was almost standing on her side, each wave pounding her hard against the reef.

Ty heard Freedom pleading. "Hurry, Omoroh! We've got to save him."

It occurred to him she might try something foolish, like boarding the foundering vessel—she who could not even swim.

"Omoroh!" he shouted. "Keep Freedom on that boat. Don't worry about me. I can hang on 'til the soldiers come. . . . Just try to make it to shore."

He had no idea if Omoroh heard him or not. The ship lifted again under him, hovered in the air a moment, then crashed down with a bone-jarring thud. He lost his grip on the mast, and a wave

158

picked him up and flung him into the sea. He somersaulted, was sucked under, and fought desperately to get to the surface for a gulp of fresh air. A terrible undertow tugged at his legs; he bumped and scraped against wood—the hull of the ship. The sea was trying to drag him beneath it. His lungs burned like fire. He kicked as hard as he could, managed to get to the surface, and inhaled a single, life-giving breath. Then something battered the back of his head with such force that stars danced in front of his eyes. He felt himself going down, down, down. . . .

With his last remaining strength, he resisted the tugging sensation. It would be so easy to just give up and succumb to the beckoning blackness. He kicked halfheartedly and flailed his arms, but it was like swimming in a bowl of oatmeal. The sea was so heavy—so thick and cloying. He couldn't fight it any longer.

Freedom, he thought. Now he never would find out if she was innocent of spying . . . never be able to teach her the pleasures of lovemaking. Life was so short and precious, so easily lost. He wished he could tell her that; he wished he could tell her he wasn't as wicked as she thought. He should have told her before . . . should have defended himself . . . should have explained things so she could understand. . . . But he had his pride. He'd never before had to humble himself for a woman. Now it was too late . . . too . . . damn . . . late. . . .

"Careful, Omoroh! I think he's unconscious. . . . Oh, I pray he's not dead."

Freedom helped the big Negro drag Tiger's inert body into the little boat—not an easy task with the waves rocking them so fiercely. The dinghy almost tipped over, but they finally managed to get Ty over the side and sprawled awkwardly in the bottom of the boat. Then Omoroh manned the oars to turn the dinghy toward shore and row it away from the *Sea Whisper*, where a fierce undertow was sucking everything under the hull. Freedom rapped on Ty's back, trying to get him to cough up any water he might have swallowed.

She hadn't the slightest idea how to administer aid to a drowning victim. But she was determined that Tiger should not die. It was inconceivable that this big, handsome, virile man should die; he was the essence of life itself, possessing a strength and vitality that enlivened everyone about him, most particularly her.

"Miss Walker! Do you need any help?"

The shout came from far across the water. Freedom looked up to see Matt and Pete wrestling the oars of their dinghy in an effort to return and help them. Beyond, the other two lifeboats were also fighting to come about. All three boats had reached an area where the waves seemed especially violent, as if they were breaking over another unseen obstacle beneath the surface. There was nothing to be gained by any of the men returning, Freedom thought. It would be impossible to shift Tiger from one boat to another, even if one of the boats had room for him, which they did not. So she waved them all away.

"Go on! We're coming as fast as we can," she hollered, not sure if they could hear her.

Pete nodded and pointed toward shore. "Look!

The soldiers are tryin' to launch boats, which means they've spotted us. Tell the cap'n if this surf dies down, we might still save the *Whisper*."

"I'll tell him," Freedom promised, again rapping Ty between the shoulder blades. "Oh, please, Ty. Breathe . . . wake up . . . give us a sign you're still alive."

She sought to lift his head but only succeeded in turning it to one side. Suddenly, Tiger coughed, and water gushed from his mouth. Freedom glanced at Omoroh in triumph. "He *is* alive."

Omoroh grinned from ear to ear, white teeth gleaming, then bent his back into the job of rowing. "Stay away from the other boats," Freedom cautioned. "Go around that spot if you can. . . . See how the waves are breaking into surf there? I think that means another reef or sandbar. A sailor might know how to get across safely, but I don't."

Omoroh nodded agreement. For a while, he rowed silently, while Freedom cushioned Tiger's head in her arms. Ty's eyes were closed but he groaned occasionally, as if in pain. She feared he had some other injury she couldn't see; he had been banged and tossed about unmercifully. Until they got to shore, there was nothing much she could do for him—except pray and hold his head and hand. She laid her hand over his and marveled that his was easily twice as large. The fingers were blunt and squarish, but oddly graceful. His nails were neatly clipped. Fine golden hairs covered the back of his hand, and he wore no rings. His was a strong, bold, masculine hand, but she knew how gently it could caress, how lightly it could stroke. . . . His hand had touched her intimately, explored parts of her body that made her blush to

161

think about it. . . . Thank God, he was still alive!

Even knowing that her feelings for him were futile and forbidden — feelings she herself did not want — she rejoiced that he still lived. A part of her wanted to sing and dance with joy, but another part wanted to weep. Yes, Ty was still alive, but what good would it do her? He didn't return her feelings, and even if he did, they had nothing whatever in common. Any sort of relationship between them was destined to end in tragedy and heartbreak. At least, she had this one last moment with him, touching his hand, remembering his caresses. . . .

She looked up to see Omoroh watching her as he pulled the oars. His dark eyes were eloquent — all-seeing, all-knowing. She snatched her hand away from Tiger's, as though she'd been caught doing something awful. Omoroh only gazed at her sadly, neither approving nor condemning. It seemed he understood her predicament — loving a man she could never have. The waves rose and fell, and the dinghy bucked and bobbed in the turbulent sea. She bowed her head to ward off the rain, falling like endless tears from the gray sky above.

When she looked up again they were nearing the shore, and new dangers loomed. She could no longer see the other boats along the fog-shrouded coastline. The only thing visible was the line of surf lying directly ahead — a roaring, tossing, angry surf that would surely dash them to pieces before they ever reached the beach. Omoroh's back was to it, so he hadn't yet noticed.

"Omoroh, look! . . . What do we do now? The captain is still unconscious, and neither of us knows how to swim."

162

When Omoroh saw the pounding surf, he became so nervous he dropped the oars. Freedom made a grab for them, but it was too late; the next wave jarred one loose from its lock and tossed it out of reach before she could catch it. The remaining oar was useless. Instead of heading straight toward the beach, the dinghy spun sideways to the surf, in which position tipping was inevitable. Freedom and Omoroh leaned hard on one side and managed to keep the boat from flipping upside down, but as they were carried closer to the beach, the surf became more powerful.

Ty's weight in the bottom of the dinghy was on the wrong side, but they couldn't spare the time to roll him over. In the absence of oars—by now, the second had been snatched away—all Freedom and Omoroh could do was hang on and hope for the best. The sea seemed determined to destroy the dinghy and dump its inhabitants before they got to shore. The crash of the breakers on the beach was deafening; Freedom could barely see through the spray.

"Don't worry, Omoroh! If it isn't too deep, we'll make it. . . . When we do tip over, try to grab hold of the captain. Between the two of us, we can get him to shore. . . ." The wind tore the words from her mouth. Glancing at Omoroh, Freedom doubted he had even heard her. His eyes were wide with fright; his big hands clutched the sides of the boat. Her own panic threatened to choke her, but she kept her tone calm and rational.

"Omoroh, listen to me. We must save the captain, do you understand?"

Omoroh never took his eyes from the crashing waves. Freedom despaired; how could she save

163

them both? How could she save herself? Looking back over her shoulder, she saw an enormous wave rushing toward them. As it approached, it towered over their heads, a solid wall of water bent on flinging itself upon the land.

"Dear God, save us!" she cried, and in the next instant, the wave engulfed them.

Water flooded Freedom's nose and mouth, clawed at her eyes, and tugged at her clothing, turning her end over end. She slammed into something hard and unyielding, tasted grit on her tongue, and felt sand give way beneath her. Then the water receded slightly, leaving her gasping for breath but aware that she could touch bottom. It wasn't all that deep. She struggled to stand in her sodden skirts, but no sooner had she done so, when another wave knocked her down and washed over her head. She came up sputtering and rubbed her eyes, trying to clear them of sand and water. Where were Ty and Omoroh?

She couldn't look for them until she escaped the waves. Each one knocked her down and dragged her back into the sea. The bottom seemed to fall off sharply, going from shallow to deep in the space of a dozen yards. Safety was so close, yet so agonizingly far. If the waves dragged her too far back from shore, she might not make it after all. Inch by inch, she fought her way toward the beach. By the time she reached knee-deep water, she was exhausted, and still the waves buffeted and clawed her.

Clearing her vision, she searched for any sign of Tiger or Omoroh. Omoroh was on his hands and knees not a hundred feet from her, fighting the same battle against the greedy waves. He was coughing and choking and looked ready to give up.

"Just a little farther, Omoroh! We're almost there." She made her way to him and helped him to his feet. He leaned on her heavily as she dragged him toward the beach. When he reached it, he sank down on the sand and began vomiting seawater. She spoke his name, but he didn't seem to hear it. Anxiously, she turned back toward the sea.

"Ty! . . . Tiger, where are you!"

She stumbled along the fringe of waves, frantically searching for him. The ocean was hurling all manner of debris onto the beach, then snatching it back again in a kind of gruesome game. Tree branches, a broken spar, the staves of a barrel, a log . . . Or was it a body? She spotted a dark shape rolling over and over, as if the waves were playing with it. A flash of whitish-yellow hinted this might be a man with pale blond hair . . . the man she wanted and couldn't have . . . the man she ought *not* to want.

Heedless of the danger, she braved the waves once more and caught hold of Tiger's shirtsleeve. The sleeve ripped away in her hand. She flung herself after him and caught him as he rolled over, taking her down with him and slamming her painfully against the sandy bottom. She refused to let go; if he was going to drown, she was going to drown with him. And she almost did. Some last spark of determination to live—and to save Tiger— gave her the strength to hold on to his body and resist the sea.

How she managed to get him to shore she never knew. Suddenly, she was dragging him onto the sand, sobbing and gasping, then falling to her knees beside him. It came to her that they were safe now. Dead or alive, Ty was free of the sea's grasp. It was all she could do. She had reached her limits. Pitching face forward onto the beach, she surrendered to overwhelming exhaustion.

Chapter Twelve

Tiger awoke to the feel of hot sun on his back and the sound of surf roaring in his ears. For several moments he didn't move, but merely savored the knowledge that somehow he was still alive — or else had reached a strange sort of paradise remarkably similar to earth. Seabirds were squawking overhead, and beneath him the sand felt warm and hard. Its grittiness penetrated every crevice of his body, but that was not his worst discomfort; he sensed that when he lifted his head, the motion would cause real pain.

It did. His temples throbbed. A huge hammer beat on the anvil of his brain, and his body ached from head to foot. He wondered how he had ever reached the beach. His last recollection was of the sea pulling him under and trapping him beneath the hull of the *Sea Whisper;* he could *not* have swam to shore, could he? Blinking against the sun's glare, he opened his eyes and looked about him. At his side, almost on top of him, lay Freedom. Her face was turned away, her body unmoving. Alarm forced him to get up. As he rose to his knees, he saw Omoroh sprawled a short distance away. The big Negro must have saved him and Freedom, and brought them both to this beach.

He scanned the area, but saw no other humans or signs of habitation. There was only sea, sky, and sand, bordered by sea grass, low dunes, and scrawny vegetation—a typical North Carolina beach. He groaned as the pounding in his head became unbearable; somehow, he must bear it. He touched Freedom's shoulder. There was no response, so he gently shook it. She moaned softly but didn't open her eyes.

"Freedom?" Her name came out as a croak. He tried again. "Mouse, can you hear me?"

She muttered something unintelligible. At least, she was alive, he thought. But he'd need Omoroh's help to carry her out of the sun and into the shade of the scrubby vegetation. He doubted he could walk that far, much less carry Freedom. He crawled to Omoroh and tapped the big Negro on the back. "Omoroh . . . for God's sake, wake up, if you're still alive."

The big man stirred, opened dazed eyes, and stared at Ty with a look of wildness. "Omoroh, it's me . . . Captain Carrington."

Omoroh blinked, then grinned and sat up. The sudden motion made him clutch his head in his hands, as if he, too, had a headache.

"I know," Ty sympathized. "It's bad, isn't it? . . . But there's no sense lying here roasting in the sun when there's shade back further off the beach. You'll have to help me move Miss Walker. . . . I can't get her to wake up. We both owe our lives to you, Omoroh. You're a fine, brave man, and I won't forget it. You've got a home and a job with good wages for as long as you care to stay with me."

For a moment, Omoroh gazed at him in puzzlement. Then he violently shook his head, denying something Ty had said.

"What do you mean?" Ty asked. "Are you saying

you *didn't* save my life and Miss Walker's?"

Omoroh nodded. He pointed to Freedom and pantomimed that *she* had rescued the two of them. Somehow, she had dragged them both from the grasp of the sea.

"My God, I can't believe it!" Ty exclaimed. "Here we are, two strong, grown men, and instead of us saving her, it was the other way around."

Omoroh regarded him solemnly, then thumped the area over his heart with his fist, as if swearing loyalty and allegiance to Freedom. Shamed by his weakness in the face of her strength, Tiger got to his feet and strode back to the inert girl. Gently, he turned her over and wiped the sand from her face with his fingers. She was paler than a corpse and looked more dead than alive. A bruise over one cheekbone was her only coloring. He smoothed back her tangled, wet hair, noted the bluish tinge of her lips, and felt something wrench inside him.

Courage alone must have given her the strength to save him and Omoroh. How else had this fragile waif pulled two men who each weighed twice as much as she did from the sea's bosom? Courage and a staunch, brave heart. He could understand why she'd risked her neck to save Omoroh, but why him? She despised him, and yet she'd saved his life. How could he repay that selfless act by turning her in as a possible spy?

Gathering her into his arms, he lifted and cradled her as he would a small child. She felt like a child, infinitely precious and vulnerable. He wished she were his child, his woman, on whom he could lavish care and affection until she bloomed again from his ministrations. He'd never felt like this before, not with any woman he'd ever known. Desire budded beneath his feelings of tenderness, but he condemned his lust

169

as another manifestation of weakness, crowding in upon his determination to guard and protect her.

"Omoroh, I'm taking her where there's shade. See if you can find fresh water—a stream or even a shellful of rainwater. After I'm sure she's comfortable, I'll try and figure out where we are."

Omoroh nodded, then strode off into the sea grass. Tiger carried Freedom away from the beach and searched for a tree large enough to cast some shade. Finding one, he kicked away the debris beneath it to make a clean place to lay her down. Barely had he settled her beneath the tree, when Freedom stirred awake. Her eyes opened. Uncomprehendingly, she stared up at him, reminding him of a dazed fawn. Kneeling beside her, he leaned over and brushed her forehead with his lips in a reassuring kiss.

"Mouse, it's all right. You're safe now. So is Omoroh. I sent him to look for water."

"Ty . . ." She reached up and touched his face with her fingertips, as if she could not believe it was really he. Tears welled in her brown eyes. "Ty, it was awful. I was so afraid. I couldn't be sure if you were alive or dead, and I was so tired I couldn't stay awake to find out."

"I don't know how you did it, sweetheart. You can't even swim. It's a miracle we're all three alive."

"You were hurt," she said. "You kept groaning."

"I still hurt," he admitted. "My head feels like a squashed melon, but other than that, I'm hale and hearty."

"I'm so glad. . . ." she whispered, then surprised him by flinging her arms around his shoulders and hugging him. "Oh, Ty, if anything had happened to you . . ."

Her voice broke on a sob. He reveled in her embrace, returning it with restrained enthusiasm so as not to hurt her by squeezing too tightly. Abruptly, she pushed away. "I'm sorry. . . . I didn't mean to be so — so forward. It's just that I was so scared. I thought for sure you were dead."

"You can be forward anytime," he tried to joke, wishing she hadn't quit hugging him. "I like forward women."

The joke fell flat. He could see her withdrawal in her huge, bottomless brown eyes. "I know you do, but I'm not one of them . . . not normally, anyway. Only when I have to be."

"Mouse . . ." He searched for the right words. Omoroh would be returning soon with water, and for what he wanted to say, he needed more than a few moments alone with her. "I — I've changed my mind about turning you over to the authorities. Instead, I want to take you home with me — to Cypress Hall. Before you refuse, stop and think. You've nowhere else to go, and I can't just let you return to Hattie Draper's to do whatever you were doing before all this happened."

Her face hardened. The light died in her eyes. "Why not, Ty? After all that's happened, do you still not trust me?"

"Trust . . ." he repeated. "I'm not sure what the word means anymore. You dragged me from the sea when you could have let me drown. . . . So I guess where my life is concerned, I trust you. However, knowing you as I do, knowing how you feel about the South, I have to say no, I *don't* trust you not to do whatever you could to aid the North. At least, if I take you home, we'll have time to explore our feelings for each other. Maybe if we both work at it, we can find some way around our differences."

She started to rise. "Oh, Tiger, it will never work! Our differences are just too large. . . . Dear God, I'm so confused! You make me feel things I don't want to feel . . . and want things I've no business wanting."

He grabbed her hands and held them to his chest. "You do the same to me, Mouse. I know what you're thinking; I've thought the same things myself. But don't you see? Whether we like it or not, there's something strong and powerful between us . . . something wonderful, magical, awesome. Can you really deny it? If you can, then why did you bother to save me? Why didn't you just save Omoroh and let me die?"

"I don't know!" she cried. "But if you *had* died, a part of me would have died with you. . . . That's why I saved you. I didn't want to live if you died."

He enfolded her in his arms. "Oh, sweetheart . . . my precious little Mouse . . . That's exactly what I'm talking about. Like it or not, you've fallen in love with a hated Southerner."

"A slaver!" she choked against his neck. "How could I love someone I hate?"

He wanted to laugh at the chagrin in her voice. Maybe now was the time to tell her that he wasn't a slaver, that he didn't keep slaves and never had. That he didn't particularly like those who did. That they had more in common than she thought . . . Then he reconsidered. Let her come to Cypress Hall and find out for herself what his life was like. Let her get to meet his people, his mother—not that his mother would favorably impress her—his friends, and experience what it was really like on a cotton plantation . . . on *his* plantation, anyway. Let her decide for herself if that life was actually so bad, so impossibly objectionable.

If, after getting to know him better, she still despised him, then there was no hope. Cypress Hall was his heritage, his livelihood. One day it would belong to his children—and hers, if she could learn to accept him for what he was.

"What was Hattie Draper paying you?" he whispered in her ear. "Whatever it was, I'll double it. You can work for me . . . be my—my bookkeeper. I need one in the worst way. It will all be perfectly proper. . . . I'll employ you for the duration of the war. After it's over, if you still can't abide me or my home, I'll personally transport you back to Boston. Now, how can you refuse an offer like that?"

She sniffed and raised her head to look at him. "A spy would certainly refuse. . . . A spy would insist on remaining in Wilmington, where news is more readily available."

"But you claim you aren't a spy. . . ."

"I thought you didn't believe me."

"I don't . . . At least, I didn't. Maybe I'm starting to. In any case, if you come to Cypress Hall, *I* can spy on *you*. I won't have to worry about whether or not I'm doing the right thing by not turning you over to the Confederacy; I'll be able to watch and make certain you're doing nothing to harm my beloved South."

She locked gazes with him. "I would if I could, Ty. You should know that before you invite me to work for you. . . . And you should know that I'll only accept your offer because Hattie Draper was paying me nothing. Even my room and board had become an insupportable financial burden for her. I have nowhere to go just now, no means of surviving, and I—I—"

"You what?"

"I need time to—to think," she finished hesitantly, avoiding the main issue, he thought with some indulgence.

"So do I, Mouse. We both need time. What we feel for each other isn't something either of us would have chosen. For now, we'll take it slow and easy. You'll live in my house, keep my books, and see for yourself

173

what an ogre I am."

"Must I live in your house? That would be improper."

"Don't worry. . . . My mother will act as chaperone. Of course, I'll never tell her I kept you chained to my bed in Nassau and on my ship. Nor will I tell her you were a stowaway. I'll claim I hired you from a British firm doing business with the Confederacy. For as long as you like, we can maintain the pretense that there's nothing personal between us."

"There isn't," Freedom stubbornly insisted. "What happened before was . . . not the way I want it to be with you or any man . . . ever again."

"It was a mistake," Ty agreed, though he had to restrain himself from trying to repeat the mistake then and there, that very moment. "I respect you too much to try and tempt you into my bed again, Mouse, but when you're ready . . . *if* you're ready . . . I'll be waiting."

"When I'm ready . . . *if* I'm ready . . . I'll gladly come," she whispered. Her eyes were luminous as stars, her mouth trembled, and she moistened her lips with the tip of her pink tongue, as if in anticipation of a kiss.

He bent toward her, intending to bestow it, but she drew away. "Here comes Omoroh! And he seems very excited about something."

Ty turned. Omoroh was indeed excited. He waved at Ty and beckoned him to come and see what was happening on the beach. He kept pointing toward the ocean; whatever it was probably had something to do with Ty's ship or his men. Reluctantly, Tiger rose and stepped out from beneath the tree. He shaded his eyes against the sun and glanced where Omoroh was indicating. Four longboats bobbed on the sea, headed for the crippled *Sea Whisper,* which had miraculously not sunk. Beyond them, the blockaders were gathered. One of the Federalists was lowering its own longboat, but before the vessel even touched the water, cannon boomed, kicking up a cloud of spray.

"What is it? What's going on?" Freedom scrambled to her feet and came to stand beside him.

"Soldiers from Fort Fisher are en route to remove my cargo," he explained. "Then it may be possible to float the *Whisper* off that shoal. The Federalists aren't too happy about it. Fortunately, there's nothing they can do. If they dare go closer, the fort's guns will blow them out of the water. What you heard was a warning volley."

"Oh . . ." Freedom said disappointedly.

Ty jerked around to look at her. She held his gaze steadily, neither affirming nor denying what she felt. But then, she didn't need to; her feelings were obvious. In that moment, he realized just how far apart they still were. While he was ready to rejoice, she was sunk in gloom. She didn't want the arms, ammunition, cloth for uniforms, and other necessities he had brought back from Nassau to reach General Lee's troops. She was sorry his cargo was going to be salvaged.

He held out his hand to her. "Come here, Mouse. . . . Come and watch with me."

She shook her head. "No—no, thank you, Ty. I would really rather not."

Three days later, Freedom found herself aboard a small river steamer, on her way to Cypress Hall. Tiger had wasted no time in Wilmington. Because of the *Sea Whisper*'s near disaster, the usual thirty-day quarantine on incoming ships had been waived. Approximately half Ty's cargo had been saved and would soon be on its way to the Confederate forces at Richmond. What remained of the *Whisper* had been towed to a nearby shipyard for extensive repairs. During that time, Freedom had stayed with friends of Ty's in town, who "thought she looked familiar" but couldn't place where they had seen her.

Having no reason to be suspicious, Ty's friends— the Willoughbys—had accepted the story that Freedom was Ty's new bookkeeper, hired in Nassau, where her father had supposedly died of consumption, leaving her to carry on his trade in that boisterous, un-safe-for-a-lady port. Tiger's lies amused and entertained Freedom, but she waited breathlessly for the truth to come out; she had recognized Mrs. Willoughby as an occasional customer at Hattie Draper's and couldn't understand why the kind but scatter-brained woman did not recognize her.

It was unnerving to discover she'd made so little impression upon Wilmington's upper class. Emma Willoughby never did recognize her, not even when she was closely examining Freedom's petite figure, prior to loaning her clothing to replace what had been ruined aboard the *Sea Whisper*. Freedom wound up wearing a gown she herself had altered for Mrs. Willoughby in the shop, a pale lemon-colored, frothy thing that made her feel like a butterfly about to float off somewhere.

Freedom had thought about contacting Hattie Draper while in Wilmington and letting the old lady know she was all right, but Ty had adamantly rejected the idea. He wanted no further communication between her and Hattie Draper; in effect, Freedom was still his prisoner. If she disobeyed his wishes, he would turn her in. His continuing distrust was annoying, but she had to concede that her own attitude had given him good cause. It was probably better that Hattie knew nothing, especially since Omoroh was still so vulnerable. Ty kept Omoroh completely out of sight, and Freedom never saw the big Negro until she boarded the little steamer that was going to take them all upriver to Cypress Hall.

"Omoroh, I'm so happy to see you again. . . . You look so much better than you did three days ago," she gushed.

Omoroh grinned and straightened his massive shoulders. He was resplendent in clean, new clothing—tan trousers and a calico shirt, even new sandals. He made motions of appreciation for her attire as well, rolling his expressive eyes and winking at her. She laughed in delight. Then Ty came to stand beside her.

"Yes, she does look pretty, doesn't she, Omoroh?" he commented. "Hardly the same half-drowned little mouse of a few days ago. In fact, I'd say she's been transformed into a delicious Southern belle."

With a swish of her huge hooped skirt, Freedom turned on her heel and strolled away from him. Tiger seemed determined to turn her into something she was not—the pampered Carolina coquette he obviously wanted for a wife. Well, he might be able to dress her like one, but in her heart she would always remain an outspoken Northerner, committed to equality among races and classes of people. A Northern woman would have recognized her from the shop at once; that Emma Willoughby had not was only further proof of Freedom's private contention that Southern women, no matter how kindhearted, paid little heed to those they regarded as their inferiors—blacks or whites. Aristocratic blue bloods many of them might be, but they had all the sensitivity of tree stumps.

"What did I say wrong?" Ty questioned, coming

after her and throwing up his hands. "All I did was pay you a compliment. You look angry enough to slap me."

"I don't consider it a compliment to be called a Southern belle," she said stiffly.

"Hush. Keep your voice down. Silas—the captain of this boat—doesn't take kindly to providing transportation for anyone who scorns Southern womanhood."

"Well, I told you this wouldn't work," Freedom clipped under her breath. "You probably should have turned me in."

"It'll work, if you try harder." Ty's voice was controlled but furious. "Give it a chance, Freedom. . . . Give *me* a chance."

"Why should I, when you wouldn't let me see Hattie Draper? Did you give me a chance?"

"That was different. I don't know if Hattie Draper is friend or foe to North Carolina and the Confederacy. If she shares your traitorous sentiments toward my state and country, then I can't chance your seeing her. . . . Besides, you're someone else now—a bookkeeper, not a shop girl. How can I explain to my mother why I brought you home with me if everyone knows you used to work for Hattie?"

"Someone is bound to recognize me sooner or later, Ty. And Omoroh, too. The more I think about it, the worse this idea gets. . . . I don't know why I ever agreed to it."

Ty's hand closed over her wrist. "Yes, you do, Mouse. You agreed to come home with me because you can't say good-bye yet . . . and I can't bear to say it, either. Shall I take you in my arms here and now and remind you of what we feel for each other?"

Freedom's spine tingled at the suggestion—rather, the threat. Something in her lower abdomen tight-

178

ened. It took all of her resolve to keep from throwing herself into his arms. "Please don't, Ty. We're taking things slow and easy, remember? . . . I'm sorry if I've made you upset, but — but don't try to change me too quickly. You can't simply refashion me into the direct opposite of what I am."

"I don't want to," he said softly, moving closer so no one could hear. "What you are is woman enough for me, Mouse. In that yellow gown, with your shoulders and half your bosom displayed so enticingly, you're like a buttercup waiting to be plucked. If I could, I wouldn't just kiss you, I'd — "

"Ty, please!" She turned her head so that the brim of Emma Willoughby's bonnet hid her burning face from his avid gaze. "Don't say such things. Don't think them. What will your mother think if she sees you trying so hard to seduce your new bookkeeper?"

"I won't try in front of her. . . . But I can't promise not to try when we're alone together."

"We're not alone now!"

"More's the pity. . . . All right, Mouse. Stop hiding behind your hat brim. I'll behave myself from now on."

"Tell me about Cypress Hall," she said, leaning against the railing and gazing down into the brown water. "Describe it to me."

"No, I want you to see and judge it for yourself, Mouse."

"Why? Will I be surprised?"

"Probably . . . You shouldn't be, but you will."

"Then if we can't talk about Cypress Hall, what shall we talk about?"

"You," he said. "Tell me the story of your life. . . . Tell me everything there is to know about Miss Freedom Walker and how she became such a rabid abolitionist."

So she did. Time flew by while she talked and talked, describing the loneliness she sometimes felt growing up without a mother, being unable to fully engage her father's attention because he was so wrapped up in The Cause. She related her own horror and dismay when she heard about the atrocities and injustices involving Negroes, and cited the times she went hungry because her father had spent his meager earnings to publish yet another "Tract Against the Evils of Slavery."

When the captain blew the steam whistle to alert the inhabitants of Cypress Hall that the master had returned, she started in amazement. It hardly seemed possible they could be there already. Ty grinned at her astonishment. "Sorry to interrupt you, Mouse, but it seems we have arrived."

"Gracious, I've rambled on. . . . I'm sorry. We've spent the entire journey talking about me."

"I'm glad. Now I feel I'm finally beginning to know you . . . and it's time you get to know me." Tiger tucked her hand under his arm. "Shall we debark, Mouse?"

She nodded, feeling extremely curious and more than a little apprehensive. What awaited her at Cypress Hall?

Chapter Thirteen

Freedom's first view of Tiger's home took her breath away. Since most visitors to the plantation came by steamer, the big house faced the river, at the end of a long drive through a tunnel of moss-shrouded cypresses. A carriage was already waiting for them when the steamer deposited them on the landing dock. With an appreciative wave at the ship's captain, Ty bounded off the vessel, embraced a short, powerfully built Negro named Jules, clapped him on the back, then herded Freedom and Omoroh into the carriage almost before she could blink twice.

Omoroh sat beside Jules, the driver, while Ty and Freedom shared the back seat. They set off down the long drive at a good clip behind a matched pair of handsome bay horses, and Freedom shamelessly gawked. At the end of the tunnel, a large two-story white house with four white pillars beckoned. There was a second-floor balcony and a huge veranda, numerous shiny windows flanked by black shutters, and a tall front door. Azaleas, camellias, and other flowering plants rimmed the house, scenting the warm air with a sweetness that challenged the tart odor of pine.

On either side of the tunnel of trees, spacious green lawns separated the property from the encroaching forest. Freedom surmised that the cotton fields must be behind the house, along with the outbuildings and slave quarters. The overall impression was one of order, symmetry, and elegance, but as they neared the end of the drive, she could see that the house was not as large as it had looked from the opposite end of the tunnel, nor was it as meticulously kept. The second story paint was peeling, and on one wing, a boarded-up window belied the image of wealth and prosperity.

"What do you think?" Ty indicated the scene with a sweep of his hand. His face glowed with pride of ownership. "This damned war has kept me from making a few needed repairs and from completing the new wing I added a few years ago, but Cypress Hall is still a grand place, wouldn't you say?"

"It's lovely," Freedom agreed. "Who planted the cypresses leading up to the house?"

"My grandfather . . . He first made his living by harvesting timber, but even before he built the house, he planted the trees. He wanted the entrance to be spectacular, and it is, I think. I've seen alleys lined with towering oaks, but to my eyes, the cypresses are every bit as beautiful."

"They are . . . but who maintains them? And who cares for the lawns and flower beds?"

He slanted her an amused glance. "Still looking for the serpent in the garden of Eden, eh? Well, the cypresses maintain themselves, and you can thank my mother for the flower beds. Her one passion in life is gardening; she permits no one to touch her roses or azaleas. Curious that—other than her gardening, she scorns getting her hands dirty."

I'm sure she doesn't need to dirty her hands at anything else, Freedom thought. She has slaves to do the *real* work.

They rode in silence the rest of the way. At the end of the tunnel, the drive circled in front of the house. In the center of the circle, a small three-tiered pond glittered in the sunlight. Water welled up from a basin in the pond's center and spilled musically over the three tiers. Borne on the breeze, the resultant spray watered a profusion of multicolored flowers surrounding the pond.

"How picturesque and refreshing!" Freedom exclaimed, delighted in spite of herself. She didn't want to be charmed by anything she saw at Cypress Hall, but it wasn't easy to despise the beauty and tranquillity of the place; she had to keep reminding herself of the underlying evil that made such beauty possible. The thick forests hemming the plantation house had been cleared by the backbreaking labor of men who had no choice in the matter, and the cotton out back wasn't picked by white hands, either.

"Jules, where's Mama?" Ty asked as he lifted Freedom down from the carriage.

"She entertainin' some ladies from de Parker place, Marse Ty. Ah 'spects dey's in de parlor or somewhere dere abouts."

Tiger's mouth tightened. "At least, she could stir herself to welcome me home. I assume she heard the steamboat whistle the same as you did."

"You knows Lady Tiff'n." Jules rolled his eyes. "She allus gots mo' important thin's to do than worry 'bout you, Marse Ty."

Freedom was surprised that Tiger allowed his slave to speak so impertinently about his mother. Ty had also surprised her by being so openly affectionate at the dock when he first greeted this squarish-built Negro with the large eyes.

"Show Omoroh around, will you, Jules? If you and Elvira don't mind, I'd like him to stay with you until I can get a house built for him. He'll need his own place eventually; he's agreed to work for me, and if one of the ladies catches his eye and he marries, he'll need his own place."

Jules did not seem in the least distressed by the request, which surely amounted to an order—nicely worded, but an order, just the same. He simply grinned and nodded. "He welcome to stay wid me an' Elvira long as you wants. Ah declare dat woman purely relishes company. . . . She gonna talk de ears off'n him."

"Well, he won't say much back. He's had a few bad experiences, Jules, one of which was losing his tongue."

Comprehension dawned in Jules's dark eyes. "In dat case, I see he keep busy away from de big house when Lady Tiff'n's guests're here."

"Good idea . . . I knew you'd understand." Ty turned back to Freedom. "Come along, Mouse. Ready or not, you have to meet Mama."

"I can hardly wait to meet your mother," Freedom murmured. "But what do I do if she doesn't like me?" Or I don't like her, she added silently.

"Just keep out of her way. . . . Don't worry. I doubt she'll notice or care what you do all day. As you've already seen, she doesn't care that her only offspring has come home from a long, dangerous journey."

Looking up at Ty, noticing how devastatingly handsome he was in the fresh clothing he'd borrowed from Emma Willoughby's husband, Freedom wondered about a woman who couldn't take time from her friends to greet her own son. Tiger's eyes held a wariness and disappointment that tore at Freedom's heart; without having met Ty's mother, she already disliked the woman.

Ty led the way up the wide steps to the enormous front porch that was part of the veranda surrounding the house. Before he got to the front door, it opened, and an old Negro in a black frock coat and creased black trousers bowed his grizzled head, then looked up, grinning widely. "Welcome home, Marse Ty. . . . When ah heard de steamboat whistle, ah knowed it was you. Ah'm glad you come home safe ag'in."

"Thank you, Ambrose. Thus far, you and Jules are the only ones who seem pleased by my return."

"Oh, everyone glad you back, suh. But dey couldn't come down to de levee to see you, 'cause Lady Tiff'n has guests t'day. She keepin' evahbody hoppin'."

"I'm sure she is. . . . Ambrose, this is Miss Walker." Tiger took Freedom's hand and drew her forward. "She's my new bookkeeper who'll be living here. Tell Elvira to ready the yellow room for occupancy. As you can see for yourself, yellow compliments her, so I think she should have that room instead of one of the others."

Ambrose's gray eyebrows shot up; clearly, it wasn't everyday that Ty brought home a young woman. The old Negro's glance swept Freedom, and he seemed curiously pleased and gratified. "Yas suh, ah do dat right away."

He bowed again, then closed the door behind Ty and Freedom. "If'n you'll excuse me, Marse Ty, ah'll go find Elvira, den ah got's to fetch more lemonade for Lady Tiff'n and her guests."

"Bring some for Miss Walker, too, Ambrose. . . . You'd like some refreshment, wouldn't you, Mouse?" Tiger smiled at her. "I know I would . . .

185

but lemonade isn't exactly what I have in mind."

To her annoyance, Freedom found that her mouth had gone exceedingly dry. Probably, it was from all her talking aboard the steamer, but it might have been from nervousness about meeting Ty's mother and her friends.

"Ty, what if one your mother's guests—or your mother herself—recognizes me from Hattie Draper's shop? What should I say? What will I do?"

"Relax, Mouse . . . As soon as you walk into that room, every female in it will be examining your gown, not your face. If they do recognize you, leave it to me; I'll think of something. . . . Now, come on. Let's get this over with."

Freedom followed Tiger across the highly polished wood floor of the front hallway. A gorgeous wood staircase beneath a sparkling chandelier dominated it; a half-dozen doors, most of them closed, opened off it. Ty went to one, rapped sharply, then opened it. Freedom had a fleeting glimpse of Turkish carpeting, gleaming wood furnishings, and solid brass gas jets and wall sconces, then Ty was ushering her into the elegant room, where a half-dozen women in hoop-skirted gowns were seated on sofas and chairs around a table of refreshments.

The women looked up, their eyes fastening first on Ty, then on Freedom. One of the women rose to her feet, a glance of annoyance on her pale, delicate features. Freedom knew immediately who she was; she had white-blond hair pulled back into the currently fashionable style Freedom herself favored, only hers was further embellished with two fat sausage curls hanging down to brush both sides of her heart-shaped face. Like Tiger, she, too, had startlingly beautiful violet-colored eyes. Her face was slightly puffy and fine lines webbed her mouth, but still, her overall appearance compelled admiration. Full, firm breasts strained at the bodice of the airy green muslin gown she wore, but the gown itself struck Freedom as too juvenile a fashion for a woman of her ripe maturity. Milky-white, blue-veined breasts threatened to spill free as she left her chair and moved gracefuly toward Ty, her gown swishing in the sudden silence.

"Well, if it isn't mah son, Tif, home from runnin' that nasty ole blockade. . . ." she said in an exaggerated Southern accent, calling Ty by a shortened rendition of his first name, which was far too effeminate for a man as masculine as Tiger. "Did you bring me somethin' nice this time, or did you do like always—stuff every last inch o'space full to overflowin' with things only the army can use?"

"Hello, Mama . . ." Ty said soberly. "Good afternoon, ladies. I won't bother you for long. I just wanted to announce my return and introduce my new bookkeeper."

Lady Tiffin's eyes fell on Freedom. Slowly, without smiling, she looked Freedom up and down. The eyes of the other women in the room fastened assessingly upon her, also, and Freedom felt a blush creeping up her cheeks.

"Good afternoon, Lady Tiffin . . . My name is Freedom Walker."

Lady Tiffin stiffened as if she'd been slapped. "Ah do declare . . . You are a No'the'ner!" she gasped. "With an exceedin'ly patriotic name!"

For the first time, Freedom questioned why Ty didn't have his mother's Southern drawl. He spoke much like she did—perhaps not typically Bostonian, but not like his crew members, his slaves, or his mother, either.

"She can't help where she was born, Mama," Ty

187

cut in. "Or what name her parents gave her. However, I'm counting on her to be an excellent mathematician. Since you can't make heads nor tails of a column of figures, and I haven't the time, I've hired her to keep our books."

"Do ah understan' she's to live here at Cypress Hall?" Ty's mother asked. "A No'the'ner beneath our very roof?"

"Where we can keep an eye on her, Mama . . . I told Ambrose to prepare the yellow room; it will be hers from now on."

"*Her* room!" Lady Tiffin's patrician nostrils flared the same way Tiger's did when he was angry or annoyed; oh, yes, Freedom could see all sorts of resemblances. "You might at least have consulted me, Ty . . . b'fore makin' such rash, peremptory decisions."

Ty nodded toward the avid-listening, hoop-skirted audience. "I could see you were busy, Mama. . . . Aren't you going to present Miss Walker and me to your guests?"

Lady Tiffin's hands fluttered about her full bosom. "Dear me, ah suppose ah must. . . . Where are mah manners? Of course, you know these ladies, Tif. As for your friend . . . ah . . . what was your peculiar name, again?"

"Walker . . . Freedom Walker," Freedom said, with emphasis on the *Freedom*.

"Ah still say that's an inflammatory moniker in these heah pahts. . . . Come heah, Miss Walker, and do meet mah friends." Lady Tiffin named each of the women in the parlor, who, like Lady Tiffin herself, were all powdered and coiffed matrons, beautifully gowned, and most refined and fragile in their appearance and mannerisms. Only one was about the same age as Freedom . . . or perhaps a bit older.

Ty's mother introduced her as Miss Stephanie Clairmont. Something about the striking young woman made Freedom look at her closely.

Stephanie Clairmont had raven-black hair, vivid blue eyes, and an hour glass figure. She exuded sensuality but could not be called pretty in the conventional sense of the word. Her predatory glance barely flickered over Freedom; instead, it devoured Tiger, and when Lady Tiffin had finished the introductions, it was Miss Stephanie Clairmont who spoke.

"How are you Tigah, honey?" she purred, her voice deep and throaty. "It's been ages since ah've seen you. This dratted war is keepin' all the good men busy. . . . How was the journey to Nassau? Did you bring back lots of gunpowder for Gen'ral Lee's troops?"

"The journey almost ended in tragedy," Ty said bluntly. "We ran aground on a shoal during a storm, I lost half my cargo, and I'm only here to tell about it because Miss Walker—this *Northerner*—dragged me unconscious from the sea."

"Mah word!" Miss Stephanie blurted out, her blue eyes darting to Freedom. "Such thrillin' adventures! No wonder you brought her home to Cypress Hall."

"Tif!" his mother exclaimed. "Ah had no idea! Why didn't say you somethin' when you first came in?"

"You never asked what kind of trip I had, Mama. Tell me, would you have come down to the levee to meet me had you known I almost died this time? Or would you merely have had a second mint julep or glass of lemonade and prettily fluttered your handkerchief, all the while bemoaning the inconveniences of this terrible war?"

"Tiffin Carrin'ton! Don't you dare talk to me like that in front of mah friends—and Miss Clairmont, too. Whatever will she think of you bein'so cruel an' heartless to your lovin' mama?"

"I don't care what she—or any of your friends—think, Mama. I'm too busy helping the Confederacy to worry about the opinions of a bunch of useless females. It's you who should be worrying what *I* think of *you* . . . sitting here gossiping as if not a one of you knows a war is going on. The least you could be doing is rolling bandages."

The women gasped, including Freedom, who could not believe Tiger's sudden rudeness or hostility.

"He's jus' tired an' exhausted," Stephanie Clairmont purred in a proprietary way. "We mustn't pay any mind a-tall to what he's sayin'. . . . Were you hurt when your ship ran aground, Ty?"

"What business is it of yours, Stephie?" Ty coldly inquired.

"Jus' the business of an ole friend of the fam'ly. After all, there was a time when our friendship ran rather deep." The way Stephanie Clairmont said *friendship* left Freedom in little doubt that something much more had once existed between the two.

"We haven't been friends for a long, long time, Stephie, if indeed we ever were. And I sincerely doubt we'll be friends in the future."

"Why, Ty . . . you wound me to the quick!"

"Tiffin!" Lady Tiffin exclaimed. Red-faced with anger, she was practically panting in her too-tight gown. "Your rudeness is intol'rable! Ah hope mah friends can overlook it. . . . This is what happens when a boy is raised with no father. Ah've had to endure such trials, ladies, as you could not imagine."

"Then why don't you enlighten them, Mama, while I show Miss Walker to her room . . . unless she'd rather remain to hear all the gritty details of

190

my neglected childhood."

"Neglected! No one can evah say ah neglected mah son. Why, ah always saw to it you were dressed as befitted a Carrin'ton, an' had plenty of pocket money b'sides. . . ."

Ty turned his back on his mother and faced Freedom. "Mouse, do you care to stay and listen to my mama's rationalizations for why she never wrote to me or showed the least concern whether I lived or died?"

Freedom felt her own cheeks flaming; she was embarrassed for both Ty *and* his mother, that they should stoop to arguing in such a manner.

With a grim smile, Tiger took her arm and led her from the room. But before he exited, he turned back once more. "I'll see you at dinner, Mama, at which time you can become better acquainted with Miss Walker. By then, I trust, all your fine, feathered friends will have departed, and you can give us your full, undivided attention."

A deadly silence ensued in the parlor, as Ty closed the door on the women's astounded, indignant faces. The only one who seemed amused by it all, Freedom noticed, was Stephanie Clairmont. The young woman's lip curled, and her eyes sparkled with suppressed laughter — a laughter that seemed somehow nasty and malicious. When the door had clicked shut, Freedom rounded on Tiger.

"That was awful of you, Ty! How could you treat your mother like that in front of all of her friends . . . and in front of me? I was mortified on your behalf."

Ty grinned and chucked her under the chin. "I'm glad somebody felt *something* on my behalf, even if it was only mortification. . . . My mama, as you may or may not have noticed, is a silly, vain, shallow, empty-headed woman who doesn't care a fig for me and never has. I get back at her whenever I can by doing the one thing that really annoys her—being rude to her in front of her friends."

He steered her toward the lovely staircase. "Don't upset yourself over it, Mouse. By dinnertime, it will all be forgotten. You'll see. Mama will go on and on about this entertainment and that, who's doing what to whom, and who wore what atrocious gown at the last tea or barbecue. . . . It's best you know now that Mama and I barely tolerate each other. I can't abide her foolish chatter, and she can't abide me, period. This always happens when I come home. Fortunately, after a few verbal jousts to reestablish our strained relationship, we settle down to ignoring each another, and life becomes tranquil once more."

Mounting the winding staircase beside him, Freedom paid scant attention to where he was taking her. "But, Ty, that must be a terrible way to live. My father was often preoccupied, too, but I didn't succumb to bitterness over it."

"I'm not bitter," Tiger denied. "I just enjoy baiting her. You must admit, she's so pitifully easy to bait."

"I can't believe she's treated you as shabbily as you proclaim. Surely, as your mother, she loves you deeply."

"The only person Mama loves is herself. . . . But you mustn't think ill of her for it. That's the way she was raised. Before Papa married her, she had never lifted a finger to do anything for herself. Her father was an English nobleman whose servants waited on her hand and foot."

"You mean, she wasn't born in the South?"

Ty gave a short laugh. "Hardly . . . Though from her accent, you'd never know it. She's become the very essence of a genteel Southern belle. I always wondered why she married my father in the first place, when she could have married British royalty. Then one day I found out."

"Why?" Freedom gasped breathlessly, pausing beside Tiger in front of a closed door on the second floor.

"She had to. She was pregnant," he said matter-of-factly.

"Oh no! With you?"

"No, with a child she miscarried shortly after she married my father."

"But how did you learn of all this? She didn't tell you, surely."

"No, she didn't, though she'll tell anyone who'll listen that she's related to the throne of England. . . . It was quite easy to find out, actually. I've made many friends among the British buyers of Cypress Hall cotton. One day, I asked an acquaintance if he'd ever heard of my mother's maiden name—though, of course, I didn't tell him why I was asking or that I was trying to learn about my own mother.

"He said yes, of course he knew the name. It's very prominent in England. He then went on to say that tragedy had struck that illustrious family years ago, when their beautiful, willful daughter fell into disgrace by conceiving a child out of wedlock. She was sent away and no one ever heard from her again, but it was rumored she got shipped off to the United States, where she met and married a gullible, unsuspecting tarheel . . . That's what my father was in those days . . . a tarheel. Not only did he harvest timber, but he made tar out of the resin from the trees and sold it."

"So that's why everyone calls her *Lady* Tiffin . . . because she's English."

"*I* never call her Lady Tiffin," Ty said. "I think it's a ridiculous affectation . . . a ridiculous name, in fact, which I've always hated, especially when she hung it on me as a first name. Unfortunately, what I think has never mattered to her one way or the other."

"Oh, Ty, that can't be true . . ."

"It is true . . . and it's a good thing she doesn't care what I think, since my opinion of her is less than flattering. . . . Well, we can't stand here all day discussing Mama. Here's your room, Mouse. I hope you'll find it comfortable."

He flung open the door, and Freedom gazed into the prettiest, most feminine room she had ever seen. Everything in it looked as if the sun had splashed it with soft, golden yellow — curtains, rugs, delicate furniture, dressing screen, the four-poster bed itself. . . . There was even a yellow-striped tabby cat curled in the center of a rocking chair with a needle-pointed seat and back featuring yellow buttercups.

"You see why I thought you must have this room," Ty said. "It was designed for a woman with your coloring."

"Doesn't your mother ever use it?" Freedom asked, stepping onto the lemon-yellow and white braided rug. "It's a wonderful room!"

"No, it's used only for guests. Her quarters are down the hallway in the other wing."

Freedom spun around in pleasure at the lovely surroundings, then stopped and eyed him apprehensively. "And where are your quarters?"

"In this wing . . ." He grinned. "But don't worry. There's no connecting door between my room and yours."

"Does my door lock?" She asked pointedly, half hoping it didn't.

"Do you want it to lock?" he asked just as pointedly. "I can have a lock installed if you insist, but I don't see the point of it. I've already told you; next time, you must make the first move. My room is just down the hall, and I *never* lock *my* door."

She studied the toes of the yellow slippers Emma Willoughby had lent her. "Oh, Ty, I'm scared. . . . I don't think I should have come here." She raised her eyes to his. "I'll never fit in . . . I'm not sure I can even keep your books properly. And your mother doesn't like me. She'll probably like me less as she gets to know me."

Tiger's violet-hued eyes softened and he reached for her, but she eluded his grasp and walked over to the chair where the cat was napping. Gently, she pushed the rocker to awaken the feline, but the cat seemed not to notice. Ty came up behind her and slid his arms around her waist.

"You're the most courageous woman I've ever met, Mouse. Don't let your courage fail you now. It's not important whether or not my mother likes you. . . . *I* like you. I want you here. Tomorrow, I'll show you how to keep the books, but for the rest of today, all I want is for you to rest and relax. I'll send up Elvira with a tray of lemonade. You can have a bath before dinner if you like, and I'll see that Elvira finds some of Mama's old gowns that might fit you. Mama was much slimmer when she was younger, and she hardly wore some of her gowns. They'll do until we can get some new ones made."

"Tiger . . ." Freedom whirled to face him. "I don't want anyone waiting on me! This Elvira is not to — to demean herself seeing to my comfort."

"Demean herself?" Ty repeated incredulously. "Do you mean as in *serve* you?"

"Yes, that's what I mean. I'm perfectly capable of

195

looking after my own needs, Ty."

Tiger's fingers suddenly dug into her shoulders. His mouth slanted downward and his eyes darkened. "Now see here, Freedom. Elvira will be insulted if you don't allow her to perform her duties. . . . She'll think you abhor having her around; her feelings will be terribly hurt."

"How can she possibly think that, when I've never even met the woman? . . . I just don't want her to wait on me."

"You'll let her wait on you, by God, or I'll—I'll lock you in this room until you do!"

"There's no lock on the door, remember? Neither inside nor out."

"You just don't want her to wait on you because you think she's a slave."

"Well, isn't she?"

"If you want to know so badly, why don't you ask her? She's got a tongue; she can speak on her own behalf."

"I *will* ask her."

"Go ahead . . . You can ask her when she brings your lemonade. She *will* bring it, Mouse. Elvira takes great pride in her work, and I won't let you trample her dignity because of your own biases."

"My biases! What about yours? You criticize your mother for wanting people to wait on her all the time, yet I don't see you fetching your own lemonade."

"I'm getting out of here," Ty gritted. "If I stay another minute, there's no telling what I'm likely to do."

"Perhaps you'd better," Freedom responded. "I'd relish some time alone."

Without another word, he stalked from the room. The tabby cat leapt off the rocker and followed, leaving Freedom by herself in the sunny chamber, which mocked her with its bright cheerfulness when she herself felt plunged into gloom. No matter what Ty said, she could not—would not—play the part of a pampered, spoiled aristocrat like his mother and those other ladies downstairs. Just because she loved the man did not mean she was willing to change her stripes for him; that would be as impossible as the tabby cat converting her yellow stripes to green ones. . . . And why did Ty want her to try, when he condemned his own mother for behaving as if she were royalty?

No, Freedom thought. This girl, Elvira, would certainly welcome having a visitor who did not expect to be treated like a queen. Freedom would try to befriend her—and to ease her burdens. After all, it could not be easy being a slave at Cypress Hall.

Chapter Fourteen

"So you're Elvira . . . Jules's wife," Freedom said as a tall, regal, light brown-skinned woman glided into the room bearing a tray of refreshments.

The woman set down the tray on a small round table in front of the tall windows and turned, affording Freedom a full view of her haughty face and slender, yet curvaceous figure. Freedom gulped back a cry of dismay; the right side of Elvira's face was beautiful, with even features and skin the color of warm honey. But the left side was grossly distorted, the skin blotched with pink and white, and the features — mouth, eye, and left nostril — pulled down in an ugly, permanent grimace.

"And you are Miss Freedom Walker," Elvira responded in a low, melodic voice that sent shivers down Freedom's spine.

For a moment, neither woman spoke. In silence, they studied each other, and Freedom recalled Tiger's warning that Elvira would take it personally if her services were rejected. Now Freedom could understand why; Elvira was watching her closely for signs of repugnance.

"Thank you for bringing me something to drink," Freedom finally said. "You'll have to excuse me if I don't seem to know how to behave in front of you . . . It's not your appearance. You're the most stately woman I've ever seen; you could be Omoroh's sister. Omoroh is the big Negro who accompanied Tiger and me to Cypress Hall . . . My awkwardness is due entirely to the fact that I've never in my life been waited on like this. I usually fetch my own lemonade . . . and usually it's well water, not lemonade," she finished with an awkward laugh.

"You from de No'th," Elvira said. "Is dat why your name is Missy Freedom?"

"My father is—was—a preacher who spent his whole life fighting the evils of slavery. Now, I'm trying to do the same."

"Den why is you heah? We got no slaves at Cypress Hall, Missy. You be better off to go someplace 'like where ah come from be'foh Marse Ty's daddy bought me and brung me home. . . . I was only six at de time. Dey had me helpin' to wash de laundry in a big ole washtub ovah de fire. Dat's how ah got mah face ruint. . . . I fell into de fire tryin' to stir de big pot. Den when ah got better, dey sold me so's dey wouldn't hafta look at me no moah."

Freedom's eyes filled with tears of sympathy and her heart with anger. "They sold you because they thought you were too ugly to have around . . . a six-year-old child who never should have been working near a big fire in the first place?"

Elvira nodded. "Dat's a fac', Missy. . . . But it was de best thing dat evah happen to me, 'cause Marse Ty's daddy bought me at a auction and brung me home to Cypress Hall. . . . his mama wasn't none too happy 'bout it, but Marse Ty's daddy, he say, 'Lady Tiff'n, dis chile needs a home, an' now she gots one, and she ain't gonna be a slave no moah neither. We's gonna pay her wages, same as we do evahbody else, and she gonna earn her keep and make us proud o' her.' "

"All the workers at Cypress Hall receive wages?" Freedom blurted astounded. "None of you are slaves?"

"No, Missy . . . Ain't none of us heah 'cause we ain't got de choice to leave. We could all leave t'morrah if 'n we wanted. . . . 'Course where could we go dat would be better'n Cypress Hall?"

"You could go north . . . after the war, I mean. In the North, you might one day be able to own your own land; you could farm it and make a living."

"Hah!" Elvira snorted. "What ah know 'bout farmin'? Jules knows, but he an' Marse Ty been friends for so long, dey ain't 'bout to quit anytime soon. Dis be home to me an' Jules. We got a pretty little white house wid green shuttahs, an' a big gawden wid a fence around it, and chickens an' ducks. Ah'm gonna get mah own milk cow one day, too. . . . Ah got all ah wants right heah, Missy, 'cept for babies. Ain't had much luck gettin' babies, for some reason. . . . But Jules 'n me keep tryin'."

"What about Lady Tiffin? How does she treat you?"

"Oh, Lady Tiff'n ain't so bad. . . . she like a li'l chile; she be lost widout me an' Jules to look aftah her. Ah ben lookin' aftah her a long time now, and she mostly do what ah tell 'er to do."

"But what about her friends? Don't they order

200

you around or make remarks about you?"

"Ah don't pay no attention to 'em, Missy. Sure, dey all keeps slaves an' acts uppity, but dey ain't mah fam'ly like Marse Ty an' Lady Tiff'n. Marse Ty got lots o' enemies 'cause he done freed his slaves, but he don't care. Jules 'n me'll stand by Marse Ty even if dem Yankees come a shootin' and tryin' to take Cypress Hall."

"You don't want the South to win the war!" Freedom was horrified. She could hardly digest these surprising and upsetting revelations. Why hadn't Tiger told her the truth?

"Ah sure don't want dem Yanks to win it! What happen to Cypress Hall den?"

"Probably nothing, if the slaves here are already freed. Don't you care what happens to the Negroes on other plantations? If the North wins, they will be freed, too."

"Ah hopes you is right, Missy, but somehow ah doubts it. Ah'm sorry, Missy Freedom, but if you believes in de genrosity of No'the'ners, you is tetched in de head. Dem bluecoats don't want nothin' 'cept de fam'ly silver. Dey's gonna come robbin' an' rapin' an' pillagin' . . . ah jus' knows it. Dere ain't a gen'leman among 'em."

Freedom was too speechless to refute Elvira; here was someone who ought to be on *her* side, yet with every word, she defended the South. If a badly scarred former slave could not understand why the North *must* win this war, how could Freedom hope that Ty might eventually understand?

"Elvira," she sighed. "You've given me much to think about, and I'm suddenly exhausted. Let's continue this discussion some other time. For now, I feel the need to rest. . . ."

"You does looks plumb tuckered out, Missy." The tall woman moved to Freedom, hands outstretched, one of which, Freedom noticed, was as badly scarred as her face. "Ah'll he'p you get undressed, so you can lie down comfo'tably."

Freedom backed away. "No, thank you! I'm perfectly capable of undressing myself."

A hurt expression crept into Elvira's dark eyes. " 'Course, Missy . . . ah can send one o' the other gals to he'p you. Mancie's a good gal, an' she got nimble fingers. Purty as a june bug, too."

"It's not that!" Freedom protested. "Honestly, I don't care about your scars, Elvira. I—I just prefer to do things for myself."

Elvira pursed her lips doubtfully. "Maybe you thinks you're too good to be waited on by de likes o' me."

"That's not it; I *swear* it's not."

"Den turn 'round, Missy, an' let me undo dat gown. . . . after you naps, ah'll send up hot water for a bath, an' den ah'm gonna do up your hair real purty. Ah got a good hand wid hair. . . . Ah'll find you a purty dress to wear for suppah t'night, too. Lady Tiff'n likes to dress for suppah."

"But this isn't at all necessary, Elvira," Freedom protested, even as the woman determinedly stepped behind her and began working on the fastenings of her gown. "I'm an employee here, the same as you. I'm going to keep the books for Marse Ty . . . I mean, Tiger . . . I mean, *Captain* Carrington."

Elvira chuckled deep in her throat. "Oh, dey's a *big* difference between you an' me, Missy Freedom. . . . You's de fust white woman Marse Ty evah brung home. So he must think purty high o' you. An' if'n he don't, he *will* when ah gets done

202

wid you. . . . It's time Marse Ty found hisself a wife, an' if the Southe'n gals won't have 'im, he'll jus' have to look No'th."

"The Southern girls won't have him? Whatever do you mean?" Freedom thought of Miss Stephanie Clairmont and doubted that *she* would reject a marriage proposal from Tiger; Miss Clairmont had eyed him like a cat about to pounce upon an unsuspecting sparrow.

"Ah've already said too much, Missy. . . . Jules says mah biggest fault is mah flappin' jaws. Now you just get into bed an' have yourself a nice nap. . . ."

After Elvira finished divesting her young charge of the yellow gown, she turned down the counterpane on the bed, and Freedom meekly climbed between cool, clean sheets and laid her head on a fluffy pillow. Never had she felt so cosseted and cared for. A bone-melting relaxation crept over her, making it difficult to ponder everything she had learned in the last half hour about Tiger Carrington and Cypress Hall. Yawning widely, she snuggled into the pillow, deciding she could sort it all out later, after she had rested.

"Ah'll wake you in two hours, Missy . . . an' then you can bathe," Elvira clucked. "Go to sleep now, an' don't bother your purty head 'bout nothin'."

Docile as a lamb—at least, temporarily—Freedom obeyed.

Several hours later, Freedom sat at a long damask-covered table beneath a glowing chandelier, in the most elegant dining room she had ever seen. Flowers graced the center of the table, where fine

203

china and shining silverware reflected a way of life heretofore unknown to her. She sat stiffly in the straight-backed chair, aware that her peach-colored gown was the most expensive she had ever worn and her upswept hairdo the most sophisticated. She felt awkward and out of place, especially whenever she glanced at Ty or his mother, both of whom appeared emminently comfortable and at ease in the gilded surroundings. Lady Tiffin was wearing diamonds in her earlobes and a spray of them in her perfectly coiffed hair, and Tiger had changed to evening attire in a dark wine color that accentuated his blond magnificence.

Even Ambrose sported better clothing than her father had ever possessed, wearing white gloves when he served the first course of soup. Freedom wasn't sure which spoon to use or where to place it when she finished the exquisite broth, which in anyone else's house would have constituted the entire meal.

"That was delicious," she murmured, hoping to break the silence.

Tiger had complimented her on the gown and elaborate hairstyle when she first entered, but since then, he hadn't said another word. His mother had ignored both of them, and neither had prayed before eating.

"Elvira is an excellent cook," Ty responded, setting down his own spoon. "Or maybe it was Mancie who made the soup. Elvira's been teaching her."

"I haven't met Mancie yet," Freedom said. "But Elvira is certainly a most persuasive person."

Ty's amused glance swept over her. "I neglected to warn you of how bossy she can be, though I'm sure by now you've discovered that—and also

204

how sensitive."

Freedom leaned back slightly as Ambrose placed a succulent-looking piece of chicken on her gold-rimmed dinner plate. "Yes, I discovered both of those attributes this afternoon. For today, I allowed her to treat me like a helpless invalid, unable to perform the simplest tasks, but tomorrow, I do not intend to let any of your employees fuss over me any longer."

Freedom put deliberate emphasis on the word *employees*.

"*Se'vants,* Miss Walker," Lady Tiffin immediately corrected, as if she'd been listening all along, just waiting to add her opinion. "Do refer to them as se'vants, won't you? Employees is much too inflammatory a term in these heah pahts."

"Now, Mama," Ty cut in. "Employees is what they are, and if Miss Walker wishes to call them that, I have no objections, and neither should you."

"Maybe if you didn't *flaunt* such liberalism in evahbody's face, Tif, you'd be happily married by now, instead of so desperate that you had to bring home a No'th'n gal for mah inspection," his mother retorted.

"She's my bookkeeper, Mama, nothing else—at least, not yet. And whomever I choose to marry will never be subjected first to your inspection. I'm a man now. I know what I like when I see it, and I hardly need your approval, in any case."

Ty shot Freedom a provocative glance that made her blush at its implications. His look was as intimate as a caress and suggestive of all sorts of devastating possibilities. Fortunately, his mother was cutting up her chicken and missed it.

"Please don't assume there's anything personal

between us, Lady Tiffin," Freedom hastened to add. "Your son and I barely know each other. I wasn't even aware that you had servants instead of slaves; Ty—Tiger—never saw fit to inform me of that. . . . Nor did he tell me I'd be eating at the dinner table with you and wearing your clothes."

Lady Tiffin's blond eyebrows lifted. She set down her fork and knife, then stared at Freedom suspiciously. "Well, where else would you be eatin' if not at this dinnah table? An' who else's clothes would you be wearin' but mine? Tif did say you saved his life, didn't he? But even if you hadn't, this dinnah table is the only fittin' place for a young white woman to be eatin' at Cypress Hall."

"I could eat in the kitchen with the ; . . ah . . . servants," Freedom offered, as Ty groaned and shook his head at her.

"Not while ah live an' breathe!" Lady Tiffin exploded. "Ah do hope you aren't one o' those bleedin' heart abolitists . . . Tiffin!" She turned angry eyes on her handsome son. "You didn't go and bring home one o' them just to spite me, did you?"

Freedom suddenly felt like a leper, intruding where she wasn't wanted. She swept her napkin from her lap and rose. "Yes, he did, Lady Tiffin, but whether or not it was to spite you, I couldn't say. . . . Ty, you can see now why this won't work. I—I just can't do it. I'll have to go someplace else to wait out this war."

Tiger rose at almost the same time. "Sit down, Mouse," he said quietly. "Mama, eat your chicken. If the three of us can't share the same table and partake of a meal without leaping at each other's throats, then what hope is there for either side in this damn, awful conflict? . . . Yes, we have enormous differences, but we also share the same human traits. We get hungry and thirsty. We want to be accepted and to fit in. We need companionship . . . . I suggest we set aside our selfish interests and try to get along. It will be good practice in case the North wins and President Lincoln forces us to return to the Union after all . . If that happens, we'll need every ounce of diplomacy and patience we can possibly cultivate — on both sides, North *and* South."

"You're right, Ty. . . . I apologize." Freedom gingerly sat down again. "Lady Tiffin, forgive me. I didn't mean to make you angry, but I can't help being what I am. Nevertheless, in the future, I'll try harder not to . . . say all the wrong things."

Ty bowed and grinned, pleased by the apology. In vain, Freedom waited for Lady Tiffin to reciprocate or at least say something placating. But Ty's mother only continued to stare angrily at her son, until some sudden thought brought a slight triumphant smile to her lips.

"Tif, if you really didn't bring Miss Walker home to introduce her to me as a possible future daughtah-in-law, then perhaps you can bring yourself to behave more kindly toward Miss Stephanie Clairmont. . . . Ah declare, but she's nursin' a badly broken heart. Ah always thought you'd marry her one day, and so did she. . . . Ah'll nevah understan' what went wrong. She's the only one among all our friend's daughters who's willin' to overlook your liberalism."

At the mention of Stephanie Clairmont, Ty resumed glowering. "What went wrong is between us and only us, Mama. You'd be doing Stephie and me a kindness if you didn't invite her to visit when

I'm home—and even when I'm not. It's time she got on with her life, just as I've gotten on with mine since our . . . er . . . relationship ended."

Tiger's uncharacteristic verbal stumbling was all the evidence Freedom needed to know that something passionate had indeed existed between Ty and the beautiful Stephanie. Freedom felt such a jolt of raw jealousy that she wanted to scratch out the girl's eyes the next time she saw her.

"Well, ah'm sorry you feel that way, Tif," his mother continued. "But you are gonna be seein' a great deal of Stephie in the comin' weeks an' months. . . . After that awful scene you created in front of mah friends this afternoon, Stephie suggested we do exactly what you suggested: meet reg'larly to roll bandages or do whatever else is needed by our brave boys stationed at the Wilmin'ton Armory."

"You don't have to meet here," Tiger snapped. "You can go to the Parker Place or even to Clairmont Gardens. I'm sure Stephie's daddy wouldn't mind his little girl entertaining at their home."

"Now, Tif . . . Stephie's got no Mama to play hostess, and the Parkah Place is too far for evahbody. Cypress Hall is the most centrally located, so what could ah do but volunteer it? Startin' next week, we'll be meetin' twice weekly to do our duty to our beloved Confederacy. Ah thought you would be pleased."

Ty threw his napkin down on top of his half-eaten chicken. "How can I be pleased when I know that the entire endeavor is merely a plot on your part and Stephanie's—and probably all your useless friends—to get me to the altar?"

"It's not a plot," Lady Tiffin pouted. "Why do

208

you always think the worst, Tif?"

"Because I'm usually right. . . . Tell me, Mama. Will you invite Miss Walker to your patriotic little get-togethers?"

"A bookkeeper from the No'th? Why, ah'd hardly think she'd want to come."

Freedom was growing weary of being treated as if she weren't there. "I don't want to come," she interrupted. "I'm sure I'll be far too busy mastering my new duties."

"And, of course, you wouldn't be caught dead rolling a bandage for a *Confederate* soldier, now, would you?" Ty pounced.

Freedom was amazed at how quickly his anger had switched to her. "Well, I—I never thought about it," she faltered.

"Then take a moment to think about it," Ty goaded, obviously trying to push her into it. "I'm sure Mama would appreciate an extra pair of hands, wouldn't you, Mama?"

Lady Tiffin pursed her lips in annoyance, while Freedom struggled to sort out her mixed emotions. "I—I suppose rolling bandages to help wounded soldiers of either army would not violate my principles. A wounded man is a wounded man, deserving of compassion no matter which side he serves."

"Well spoken, but not a very realistic sentiment . . . Ah certainly couldn't roll bandages for the Union Army," Lady Tiffin sniffed.

"It isn't a matter of loyalties," Freedom enunciated carefully. "It's more a matter of—of—Christian charity. One of my favorite parables has always been that of the good Samaritan who stopped and aided an injured man when others passed him by."

Lady Tiffin gave an inelegant snort. "We're

hardly passin' by our fine Rebel soldiers."

Ty broke into a grin. "I'm glad you feel the way you do, Mouse . . . because I think you *should* join the ladies in rolling bandages. Your bookkeeping duties won't take up all your time, and you need some nice female companionship—if Mama and her friends can be called nice."

"Tif! You are such a—a crass manipulator!" Lady Tiffin burst out.

"Oh, but I can hardly compete with *you,* dear Mama. . . . Now, if you ladies will excuse me, I've business to attend to with Jules."

Ty left Freedom and his mother sitting alone in the big dining room, where they finished the meal in strained silence, Freedom wondering anew how she would ever adjust to living among the enemy and Tiger's mother wondering God-alone-knew-what.

Later that night, as Freedom prepared for bed, a light knock sounded on her door. Sighing, she went to answer it. Probably, it was Elvira with a midnight snack of hot milk and cookies. Since she had just taken down her hair and wore only her night shift, Freedom hid behind the door and peaked around as she opened it.

"Ty! Why are you knocking on my door at this late hour?"

He was still wearing formal dinner dress—a snowy-white shirt, untied cravat, and slim-fitting black trousers—but had discarded the wine-colored jacket. He waved a brandy snifter under her nose and grinned lopsidedly. "I was lonely, Mouse, and I thought you might be lonely, too."

Freedom did feel a pang of desperate longing for his company, but she resisted it. "I'm most definitely not lonely, Ty. It's very late. You should be in bed."

"That's correct . . . *your* bed. Or you should be in mine."

She pushed against the door to keep him from entering. "No, Ty. . . Please, you promised. You said it was up to me when or *if* I came to your room."

"I just stopped by to reissue the invitation," he drawled. "I was down in the study drinking brandy when suddenly I became unbearably lonely for you."

"You're drunk," she accused.

"No, not from brandy, but maybe from frustrated passion. I want you in my arms, Mouse. I want you in my bed beside me."

Freedom wrestled with her own desires, reminding herself that she had been up and down all day—one minute, determined not to be absorbed into this enticing but alien culture, and the next, trying to compromise and make her new life work. Ty didn't keep slaves, so a major hurdle had come tumbling down. But other hurdles had gone up in its place. He still lived in a manner she was finding difficult to accept.

"Ty, please give me time. . . . We're so different. You can see that now, can't you? I don't know if I can adjust."

"You've already adjusted, Mouse . . . quite admirably, I might add. You've only been here one day, but already you've promised to roll bandages for the Confederacy, you've let Elvira prepare your bath and do your hair, you've put up with Mama—and

211

God knows, if you can put up with her, you can put up with anyone and anything."

"I'm not sure I can put up with *you!*"

"Yes, you can, Mouse. . . . Let me come in and I'll prove it to you."

"No!" Freedom pushed harder against the door. "Ty, as you've just pointed out, I've only been here one day. This is all so strange to me . . . so difficult. It isn't at all what I expected. In some ways I'm relieved, but in others I'm still worried and afraid I'll always hate certain things. Elvira, for instance . . ."

"You hate *Elvira?*"

"No, not Elvira herself, but what slavery has done to her—and then what you've done."

"What have I done but make her feel like she's a part of my family . . . that she's necessary to the success of Cypress Hall? I should think that's what you'd want for all slaves . . . to regain their dignity and self-respect. To feel competent, worthwhile, and needed."

"But she doesn't seem to care about all the other poor slaves, Ty! After all she's suffered, she still wants the South to win."

There was a sudden silence behind the door. Furtively, Freedom peeked around it to confront Tiger's furious gaze. "So do I," he grated, nose to nose with her. "North Carolina isn't the cesspool of evil you still think it is, Freedom, nor is the Confederacy. We have our own cherished beliefs and values, our own ideals, our own pride . . . I thought that once you saw Cypress Hall, you'd realize that we aren't all heartless monsters."

"I do realize it, Ty, but . . . how can you expect me to give up all my own beliefs and values in a single day?"

He straightened and stared at her, his face hardening to stone. "All right, I guess you can't. I guess I expected too much. . . . So I'll say good night, Miss Walker. Don't worry, I won't bother you again."

"Ty . . .!" She flung open the door, but he was already stalking down the darkened corridor, his rigid shoulders betraying his anger. "Oh, Tiger . . ." she muttered softly, retreating back inside her room. "I keep forgetting that you really are a tiger, not a little tame housecat. . . . Unfortunately, I'm not sure I can handle either one."

Chapter Fifteen

"Please excuse me, ladies, but I see that Captain Carrington has just come in, and I must consult with him on a bookkeeping matter." Freedom smiled at the dozen or so women gathered in the front drawing room. Then she set down her sewing on the chair she had just vacated and wove her way through the midst of the huge hooped skirts that billowed in every direction, taking up all the space between her and the doorway.

As she reached the hallway, the women's chatter floated out after her. She inhaled the flower and perfume-scented humid air as if she couldn't get enough of it to fill her lungs. The drawing room's close confines were stifling. The windows had been flung wide open, but summer had arrived during the past several weeks, bringing with it an oppressive heat.

Freedom relished the opportunity to escape the hateful task of sewing buttons on Confederate uniforms—not quite the same thing as rolling bandages for wounded boys—and she did need to see Ty. Several of his recent entries in the large leather-bound book recording all purchases for Cypress Hall were illegible. She could decipher neither the amounts spent nor the items bought. Someone had also stuffed a handful of receipts into the ledger but had neglected to identify the purchases or to date them, though a goodly sum of money had been spent.

Consulting Ty during the daytime was a far safer prospect than cornering him during the evening hours, Freedom had learned from experience. At night, Ty flatly rejected talk of the business that consumed his attention during daylight hours. When the sun went down, all he could seem to think about was luring her into his bedroom. She was still resisting, all the while suffering her own private hell of tormented longings. Yes, it was definitely better to discuss things with Tiger in the daytime. Danger haunted the dark, becoming especially potent after Ty's mother had retired to her wing of the house or gone out to visit friends.

Freedom hurried quickly to the back of the house to get the current ledger. There, an office had been fashioned out of an unused pantry. In it were kept the records and documents related to the financial transactions of the plantation and also to Ty's blockade-running ventures. Freedom worked in the office every morning until noon and for several hours each evening, yet she still had much to learn. Ty wanted her to manage his financial affairs so that she could tell him at a moment's notice his exact profits, losses, projected income and expenditures, and possible savings.

He had kept fairly careful records in the past, before the war, but from the moment the *Sea Whisper* had been launched, Ty's ledgers had suffered neglect. What entries there were, Freedom had difficulty deciphering. Mostly, Ty tossed receipts in an empty drawer and, when it filled to overflowing, started on another. She spent nearly all her time going through old receipts and recording them. Ty was now making a better effort to keep track of current transactions, but his mother refused to make any effort whatsoever. Lady Tiffin demanded money when she needed it and declined to account for anything she spent. Something would have to be done about that, Freedom knew, but she wasn't ready to suggest to Tiger that his mother's access to funds be curtailed if she did not cooperate. Freedom suspected she had already antagonized Lady Tiffin too much; the blond matriarch was leaving no stone unturned in her efforts to find Ty a suitable Southern wife.

Arriving in the office, Freedom unlocked the bottom drawer of the desk, withdrew the current ledger, and relocked the drawer, all the while musing on the fact that every time Lady Tiffin invited friends to roll bandages or sew buttons for the Confederacy, she also invited a pretty, unmarried girl to help and often asked her to stay for dinner. Stephanie Clairmont had been invited three times in a row, but when Ty all but ignored her, Lady Tiffin began issuing invitations to other girls—and mere girls they were, too. The last had just turned fifteen, and the one today could not be much older. Young Millicent didn't even know how to thread a needle, and she blushed furiously every time Ty's name was mentioned. The poor child had looked more in need of a schoolroom tutor than a husband, Freedom thought, hiding the key again inside a nearby potted fern.

Ledger in arms, she retraced her steps to the hallway, then knocked on the door of the library, which was where she had seen Ty disappear. Without waiting for an answer, she opened the door and peered inside. Standing behind the large desk, Ty nonetheless dwarfed it with his big, powerful body. He was sweaty and dirty, dressed for riding his Plantation Walking Horse, but he still caused her heart to flutter at the mere sight of him. Her eyes clung to his damp shirtfront, which revealed ridges of muscle beneath. Her prurient interest wasn't lost on him, and his mouth stretched into a wide, knowing grin.

"Come in, Mouse. . . . Feel free to close the door behind you, so we can escape the chatter of your competition."

Closing the door with one hand and clutching the ledger to her chest with the other, Freedom chose to ignore the crude reference to her rivals. The library was cool, dim, and quiet in comparison to the noisy, overcrowded drawing room; it was also decidedly masculine, with its heavy dark furnishings and massive stone fireplace. She feasted her eyes upon him for a moment before speaking; they saw each other at least once every day at the evening meal, but for Freedom it wasn't enough, not when she wanted to spend every moment of every hour of every day in his company.

"To what do I owe the pleasure of this visit?" he inquired with a lift of his blond brows. "You don't usually seek me out like this. Most of the time, you avoid me."

"I'm not avoiding you. I'm just busy, and you aren't helping matters any. If anything, you're making my work more difficult." She held out the ledger. "I can't read what you've written here, and you left receipts with incomplete information."

He frowned. "I should have known you only sought me out for the sake of business. . . . Here I was hoping you'd come for a kiss instead."

"If you're so desperate for a kiss, there's a dozen females right next door," she reminded him, placing the ledger on the desk where he couldn't help but notice it. "I'm sure one of them might be willing to oblige you."

His violet eyes probed her; she had the unnerving sensation that her skull was transparent and he could read all her thoughts. "Aren't you afraid you'll drive me to one of them if you keep saying no?"

The only response to such a difficult question was to toss back another question—something she found herself doing quite often with Tiger. "Should I be afraid?"

"You should at least be concerned. Mama's very determined. . . . Not a day goes by that I'm not bombarded with the attentions of some nubile young female."

"You poor, besieged fellow . . . You once said I was quite forgettable, so why is it you haven't forgotten me?" She kept her tone mocking, masking the hunger she felt to hear him restate his feelings for her. She was hungrier still to feel his arms around her.

Another grin tugged at his mouth. "You damned well know I can't forget you, Mouse. Far from it. With each passing day, I'm becoming more and more obsessed with you."

"Good! If that's the reaction I get by avoiding you, imagine what would happen if I left Cypress Hall tomorrow."

His eyes darkened. "Don't even joke about that, Mouse. You're staying here at least until the end of the war—and I hope for a very long time after."

She lowered her eyes, suddenly unable to maintain her flippancy. One part of her wanted to fly into his arms and never leave, but another part—the cool, rational, logical one—hung back, urging caution, warning her that nothing had really changed between them. He was still a loyal, patriotic Southerner, and she was still a Northern zealot, committed to destroying everything he stood for.

"About those entries in the ledger," she said, changing the subject. "You'll have to translate them for me. And I do hope you remember what those receipts were all about."

He sighed. "I'm afraid I don't remember putting any receipts in there. It must have been Mama who did it."

"Oh, dear . . . She'll never remember, or if she does, she won't tell me."

"Why don't you ask Jules what she bought? He took Mama somewhere in the buggy the other day, and when she came back, the buggy was loaded with all sorts of things. She probably made purchases at one of the other plantations. I believe I heard that the Parker vessel made it safely through the blockade, so she might have been buying the luxury goods it brought back. . . . No, on second thought, it couldn't be the Parker ship. That vessel would still be anchored in the middle of the river under the thirty-day quarantine. At least, it better be. We don't need another outbreak of yellow fever in town. Last year's was bad enough. . . . Well, maybe Jules will remember."

"Thank you, I will ask Jules. He's very good at keeping track of things like that, isn't he?"

Ty nodded. "He has to be. When I'm gone, he's the man in charge. I depend on him—and Elvira, too—to keep a rein on Mama, or else she'd buy every feminine frippery still available in these tight times."

"Tight for everyone else, you mean, but not for the high and mighty Carringtons."

"No, not for the Carringtons . . . at least not as tight as it is for some people. That really bothers you, doesn't it, Mouse? You're uncomfortable with the Carrington wealth."

Freedom lowered her eyes and refused to look at him. "I—I suppose I am. Never having been wealthy, I don't know how to deal with it. It *does* bother me to eat so well every evening, when I know that others are not so fortunate."

"Starving yourself wouldn't feed them, Mouse."

"I know . . . so why are we discussing it?" She dared a small smile. "Why don't I go find Jules, while you rewrite your entries in the ledger? I'll stop by later to fetch it."

Ty didn't return her smile. Instead, he regarded her sadly. "Maybe if you were more willing to discuss the things that are still bothering you, we could do something about them, Mouse. I'm willing to try. . . . How about you?"

"I guess I'll have to make a list," she half teased, but he resisted the attempt to reestablish levity.

"Maybe you should. I can't begin to guess all the things that might be bothering you, but I'd welcome the chance to change whatever might be possible."

"That's exceedingly kind and generous of you," she said, and meant it. No one else had ever bothered to care that much what she thought or felt. "I'll start on my list as soon as I have time."

"Don't wait too long, Mouse. After all, I'm only human. I can't put off kissing forever."

She glanced up to see him smiling. He was so boyishly appealing that she wished she could kiss him then and there. "I'd better go find Jules," she murmured, and fled the room before she could change her mind.

It took Freedom more than an hour to locate Jules and listen patiently while he struggled to remember every item Lady Tiffin had bought that day at the Parker plantation, then had him load in the buggy. Apparently, the Parker vessel, the *Sylph,* had found some way around the regulation requiring all incoming ships to anchor in the river for a thirty-day period, as a precaution against the spread of yellow fever. Recalling the terrible epidemic of the year before, Freedom was aghast at the risks the Parkers were taking.

In September of 1862, the side-wheeler *Kate,* one of the first nonlocal blockade-runners to use the harbor, had off-loaded yellow fever, along with her cargo of war supplies. By early October, there had been almost four hundred cases of yellow fever in the city and over forty deaths. By the time the epidemic had run its course, halted by the arrival of winter, seven hundred people had died in the town and over one hundred in the surrounding countryside. After that, the quarantine had been instituted, and unless some dire circumstance occurred—such as the near sinking of the *Sea Whisper*—all ships had to honor the thirty-day waiting period before their cargoes could be unloaded.

In her eagerness to get first pick of the *Sylph*'s offerings, Lady Tiffin could have brought contaminated goods into Cypress Hall. After all, no one really knew how the disease was spread. Since the plantation was so isolated, Ty's mother might not have realized the chances she was taking; she might never have personally witnessed how devastating the disease could be. But Freedom very well remembered the terror of those autumn months, when she and Hattie Draper had closed the shop and lived behind latched shutters, dreading that one or the other of them would contract the deadly disease.

Freedom's concern about the receipts paled beside

the greater fear that Lady Tiffin's foolishness might have endangered them all. It was bad enough that she and Ty had not honored the quarantine, but at least none of the *Sea Whisper*'s goods had been brought to Cypress Hall. Ty had locked them in his warehouse in Wilmington, pending delivery to the Confederacy. Hurrying to the library, Freedom was anxious to tell Tiger what had happened and to urge him to forbid his mother to take such risks in the future. She was so preoccupied that she did not bother to knock on the door; she simply opened it and swept inside. A shocking sight greeted her: Ty and Stephanie Clairmont locked in a torrid embrace!

For a moment, Freedom was too stunned to do anything but stand there, gaping. Stephanie was tearing at Ty's clothes, and her own clothes were in great disarray. One shoulder of her gown dipped down to reveal a firm, round globe of flesh, with a darkened areola and a nipple budded to a point. Neither seemed to notice that they were no longer alone, until Ty tore his mouth away from Stephanie's and gasped aloud. "Stephie! For God's sake. Someone may come upon us at any moment."

"Ah don't care, mah darlin'. . . . Ah'm mad for you," Stephanie Clairmont rasped in her throaty voice. "Ah hope they do find us. Then the whole world'll know that handsome, sexy Ty Carrin'ton belongs to me. . . ."

It was then Ty discovered Freedom standing there with her mouth open and her heart breaking. His eyes widened; every muscle in his body tightened as he thrust the beauteous Stephanie away from him. "Mouse!" he cried. "I didn't know you were there."

"Obviously . . ." Freedom whispered. "I should not have intruded without knocking. Forgive me, but I thought you were alone. . . . You may carry on.

I'm leaving anyway."

Stephanie Clairmont turned around to face her, uttering a feline purr of triumph. The stunning girl made no effort to hide her dishevelment, not even to cover her breast. "Don't look so shocked, Miss Walker. . . . Tigah an' ah were just renewin' a very old an' intimate frien'ship. Do go out an' tell his mama an' all the other ladies jus' exactly what you saw us doin'."

"She'll do nothing of the kind, Stephie," Ty snapped. "Mouse, this isn't at all what it looks like."

"Oh, isn't it, Ty?" Stephie interjected. "Then jus' how do you explain *this?*" She looked down at her exposed bosom. "This heah gown didn't rip itself, did it?"

"Don't believe a word she says, Mouse."

Freedom didn't want to believe it; she *had* seen Ty pull away from Stephie. But there was the proof of his runaway passion before her very eyes. Stephanie's gown was ripped, not just pulled down. And her mouth had that soft, bruised look that came from unrestrained kissing. Her cheeks were flushed, her hair had tumbled down, and her eyes had that sleepy, glassy look that Freedom had seen in her own mirror *after* Ty had made love to her. Had she interrupted this scene of passion at the beginning or at the end?

"What you do behind closed doors is your own affair," she heard herself say stiffly. "It's not for me to expose your indiscretions to the entire household. . . . Excuse me, but I have work to do."

"Freedom!" Ty shouted.

"Now, Ty . . . surely, you don't want her to stay. Not when we still have unfinished business between us."

Freedom didn't wait to hear more. She spun on

her heel and ran from the room, slamming the door on Tiger's angry outburst. "Damn it, Steph! Have you no decency or morals at all?"

That night, Freedom hid in her room at dinnertime. When Elvira came to get her, she pleaded a headache and insisted that all she wanted or needed was to be left alone to sleep.

"Ah'll bring dinnah on a tray den," Elvira clucked sympathetically. "Mus' be de summer miseries startin' already . . . Lady Tiff'n don't feel so good neither, an' ah's takin' her a tray, too."

"Honestly, Elvira, I don't need dinner. . . . I just want to be left alone to sleep."

"Ah'll bring chicken soup," Elvira said stubbornly. "Mah chicken soup is de best thin' for de summer miseries."

"Fine, then bring me chicken soup, but I probably won't be able to eat it," Freedom said crossly.

True to her word, Elvira sent up a tray with Mancie, the shy, big-eyed girl who helped in the kitchen and house. Freedom had already discovered that Mancie was none too bright, but the girl made up for it by being sweet, pretty, and eagerly helpful. "Ah don't know what's wrong wif evahbody tonight, Missy Freedom," Mancie said, setting down the tray on the table in front of the windows.

"What do you mean, Mancie?" Freedom sighed, wishing she could indulge her misery in private.

"Marse Ty don't want no dinnah neither. . . . He's jus' sittin' in de library drinkin' brandy an' lookin' real mean an' nasty."

"Didn't Miss Clairmont stay for dinner?" Freedom shamelessly quizzed, hating her curiosity but unable to keep from asking.

"No, Missy . . . All de ladies done gone home 'cause Lady Tiff'n was feelin' poorly. Only one who look happy when she lef' was Miss Stephanie. . . . Ah sure hopes Marse Ty don't marry *her*. She trouble for certain."

Mancie's remark both surprised and dismayed Freedom. It seemed too astute to be coming from a girl who gave the impression that her mind was out somewhere picking daisies. "Why do you say that, Mancie?"

"Oh, ah prob'ly should keep mah mouf shut, Missy Freedom, but Miss Stephanie don't like black folks to be free like we is at Cypress Hall. If'n she marries Marse Ty, she gonna make us leave heah an den she gonna get some slaves to do de work."

"Marse Ty—Tiger wouldn't allow her to do that. I'm sure you've nothing to worry about, Mancie."

"But Miss Stephanie know how to get her way real good, Missy Freedom. Ah heard her an' Lady Tiff'n already plannin' Marse Ty's weddin'. . . . Dey laughin' and jokin' togethah, talkin' 'bout how things gonna be when Miss Stephanie comes to live at Cypress Hall. . . . It be plumb hard for Marse Ty to resist a pretty lady like Miss Stephanie. She knows how to twist a man roun' her little fingah. . . . Ah bet she won't let you work for Marse Ty neither when she becomes mistress heah."

"Perhaps you'd better go back to the kitchen now, Mancie," Freedom said. "Elvira will be looking for you. . . . thank you for bringing me the dinner tray."

Mancie grinned and dropped a curtsy. "Ah like waitin' on you, Missy Freedom. . . . Y'ain't uppity like Miss Stephanie."

Freedom swallowed back the sudden tears clogging her throat. "Is that why you call me 'Missy' and Miss Stepanie 'Miss'?"

"Ah don't know. . . . Ah 'spects so." Mancie flashed her innocent smile. "Elvira say you is mos' peculiar for a white person, but ah don't think so. . . . Ah thinks you is nice—an' purty, too. Maybe not purty as Miss Stephanie, but den nobody is purty as Miss Stephanie. She be de purtiest belle in Bladen County. Evahbody been expectin' her an' Marse Ty to tie de knot for yeahs and yeahs, an' ah think maybe dey do it one o' dese days."

Freedom put her hand to her head, which really was throbbing now. What a fool she had been not to recognize the threat Miss Stephanie Clairmont represented! But she *had* recognized it; she just hadn't wanted to believe it. Tiger could deny it all he wanted, but the fact remained: He desired the beautiful, raven-haired Stephanie. Maybe he hadn't initiated what had happened this past afternoon, but he had succumbed, been swept away by it, had even torn the girl's gown!

"You bes' go to bed, Missy Freedom." Mancie was watching her with concern. "You's lookin' worse n' worse."

"I'm afraid I'm feeling worse and worse."

Freedom could hardly hold back her tears until Mancie had left the bedroom. When the girl had gone, she sank down on the bed, her mind spinning with images of what had been going on in the library before she opened the door. Ty kissing that gorgeous girl . . . his hands stroking her voluptuous figure . . . the kisses growing warmer, deeper . . .

Tiger was a passionate man; nobody knew that better than Freedom. He hadn't touched her since that night in Nassau, but he didn't need to in order for her body to respond to his presence. Whenever he so much as looked at her, she felt the vibrations between them—felt his need, his wanting, his desire

226

to possess her again. She had denied him over and over, fought her own desires, so he had finally turned to another woman — or returned to her. He'd warned that he might do it, and she — Freedom — had ignored the warning!

Had she been wrong to resist? What if she lost him because of it? But what if she gave in, only to discover that their love turned to ashes anyway? Tiger couldn't love her very much if he was willing to tumble the first female who offered herself. She thought of Ty caressing the round white globe of Stephanie Clairmont's breast, taking the girl's nipple into his mouth, licking and sucking it . . . and she felt sick to her stomach. Hurt beyond belief, she collapsed on the bed and sobbed into the pillows.

She didn't want Ty Carrington touching any girl's breast but her own! She didn't want him to *want* to touch it, but he had apparently desired Stephanie so badly that he had ripped the gown off her shoulder. Damn him, anyway! He had no more control than a male dog sniffing after a bitch in heat. Curled into a tight ball of dejection, Freedom finally cried herself to sleep.

Chapter Sixteen

Ty was on his fourth glass of brandy when Elvira, more upset and distraught than he had ever seen her, burst into the library. "Marse Ty! You gotta get de doctor. Lady Tiff'n be mighty sick. Look to me like she got yellah fevah."

"Yellow fever!" Ty jumped to his feet. "No, she couldn't have; where would she have gotten it this early in the shipping season? Every vessel that comes into port is quarantined. The only exception I know of was mine, but neither my crewmen nor I have come down with it. You must be mistaken."

Elvira shook her head. Terror distorted her already scarred features, and she looked as if she might burst into tears at any moment. "Ah ain't mistaken. We was lucky las' year, Marse Ty. When half o' Wilmin'ton was dyin', nobody got it at Cypress Hall. But ah still knows de symptoms. Lady Tiff'n be burnin' up, an' de whites of her eyes is gone yellah. In a few days, she gonna be jawndiced somepin' awful and vomitin' blood. . . . Ah don't know where she got it, but it gonna spread to evahbody in no time. . . . We's all gonna die, Marse Ty!"

"Calm yourself, Elvira. . . . It isn't like you to panic. We can't help her or anyone else if we don't get a firm grip on our emotions."

Tiger struggled to sort out his own whiskey-muddled thoughts. What had happened this afternoon—Stephanie clawing at her gown and shamelessly throwing herself into his arms, then Freedom walking in on the scene—paled in comparison to the threat of another outbreak of yellow fever. Could his mother possibly have contracted it, despite all the precautions taken since the epidemic of the year before?

"Listen, Elvira. . . . No one is to go near Mama except you and me. If she has it, you've already been exposed. As for me. . . . well, I'm her son. I'll have to take my chances. . . . you and I are the only ones who should enter that wing of the house. If anyone else comes down with it, we'll bed them in the old stable, where they can be isolated from the rest of the plantation workers."

"Awright, Marse Ty, but you gonna have to order Jules to stay away. Long as ah'm heah, he gonna wanna butt his nose in. Fact is, he don't need to set foot inside de door. You best tell 'im dat ah'll see 'im soon's ah can."

"Don't worry, Elvira. I'll warn Jules to keep his distance. To make sure he does, I'll send him downriver right away to fetch the doctor at Wilmington. If it is yellow fever, maybe there's something we can do to stop it before it gets out of hand."

"Ah knows what ah'm gonna do . . . make sassafras tea an' lots o' chicken soup. Best thing ah can think of is to treat dis sickness before it starts."

"If more than Mama gets sick, you're going to need all the help you can get. Put Mancie to work. I'm sure Miss Walker will lend a hand, too. . . . Why, she was in Wilmington last year during that siege! Perhaps she knows something we can do until the doctor arrives."

"Why don't you go talk to her, Marse Ty, an' let me send Jules for de doctor. He can wring a few chickens' necks before he leave — or get Omoroh to do it. Omoroh can put fresh straw and some mattresses in de ole stable, too, in case we need it."

"Good idea, Elvira . . . You talk to Jules while I consult Miss Walker."

Moments later, Tiger was standing in front of Freedom's door, a three-branched candelabrum in hand to illuminate the darkened hallway. The last thing he wanted to do tonight was to face Freedom's accusing, hurt expression, but he had no choice. A possible yellow fever outbreak outweighed personal problems. He just wished he could forget how wounded she had looked when she saw him in Stephanie Clairmont's arms — with Stephanie gleefully displaying herself so as to make it seem worse than it really was. He knew exactly how Freedom felt. Two years ago, discovering Stephanie in the arms of another man had almost driven *him* to murder. It was fortunate the young man had been leaving town, or Ty would undoubtedly have had it out with him at pistol point.

Holding the candelabrum in one hand, Ty rapped smartly on the door. There was no answer, so he turned the knob. The door did not budge. Freedom must have pushed a chair or other heavy object in front of it to keep him out. "Freedom!"

230

he bellowed, in no mood to play silly games. "Open this door! It's an emergency. I need to speak with you this instant."

He pressed his ear to the smooth wood but heard nothing. "If you don't open this damn door, I'm going to get an axe and chop it down. You haven't given me a chance to explain what happened this afternoon. . . . I assure you, I'm perfectly innocent. Stephanie maneuvered the whole thing — only she was expecting someone else to walk in on us, not you. Had Mama or one of her lady friends discovered us, I'd have had to marry the little whore or else face her father over the barrel of a gun. Like you, he probably wouldn't grant me an opportunity to defend myself."

The door suddenly opened, and Ty found himself staring into a pair of velvet-brown eyes that skewered him without mercy. "If Stephanie Clairmont is a whore, then so am I, because I, too, have desired your kisses, Ty Carrington — probably more than she has. I, too, have undressed for you — or permitted you to undress me. But I would have thought that tearing a woman's bodice was beneath you. Were you so carried away by passion that you couldn't help yourself?"

"I didn't tear the bodice of her gown! She tore it herself, so she could offer a temptation she was sure I couldn't resist. But I did . . . I swear to you I did."

Freedom tossed her head contemptuously. Her long, unbound hair swirled about her shoulders, then fell rippling down her back like a burnished amber curtain. He was distracted by its look of softness; his fingertips had not forgotten the silky texture of her hair. He longed to run his hands

231

through it, capture her head, and kiss away her doubt, jealousy, and anger.

"Do you honestly expect me to believe that?" she coldly queried. "It didn't look to me as if you were refusing anything. You warned me you couldn't put off kissing forever. Apparently, you couldn't even survive the afternoon without a few kisses. . . . There's no sense lying, Ty. If Stephanie Clairmont is the wife you want, then you can have her. . . . You and she obviously have much more in common than you and I will ever have."

Tiger raked his free hand through his own hair, since he dared not touch Freedom's. He wondered what more he could say that would persuade her to trust and believe him. In similar circumstances, he hadn't been able to accept Stephanie's apologies or explanations. He had believed the worst of her—and still did. Her efforts to seduce him had only further demonstrated her guilt and shamelessness.

"Look, Mouse, I wish I knew how to convince you that Stephanie means nothing to me. Once she did, but then I discovered what sort of woman she really is. The only thing we have in common is that we were both born in the South. . . ."

"I'd say that's plenty. In fact, I'd say it's all you need."

"Will you please stop talking long enough to listen? I didn't come here to argue and fight with you tonight, Mouse. Nor did I come to apologize for something I didn't do."

"Then why did you come, Ty? I don't want to see or talk to you. I don't want to hear your lies and rationalizations. Stephanie Clairmont is a beautiful woman—and she's a Southerner. You two are perfect for each other. Your children will be stunning. You and she can—"

"For God's sake, I came because I need your help! My mother is sick with yellow fever. At least, that's what Elvira thinks it is. We can't be sure until the doctor comes. Jules will be leaving soon to fetch him, but the earliest the man can possibly get here is tomorrow. In the meantime, I was hoping you might know what to do. . . ."

"Yellow fever!" Freedom's face crumpled as the horror of his words sank in. "Oh, Ty, no! I was afraid something like this might happen. That's what I was coming to the library to tell you. Your mother was at the Parker place a few days ago. Their ship somehow avoided the quarantine, and she wanted first pick of the merchandise it brought back from Bermuda. I was coming to complain about the risks she had taken, but after I saw you and Stephanie together, I quite forgot what I had come for."

"Dear God, it's true then. She *must* have yellow fever. I told Elvira it couldn't be possible, because I couldn't imagine where she might have gotten it. Now, I know. The Parker ship. And if Mama has it, then all the Parkers will get it—and all their slaves, *our* people, Elvira and Jules, you and me, everybody who was here today. . . ."

As he turned away, appalled at the possible consequences, Freedom grasped his shirt sleeve. "Not necessarily, Ty. The disease seems to strike at random. It might take only one person out of a dozen in a household—or it might wipe out every last one of them. Ahead of time, there's no way of knowing."

Tiger turned back to her. "But what can we do? How can we stop it? You were in Wilmington;

what did they do in town last year?"

Freedom shrugged helplessly, her dark eyes bleak. "We closed our shops and hid in our houses. We prayed that we might be spared."

"God help us, but we've got to do more than that! First, I'm going to go see Mama, and then — wait a minute. Would you recognize the disease if you saw it in its early stages?"

She nodded. "I'm sure I could. Before we knew how contagious it was, Hattie and I helped nurse a family of five, every one of whom came down with it."

"What happened to them?"

Freedom's expression revealed the answer before her mouth could form the words. "They all died. By then, a proper funeral was out of the question. They were buried in a communal pit, along with dozens of other victims."

"Stay here while I see my mother," Ty said. "When I come back I'll describe her symptoms, and you can tell me if you think she has it. I don't want you to set foot in that wing of the house or to go down to the old stable either."

Freedom grabbed his hand before he could leave. "Don't try to keep me away, Ty. I'll go with you to see your mother. . . . I survived one epidemic; I'm sure I can survive another. She may not even have yellow fever. I'd like to judge with my own eyes. . . . Besides, the sooner we know what we're facing, the better."

"All right," Ty conceded out of desperation. "But you mustn't get too close to her."

"I won't. Come, let's go now." Freedom laced her fingers through his, and Ty was halfway down the hallway before he realized that Freedom was no longer angry. She had forgotten all about Stephanie Clairmont—or else had decided to save her anger for another day. Yes, that must be it. She was postponing the issue until this crisis had passed. Still, the feel of her hand in his gave him hope and strength to confront whatever lay ahead. With Freedom at his side, he knew could face anything.

Freedom softly closed the door to Lady Tiffin's rose and cream room, then sighed and shook her head regretfully. They had just finished examining his mother, who was lying like a queen in the huge four-poster with its ivory satin pillows and rose-colored coverlet, which matched her elegant lace-trimmed dressing gown. Even from the doorway, which was as far as Tiger would let her go, Freedom had no trouble discerning the indisputable signs of the disease. Not only was Lady Tiffin flushed with fever, but she exhibited the reddened nostrils, lips, and tongue of the typical yellow fever victim. Her pale blond hair masked the jaundice associated with the illness, but in time, the characteristic hue would become more pronounced—and if she began to vomit blood, death was inevitable.

"She didn't even know me," Ty whispered, looking stunned. "And she kept muttering nonsense."

"She's delirious, Ty. She doesn't realize what she's saying. You must let me go in and bathe her; bathing helps bring down the fever."

"No! Elvira will look after her—or I will. There's no sense in three of us exposing ourselves to this scourge."

"There will be other cases, Ty. You'll have to let me help some time."

Tiger set his jaw in the stubborn manner that was all too familiar. "Not yet. You can make soup and tea, but I don't want you in direct contact with those who fall ill. Not unless it becomes absolutely necessary."

"It will be necessary," Freedom quietly asserted. "I've seen it all before."

"Damn!" Ty shook the candelabrum so that flames danced at the end of their wicks and wax dripped on the varnished wood floor. "Why did she do it? If I'd known she wanted bolts of fine lace and muslin that badly, I myself would have transported them—even if it meant sacrificing cloth for Confederate uniforms."

Freedom thought it best to say nothing. Lady Tiffin's priorities were clear—and they were likely going to cost her life. Every last item she had bought from the Parkers was something she could have done without.

"Let's find Elvira," Ty muttered. "We'll have to get the stable ready. She and I already discussed it. Omoroh and a few of the field hands can pile straw, mattresses, and bedding in there, and we'll isolate the sick from the well. I hate to say it, but we probably should start making coffins. I don't want to have to do what they did in Wilmington last year."

Remembering the big burial pit where bodies had been dumped wrapped only in sheets or squares of canvas, Freedom silently agreed. She followed Ty through the darkened house and swept down the front staircase, confronting a nearly hysterical Elvira at the bottom of it. "Oh, Marse Ty! I wuz jus' comin' to get you! I cain't send Jules to fetch de doctah, 'cause he comin' down wid it, too."

"Jules is sick, too?" Ty exploded. "Who else? Are any of the other workers ill yet?"

Elvira half-sobbed her answer. "I don't know, Marse Ty. . . . Ah can't take time to find out. Jules done gone to bed at de house, an' dat's where ah'm goin' back to. Ah jus' wanted to tell you. Mancie'll have to look aftah Lady Tiff'n."

"Don't worry. . . . *I*'ll take care of her," Freedom promised. "You just see that Jules gets better. . . . But send Omoroh to me if you can. Between the two of us, we'll set up some sort of system for nursing the sick."

Ty handed Freedom the candelabrum. "I'll have to fetch the doctor myself. There's no one else I can trust to send, especially at night. Will you be all right here until I get back?"

Freedom felt a stab of dread, but to Tiger, she gave a smile of encouragement. "Don't worry about us. We'll be fine until you return."

Ty bolted for the front door. "In the morning, have someone post warning signs on the dock and near the dirt road leading to town, and the other plantations between here and there. No one but me and the doctor is permitted to enter Cypress Hall land, and no one is allowed to leave."

Freedom hurried out the front door after him. "What about the Parkers? And Stephanie Clairmont and the other ladies who were here today? Shouldn't they be warned?"

"What for? If they don't know it already, they'll find out soon enough that yellow fever has broken out. . . . I'm sure the Parkers must know by now; it's *their* greed and foolishness that caused this whole mess!"

Ty disappeared into the darkness between the

house and the stables—the new one, where the horses were kept, and the old one, which was now being used to store hay and grain but would soon become a hospital. Elvira had vanished, and Mancie had not yet arrived. For the moment, Freedom was alone in the big house, except for Lady Tiffin. As she turned to go back inside, a tall, familiar figure approached the veranda. It was Omoroh, his sympathetic eyes offering comfort as clearly as if he had spoken.

"Oh, Omoroh! I'm so glad you've come. . . . So much has happened. Come into the house and I'll tell you, though you probably already know. . . . Yellow fever has broken out. Ty has gone to fetch the doctor, Elvira's left to nurse Jules, and Lady Tiffin is upstairs ill and possibly dying—and—and—" She almost broke down in tears, but checked herself and swallowed hard. "Don't mind me. I'm just feeling overwhelmed at the moment."

Omoroh gruffly patted her shoulder, and Freedom sniffed and dabbed at her eyes. "I'm sure we can handle it together, Omoroh. . . . The first thing I want you to do is find Mancie. Bring her to me, then I'll assign you both some tasks."

Omoroh nodded.

"The second thing you must do is pray, Omoroh. Maybe Allah will show more mercy to Cypress Hall than God showed to Wilmington last year . . . and I hope I'm not blaspheming by saying that."

Omoroh gave her a sad smile, then folded his hands, closed his eyes, and bowed his head. He appeared to be meditating, but only for a minute or two. Afterward, he quietly left to find Mancie. Gathering what she needed to bathe Lady Tiffin, Freedom again mounted the big staircase and entered the wing of the house where Ty had forbidden her to go. Now, there was no other choice—nor had Ty repeated the order. In the days to come, everyone at Cypress Hall would be exposed to the terrible malady. How many would die from it? . . . And all because Lady Tiffin had wanted to be fashionably dressed.

A full day, another night, and half of another day passed before Tiger returned with the doctor, a haggard-looking man in a dusty frock coat, who complained he'd had no opportunity to sleep during the past two nights because a woman downriver had almost died trying to give birth to twins. Freedom had little sympathy for him. She, Omoroh, and Mancie hadn't gotten much sleep either, and neither had Ty from the looks of him.

"Well, I'm glad you finally made it, Doctor—what did you say your name was?"

"Koontz," the man replied. "Dr. Harrod Koontz is my name."

"We have seven cases so far, Dr. Koontz, but only two are vomiting blood."

"Who?" Ty cut in.

Freedom hated to tell him. "Your mother and Jules. Elvira and I have done the best we can—indeed, Elvira herself is sickening—but no matter what we've done, we can't seem to help them. They just keep getting worse."

"If they're vomiting blood, they won't make it," the doctor said flatly. "I'll do what I can to ease their pain, but you might as well prepare for the worst. If I could trouble you for something to drink before I start, I'll get busy right away."

"Of course," Freedom murmured. "Go into the drawing room and I'll get you something."

Ty followed her into the bowels of the house. "Are they really that bad, Mouse? . . . Is there no hope at all for them?"

He seemed to want a retraction of what she'd said — for her to refute the doctor himself. She stopped walking and gazed at him in helpless frustration. "I'm sorry, Ty. . . . You should go see your mother. I doubt she'll last another day. She doesn't seem to know any of us, but she might recognize you . . . . Mancie's with her now."

"And . . . Jules?" Tiger's handsome face sagged with exhaustion and grief; Freedom ached to take him in her arms and soothe him.

"Jules was stronger to start with, so maybe he still stands a chance, despite what the doctor says. . . . Sit with your mother first. There will be time later to sit with Jules."

"Mama and my best friend . . ." Ty's voice was hollow. "For some reason, I never thought this could happen."

And Elvira, too, maybe, Freedom added silently. Aloud, she said, "I know how you feel, Ty. When my father died, I couldn't believe it either. Then, when the shock wore off, I was angry. That lasted for a while. But finally, I learned to accept his death as a natural consequence of living. If you live, you're going to die one day."

"But not yet! Not until you're old and feeble. Jules is no older than I am. And half of Mama's friends are older than she is. How can you meekly accept it? . . . I never accepted it when *my* father died. He fell off his horse trying to jump a stone wall. Did I ever tell you that . . . I was only a little

240

boy at the time, but even then, I knew it wasn't fair. He was the only one who ever cared about me—besides Jules, that is. And now Jules is dying because of something stupid that Mama did!"

"Ty, don't be angry with her. Don't hate her. She's dying, too. Whatever wrong she's done, whatever foolishness, she's paying the price for it. . . . Go to her, Ty. She needs you. This may be your last chance to see her alive."

Tiger's mouth thinned into a hard, angry line. "You don't have to tell me my duty, Mouse. I'm going. I'll hold her hand, though she never held mine when *I* was lonely and afraid . . ."

His bitterness shocked Freedom. Someday, she'd make him tell her more about his childhood and his relationship with his mother; the woman must have hurt him terribly for him to feel so hostile when he knew she was dying.

"Don't judge her, Ty. Leave that to God. You can't know with certainty what was in her mind or heart."

"How strange to hear that coming from *you!*" Ty sneered. "Aren't you the one who goes around *judging* people?"

"Me?" Freedom gasped, but the truth of the accusation struck home hard.

"Yes, you, Mouse. . . . Think about it." With that, he strode off in the direction of the staircase.

Chapter Seventeen

Cypress Hall remained under quarantine for over a month. Tiger's mother was the first to die, Jules the second, followed by a half-dozen plantation workers and old Ambrose. Elvira hung on until the very last, and after her death, there were no more new cases. All but Lady Tiffin, Jules, and Elvira were laid to rest in a pleasant meadow, beneath a large apple tree. Ty insisted upon burying his mother, his best friend, and his best friend's wife in the Carrington family cemetery, where his father and grandfather were buried.

When it was finally safe to lift the quarantine, a memorial service was held, to which Ty invited the remaining workers but none of Lady Tiffin's friends nor any of his own, not even his crew members from the *Sea Whisper*. The disease had apparently run its course, he told Freedom, but it was best not to take chances. The minister, a dour-faced reverend from Wilmington, mounted his horse immediately after intoning a last blessing over the new graves. His remarks had included some sharp criticism of Ty's burial arrangements, which Freedom already knew were unusual. Whites and Negroes were rarely interred in such close proximity, and Negro slaves—or in this case, servants—*never* shared the same burial plot as their white masters.

Since Ty had regarded Jules and Elvira as family, nothing anyone said could have made him change his mind about where they would be buried. Freedom suspected that he was grieving more for them than he was for his own mother. Before the minister had finished praying, Tiger left the gathering, his eyes so bleak that she was certain he was going someplace where he could mourn in private. She expelled a sigh of relief when the frowning reverend finally departed. Had he remained much longer, she herself might have spoiled the occasion by telling the minister exactly what she thought of *him*. She and Mancie cleared away the remnants of the feast Ty had authorized but not attended, and the mourners soon drifted back to their cabins, located in a copse of pine trees some distance behind the big house.

When they had finished cleaning up, Mancie came to her in the pantry and said, "Missy Freedom, is ah gonna have to spend every night in de big house from now on?"

The girl had been staying there ever since Elvira took sick, but she plainly did not wish to continue the practice. Freedom paused in removing the apron that protected her somber-hued muslin gown. "Is there some reason why you don't want to?"

"It's lonely heah, Missy Freedom. An' ah got's to tek care o' mah poor ole mama. She half blind an' cain't move aroun' so good anymoah. It's a wonder de yellah fevah didn't tek her."

"Who's been caring for her while you've been assisting me with the household and nursing chores?"

"Oh, evahbody hep's out evahbody else down in de quarters. . . . But now dat de yellah fevah's gone, ah was hopin' ah could stay wid Mama ag'in."

"Of course, you can. You go along home now, Mancie. You've been a wonderful help. I don't know what I'd have done without you these past several weeks. When Captain Carrington feels more like himself, he'll probably tell you what a good job you've done, too."

Just then Omoroh entered the pantry and gestured that he, too, was leaving, returning to the empty little house that had once belonged to Jules and Elvira but now belonged to him. Freedom had heard Ty tell Omoroh that he was to live there and consider it his own, so the first thing the black man had done was to put smudge pots all around it. No one really knew why, but Freedom guessed that it had something to do with chasing away the evil spirits responsible for the yellow fever. Omoroh had also put smudge pots around the big house. Tiger endured it for almost week, then finally ordered Omoroh to remove them, saying he couldn't abide the thick, dense clouds of smoke produced by the smudge pots. Freedom hadn't minded the smoke; at least, it helped to dispel the mosquitoes, which had become quite bothersome since the arrival of hot weather. She herself wore long sleeves during the daytime and slept beneath a mosquito net at night, in order to avoid being bitten.

"Good night, Omoroh," she said to the tall, regal black man. "By the way, I'm indebted to you as well as to Mancie for your hard work and support during this difficult time. The two of you deserve a bonus, and I intend to mention it to Captain Carrington as soon as I get the chance."

A beaming Mancie shyly peeped at Omoroh from beneath the fringe of her dark lashes. Omoroh adopted a pleased expression but did not return Mancie's longing glance. Watching the two depart together, Freedom speculated on the possibility of a relationship between them. Mancie was clearly open to receiving Omoroh's attentions, but he did not seem excited about the prospect. Maybe they were like her and Ty—too far apart on important issues. Too dissimilar. Omoroh was an intelligent, literate, complex man, while Mancie had trouble following any but the simplest directions. But despite her limitations, Mancie was willing and hardworking, and Freedom had developed a real affection for her. She liked the girl almost as much as she liked Omoroh and could only hope that both of them found happiness in their increased responsibilities at Cypress Hall.

With Elvira and Jules gone, there was no one left but Mancie and Omoroh to take over the tasks the other two had so capably performed. Freedom's own responsibilities had increased alarmingly in the wake of Lady Tiffin's death. Everyone now looked to her to tell them what needed to be done; Ty was too busy running the plantation itself to worry about meals, laundry, nursing chores, and house cleaning. Feeling tired and depressed, Freedom hung her apron on a peg, then walked through the silent, darkening house, checking to see that all was in order for the night.

For the first time since her arrival, she was alone

with Tiger—or would be as soon as he returned from wherever he had gone following the services. Even if Mancie had stayed, Freedom risked her reputation by continuing to live at Cypress Hall. Among the Southern aristocracy, a Negro serving girl did not count as a proper chaperone. Freedom wondered if there was anyone Ty could invite to stay in the big house. In the absence of a chaperone, she ought to be thinking about leaving. Yet, how could she abandon Ty now when he needed her more than ever?

Mancie couldn't run things without supervision; she could barely keep up with the work now. Another girl should begin training at once to work in the big house. The workers' wives and daughters helped out in the cook shed behind the house, but most labored beside their menfolk in the fields or else performed the more menial household tasks, such as doing laundry, gardening, or scrubbing floors. There was no one to make decisions and see that necessary tasks got done, Freedom realized—except *her.*

As Freedom passed the library on her way to the staircase, she heard a slight sound coming from within. Her stomach knotted with apprehension. She had not seen Ty enter the house; if it wasn't him, who could it be? Summoning her courage, she peeked around the door, which was ajar, but could see nothing or no one in the deep gloom of the shadowed room. The sound came again, almost as if someone were choking. Freedom's gaze flew to the wide, heavy sofa in front of the stone fireplace. A man—Tiger—was sitting there, elbows on knees, head propped in his hands, shoulders shaking, as he struggled to hold back ragged, heartbreaking sobs.

Freedom debated whether or not to reveal her presence; she had never before witnessed a man weeping—especially not a man like Ty. He was masculinity personified and might not want her to see him in his present state of bereavement and despair. He had kept a tight rein on his emotions during these awful weeks, politely consulting with her when necessary but otherwise burying himself in work from morning until night.

Her desire to comfort him grew stronger with each muffled sound, until she could bear it no longer. Striding purposefully into the room, she went to him and gently touched his shoulder. "Tiger . . . if there's anything I can do for you, you've only to ask."

His head jerked up, and he swiped at his tear-stained cheeks as if embarrassed to be caught with his guard down. "What are you doing in here? I thought I was alone."

Freedom withdrew her hand, hurt that he was rejecting her sympathy. "I—I was on my way to bed when I heard a noise. I came to investigate and discovered you. Forgive me for intruding, Ty. . . . I should have knocked before entering."

"It's not your fault," he muttered, turning away. "I should have locked the door. I didn't, because I thought you'd already retired for the night."

Gingerly, she sat down on the sofa beside him. "Ty, I'm so very sorry. I know that words can hardly heal your pain, but please know that I share your sorrow. I'd do anything to spare you this unhappiness; I just wish there *was* something I could do."

He glanced at her in the semidarkness, his violet-colored eyes reddened and puffy from weeping, his mouth more tender and vulnerable than she had ever seen it. "Thank you for your concern," he said with quiet dignity. "But really, there's nothing you can do. . . . Jules and I grew up together, you see. We were closer than brothers. I feel as if a huge chunk of my heart has been torn from my chest."

"I know," Freedom whispered, sliding one arm around his broad shoulders. "He can never be replaced. At least, you can take comfort in the fact that you and he had a wonderful friendship. Most people never get that close to anyone. . . . I've never been that close. I've had friends, yes, but none who meant as much to me as Jules did to you."

"And Elvira," Tiger said. "How will we manage without her? It wasn't Mama or me who ran this place; it was really Elvira. That woman was a master of efficiency. Even Mama, an expert at getting her own way, couldn't stand up to Elvira. Whenever they argued about something, Elvira always won."

"I know," Freedom repeated. "I've been trying to take Elvira's place for the past few days, and I marvel at how smoothly she was able to run a household this size. The house hasn't been cleaned properly nor have we had a decent meal since the day she took sick."

"And Mama," Ty continued, only half aware of his surroundings, including her. "I never thought I could miss her. When I was a boy, I often wished she had been the one who died instead of my father. She was cold and selfish, resenting me for providing proof of how old she was getting, while I was busy resenting her for saddling me with her maiden name, among other things. . . . But when I held her hand as she lay dying, none of that seemed to matter anymore. All I could think of was that I never really knew her—and now it's too late. The few times when she did reach out to me, I cut her off. I *wanted* to hurt her in retaliation for all the times she had hurt me. . . . I'm a grown man, but I still blame her for things that happened when I was a child."

"We all behave stupidly sometimes, Ty. Then we look back and wish we had acted differently. We wish we hadn't wasted so much time nursing grudges and feeling sorry for ourselves. . . . Unfortunately, regretting what we've done doesn't help much. Your mother feels no pain, suffering, guilt, or unhappiness. Instead of being sad that she died, we should be glad for her. Wherever she is, it has to be a better place than this. . . . She's at peace now."

"Are you saying you don't believe in heaven and hell? How do you know she's at peace? What about punishment and reward in the hereafter?"

"Oh, Ty, I'm not sure what I believe anymore," Freedom admitted. "Once, I thought bad people went to hell and good ones went to heaven. Now, I question whether there is such a thing as absolute good or evil. We are all mixtures of good and bad. . . . I guess I've finally learned not to judge people so harshly. I'm sure God understands your mother better than you or I ever could."

Ty took her hand and laced his fingers through hers. "Thanks for comforting me, Mouse. What you say makes sense. Even if it didn't, it makes me feel better."

"It's my pleasure," Freedom said lightly, though

his touch produced a sensation that vibrated through her body. "Do you really hate your name so much, Ty? Why, may I ask? Tiffin isn't as strong a name as Tiger, but it really isn't all that bad."

"You only say that because you're not a boy." He gave a short laugh. "I grew up having to defend it all the time. . . . You must admit, it's not the most masculine of names. Up North where I went to school, my classmates bedeviled me over it. Together with my blond hair, my name had some fellows convinced I was really a girl. Only the judicious use of my fists persuaded them otherwise."

So that accounts for your lack of a Southern accent, Freedom thought, as well as for the name by which you now are known. "Maybe your mother did you a service after all, Ty," she mused aloud. "Defending your name made a man of you. Did you ever consider that?"

His violet eyes caught hers. "No . . ." he said softly. "But I've been wondering: Am I man enough for *you?*"

Their gazes held for a long, breathless moment. Freedom had never doubted Ty's masculinity; no woman in her right mind could. From the soles of his feet to the top of his blond head, he radiated strength and a potent sexuality. He possessed an undefinable power that prickled her flesh with goose bumps. Hardly conscious that she did so, she leaned toward him. Very slowly, he leaned toward her. Their lips met tentatively at first, pressing briefly together as if the slightest disturbance would catapult them back into their separate worlds.

Freedom savored the gentle kiss more than she had savored all their previous kisses put together; this time, there was something behind it . . . a depth of understanding they had never had before. Shared sorrow had forged a tenuous bond between them. They had survived the epidemic and buried its victims; they had worked side by side to keep Cypress Hall intact and to bolster the hope of its other survivors. They had endured weeks of loneliness and yearning, wanting to be closer to each other but uncertain how to bridge the chasm between them. Now, suddenly and miraculously, the gap had closed, seemingly of its own volition.

When Tiger rose to his feet, Freedom did, too. They stood facing each other in the semidarkness. Ty pulled her into his arms and kissed her with less gentleness and more urgency, but it was an urgency she herself felt bubbling deep within. She parted her lips for the sweet assault, granting him access to her mouth just as she intended to grant him access to her body, if he so desired. He did desire. He broke the long, passionate kiss just long enough to sweep her off her feet and lift her in his arms, cradling her as he might an infant.

She did not have to ask where they were going. He carried her out of the library, into the hall, and up the darkened staircase. She snuggled against him, unafraid, her body tingling in anticipation of what was sure to follow . . . what had been inevitable since the day they first met and argued aboard the *Sea Whisper*. This time, she would not resist him, would not fight, would not spoil everything with thoughts of duty or self-recrimination. The vast differences between them no longer mattered — not tonight and maybe not ever again.

Love and desire were such fragile, fleeting, precious things. Why did it take sudden, senseless death to remind her of how short was the time of honey-making upon the earth? Bees knew it; they never wasted an hour of golden sunlight. Only humans seemed prone to denying themselves and postponing all that they might enjoy today. Freedom was done with self-denial and postponement. She wanted Tiger, and he wanted her. Tonight, they would love, comfort, and pleasure each other. They would do what she had been wanting to do ever since that first, painful episode when she had surrendered her virginity for all the wrong reasons—not because she loved Ty, but because she sought something from him. Tonight, she desired only to *give* him things—tenderness, solace, escape from his bereavement . . . and most of all, love. Joyous, unconditional, healing love.

He bypassed her room and carried her down the upstairs hallway to his own bedroom, where he kicked open the door, entered, and went directly to the bed. She had seen the chamber once in daylight, when she had helped Mancie to change his sheets. It was a large, airy, masculine abode reminiscent of the library below. The furnishings were all dark, heavy wood, and the Brussels carpet was thick underfoot and veined with a design done in gold, royal-blue, and poppy-red.

She could see little of it now. Night was filling the corners with dark shadows; Ty himself was a dark shadow leaning over her. As he deposited her in the center of the big bed, she twined her arms around his neck and pulled him down, arching her body to meet his. Uttering a low growl, he fell upon her. They tangled the sheets and bedding in their wild, unrestrained embrace. Articles of clothing flew in all directions as they struggled to remove whatever blocked skin from touching skin.

When they were both naked, they rolled together, locked in each other's arms. First he was on top, then she, touching, tasting, teasing . . . stoking the fire of their need higher and higher. Then he pinioned her to the bed and began to kiss her in a more leisurely fashion, as if he didn't want to be rushed. She restrained her impatience and submitted to his ministrations with a small sigh. He seemed determined to leave no part of her unloved; every inch of flesh had to have its kiss. As the kisses became more intimate, circling nearer and nearer to her feminine core, she had the sensation of being turned inside out.

She wanted him desperately. He teased her with his mouth, lips, and fingers, making little forays into every crevice of her body. She cried his name aloud and clawed the sheets in her urgency. Only then did he respond to her entreaties. When he finally pierced her, he thrust deeply, holding nothing back. She received him in an explosion of ecstasy. There was no hint of discomfort. She rocked with him, catching his rhythm, spiraling upward to an even greater rapture. They scaled a peak of shuddering pleasure, conquered its summit, then climbed it again.

Mouths joined, hearts thundering in unison, they lay entwined as one. They breathed as one. They wept as one. Freedom felt a dampness on her cheeks but could not tell if had come from her tears or his. Their emotional unity transcended the physical. In that shining, perfect moment, she was absolutely certain that nothing or no one could ever come between them. She fell asleep in Ty's arms, the scent of him strong in her nostrils, mingled with the odor of their lovemaking, sweeter than any perfume.

Several times during the night, she awakened to his kisses and caresses. As starved as he, she responded with all the pent up ardor that had tortured her for so many long weeks and months. When his energy finally waned, she became the aggressor, reveling in her ability to make him want her even when he was exhausted from hour upon hour of lovemaking. Lust fed upon lust, rapture upon rapture. At last, neither could resist sleep any longer. Sated and content, they sank into oblivion, but it did not last long. Barely had Freedom closed her eyes, when she heard footsteps on the stairs and a voice outside the bedroom door.

"Ty? Are you up heah? Ah declare, ah've been bangin' and bangin' on that front door until mah poah knuckles are bruised. But nobody came to answer it."

The throaty, feminine drawl sounded familiar, and Freedom half thought she was dreaming. What would Stephanie Clairmont be doing at Cypress Hall in the middle of the night? She opened one eye. It wasn't night; it was morning. And the voice wasn't a dream; it was real—and right outside the door.

"Ty? Tigah, where *are* you? It's me . . . Stephanie. Ah've come to offer mah sympathies on the death of your poah mama. . . . Ah would've come sooner, but ah jus' got back to town aftah visitin' with relatives down in Georgia. Ah brought the latest war news, too. . . . Ty, honey?"

Freedom didn't wait to hear any more. She

leaped out of bed, snatched up clothing left and right, and scurried behind the dressing screen — not a moment too soon. The door creaked open.

"Ty, sugah . . . so heah's where you are! Probably exhausted from grief, poah lamb . . ."

"What?" Ty mumbled, only just now awakening.

Freedom froze behind the screen, praying he wouldn't mention *her*. The rustle and swish of petticoats sounded loud as Stephanie entered the room, bringing with her the fresh scent of lavender.

"Mah word, but it's stuffy in heah! Ty, ah'll just open the shutters if you don't mind. Ah can see ah came not a moment too soon. . . . You mustn't take on so over this tragedy. Ah'm heah now, an' ah'll jus' dedicate mahself to helpin' you recover."

Chapter Eighteen

An hour later, Freedom joined Tiger and Stephanie on the veranda where Mancie was serving coffee, tea, and buttermilk biscuits, the one thing the girl could make well without close supervision. Freedom feigned surprise as she greeted the beautiful Stephanie; Ty had ordered his unexpected guest to leave his room and wait downstairs in the parlor while he dressed—an order Stephanie had coyly tried to ignore until Tiger threatened to throw her out bodily.

No harm had thus been done, except that Freedom felt robbed of the pleasure of awakening in bed beside Ty and sharing another few moments of tender intimacy before having to face the demands of another day. Instead of exchanging kisses with Ty, she had been forced to sneak down the hallway to her own room and there stew in the juice of her own frustration, until such time as she could make an innocent-seeming appearance downstairs. She hated having to be polite and act surprised to see Stephanie . . . hated even more the proprietary way that Stephanie was pouring Ty his second or third cup of coffee.

"Why, I didn't know you were here, Miss Clairmont," Freedom lied, smoothing down her plain, dark muslin gown. "I haven't seen you since the day I surprised you and Ty in the library."

There was no sense pretending an excess of cordiality, Freedom decided. Tiger was hers now and she intended to keep him, whether or not Miss Stephanie Clairmont approved. Ty shot Freedom a wry grin behind Stephanie's back, while Stephanie straightened and glared at Freedom, her annoyance obvious.

"Seems like you relish surprisin' me an' Tigah t'gethah," she drawled.

"Come in, Mouse," Ty said, when Stephanie failed to invite her. "Or should I say . . . sleepy-head? I was wondering when you were going to join us this morning."

"Had I known we had guests, I would have hurried right down." Before being seated, Freedom helped herself to a cup of raspberry tea. "It's rather early in the day for a social call, isn't it, Miss Clairmont? And a bit overdue for a sympathy visit."

Stephanie leaned back in her white wicker chair. In total disregard of the austerities brought on by the war, she was wearing a frothy white organdy gown trimmed with pink rosebuds. The bodice of the gown pushed up her bountiful breasts, beneath which a rose-colored ribbon was daintily tied. A wide straw hat trimmed with a matching ribbon lay on a nearby chair. Freedom picked up the hat and handed it to Stephanie. The chair was the only one available, but Stephanie seemed not to notice. The raven-haired beauty took her hat most reluctantly, as if she wished Freedom would sit elsewhere—

preferably out of sight.

"Ah came as soon as ah could," Stephanie defended herself, batting her long black lashes. "Ah've been in Georgia all this time. You can't imagine mah distress when ah returned an' heard that yellah fevah had broken out at Cypress Hall and claimed the life of Ty's dear mama. Why, ah've been cryin' mah eyes out evah since."

I'll bet, Freedom thought, noting that Stephanie's lovely, petulant face did not look at all as if she'd been weeping. "How fortunate that you yourself did not contract the disease, Miss Clairmont. You were certainly exposed to it that day when all the women were here."

"It's a downright miracle ah didn't! You've probably heard that Nellie Parkah came down with it, too, but she's recovered now, ah understand. . . . The Parkahs lost a few Nigras, but no one else in the fam'ly got it. And not a single othah guest that day took it home with them. . . . It's such a tragedy 'bout Lady Tiff'n. But we can all thank ouah lucky stars that the epidemic was confined to Cypress Hall and the Parkah place."

"We can thank the quarantine," Ty snorted. "Or better yet, we can thank Miss Walker here. She recognized the signs of the disease right away, even before the doctor arrived, so we were able to start doing something to contain it almost immediately."

"Elvira was the first to recognize it," Freedom corrected. "Then when Jules got it, we knew for certain what we were up against."

"Too bad about all your Nigras, Ty," Stephanie said, acknowledging their deaths for the first time. "Papa says you can borrow any of ouahs that you'd like, until you have a chance to replace what was lost. We've got plenty of house Nigras and

258

field Nigras; jus' tell me what's needed an' ah'll send them ovah—no charge, of course."

"That's very kind of you, Stephanie, but I really don't think that will be necessary."

Freedom waited for Tiger to say more . . . to protest the casual lending of human beings and the reference to them as property that could be replaced with new purchases. When he said nothing, she took a swallow of hot tea and promptly burned her mouth. Oh, but it was difficult to keep from telling Stephanie Clairmont to get off the veranda and go home to her slaves!

"Ah'm more than happy to do anything ah can to help out, Ty," Stephanie murmured in her throaty voice. "Now that Miss Walker has to leave, you're gonna need mah help more than evah."

Freedom's head jerked up. "Leave? Who said anything about my leaving?"

Stephanie turned guileless eyes on her. "Well, nobody did . . . ah just assumed you would. Now that Lady Tiff'n's gone, a young lady can't stay heah alone in the house with Tigah. It wouldn't be propah."

"She can stay here," Ty interrupted. "And it will be perfectly proper, because I'm the one who's leaving."

Freedom's tea cup rattled as she set it down. Stephanie looked as stunned as she felt, and it was she who voiced the question uppermost in Freedom's mind. "Why, what do you mean, Ty?"

"By now, the *Sea Whisper*'s repairs should be completed." Ty's violet-colored eyes sought Freedom's. "And if everything I've heard this morning about the war is true, supplies will be needed more desperately now than they ever have in the past."

"What have you heard?" Freedom whispered, ig-

259

noring Stephanie's presence between her and Ty.

During the last month, the war had seemed far away. The latest news they had received had been at the end of May, and it was now the second week of July. In May, Generals Lee and Jackson had trapped the Union general, Josiah Hooker, near the small village of Chancellorville, Virginia and defeated him. Following the Confederate victory, Lee had assembled his forces and struck out for Pennsylvania. No word had arrived as to the outcome of that bold move and Freedom had half forgotten about it, assuming that either Lee had changed his mind and returned South or been routed by the Unionists.

Ty was watching her closely, as if dreading to reveal all that had happened during the time of the quarantine. "Stephanie says word has just come of a three-day battle held at Gettysburg, Pennsylvania during the first week of July. The casualties on both sides were enormous."

Freedom could barely catch her breath. "Who won?"

"Not us," Stephanie said bitterly. "If we had, this heah war would be ovah. There'd be nothing stoppin' us from marchin' straight through to Washin'ton and runnin' that ugly ole Abe Lincoln out of town."

"Meade—that's the Union general—held firm," Ty informed Freedom. "And the Confederate Army has returned to Virginia."

"I see. . . ." Freedom was careful not to betray her relief. She kept her voice noncommittal and lowered her eyes so as not to let Ty or Stephanie see how she felt.

"That's not all the news," Ty continued. "It's rumored that General Grant is laying siege to Vicksburg. If he takes it, the Mississippi River will belong to the North, splitting the Confederacy in two. That means guns and food will no longer get through to us from the West."

"They intend to stahve us to death, the beasts!" Stephanie cried. "Honestly, Ty, ah don't see how you can harbor a No'the'ner under this very roof. . . . Your dear mama probably died of a broken heart, not yellah fevah. She confided in me how much she hated havin' to be polite to an enemy of ouah beloved South!"

"Miss Walker is no enemy, Stephanie. She's my bookkeeper and my friend. I'd appreciate it if you ceased insulting her. If you don't, I'll be forced to ask you to leave."

"Me! You would send me away and keep *her?* Lord Almighty! Your Mama was right. It seems she did have somethin' to worry about. . . . Ah'm insulted by such an attitude. Ah came rushin' all the way ovah heah to offer help an' comfort, an' all ah get for mah efforts is nasty threats." Stephanie jumped to her feet, crumpling her straw hat against her ample bosom. "You've been a curiosity in these heah pahts for yeahs, Ty, but we all ovahlooked your peculiarities on account of your mama. Now that she's dead an' gone—God rest her soul—it wouldn't surprise me a bit if people went out of their way to avoid you from now on, Ty Carrin'ton."

"I wouldn't mind it a bit if *you* went out of your way to avoid me, Stephanie." Ty threw his napkin down on the table. "Your efforts to entrap me into marriage have embarrassed me for the last time. Now that mama's gone, there's no reason for you to visit Cypress Hall ever again. . . ." He pushed back his chair and stood. "Let me escort you to your carriage so you can hurry back to your boring friends and tell them what an ingrate I am."

"That's exactly what ah'm gonna tell 'em! An' there's no need for you to accompany me to mah carriage. I can find it by mahself! You just stay heah with this little No'the'n tramp. No self-respec-tin' South'n belle would consent to live alone in this house with you, like she's been doin'."

"I've already told you: She won't be living here alone with me for much longer, because I've got to get back to running the blockade. If I don't, you may not eat this winter, Stephanie. It's people like me who've been feeding the South and arming her soldiers, while people like you have been draining her dry, causing precious cargo space on the block-ade-runners to be crammed with luxuries instead of necessities."

"Ah don't do nothin' your Mama didn't do first!"

"Well, Mama died because of her expensive tastes. Are you willing to die for them, too, Stephie?"

Stephanie whirled about with an angry swish of skirts. "Ah will not stand heah an' be insulted for anothah minute! Good-bye, Ty Carrin'ton! What-ever once existed between us is dead now, an' can't be resurrected! You will nevah see mah face again at Cypress Hall!"

"Thank God," Ty muttered as Stephanie flounced away.

When she had disappeared around the corner of the house, Ty sat down again opposite Freedom. His eyes probed her face. "You haven't said much in the last few minutes, Mouse. What are you thinking?"

Freedom carefully retrieved her teacup, her emotions churning. "Must you really return to block-ade-running, Ty? You needn't do it on my account. Stephanie's right. I ought to find somewhere else to live now that your mother is gone."

He took the cup from her hand, set it down, lifted her fingers to his mouth, and brushed a kiss across them. "Weren't you listening, Mouse? I'm not doing it just to get out of the house or to pro-tect your reputation. I'd much rather marry you than send you away. . . . That's what I intend to do eventually. But first, I must do my duty to the Confederacy. I'm needed now more than ever. The battle at Gettysburg has depleted our war materi-als, and if we lose Vicksburg, widespread famine is a real possibility. . . . I've been away far too long. Now, I must get back to work."

Freedom clung to his hand, pressing it to her breast. "Ty, what if I begged you not to go back to blockade-running? What if I got down on my knees and pleaded with you? You aren't like Stephanie or your mother or the rest of their friends; in your heart, you're more a Northerner than you realize."

He looked straight into her eyes, his own eyes dark as smoke. "No, sweetheart, I'm not. Don't make the mistake of thinking I can abandon the Confederacy in her hour of need. Just because I love you and don't believe in slavery doesn't mean I can sit back and do nothing while North Carolina fights a desperate, losing battle. No matter what happens—sweet victory or bitter defeat—I'll stand by the Confederacy until the end."

Freedom felt tears gathering in her eyes. "All you're doing is prolonging this war, Tiger, can't you see that? The more guns you bring back, the more cloth for uniforms, the more gunpowder and ammunition — "

"The more food," he added. "Yes, Mouse, I'm prolonging it. I'm giving us a chance to win. Neither Abe Lincoln nor his Congress has a right to tell North Carolinian tarheels how to live. It's like King George trying to rule the colonies, forcing them to pay taxes for things they didn't want and would never see."

"It's not like that at all, Ty! You can't begin to compare the two. North Carolina is a part of the Union — or at least, she was before she broke away. The Union must decide what's best for us all; each state can't just make its own laws."

"Why in hell not?" Ty shouted, jerking away from her. "Nobody from Boston, Baltimore, or New York is going to come down here and tell me how to run Cypress Hall. That's what this war is all about, Freedom . . . it's about your name! I'm a free man who won't be ruled by a bunch of Northerners who don't understand my culture or my problems."

"But you don't even believe in slavery!"

"Slavery isn't the only issue! And you Northerners aren't the only people in the world who know what's right! Damn it, if it weren't for your Northern arrogance, Jules, Elvira, and my mother would still be alive today."

"You're blaming *me* for their deaths?"

"I'm blaming this whole damn war and what it's done to all of us. If it weren't for the North trying to rule the South, there wouldn't be a war — and no blockade, no blockade-running, no importation of yellow fever, no young men dying on bloody battlefields. . . . This whole thing is the fault of the North, Freedom, do you dare deny it?"

"Of course, I deny it! You talk about Northern

arrogance; what about Southern pride? Just what is it that prompts you stubborn Southerners to think you're better than Negroes or Northerners. . . . better than anyone, in fact? This war *your* is fault, not ours! I hope Grant does take Vicksburg and the Confederacy is split in two! And I hope we're all so hungry this winter thàt the South is forced to concede to the North!"

"If I have anything to say about it, it won't happen. And I *do* have something to say about it." Ty stood and towered over her. "You can stay here and wait for me until this war is over, Freedom, or you can be true to your misguided beliefs, leave, and go elsewhere. The choice is yours. . . . I'm a Rebel, and I'll *be* a Rebel 'til the day I die. What you have to decide is whether or not you can love a Rebel."

"Can you love a Yank?" she shot back.

"I already do," he said levelly. "And I'll go on loving her, provided she doesn't attempt to change me . . . and doesn't betray me behind my back."

Freedom clenched her fists in mute anger and frustration; all their arguments came to this—to a not-so-silent challenge. They kept returning to where they'd started, with her on one side and him on the other, hurling their differences in each other's faces. She refused to look at him . . . did not look up even when he strode away from her and entered the house. She sat for a long time on the veranda, listening until she heard distant hoofbeats departing the stable at a gallop.

She sat until Mancie came to her, wringing her hands in her apron. "Marse Ty gone to Wilmin'ton, Missy Freedom. Gone back to runnin' de blockade in de *Sea Whisper*. He say you in charge now. He say we all gotta do what you tell us just as if you was de new mistress heah. . . . What we gonna do now, Missy Freedom? What we gonna do now dat Marse Ty an' all de other white folks 'cept you is gone from Cypress Hall?"

The rest of July passed slowly at Cypress Hall—hot, muggy days when the only things that stirred in the heat were the human beings, Freedom struggling to run the plantation in Ty's absence, and the Negro men, women, and children who looked to her for supervision and guidance. Managing the big house was the easy part, since no one lived in it except Freedom, but managing the plantation was another story.

Freedom hardly knew where to begin. Fortunately, Omoroh came to her aid, his experience on a cotton plantation in Georgia standing him in good stead. Each morning, he pantomimed the various tasks that needed to be done—hoeing the cotton fields, vegetable patch, or flower gardens, repairing this or that, caring for the livestock, and so on. Freedom appointed a quick-witted lad named Billy Bob to convey her orders to the hired workers. Billy Bob had worked under Jules, and Freedom soon discovered that the tall, lanky young man knew almost as much about what needed to be done as Omoroh. Under Omoroh's sober, watchful eyes, Billy Bob performed quite well, his only faults being a carefree attitude toward work and a roving eye for the ladies. Billy Bob constantly found excuses to seek out Mancie and the other girl, Tillie, whom Freedom had assigned to help Mancie in the house.

A good-looking lad, he was always flirting, playing the two girls against each other and provoking jealousy, so that Freedom often had to intervene when sudden tears and name-calling erupted. Much as Freedom hated to admit it, it did seem as if the Negroes often behaved like children, running to her as the authority figure who must settle petty disputes and arguments. Freedom longed for someone with whom she could discuss this situation, but the likeliest candidate, Omoroh, remained locked in his world of silence. His limited ability to communicate was as great a frustration to Freedom as it must have been to Omoroh himself.

Then one sultry evening in August, Omoroh approached her as she sat fanning herself on the veranda. He had two books in hand. Freedom was amazed to discover that one was an English copy of the Muhammadan bible, the Koran, and the other was apparently an Arabic version. Omoroh pointed to identically placed passages in each book, telling Freedom with animated gestures that he was learning to read English by comparing such passages. He pantomimed that he wished to obtain writing materials so that he could practice forming the English symbols that matched the Arabic ones.

Freedom was stunned. Suddenly, she knew what she wanted to do—teach Omoroh to read and write English, and teach the other Negroes as well. A door of understanding abruptly opened in her mind. The reason Ty's workers were so childish was because they had never been educated for any but the most simple, menial tasks. Mancie's cooking skills were limited because she was unable to read recipes and could not always recall the ingredients of a particular dish. Billy Bob wasted so much time chasing females and playing juvenile pranks because he'd never learned mental discipline. These people were unprepared for freedom because they'd never been to school and could not read or write even their own names!

Unless they became literate, Ty's workers would always be relegated to boring, mundane tasks. Resigned to lifelong ignorance, they'd always feel inferior, a kind of slavery in itself. A great excitement and determination took hold of Freedom; this was her chance to really do something to improve the lives of the downtrodden. Not that Ty's workers were downtrodden in the same way as actual slaves, but neither were they fulfilling their full potential.

The very next evening after supper, before it got dark, she gathered all of the plantation workers together beneath a huge magnolia tree and instituted classes designed to teach them their letters and enable them to learn to read. After that, the days sped by. Not content to give simple lessons on the ABC's, Freedom also attempted to discuss current events happening outside the plantation. She was amazed to learn that few of the workers had ever ventured beyond the gates of Cypress Hall. Some had been to Wilmington or could recall distant places of birth before they came to the plantation, but most had lived all their lives upon Carrington land. Few understood what the war was all about.

Unable to read newspapers, they knew only what they heard white folks saying. In times past, news had also spread via visiting slaves from neighboring plantations, but now that visitors were no longer coming to Cypress Hall, Tiger's people were completely ignorant of what was happening elsewhere. Freedom regularly sent Billy Bob to town to buy newspapers, so she began reading them to the workers, too. They were a fascinated audience, and it was during such a reading session that they all learned that Vicksburg had indeed fallen, and

Union gunboats were now patrolling the Mississippi.

Fearing that shortages would soon worsen, Freedom carefully counted the household money Ty had left behind in a locked drawer in the library. She intended to spend it only when absolutely necessary. The vegetable garden was producing enough sweet potatoes and greens to feed everyone, the flour supply was abundant, and occasionally, she permitted an old hen or duck to be killed to make a nourishing soup. The smokehouse still held a few hams, lots of fatback, and a number of other items useful for flavoring greens, so there was no reason why they couldn't manage until such time as Ty finally returned.

What she would do then, Freedom had no idea. For now, it was enough to teach her classes and read the *Wilmington Journal* to the workers, who were slowly but surely learning their letters and taking an avid interest in the outside world. When Ty did return, he probably wouldn't stay long anyhow. As for her own immediate future, she couldn't imagine abandoning Cypress Hall and its inhabitants now; they'd never survive without her tender care.

As August gave way to September, Freedom found herself listening for the pound of hoofbeats or blast of steam whistle that might indicate Ty's arrival. Billy Bob had taken a bargeful of Cypress Hall cotton downriver and delivered it to the usual storage place, but he'd neither seen nor heard anything of Ty. Freedom figured that Ty would need at least six weeks to make the round trip to Nassau, allowing thirty days for honoring the quarantine imposed on incoming ships, which the Parker vessel had ignored with such dire results. But September unfolded with nary a sign of Ty. Near the end of the month, Freedom sent Billy Bob to town to fetch the latest news. When he returned, she almost wished she hadn't sent him; the news was far too worrisome and upsetting.

According to Billy Bob, Wilmington was crammed with blockade-runners—more than had ever previously used the port. The number of Federal blockaders had correspondingly increased. The reason was that Charleston, South Carolina had all but shut down as a port, following the fall of Morris Island, the fortification guarding Charleston harbor. The Unionists had taken Morris Island on September 7, and Wilmington was now the last Southern port open to blockade-runners.

Billy Bob regaled her with tales of the young Englishmen accompanying the blockade-runners; they occupied a large house on Market Street, where they fought cocks on Sundays, kept their gas jets lit until all hours of the night, and regularly enjoyed the music of a band of Negro minstrels. While the Englishmen had money to pay the exorbitant prices being demanded for everything in Wilmington, the townspeople didn't. Coffee was now being made from parched corn or acorns, and meals often consisted of wheaten biscuits or corn muffins and hominy, with no meat or fresh vegetables to round them out.

Salt was in such poor supply that many of the estates along the lagoon in the Wilmington area were boiling seawater in huge kettles day and night in an effort to produce it. Rice continued to be supplied by the large plantations along the Cape Fear River, and cotton, turpentine, resin, tar, and pitch were still available for shipment to Nassau, but the goods bought with these items commanded too high a price for the common people to pay.

"Dey's growin' hungry in Wilmin'ton, Missy Freedom," Billy Bob told her, rolling his huge dark eyes. "We's shore lucky Marse Ty runs de blockade. Least we knows we won't stahve to death. But ah shore feels sorry foh de Rebel soldiers. De ladies is cuttin' up cahpets to make army blankets now, 'cause cloth cain't be had at any price. Dis wintah, de poor in Wilmin'ton an' de surroundin' countryside is gonna be mighty cold."

Freedom felt a momentary pang of guilt; what she had wished for was coming true. Then, remembering where her loyalties lay, she snapped, "But I suppose the social life of Wilmington hasn't let up in the least, has it?"

"Ah wouldn't know bout dat, Missy," Billy Bob responded.

Flipping through the *Journal,* Freedom saw ads for the Thalian Association and was able to answer her own question. No, the social life had not diminished. Wilmington's town hall boasted a full-size theater, in which all the town's notables regularly staged theatrical dramas for the edification of the entire populace, who flocked to see them. Despite the war and its shortages, the prestigious Thalian Association was staging one of Shakespeare's plays and inviting everyone to attend.

Other ads told a similar story: The common folk might be going hungry and shoeless, but the wealthy could still buy silks, merinos, alpacas, and the latest French millinery at M. N. Katz's emporium, which had always been a cut or two above Hattie's shop, and William Patton, the baker, was still offering to execute "all orders for cakes and so forth for weddings, parties, and funerals in the most approved manner and on the shortest notice."

Freedom threw down the paper in disgust. What would it take to make the proud South come to her senses? How many deaths must occur? How many people suffer? She thought of the Rebel soldiers deprived of decent clothing, boots, and blankets — and probably also of food. She could understand why Ty wanted to help them, but at the same time she wished he'd quit, so the whole thing might end sooner. It would never end, she suspected, as long as the planter class continued to enjoy their affluence.

In a fit of pique, she went through the empty house gathering unused bed linens, stripping closets of old clothing, even tearing down drapes that could be made over into dresses, shirts, or trousers. First, she decided, she'd make sure that Cypress Hall workers had enough bedding and warm clothing to last the winter, and then she'd send Billy Bob to town in a wagon with the excess. She didn't want the items to fall into the hands of the Confederate Army, but there was no reason the poorer townspeople could not benefit from them. In a fit of inspiration, she penned an anonymous letter to Hattie Draper, requesting that the shop owner make the items available for sale to the neediest of Wilmington's residents.

"Inasmuch as poor women of Wilmington cannot afford to decently clothe themselves and their families," she wrote, "I am requesting that you sell these things at prices affordable to the poorest of the poor. The profits you yourself may keep — or with them, you may purchase food to distribute to those who are hungry. I have heard you are a kind-hearted woman; that is why I have chosen you to undertake this responsibility. . . ."

Freedom signed the letter: "Sincere Regards From

a Northern Sympathizer Who Nonetheless Cannot Bear to Witness the Suffering of the South."

When she had finished writing the letter, she retired to her room for the night. She had just finished donning her long, white nightdress when she heard footsteps on the stairs.

"Mouse? Where are you? It's me, Ty. I've come home."

Chapter Nineteen

Ty bounded up the remaining stairs two at a time. He had missed Freedom dreadfully; the lonely, boring weeks spent waiting for the quarantine to lift had been the worst. Even when danger threatened—those tense moments when he had guided the newly refurbished *Sea Whisper* through the Federal cordon—Freedom had been on his mind; the memory of her sweet smile, liquid brown eyes, and softly shining hair had tormented him unbearably, and he damned himself for the worst kind of fool. Why did he always provoke a fight between them when all he really wanted was to take her in his arms and make passionate love to her?

He raced down the hallway to her room, skidded to a stop, and considered whether or not he ought to barge in on her. After all, she might still be angry with him. And she had reason to be, since he'd behaved like a perfect jackass. Instead of rejoicing in the concessions she'd already made, he had demanded more than she was ready or able to give. If she could never go another step he'd still love and cherish her, still beg her to stay in North Carolina after the war ended, still plead with her to marry him. Somehow, they'd find a way to make it work. It *had* to work. Without her, nothing seemed to have any purpose. He saw his days stretching endlessly ahead of him, devoid of humor, love, and laughter, filled only with duty and painful regrets. He loved her so much that he was even willing to consider selling Cypress Hall and going North, if that's what it would take to make her happy!

Unable to wait another moment, he burst through the closed door, praying he'd find her smiling that sweet, shy smile of hers. But she wasn't smiling when he finally saw her, standing in her prim nightgown, her delicate curves outlined by the light of a gas jet on the wall behind her. Instead, she had an oddly questioning expression, as if wondering what he was doing there.

She didn't say a word, and neither did he for the first few moments. The sight of her momentarily robbed him of breath. She was lovelier than he remembered, more fragile and innocent-looking, her translucent skin glowing as if lit from within, her hair shinier than memory had conjured. He walked into the room, fell to his knees in front of her, and wrapped his arms around her waist. Burying his face in her soft bosom, he held her tightly, willing her to forget the things he'd said the last time they were together.

"I'm sorry for all the times I've hurt you, Mouse," he whispered against her breasts. "It's not you I despise; it's never you. I don't know why I heap my anger on your pretty head. I know you're not to blame for all the things the North has ever done to the South."

"And you're not to blame for all the evil I've

275

seen or read about involving slavery," she replied, hugging him to her. "Oh, Ty, what will become of us?"

"We'll triumph over everything," he said. "We'll confound the cynics who say love can't conquer all; we'll prove that it can by loving each other until we're so old that even we can't remember why we ever fought."

"Oh, my love, do you think that's really possible?" Entwining her fingers in his hair, she tilted back his head and gazed down into his eyes. "I dream of such a thing. . . . I dream of it every night. But somehow, I can't quite convince myself it will ever happen."

"Hush," he whispered. "We'll make it happen."

She slid downward and joined him on his knees in the center of the floor—a floor where once a yellow and white braided rug had cushioned the hardness, he dimly recalled. Since now was hardly the time to ask what had happened to it, he took her in his arms and kissed her. Kneeling on the hard wooden floor, he rejoiced in the taste and feel of her. Then, thinking of her comfort, he rose and pulled her up after him, steering her toward the bed. She went willingly, a small smile tugging at the corners of her mouth.

The curtains were gone, too, he noticed, and the bed coverings were different—old and worn. But even that discovery did not deter him from the pressing need to possess her again, here and now. She could rearrange the entire house, sell off all the furniture, do whatever she fancied—he didn't care! All he wanted was to feel her body beneath him once more, hear her gasp his name as she scaled the heights of ecstasy, revel in her total surrender. Most of all, he wanted everything to be right between them, with no more anger, hurt, or bitterness.

"Mouse, sweet Mouse, I've missed you so," he murmured, easing her nightdress over her head.

"And I you, Ty." Naked but unabashed, she lay back on the bed and held out her arms, welcoming him into them. "I'm so glad you've come home."

As he embraced her, he felt as if he'd come home in a way he never had before; this time, he was truly home. Home was her arms, her mouth, her legs opening to receive him. . . . He bent his head to taste her breasts, and hunger drove him to devour them with kisses. He could not get enough of her. He filled his hands with her satiny softness, his mouth with her tender succulence. Still, it was not enough. He wanted more; he wanted all. She gave all. She gave more than he had ever dared dream of receiving. With lips, hands, and body, she told him of her love. Her caresses drove him wild with wanting. Her kisses intoxicated him. He tried to prolong the exquisite agony, but she wouldn't let him. Her need was as great as his.

Driving into her, he possessed her totally, and they clung together in mounting rapture. As he began to move within her, the impact of their joining struck him to his very soul. He could never give her up, never live without her. Whatever she wanted, he would do. Nothing mattered but that she agree to marry him, to love him always, to bear his children, to grow old with him. She who so much hated slavery had enslaved him utterly.

When Freedom awoke the next morning, everything was exactly as she had wanted it to be the first time she slept beside Ty. There were no interruptions, no rude intrusions. Ty's arm and leg pinioned her to the bed. As soon as she stirred, he stirred, then started nibbling the back of her neck.

"Ty . . . don't. We must get up before Mancie or Tillie comes looking for us."

"If they do come looking for us, we'll send them away. You're not getting out of this bed, Mouse, until you agree to marry me."

"All right, I'll marry you. . . . Now, please let me up."

He tightened his grasp on her. "Oh, no you don't, Mouse. That was too easy. *When* will you marry me?"

"After the war ends, I suppose. . . . Or did you have some other time in mind?"

"Mouse . . ." he growled. "You're not taking this seriously."

He turned her over to face him, and her heart leapt at the sight of his rumpled handsomeness. She loved how his hair dipped over his forehead, half concealing one of his remarkable eyes. She loved the width of his muscular shoulders, the play of muscles across his powerful chest. She loved the way he was looking at her, with mingled exasperation and indulgence, half angry because she was treating the subject too flippantly. . . . Well, really, it was *his* decision. He was the one running the blockade and prolonging this war.

"I'd marry you today if I could, Mouse, but today I have to go back to Wilmington."

"You're leaving for Nassau again, I take it."

"I'm supposed to, yes, but if you beg me to stay, this time I might change my mind."

278

She studied him closely; he actually meant it. If she asked him to stay, he'd do it. He'd quit running the blockade. But was that what she really wanted? "Tiger. . . what did you bring back on this trip?" she found herself asking.

"More food than I ever have before . . . and medicines, though I had to pay a fortune for them. This time, I didn't bring guns, Mouse. I think you would approve of my cargo; you were on my mind when I chose it."

"Then I won't ask you to quit now, Ty. People are suffering for lack of necessities. In fact, I've collected all sorts of items we don't really need here at Cypress Hall, and I'm sending them to those who do need them."

"So that's where the carpeting went . . . and the curtains and the bedding that used to be in this room.

"I—I didn't think I could sleep at night knowing that others might be freezing or hungry this winter. I hope you don't mind my taking things without your permission."

"I left you in charge, didn't I? And I'd say you're doing a wonderful job. . . . When I stopped by my warehouse in Wilmington and saw the cotton, I was amazed. I know my workers didn't produce that fine harvest all by themselves. Someone had to oversee it." He kissed her very gently on the lips, then playfully tweaked her nose. "So I guess we won't get married today, after all. But as soon as this damn war is over, I'm dragging you to the nearest preacher and making an honest woman of you."

She sighed, wishing the delay wasn't necessary but knowing it was what Ty actually wanted, even if he was pretending he didn't. "It will be over soon, won't it, Ty? With Charleston closed to blockade-runners, how much longer can the Confederacy hold out?"

He sat up beside her, his mouth tightening. "It's not over yet, Mouse. Before I came here, I also stopped to see General Whiting, the army commander in Wilmington. He's awaiting word of the outcome of a battle in Tennessee, somewhere near Chattanooga. General Braxton Bragg commands our forces there, and I wouldn't be surprised if we won this one."

"I can hardly keep all these battles straight," Freedom complained. "I just want it to be over. I hate this war."

"So do I, sweetheart. . . . Let's not talk about it anymore, all right? If I'm going to leave, I'll have to leave soon, and the last thing I want is another argument before I go."

"No more arguments," she agreed. "Let's discuss the plantation instead. There's so much I have to tell you — and to ask you. You took a great risk going off and leaving me with no instructions whatever; it's fortunate Omoroh and Billy Bob know something about cotton, even if I don't — or rather, didn't."

His rakish grin flashed. "Ah, but I knew you could cope, Mouse. All the while I was gone, I never once worried about Cypress Hall, my cotton harvest, or any of my people. I knew you'd take care of everything. After all, I've seen you in action. Anyone who can handle a yellow fever outbreak as well as you did can certainly manage a plantation."

"About your people, Ty . . ."

Freedom told him of her literacy lessons and all she had been doing to educate his workers. Surprised and pleased, Tiger seemed especially glad that she was making so much progress with Omoroh. He listened to her theories about teaching Negroes and never once protested or disagreed. They talked for over an hour, then he suddenly reached for her, and she forgot what she was going to say next. They spent half the day in bed, and neither Mancie nor Tilly came to look for them, causing Freedom to wonder why. When she and Ty finally got dressed and went downstairs, they found a meal laid out for them in the dining room, as if the two girls had guessed what was happening upstairs but were being discreet about it.

They ate, talked some more, then said good-bye. Locked in Tiger's strong arms, Freedom struggled to contain her tears, consoling herself that at least this time the parting was sweet, not bitter. "I'll be waiting for you, Ty," she promised, swallowing hard. "Please be careful and come home to me soon."

"I will, Mouse. . . . You don't know what it means to me to have you here, waiting for me, taking care of things. . . ." He held her tightly. "It's such a relief to know I can trust you. I was such a fool ever to question or doubt it."

She almost reminded him she was still a Northerner—and still wanted the Yanks to win—but such a comment might precipitate another argument, so she just hugged him and teasingly whispered, "You mean you're finally convinced now that I'm not a spy?"

He laughed. "When would you have the time? Between teaching and running the plantation, not to mention clothing the poor, you're far too busy. Besides, other than what you read in the newspapers, you don't know a thing that's going on in this war."

"That's true," she said. "I don't. . . . So that's why you're so sure of me!"

He laughed even harder. "No, Mouse, I'm sure of you because you've proven yourself to me. In all these months, you haven't done a thing to harm me or mine, so how can you be a spy?"

"As far as you know, I haven't!" she snapped, not at all pleased to be taken for granted, her most cherished beliefs made light of.

"Now, don't go and lose your temper. . . . Guess I better get out of here before we go at it again."

"Yes, you'd better!"

They kissed one last time, and Freedom's tears finally spilled over and ran like rain down her cheeks. She wondered if she was sending him off to die. After all, he could be shot and killed while running the blockade. His ship could be sunk. He could drown in a storm. A hurricane could blow him off course and smash the *Sea Whisper* against a reef.

"Wait for me," he whispered hoarsely, and then he was gone.

General Braxton Bragg won the Battle of Chicamauga, as it came to be called, and the Confederate victory made banner headlines, enlivening the flagging spirits of the beleaguered South's inhabitants, who were still reeling from the Gettysburg defeat. In November, however, the Union Army under General Ulysses S. Grant trounced the Rebels at

Chattanooga and drove Bragg back into Georgia. As the days grew shorter and colder, a deep gloom settled over everyone in Wilmington and at Cypress Hall.

Only Freedom was happy. She sang as she went about her chores or taught Omoroh and the other workers how to read and write. Up in the attic, she discovered a trunk filled with Ty's old schoolbooks; there were also writing materials, an old slate, and other things that had been packed away, presumably for Tiger's children or any other offspring his parents might have. Freedom made good use of it all and even sent Billy Bob to Wilmington with precious household funds to buy more writing slates being auctioned off at a special event to raise funds for North Carolina soldiers.

She dreamed of the war's end and of marrying Ty and of one day teaching their children to do simple sums and to learn their ABC's. The world of Cypress Hall was a warm, cozy little cocoon shielding her from the war and from everything she had ever hated about the South. She was busy doing work she loved and had begun to think of Cypress Hall as becoming a beacon of light in a sea of darkness, guiding the way for other plantation owners to see how much better life could be if the slaves were freed and educated.

She could almost picture herself spending her life in North Carolina; as long as she didn't have to socialize with people like Stephanie Clairmont, she could be perfectly happy on the plantation. She even relished gardening and looking after the livestock. The horses, especially, were a source of joy and satisfaction to her. Recognizing a horse's usefulness in enabling her to check on the more distant cotton fields from time to time, she had convinced Omoroh and Billy Bob that she must learn to ride. Billy Bob had been teaching her the rudiments on a gentle old mare, and she was eagerly anticipating the day when she could confidently swing one leg over Ty's beautiful, spirited Plantation Walker and set off across the now-dormant fields by herself.

She had altered two skirts to accommodate riding astride, and she took pride in grooming the animals herself and currying their coats to a glossy sheen. One day in late November, following a lonely, quiet Thanksgiving, she walked into the stable and discovered Ty's lovely chestnut stallion sweating in his stall and pacing, acting as if he had a monumental belly ache. Quickly, she found Li'l George, the stableboy, and sent him to fetch Omoroh and Billy Bob.

The two men came quickly, took one look at the big Walker, and began arguing over what should be done. Omoroh's hands flew as he made gestures, and Billy Bob countered each one with shouts of disagreement. They finally settled on giving the horse a bran mash and walking him until the discomfort passed. The remedy seemed to make him feel better, and Freedom went to bed that night certain the valuable animal was out of danger.

About midnight, she abruptly awoke, seized with a terrible premonition that something was wrong. Throwing a heavy dressing gown over her nightdress, she shoved her feet into sturdy shoes, snatched up a whale oil lantern, and went out into the gusty night. It was cold and dark. The sky was moonless. There were no stars. The wind cut through her clothing, making her shiver, and she thought of Ty, wondering where he was on this frigid eve.

Hopefully, he had already finished his business in Nassau, run the blockade on the homeward trip, and was patiently waiting out the quarantine. When he came home the next time, she intended to ask him to stay at Cypress Hall through the Christmas holidays and maybe through most of January. This far South, shipping was still possible during the winter months but it wasn't pleasant, and she longed to spend more time with him. The matter of her reputation had ceased to bother her; they would marry one day, anyway, so if people gossiped, what did it matter? The war might drag on forever; she and Tiger were entitled to grab a little happiness along the way.

Arriving at the big wooden doors to the long, low stable, Freedom saw that one side of the door had been pushed back and left open, when it was normally kept closed at night. She frowned, blaming Billy Bob or Li'l George for such carelessness. Entering, she went straight to Zephyr's stall and looked inside, holding up the lantern so she could see better. The big chestnut was placidly munching hay and paid her no attention, other than to toss his head at the sudden intrusion of light.

He looked perfectly fine; whatever had been bothering him earlier in the day was obviously not bothering him now. Freedom sighed at her foolish misgivings. It seemed that she had left her warm bed for nothing. Turning to leave, she heard a slight sound, almost like a moan coming from the dark shadows farther back in the barn. Her throat constricted with fear, but she knew there had to be some logical explanation for the strange, half-human sound.

Holding the lantern aloft, she walked down the aisle. Nothing seemed out of order, and she supposed it must be her imagination playing tricks on her. Then the sound came again. "Water . . ." a voice said clearly. "Help me, please . . . I must have water."

Freedom hurried toward the empty stall from which the summons was coming. She shone the lantern into it and was startled to see a young man lying crumpled on the clean straw. He lifted his tousled head, gazed at her from bleary, bloodshot eyes, and croaked, "Water, for the love of God . . ."

Slinging the lantern from a hook on a nearby post, Freedom ran to the watering trough at the far end of the aisle. A dipper hung on the wall to serve the needs of thirsty stable workers, and she filled it to the brim with the stale, brackish water from the trough. Then she returned to the man, who was either unwilling or unable to move from the spot where he had collapsed on the straw. Kneeling beside him, she held the dipper to his cracked lips. The man drank thirstily, dribbling much of the water down his chin. Seeming not to notice, he fell back, moaning. "Oh, God . . . God, have mercy on me."

Freedom set down the dipper and felt the man's forehead. It was burning hot. She examined him closely, but there was no redness of the nostrils or yellowing of the eyeballs, no telltale signs that this was yellow fever. It was too late in the season for it, anyway, Freedom reminded herself. Feverish the man may be and he might have something else that was contagious, but she wasn't looking at another case of yellow fever. Still, she would take precautions and keep him isolated here in the barn, until she knew for certain what it was that made him so ill and also what had caused him to go skulking about the plantation in the dark.

"Sir . . . what's your name? How did you get here?" Her eyes roved over his clothing; he was well-dressed, like a Southern gentleman, but one who lived in the city not the country. His fashionably cut dark blue coat was of the finest fabric, and his trousers and boots were equally fine. Only the bits of straw clinging to his attire and the wrinkles in it marred an otherwise elegant appearance.

"My horse . . ." he rasped. "Where is my horse?"

The man spoke with a Northern accent, similar to Freedom's, and she blinked in surprise. Who was this stranger and what he was doing at Cypress Hall? Lifting her head, Freedom glanced down the aisle, counting the noses poking out over the half doors of the stalls. The number matched her expectations.

"I've no idea where your horse is. . . . Did you bring him into the barn?"

"I—I tried. . . ." the man replied. "But . . . he got away from me. And I—I was too weak to go after him."

Freedom studied the young man who so aroused her curiosity. He looked to be in his twenties, she guessed, and he had brown hair and blue eyes. Were he not so pale and trembling, his eyes not so bloodshot, he might have been most attractive. "You're very ill," she said. "Why don't you lie here and rest, while I see if I can find your horse? Then I'll get you some blankets and something hot to drink."

"You won't tell anyone I'm here, will you?" He suddenly grasped her hand, his face anxious, his eyes panic-stricken. "If I'm caught—especially with these documents on my person . . ." He flopped back into the straw. "Oh, God, what does it matter, now? I'll never make it to the next checkpoint in time. I'm way off course, anyway. . . . I should have known better than to try this."

Freedom leaned over him, trying to get him to look at her. Was he delirious? Did he know what he was saying? "What's your name?" she asked. "Tell me who you are and where you're going."

"When you see Maeve," he mumbled, "tell her I'm sorry . . . so terribly sorry. I've bungled everything."

"Who is Maeve?" Freedom pursued.

"I only did this because of her. I'm not cut out for this kind of work. She'll be so disappointed. . . . I tried to keep going, honestly I did. But I felt so ill, so very ill." He closed his eyes, his breathing rapid and shallow, every breath an effort.

Freedom grew more and more alarmed. The young man was slipping away from her; he had that look about him. She had seen it too often during the yellow fever epidemic to be mistaken about it now. By morning, he might be too ill to speak. He might even be dead. She grasped his lapels and shook him.

"Wake up! You must tell me more. What are these documents you mentioned? Were you taking them somewhere?"

When he didn't answer but only lay there with his eyes unfocused and his mouth half open, she reached into the front of his coat, where a slight bulge over his heart indicated that something was hidden. Her hand found a leather-bound packet. Trembling, she withdrew it and undid the leather thong tightly binding it. Inside was another packet, this one of the finest vellum and sealed with wax. She turned it over in her hands. Something was written on the outside. It was a name. The name, incredibly, was General Ulysses S. Grant.

Chapter Twenty

Freedom dared not open the packet; she wasn't sure she wanted to know what was inside. But she knew what Ty would think if he were there. The man was a Northerner, carrying papers addressed to a Union general, and he was muttering about checkpoints, which probably meant the same thing as "stations" on the Underground Railway. One did not have to be a genius to realize that this man was involved in some kind of spy network, relaying information from one location to the next. It was exactly the sort of thing she had been doing with slaves before the war began.

Thank God Ty wasn't home now, Freedom thought, hiding the packet in a corner of the stall beneath the straw. She must keep the man's presence a secret for as long as possible. The fewer people who knew about him, the better. She could use his illness as an excuse for ordering everyone away. Billy Bob and Li'l George needn't hear the fellow's ravings about his precious documents or his disappointed Maeve. The only person she could trust to help her care for the man was Omoroh.

Leaving the stranger where he lay, Freedom went to Omoroh's house to awaken the big African. After she told him what had happened, omitting only the part about the sealed papers, Omoroh grabbed blankets and a pillow from his own cupboard and hurried back to the stable with her. They found the man still unconscious and moaning in his troubled sleep.

"Make him comfortable, Omoroh, while I brew some sassafras tea. We'll try to get his fever down and maybe, when he awakens, he can tell us more about himself."

Freedom and Omoroh worked until the wee hours of the morning, trying to halt the man's raging fever. About an hour before dawn, their patient opened his eyes and glanced about lucidly, as if seeing everything for the first time.

"Where am I?" he muttered. "How did I get here?"

"Apparently, a horse brought you, but we were waiting until morning to go looking for it," Freedom said, kneeling beside him in the straw.

"Ah have to get up an' find 'im." Affecting a Southern drawl, the man tried to rise. "Ah must be in Fayetteville or thereabout befoh mornin'."

Freedom stayed him with one hand on his blanket-draped chest. "You're in no condition to go anywhere . . . and you needn't pretend to be a Southerner in front of me. If I'm not mistaken, you hail from Boston."

The young man lay back and warily scrutinized her. "Not Boston," he said, "but a little town near there . . . If I weren't so sick, I'd have noticed *your* Northern accent immediately. Ah well, pretty lady . . . I know why I'm so far from home. But why are you?"

"You first," she said, glancing at Omoroh. "And don't worry about my friend here. He'll never repeat a word you say."

The young man waved his hand and tiredly sighed. "It's too long a story . . . and there isn't time to tell it. To be perfectly frank, I feel too awful to tell a long story. So I guess I should get right to the point. If you're from Boston, does that mean you're loyal to the North, even though you live on a Southern plantation?"

"Yes, I'm loyal to the North. I'm just . . . staying here until the war ends."

"Then I guess the good Lord led me to the right place. . . . You see, I'm carrying documents that could help bring about a Northern victory."

"I've already seen those documents. They were tucked inside your coat."

The young man paled more than he was already. "You *found* them? My God, where are they?"

He started to paw his chest, but again, Freedom stopped him. "Don't worry. They're safe. And I haven't read them. I saw to whom they were addressed and knew they must be important. . . . What's in those documents, anyway?"

"Damned if I know. I'm just the courier. But I suspect they've got something to do with taking Richmond by way of Petersburg. Grant's the man to handle an assignment like that. He'll have to wait 'til spring, of course, but then—" The young man stopped talking and gasped for air, wheezing as if his lungs were clogged. Omoroh lifted him by the shoulders, so he could breathe better and resume speaking.

"Lord! I don't know what's wrong with me, but I sometimes feel as if my chest is being squeezed in a vise. It started out as a chill, with a sore throat and cough. I ignored it, and instead of going away, it got worse. I should never have gone out tonight in this wind and cold. But I was trying to get those papers to a place upriver near Fayetteville. Another courier is supposed to pick them up there and see that they reach the next stop."

"Then your spy ring—or whatever you call it—does operate like the Underground Railway," Freedom said. "I knew it must."

"Where do you think the idea came from? The South is crawling with Northern sympathizers . . . people like you and me who got stuck here after the war broke out. We've got to do something to help. At least, that's what Maeve, my lady friend, said. . . . Fool that I was, I believed her. I thought all I had to do was ride from Wilmington to Fayetteville carrying a pack of papers. . . . Now, look at me—flat on my back, sick, in a heap of straw."

Freedom sought to cheer him. "Yes, but at least, it's clean straw. . . . You're living in Wilmington?"

"No, just visiting . . . Came in on a blockade runner that started out in Charleston but couldn't return there, so it came here. Suited me fine. After all, Wilmington is farther north, and besides, I met Maeve, a girl who talks like a Southerner but thinks like a Northerner."

"She must be a wonderful person." Freedom was touched by the brightening of the young man's face whenever he mentioned the girl's name.

"She is. She recruited me and gave me the papers. I'd take them back and tell her I failed to make the checkpoint in time, but I'm afraid I can't."

"Why not? Didn't you say she was living in Wilmington?"

"Yes, temporarily. She arrived a few weeks before I did on another runner, but she left yesterday on an outward-bound vessel headed for Nassau. Said she had friends there. I was going to try and follow her, but she also told me she was in love with someone else, an officer in the Union Navy. . . . Can you believe it? I've risked life and limb to impress a woman who doesn't care whether I live or die!"

"I'm sure she cares, though maybe not in the way you want," Freedom disputed. "Still, you mustn't think negative thoughts. They will only make it harder for you to get well again."

"*If* I get well," the young man said glumly. "God, I'm so tired, and my chest hurts so bad. . . ."

"You need to rest," Freedom said. "Since it's already too late to make your checkpoint, why not forget about it and go to sleep?"

"It wouldn't be too late if I were stronger and had a good horse. . . . That nag I was riding pulled up lame on me. That's what took me so long coming from Wilmington. I was going to stop here, rest and grain him, hoping he'd recover. If not, I was going to steal another horse . . . well, borrow it, anyway, so I could get to Fayetteville."

"What time were you supposed to be there?" Freedom questioned. "Fayetteville isn't that far from here."

"Before daybreak . . . I was supposed to put the packet in a hollow tree a half mile downriver from Fayetteville. The tree is a big, twisted oak with a heart carved into its trunk. It's located on the riverbank just past a plantation belonging to a family named Owen."

"I know where the Owen place is, though I've never been there," Freedom added hastily as she saw the flare of speculation in the young man's eyes. "I've only heard mention of the family. They own a cotton plantation as big as Cypress Hall."

"Couldn't your friend here take it? If he galloped all the way on a fresh horse, he might still make it before the next courier arrives to pick it up."

"Oh, I don't think so. . . . Omoroh doesn't dare leave Cypress Hall. He's a runaway slave from Georgia, and the slavecatchers are looking for him."

"Doesn't talk much, does he?"

"He *can't* talk, which means he can't answer questions or explain that he belongs at Cypress Hall, if someone stops him."

The young man fixed pleading, feverish eyes upon her. "I don't know what your situation is here — or if you could get away without anyone seeing you — but couldn't *you* take it? That is, if you have any idea how to ride."

Omoroh violently shook his head no, but Freedom carefully pondered the request. She wanted the documents to get into the right hands, especially if the information they contained could help end the war. Her only hesitation was because of Tiger. He would see this as a betrayal of the Confederacy, not to mention an abuse of his trust. It *was* spying of a sort, even if the packet's actual contents were a mystery to her.

"I can ride, but — but I just don't know if I can take your papers," she demurred.

"There's no reason to be scared," the young man said. "All you'll be doing is putting a packet inside a hollow tree. There's no danger, no one's trying to stop you. No one even knows about it, except you and the courier who has instructions to pick it up later in the morning."

"I suppose Zephyr could make it to Fayetteville before it gets light enough to be seen," Freedom mused. "He's our best and fastest horse. If I rode

Zephyr, we could probably be back before anyone realizes we're gone."

Again, Omoroh shook his head, warning her it would be too dangerous.

"Please go," pleaded the young man, his glassy eyes tearing at her heart. "The information is terribly important. It could mean victory for the North and an end to this blasted conflict."

"What happens if I'm too late and the other courier has already been there?"

"If there's no packet in its prearranged place, we couriers have instructions to abandon the entire effort. Similarly, if we spot anyone within a mile radius of our checkpoint, we're to turn around and flee. We're not to trust a single soul."

"You're trusting me," she reminded him.

He smiled a wan smile. "I have no choice. Besides, you discovered the packet on your own. Even if I'd never mentioned it, you would have known about it."

Freedom turned to Omoroh, "Saddle Zephyr please, Omoroh, while I go change into my riding skirt."

Omoroh made several violent gestures of disapproval. Then, in desperation, he scraped away the straw and scratched a message in the dirt with one long finger. "Do not go," the message read.

"Omoroh, that's wonderful! You've just written your first sentence in English. . . . But I'm afraid I have to go. There's no one else to send. Please don't tell Billy Bob or anyone else where I've gone, and keep them out of the stable. That way, they won't know Zephyr is missing and won't discover that we're sheltering a sick spy . . . By the way, what's your name?"

Turning back to the young man, Freedom saw that

he had lapsed into a fitful sleep. All that talking had probably exhausted him. Well, there'd be plenty of time to find out his name when she returned. If she was going to make it to the checkpoint before daylight, she had to hurry.

Freedom encountered no serious difficulty riding Zephyr, finding the big oak, dropping the packet inside a hole in the tree, and escaping the area unseen. Her only problems occurred on the homeward journey. The wind knifed her clothing, chilling her to the bone, and her legs and bottom ached from so many long hours in the saddle. Other than jumping once or twice at the wind, Zephyr minded his manners and brought her home at a steady, ground-eating pace, which would have been comfortable to ride had Freedom not been freezing to death.

Her hands were stiff and her teeth chattering when she finally rode up to the stable and dismounted. It was near noon, still overcast and windy, with great dark clouds racing across the sky. As she led Zephyr through the open stable doors, the big horse whinnied a greeting to his stablemates. Freedom peered into the gloom, searching for Omoroh. Other than the noises the horses were making, the barn was strangely quiet.

"Omoroh?" she called.

There was no answer. Quickly, she unbridled Zephyr in the aisle, slipped on his leather halter, and without taking time to unsaddle or rub him down, put him in his stall. Then she raced down to the far end of the stable where she'd left the courier in the empty stall. He wasn't there. Pillow, blankets, and nursing items had all been removed; only a slight indentation in the straw gave evidence that he had ever occupied the spot.

Freedom's heart began to thump against her rib cage. Omoroh would not have disobeyed her orders without a very good reason. Could the man have died in her absence? But she hadn't been gone that long! And where would Omoroh have taken the body?

Whirling about, she caught sight of a tall, dark figure striding toward her down the aisle. She gasped in surprise, then her throat closed. It was Ty, and he was very angry. As he came closer, she took in his tall black boots, gray trousers, and slate-colored coat. Beneath the tousled blond hair, his eyes were a stormy violet, his mouth a slash of rage.

"He's gone, Freedom," Tiger grated. "Your coconspirator died of lung congestion about an hour and a half ago. I arrived just in time to see him breathe his last."

"My . . . co-conspirator? Ty, don't be ridiculous! I don't even know the man's name."

"Where have you been, Freedom?" Ty quizzed in the same deadly quiet tone.

"Where have you put the man's body?" Freedom countered.

"He's laid out on a door in the carpentry shed. Omoroh and Billy Bob are making his coffin. As soon as they've finished, I'm taking him downriver to General Whiting at the Army post. Obviously, I can't trust you to tell me who he is, but maybe someone there will recognize him before he's buried. I only found out his first name—Albert."

Freedom's mind whirled. Tiger had to be guessing about what had happened; other than the packet she had just delivered, there was no proof that the man was a spy or a courier. Maybe she could bluff her way out of this yet. "I know what you're thinking, Ty, but I assure you, this is all perfectly innocent. . . . It isn't what it seems."

Her argument sounded both weak and familiar. Hadn't Ty said nearly the same thing that day when she had confronted him and Stephanie in the library?

"Don't lie to me!" Ty snapped, reaching into his vest pocket. "I found this letter in Albert's boot."

He withdrew a small, folded sheet of parchment, opened it, and began reading: *"To my darling Maeve . . . I can't let you go without trying one more time to change your mind . . . We were made for each other, dearest. We share the same loyalties, the same sympathies, the same burning desire to see the North triumph. Before we met, I may not have known my duty, but I know it now. One need not be wearing a blue uniform to fight the cause of justice. Why can't we fight it together? As soon as I complete this mission, I'm coming for you. This time I won't take no for answer. Devotedly, Albert."*

Ty crumpled the letter and threw it at her. "Do you take me for a fool? The man's a spy, and you're in league with him!"

"No, Ty, that's not true!" Freedom rushed to his side. "You must listen to me! Let me explain."

"You mean I should let you spin a web of lies and trickery? How long have you known Albert? How often has he come here, bringing information for you to carry to the next station?"

"This is the first time. I swear it! I never saw the man before last night. I didn't even know his name was Albert."

Tiger's eyes bored into her, his glance like a shaft

299

of steel plunging into her breast. "But you did go somewhere and deliver something that he was too ill to take any farther."

"Yes," she admitted. "I took a packet of papers upriver and left them at a spot near Fayetteville. I've no idea what was in the papers, and Albert didn't know either. He simply thought the information might help to end the war."

"You betrayed the Confederacy. . . . Worse yet, you betrayed *me!*" Ty shook her hand from his arm. "All this time I've been trusting you, loving you more each day. . . . You said you loved me. How could you have lied like that?"

"I didn't lie, Ty! I do love you. . . . I never meant to betray you, but the man was dying and he needed help. I couldn't say no. It was only a packet of papers, for God's sake. How harmful could they be?"

Tiger eyed her with virulent scorn. "They could reveal Confederate troop movements, battle plans, all kinds of important things. . . . Don't tell me you didn't know what you were doing, Freedom. You knew, and you did it anyway. You chose your precious North over me and everything we've become to each other."

"All right!" she screamed. "I did know what I was doing. He begged me to fulfill his duties as a courier, and I fulfilled them. That doesn't mean I don't love you!"

"Just what in hell does *love* mean to you? Is it only going to bed together . . . with a few sweet words thrown in to make us both feel better about it? Is that all it is, Freedom? . . . Strange, but I thought it was more than that. I thought trust and loyalty had something to do with it."

"Ty, you know I love you, but you also know who

300

I am and what I feel. You can't expect me to change all that just because we fell in love."

"Then I ought to hand you over to General Whiting, along with Albert's body, shouldn't I? You're a spy and a traitor; you deserve to be punished—or at least locked up where you can't do any harm."

"This was an isolated instance, Ty! The man's dead now, so it'll never happen again. He only stopped here because he was sick and his horse was lame. Surely, you understand how it happened . . . that I never once meant to go behind your back and do anything that would hurt you."

"But you *have* hurt me, damn it! I came rushing home to see you, to hold you. . . . I was even going to stay over the holidays. . . ." Ty's voice cracked. "And what did I find? A spy dying in my barn, and the woman I love out peddling secrets to my enemies."

"I'm so sorry, Ty. Oh, God, I'm sorry. Not sorry that I did it—God knows, I had to—but sorry that I hurt you. Please forgive me, Tiger, *please* . . ."

"Some things," he said, turning and walking away from her, "can't be forgiven."

Chapter Twenty-one

Tiger did not sleep the entire night. He sat in the library with the door closed, staring at a half-filled bottle of brandy and a brimming glass from which he never drank. Whiskey only dulled the mind; it didn't shut out pain. He'd learned that from experience. Getting drunk never helped one to make decisions, either, and he had a big decision to make tonight: Should he tell General Whiting everything, revealing what Freedom had done and turning her over to the Army commander?

It was his duty to do so, but he'd been flaunting duty ever since he met Freedom. That was his problem. He'd been flaunting it for so long that it had become a habit. Over and over, he weighed his choices: deliver Albert's body minus the letter, thereby protecting Freedom, or deliver everything to-gether—Albert, Freedom, and the damning letter. Let General Whiting draw his own conclusions, which might very well mean prison or a hanging noose for Freedom.

Ty had few delusions about what might happen to her; sentiment against the few Northerners still left in town was extremely hostile. Rocks were being thrown at their windows, the riffraff were calling them names, and even the upper class was talking about confiscating their properties—and these were Northerners who'd lived so long in the South that they'd developed Southern accents! What would happen to a Northerner caught red-handed in covert activity against the Confederacy? Ty could only speculate and shiver.

Toward dawn, he finally decided he couldn't turn Freedom in, but he would hand over Albert's body and the letter, claiming the man must have been homeward-bound, having already completed his mission, because no other damaging papers had been in his possession at the time of his death. This was mostly true, so he wasn't lying. As for what to do with Freedom herself, Ty was still in a quandary. Only one thing was abundantly clear: He had to end their relationship.

He had to end it once and for all. There wasn't the remotest possibility they could ever marry and lead normal lives. No matter which side won the war, problems would arise, the greatest of which was their own strong feelings. If the North won, Ty would be bitter—especially when his lands and home were destroyed or stolen. If the South won, Freedom would rage about the continued injustice of slavery. She'd never be able to settle down in a state where the institution still prevailed and was practiced by all their neighbors. The situation was impossible. For a brief time, he had allowed himself to hope, but this latest incident had opened his eyes to reality. It was better to end it now than to risk hurting Freedom later, and the longer it dragged on, the more she would be hurt.

Thus resolved, he rose, left the library, and went upstairs to awaken and tell her. He didn't knock, but simply entered her room and walked over to the bed. She was lying on her side, curled into a ball, looking more like a child than a woman in the dim, grayish light. He stood watching her for several long moments, wanting nothing more than to crawl into bed beside her and fit his body around hers. He wasn't conscious of making any sound, but suddenly she opened her eyes and raised her head.

"Ty?" Hope and disbelief tinged the question. She held out her hand to him. Coward that he was, he took it, allowing himself to be drawn nearer.

Now was the time to say the words that would bar him from touching her ever again. He opened his mouth, but nothing came out. She sat up and held out her arms, inviting, luring, seducing him. . . . Just as in the past, he couldn't resist. Reaching for her, he uttered a low growl—half-passion, half-protest. She pulled him down on top of her, and the magic began anew. Kissing, caressing, and undressing her, he could think of nothing but making her his.

There was no hesitation, no preliminaries. They both knew what they wanted and wasted no time getting there. Within several breathtaking minutes, he was inside her, moving swiftly and confidently, knowing exactly how far and fast he could go to push her over the edge of sanity into mindless ecstasy. She threw back her head and arched her body, straining against him, wrapping her lovely legs around him. He drove into her more deeply, more brutally than ever before; he wanted to leave his mark on her, brand her as forever his, possess her totally.

He held back, delaying his pleasure until he knew she was growing frantic. He wanted her to want him more than she ever had in the past. He wanted to plant his seed in her, bind her to him by making her pregnant. At the last possible moment, he came to his senses. Just as she clutched him and cried out, he pulled back and wasted his seed in the bed linens. The last thing they needed to confuse and complicate the issue was a child. . . .

"Tiger?"

This time, his name on her lips was a tearful plea. He ignored it and rose from the bed, picked up his clothing, and left the room, shutting the door softly behind him.

When Freedom finally found the courage to rise from her bed, it was well past daybreak and the house was silent. She knew Ty had gone; she had heard him cross the hall to his room and, moments later, descend the stairs. He might never be coming back. She wouldn't be surprised if he didn't. He had kissed and made love to her like a man saying good-bye. She loved him too much not to know what he was thinking and feeling when he denied her his very essence. That denial was meant to tell her they had no future. He hadn't wanted to create a child, because he no longer intended to marry her.

She rose, washed, and dressed in a haze of pain and regret. Then she walked through the house touching things—the bannister where his hand must have rested as he passed down the staircase, the doorknob he had used to open the front door, the doorknob to the library, his favorite room. . . . In the library, she found a letter on the desk, a single sheet of paper containing a short, brusque message in Ty's handwriting: *Don't look for me again until*

305

the war ends. I will fight until the last shot is fired,
the last ship sunk, and the last Southerner draws his
final breath. I will be that last Southerner . . . I will
never give up, . . . Yours, Tiger.

Freedom sank down into Ty's chair. Slowly, she
crumpled the message in her hand. There was no
sense weeping; she'd brought this on herself. When
he came back — *if* he came back — she would be here
waiting for him. . . . That was all she could do: wait
and hope. She wasn't the sort to give up, either.

Christmas and New Year's Day passed quietly.
Freedom barely noticed them. She wasn't in the
mood to celebrate the arrival of 1864. Winter
dragged on interminably. In March, General Ulysses
S. Grant became the new Commander-in-Chief of
the Union forces. On the western front, William T.
Sherman assumed command. Of the two Yankee
leaders, Sherman made Freedom the most uneasy.
He was reportedly a ruthless man; Southerners hated
him for his arrogance and rabid patriotism. They
were sure he meant to crush the South and crush it
mercilessly.

That was what Freedom wanted, yet she dreaded
the thought of more bloodshed and violence. Trying
not to think about it, she marked the passage of
time by the progress of her students. Omoroh could
now write whole paragraphs, and Billy Bob could
read from the newspaper. Mancie was able to follow
the recipes in a book that had belonged to Ty's
grandmother. The seasons unfolded with all their
usual beauty and demanding activity. Cotton was
planted, the vegetable and flower gardens weeded
and hoed, the horses exercised, and Freedom man-

aged to keep everyone fed and clothed despite running short on everything that wasn't produced at Cypress Hall.

From time to time, deliveries arrived from town: a wagon or steamboat loaded with barrels of flour, dried meat, and slabs of fresh mutton; maybe a bolt or two of cloth or a keg of nails; and once, there were several pairs of men's sturdy leather boots, which didn't fit anybody. Everything was from Ty, Freedom knew, but he sent no messages. As isolated as she was, she had no way of knowing when he was in town, and there was too much to do at Cypress Hall for Billy Bob to make the journey very often. She only sent Billy Bob when she grew desperate for news and simply had to buy a newspaper to find out what was happening.

In June, she learned of Grant's drive toward Richmond and Lee's desperate fight to stop the Union Army of the Potomac. Grant then circled Richmond and attacked Petersburg, twenty-two miles south of Richmond. Albert's packet must have done some good—or bad, depending on how one looked at it. It unnerved Freedom to think that everything Albert had predicted was coming true: Grant's appointment, the attack on Petersburg . . . But instead of rejoicing over the Union's progress, she felt responsible for every death and wished she hadn't gotten involved. The summer was long and hot, filling her with a dark foreboding, but nothing quite prepared her for the tragic events of the fall.

On the first of September, Sherman captured Atlanta, a devastating blow to the Confederacy. Capitalizing on the victory, he swept toward the sea, destroying everything in his path and striking abject terror into the hearts of everyone. Southern newspapers detailed horror after horror wrought by the vicious invaders. Fearing Sherman's arrival on their doorsteps, panicked refugees fled their homes and plantations, leaving them to be burnt and plundered. Many came to Wilmington—and eventually, to Cypress Hall.

On a crisp, clear day in late October, a steamboat announced its presence with a shrill whistle blast from the river. Billy Bob quickly fetched a horse and buggy, and Freedom leaped inside. The blast was a signal that either guests or goods were arriving— probably goods, since no guests had come calling since the day Ty had clashed with Stephanie Clairmont. Freedom was therefore most surprised when she arrived at the dock and discovered a party of eight people waiting for her, none of whom she recognized from Wilmington. Warily, she stepped down from the buggy.

"You must be Miss Freedom Walker," said a plump, kindly-looking woman with gleaming silver hair. Wearing a gown reminiscent of a Confederate uniform, she greeted Freedom with a hug, pressing her to a massive bosom clad in sturdy gray broadcloth. Her smile was broad and genuine-looking, taking Freedom by surprise.

"Why, yes, I am. . . . But who are you and these others?" Freedom indicated the group with a wave of her hand.

It was comprised of a tall Negress dressed in a plain calico gown, a short, dapper bald-headed man accompanied by a pale woman and two boisterous children—a girl and a boy—and a matched pair of tall, thin white women with pinched features and nervous hands. The two women were almost mirror images of each other, except one was noticeably older, and both wore shabby but elegant gowns that had seen far better days.

"Ah'm Peonie Harkness," the plump silver-haired woman chirped. "An' these are mah frien's in misfortune. . . . Let me introduce 'em all."

The tall Negress turned out to be a freedwoman named Mary Brown, who was Peonie's devoted servant. The rest were people Peonie had met while fleeing Sherman's massacre. The short, dapper baldheaded man bore the distinguished name of Percival Abraham Goff, his wife was Martha, and his children, ages eight and ten, were named Abner and Isabelle. Peonie introduced the tall, thin women as the Butler sisters, Daisy and Hortense.

They had all fled Georgia, having lost homes, crops, livestock, and slaves to the wrath of William T. Sherman. "An utter madman, mah deah," Peonie Harkness said. "Not at all a No'the'ner of yore caliber."

"But why are you here? How did you know I was a Northerner?" Freedom questioned, while Martha Goff darted nervous glances in every direction and warned her children not to fall off the dock into the river. Abner and Isabelle were running up and down, paying no attention to their distraught mother or their father, who was listening intently to the exchange between Peonie and Freedom.

"Why, Captain Carrin'ton invited us to stay. . . . Didn't he send word ahead? We met him in Wilmin'ton, which is positively overrun with refugees. He also sent supplies that he just bought in Nassau and told us we were welcome to visit as long as we liked." Peonie gestured to the crates heaped high on the dock. "He could have sold the food in those boxes for a fortune, but he was mos' con-

309

cerned that we all have enough to eat. 'Pon mah word, that man's a saint!"

Freedom was stunned. Her face must have revealed her amazement, for Peonie Harkness slid her arm around Freedom's shoulder and gently patted her back. "Ah'm jus' sorry we're such a surprise, mah deah. We'll help out in any way we can; the truth is, we're homeless an' destitute. Ah've got all mah money tied up in Confederate war bonds and script, neither of which is worth a hoot nowadays. . . . Mr. Goff and the Butler sisters are in much the same straits, ah fear."

"We won't be stayin' long, howevah," Percival Goff interrupted. "Martha and ah have relatives in Richmond, an' the Butler sisters have kin in Petersburg. One of these days, it'll be safe to go there. We're countin' on Lee to make it safe."

"That's right," Daisy Butler chimed in. "Soon as it is, mah nephew an' his wife will be only too happy to take us under their roof. Ah'm his son's godmother."

"And ah'm godmother to *both* his daughters," Hortense smugly added.

Peonie Harkness flashed her charming smile. "The plantations all along the rivah have kindly opened their doors to friends and kin fleein' that monster, Sherman. . . . Since Captain Carrin'ton doesn't have any kin, he was kind enough to offer his house to us poor strangers."

"Ah understan' that you're the Captain's bookkeeper," Mr. Goff drawled. "It's rathah unusual to meet a woman who's good with figures."

"I also run the plantation, Mr. Goff," Freedom quietly announced. "And as long as you don't speculate about the nature of my relationship with Captain Carrington, you're all most welcome at Cypress Hall."

The Butler sisters gasped audibly, and the Goffs exchanged startled glances. After a moment's pause, Peonie Harkness covered the awkwardness by taking Freedom's arm and strolling unconcernedly toward the buggy. "Why, the captain thinks the world of you, Miss Walker. . . . Whatevah your relationship is, that's your business. We're startin' out as guests at Cypress Hall, but we're all hopin' to become fast friends."

They couldn't all crowd into the buggy at once, so Peonie volunteered herself, Mary, and the Butler sisters to wait until the second trip, while Freedom went ahead with the Goffs and their children. As the buggy bumped and swayed up the cypress-lined drive, the delighted cries of Abner and Isabelle assaulted everyone's ears. "Oh, Mama, lookit the pretty fountain . . . lookit the house!"

Martha Goff burst into tears, and her husband gruffly patted her knee. "There, there, Martha . . . Ah know it reminds you of our place b'fore Sherman burnt it to the ground, but that's ovah and done with. We're lucky to still be alive. You gotta count your blessin's."

"You say you're from Georgia?" Freedom asked, suddenly remembering Omoroh and worrying that these people might recognize him.

"Yes," Martha Goff answered in a little girl voice. "Close to Atlanta . . . It was pure chaos aftah Sherman took the city. We knew it'd be awful, but we nevah dreamed it would be as bad as it was. Them Yankee cutthroats stole everything they could lay hands on, then burnt the rest. They raped and pillaged all ovah the countryside, like beasts

311

gone wild."

"Now, Martha, remember the children," her husband reminded.

"Oh, fuss an' bother! They know as well as you an' ah do what happened — and is still happenin'. Sherman might even come heah. . . . They say when he gets to Savannah, he's gonna turn No'th an' start through South Carolina."

Overhearing, Isabelle erupted in a wail, her big blue eyes round with terror. "Oh, Mama! He won't come this far, will he? They say he eats li'l Southern girls for breakfast."

"Oh, Isabelle, where did you heah such ridiculous nonsense?" Martha exploded.

"Probably from you, deah," Percival said.

"*Me!* Ah never said such a thing. . . . Now, Isabelle, don't you go cryin' again, honey." Martha Goff shot an apologetic glance at Freedom. "She cries at nothin' an' everythin' these days. She cried all the way from Georgia, but then ah guess ah did, too. It's hard not to cry when you've lost everything you've evah had."

"I imagine so," Freedom agreed, appalled that a little girl should have to suffer so.

They drove the rest of the way in silence, except for the muffled sobs of Isabelle, who hid her face in her mother's skirt. The child's sobs cut Freedom to the heart. She spent the rest of the day trying to make the newcomers feel welcome and comfortable at Cypress Hall.

Chapter Twenty-two

In a matter of weeks, it seemed as if the Goffs, the Butler sisters, Peonie Harkness, and Mary Brown had always lived at Cypress Hall. Freedom hadn't realized how lonely she had been until the house was full of people. To her surprise, she found that she enjoyed having so many around; their presence kept her from brooding so much about Ty or working so hard in an effort to forget him. Suddenly, there was someone to talk to and share the burden of her responsibilities.

It was obvious from the very beginning that the Goffs did not approve of the way Freedom — or for that matter, Ty — ran things. But they bent over backward not to criticize and they treated Omoroh, Billy Bob, Mancie, Tillie, and all the other Negroes with studied politeness. Their slaves had all run away when Sherman came and they remembered them fondly, but always as nothing more than slaves — people who had waited upon them hand and foot and had belonged to them the same as their horses, pigs, or chickens. The Butler sisters had had much the same experience; they were two old maids who had been living in their family home, dependent upon the good will of their eldest brother. Ephram Butler had died trying to defend his inheritance, while Daisy and Hortense had escaped into the woods. Now, their youngest brother, an attorney in Petersburg, was awaiting their arrival, as soon as it was safe for them to travel to the besieged area.

Such an odd little group we are, Freedom often thought. None of us really belongs here, so maybe that's why we all try so hard to get along.

Peonie and Mary helped Mancie and Tillie with the cooking and baking, and the Butler sisters cleaned industriously if not always effectively. Percival Goff, or Percy as they came to call him, assumed the task of exercising the horses and riding out into the fields, even though there was nothing to see at this time of year. Martha had her hands full with the children, but even she tried to help. Sewing was her specialty, and she gleefully tackled the cloth Tiger had regularly sent and began making and mending clothing for whoever needed it.

The only disagreement Freedom had with any of them occurred on the day when she invited Abner and Isabelle to join in the daily reading and writing lessons. The chilly November weather had caused her to move the lessons into Omoroh's house, where the workers crowded into the big front room and sat on the pinewood floor with their writing slates in their laps. Abner and Isabelle were excited about attending. Spoiled and impetuous, the Butler children found it difficult to fasten their attention on anything for long periods. This, however, was something new — attending lessons with darkies — and they were eager to show off their superiority.

When she heard where her children were going,

Martha Goff jumped up, spilling a lapful of fabric to the floor. "Ah won't have it!" she cried, confronting Freedom at the front door, where she was waiting for the children to meet her for the walk to Omoroh's house.

"Mah babies can't be mixin' with no colored folk to practice their letters; it ain't propah! Nigras shouldn't even be learnin' to read an' write."

"Why not?" Freedom inquired. "They can learn as well as you and I. Omoroh writes beautifully now, and if he could speak, I've no doubt he'd speak beautifully." Freedom had already established that no one knew Omoroh, so she felt confident in singling him out. "Nothing will happen to the children, Martha. I'll keep a close eye on them."

"No!" Martha cried. "They mustn't go. Ah forbid it."

Behind her, Abner and Isabelle simultaneously started wailing. "Mama, that's not fair! We want to go! We'll be good . . . honest!"

Martha whirled to face them. "It's not a matter of bein' good or not. . . . Ah just don't like the thought of mah two precious babies bein' all alone in a roomful of strange Nigras."

"They *won't* be alone . . . *I*'ll be there," Freedom snapped.

"You will be too busy teachin' to keep an eye on mah babies," Martha protested.

Just then Mary came into the hallway, carrying a shawl flung over one arm. Tall, handsome, intimidating Mary reminded Freedom of Elvira; she was every bit as regal, but not nearly as talkative or bossy. But Mary knew how to get her way, just as Elvira had known. "If it's all right wid you, Miz Goff, ah'll take the chillun an' look aftah 'em.

Ah've a mind to learn to read an' write mahself. Won't none of them niggers say a word to Miss Isabelle or Master Abner if dey's wid me."

Martha Goff's face lit up. To Freedom's astonishment, she exclaimed, "That's the perfect solution! Of course, you can take them, Mary. . . . Now, children, you best mind Mary an' not give her any trouble."

"We won't, Mama," the children chorused.

Freedom almost laughed out loud. Mary was the only one in the house who seemed able to control the two little hellions; when she spoke up, they always quieted and did whatever they were told. Behind Martha's back, Mary winked at Freedom, then held out her hands, and the children rushed to grab hold of them.

"It's time y'all got back to your lessons," Mary scolded. "Ah bet ye've forgotten everythin' y'evah learned."

"No, we didn't, Mary!" Eight-year-old Abner piped up. "Ah can still write mah name an' do mah sums."

"We'll see," said Mary, following Freedom out of the house.

Thanksgiving of 1864 was a more joyous occasion for Freedom than it had been the year before, mainly because she had friends to share it with. But it was still a sad day. Sherman was pushing toward Savannah and would probably take it by Christmas. Mile upon mile of destruction lay in his wake. After Savannah came South Carolina, and her inhabitants were already trembling with fear. Freedom no longer had mixed emotions about it;

she thought Sherman's cruelty was utterly barbaric. It shamed her to think that they were both on the same side.

"But that's war, mah deah," Percy said at dinner. "Ah expect Lee will be no kindah to the folks 'round Washin'ton if he evah makes it that far."

"Then war is an abomination no one should tolerate for any reason!" Freedom said in a shaking voice. "You all know where my sympathies lie. I haven't tried to hide the fact I was born in the North and favor a Northern victory, but I can't condone ruining the land nor raping and killing helpless women and children in order to win. Sherman's gone too far. . . . I wish there were some way to stop him."

"Atrocities have been committed on both sides, deah Freedom," Peonie observed. "But there's still hope for us all. . . . If it's possible for a patriotic No'the'ner like you and die-hard Southe'ners like us to peacefully coexist beneath the same roof at Cypress Hall, then there's hope the two sides may yet resolve their differences."

Freedom smiled gratefully at Peonie; the silver-haired lady always knew what to say to make her feel better. In Peonie, Freedom had found a friend and confidante; the Goffs and the Butlers didn't know her past, but Peonie did, and she also knew of her dilemma with Ty. Her comment seemed to cover that situation as well as the war.

"Mah word, but this was a grand dinnah, Freedom," Hortense announced from across the table. "It's just a cryin' shame that Captain Carrin'ton couldn't have made it home to enjoy it, especially aftah sendin' us all these delicacies."

The meal had included many things Freedom

hadn't enjoyed in a long time: a round of roast beef, real coffee, even a bottle of fine Madeira. . . . She felt guilty consuming such luxuries, but then she felt guilty about everything these days. Nothing was black and white anymore. Two years ago—even one year ago—she never could have imagined sitting at a dinner table with a bunch of Southerners and bitterly criticizing a Northern leader. In those days, she would have defended William T. Sherman to her last breath. She would have thought that since the slaves had suffered so much, it was only fair that their white masters should have to suffer, too.

Now, her thinking had drastically changed. One evil did not justify another. In its own way, the war was every bit as evil as slavery had been. In the name of patriotism, men were killing each other—in some cases, killing those who had once been their friends. So many lives had been lost, so much property destroyed, so many people had suffered and were suffering still. . . . Freedom felt sickened by it. She hated having been a part of it, even if only a small part. At the same time, she wondered if she might have done more and thereby helped to end the whole thing more quickly. . . . Only one thing was certain: There were no easy answers.

She still wanted the North to win, but she wished they'd do it more honorably. She still wanted all the slaves to be freed, but she didn't want them to be abandoned before they were ready to stand on their own. She still wanted . . . Tiger, even if he no longer wanted her. Glancing up from the dinner table, Freedom spied Mary coming through the doorway of the dining room, her handsome face aglow with happiness. Freedom knew the reason for that happiness, and try as she might, she could not help feeling a trifle jealous. Earlier in the day, Omoroh had given Mary a present—a small wooden box with a lovely carved lid that he had made in the carpentry shed especially for her.

Mary was now floating when she walked. The two regal-looking Negroes seemed ideally suited to each other. Despite Omoroh's inability to speak, he had no problems communicating with Mary, at least none such as Freedom experienced with Tiger. Whenever they were in the same room together, their eyes sent silent, heartfelt messages. Freedom had been aware of their mutual attraction from almost the first day Mary had arrived. Oh, why couldn't she and Ty love as easily and tenderly?

Tears gathered in her eyes and she lowered her head, so no one would see them. It would soon be a year since she'd seen or heard from Tiger. If he really loved her, he wouldn't abuse her this way. Whatever hurt she had done to him had been repaid by the enormous hurt he had inflicted upon her—not writing, not visiting, not even inquiring after her health. Nor did he send word of his own well-being or lack of it. In his house, she was just another refugee of the war; he could not have made that plainer if he'd engraved it upon a stone tablet.

Her throat tightened threateningly. As she so often did when she thought of Tiger, she swallowed hard and tried to think of something else. Tomorrow, she decided, she'd send Billy Bob to town for the latest newspapers. One of the shopkeepers in town had begun keeping them for her, though no one had yet guessed that the little bookkeeper out at Cypress Hall was the same young woman who'd once worked at Hattie Draper's Fine Fashion Emporium.

"Dessert, Miss Freedom?" Mary asked, standing at her elbow with a platter of cakes made from ingredients Tiger had sent for the Thanksgiving Day meal.

"No, thank you . . ." Freedom started to say, then changed her mind. She must keep up her spirits and not become moody and withdrawn. The others depended upon her enthusiasm to lift them out of their own occasional bouts with depression. Besides, when so many in the South were hungry this holiday, it was wrong to snub precious food. "Yes, please . . ." she answered instead. "And be sure that all the workers get a piece, too, Mary, will you?"

"Yes, Ma'am. Omoroh already done seed to dat. Soon as ah finish servin' you, ah'm goin' to his house foh a celebration we's gonna have."

"That sounds lovely, Mary," Freedom said sincerely.

"Hmph!" snorted Percy disapprovingly. "It's all right for us white folk to keep traditions, but in times of want, coloreds should know their places and not presume to act like white folks livin' high off the hawg."

"Now, Percy," Freedom remonstrated. "You know we do things differently at Cypress Hall . . . and, really, don't you agree we do them better?"

"Well, ah must admit ah've learned a few things since ah've been heah," Percy conceded. "Still, it's not the best policy to coddle Nigras the way you do."

"I'm only treating them the way I know Ty

Carrington would treat them if he were here."

"Then ah'm gonna have a li'l talk with him when he returns, Miss Walker."

"You do that, Percy. Meanwhile, have another piece of cake. . . . We should all thank the good Lord we have *anything* to eat this day."

The next day Billy Bob left for Wilmington. When he returned two days later, he had a stack of the most recent papers and a letter a stranger had pushed into his hands, saying it was for Freedom. Praying the letter might be from Tiger, Freedom took it with trembling fingers and rushed upstairs to her room where she could open it in private. To her great disappointment, the letter began with a strangely formal address: *To Miss Freedom Walker.*

Her eyes skipped to the bottom of the page; there was no signature, no clue as to who had written it or why. Sitting down on the bed, Freedom began reading.

"It has come to my attention that you are a Northerner, born and bred. I therefore hope you might find it in your heart to undertake a difficult and perilous mission, the purpose of which will benefit the cause of victory for our Beloved Union. More cannot be committed to writing until I know that you do not oppose the idea. If you do not, come to the levee tonight at midnight. I will tell you what must be done. Bring no lantern and tell no one where you are going. When I am certain it is safe I will make myself known."

Freedom stared at the letter in growing consternation. Obviously, it wasn't from Tiger — or was it? Was he testing her, trying to find out if she would betray him a second time? Small beads of perspiration popped out on her brow. She wiped her damp hands on her dark blue skirt—a work dress Martha had made for her—and pondered what she should do. If the letter wasn't from Ty, it had to be from someone who wanted her to carry information, perhaps to the same spot where she had carried it before. The person must be truly desperate to risk contacting her like this; he or she knew nothing about her, except that she was a Northerner. Had Billy Bob mentioned something in town? Or had Stephanie Clairmont spread the rumor?

She supposed it wasn't so surprising that this mystery person had discovered her origins; what *was* surprising was that she *hadn't* been contacted—or even threatened—before this. Billy Bob had told her what had happened to several known Union sympathizers in Wilmington; their homes had mysteriously caught fire and burned. Here at Cypress Hall, such violence seemed far away, but apparently, the plantation wasn't far enough. Someone in Wilmington knew about her.

Holding the letter as if it might erupt into flames at any moment, Freedom rose from the bed and paced the room, wondering what she ought to do. It wasn't fair to be put in this terrible position. No matter what she did, she'd be wrong. No longer was her loyalty to the North a foregone conclusion. Sherman's march to the sea had caused too much suffering for her to want the North to win at any cost . . . and then, there was the matter of Ty. If she betrayed him again, she'd never be able to look him in the eye when he returned. Her face would be stamped with guilt; this time, there'd be no excuses—and surely no forgiveness. He hadn't forgiven her for the last time.

Stuffing the letter beneath her pillow, she decided she wouldn't go. If the North needed a courier or a spy, let them find someone else. But as the day wore on, Freedom performed her chores in a daze, endlessly debating the issue.

"Is somethin' wrong, deah?" Peonie Harkness inquired.

"Wrong? No, nothing's wrong, Peonie. I guess I'm just . . . tired."

"Or heartsick," Peonie observed with a shrewd shake of her silver head. "Ah'm guessin' you are thinkin' about the captain. Ah've seen that look on your pretty face many times."

"What look?" Freedom was surprised, unaware that she had a certain look whenever she was thinking about Tiger.

"You're missin' him, wonderin' if things can evah work out between y'all."

"I don't think they can, Peonie. . . . Despite your kind encouragement, I don't think Tiger Carrington and I stand a chance."

"Maybe not," Peonie sighed. "It is difficult to retain one's optimism when the war news is so bad. Ah was readin' in them newspapers Billy Bob brought back that Lee's army is bein' hemmed into a smaller and smaller circle 'round Richmond and Petersburg. Ah don't know how long he can hold out against Grant. And in the Shenandoah Valley of Northwestern Virginia, General Philip Sheridan, the Union cavalry leader, is doin' the same thing as Sherman, destroyin' everythin' he can."

"Oh, Peonie, when will it all end? I can't go on much longer being torn in two like this! If Sherman comes to North Carolina, I swear I'll take a pitchfork and drive it through his black heart before I let him harm anyone at Cypress Hall."

"There, there, deah . . ." Peonie soothed in the tone of voice she used to calm Isabelle. "Why don't you get to bed early t'night and have a good rest? You will feel bettah in the mornin'. A good rest can work wonders for a tired mind an' body.

"Perhaps, I will, Peonie. Maybe that's all I need. A good night's rest."

Freedom did go to bed early that night, but at eleven o'clock she was wide awake. Quickly, she rose and dressed, determined to at least find out what she was refusing to do. Wrapping herself in a warm black cloak, she crept down the darkened staircase toward the front door. Everyone had gone to bed and the house was silent, steeped in shadows, with only the wind tugging at the shutters outside. If this was indeed a test of her loyalty, Ty had chosen a good night for it. Slipping out the front door, Freedom caught the scent of rain. The chill penetrated her clothing, reminding her of the night last year when she'd engaged in clandestine activities.

It was a long walk to the levee, but she did not want to saddle a horse and ride down the length of the cypress-lined drive. She'd be too visible to whoever was waiting at the other end on the dock beside the river. Darting from tree to tree, she kept herself hidden as much as possible and finally arrived at the levee just as it was starting to drizzle. Scanning the inky blackness, she waited for the author of the letter to come forward and identify himself. No one came. Freedom took shelter beneath the huge trees and anxiously searched the area with her eyes.

Her feet were wet, and her cloak was becoming damp. She felt chilled to the bone. This was foolish, she decided. Five minutes was all she would wait. Suddenly, a tall figure clambered onto the dock from what must have been a small boat tied up beneath it. Freedom suppressed a shiver of fear as a man in black clothing straightened, looked around, then hissed softly, "Miss Walker?"

The voice wasn't Tiger's. Freedom heaved a sigh of mingled relief and disappointment. Then she stepped out from behind the tree. "Over here," she called softly. "Please identify yourself and tell me what this is all about."

Chapter Twenty-three

"I can't reveal my name," the man said, coming toward her. "In a situation like this, I dare not even show my face."

Freedom gasped as she saw that the man wore a black hood and was dressed all in black. In the darkness, only his hands were visible — large, squarish white hands that gleamed when he gestured. "Are you a spy for the Union?" she asked. "Surely, you can tell me that much."

The man chuckled behind his hood. "Yes, I can tell you that much. . . . I'm a spy. I gather what information I can in Wilmington and pass it on to the next checkpoint, so that eventually it reaches General Grant and other influential Union leaders."

"What sort of information?" Freedom demanded, not quite trusting him.

"Oh, anything I think might be of interest. I started out tattling on the blockade-runners, telling who was getting ready to leave and when they might be expected to return. But my information never seemed to arrive in the proper hands in time. Now, I simply pass on what I hear regarding troop movements, and also what I receive from another checkpoint."

"Do you know anyone named Albert?"

There was a slight hesitation. "Yes, I'm afraid I do—or rather, did. He was a courier recruited by my wife. We needed someone to help us, and she convinced him to volunteer. Unfortunately, Albert died about a year ago, after completing his last mission. Someone found his body on the road to Fayetteville and turned it over to General Whiting in Wilmington. Albert had an incriminating letter in his possession at the time, and some inquiries were made about my wife, to whom the letter was addressed. Luckily, nothing further ever came from the incident."

"Then your wife's name is Maeve." Freedom could not keep the contempt from her voice. "And she lied to Albert—lied and disappeared, forgetting all about him."

"She lied, yes, but she didn't forget him. Nor have I. . . . But how do you know about all this? Who told you about Maeve and Albert?"

"Albert did not complete his mission," Freedom informed the man. "I did. Albert was too ill. I found him in our stable, and I carried his papers to the next checkpoint."

"*You* carried them! Then surely, you'll help us again!" the man cried excitedly.

"Don't be too certain of that. Is that what you want me to do . . . carry more papers?"

"Yes . . . We desperately need another courier. I'd do it myself, but I can't risk another unexplainable absence from Wilmington. I shouldn't even be here tonight; lately, I'm being watched, and people are whispering about me behind my back. . . . Even if that weren't true, I need to stay close to home in order to keep an eye on things. The news

327

changes daily, and I never know what important tidbit I might overhear."

"Why can't Maeve be your courier? . . . Or hasn't she returned from Bermuda?"

"Goodness, but you're well-informed. . . . Did Albert tell you that my wife suddenly lost her nerve and realized that what we were doing was extremely dangerous? Overnight, it seemed, she decided to wait out the war in Bermuda."

"I'm not sure he knew all of that. But poor Albert was in love with your wife and hoped to convince her to marry him. She had not, of course, told him she was already married."

"I see. . . . But before you judge her—or me—too harshly, you must realize that as a single woman, Maeve was able to collect all sorts of information she never could have learned as my wife. No one in town knew of our marriage. . . . It has been a terrible strain. Her sudden departure a year ago nearly destroyed our relationship, but I hope that one day we can be together again."

"You've paid a high price for your political beliefs," Freedom observed, remembering that Albert had said Maeve was in love with a Naval officer. Was that why she had fled to Bermuda? Whatever the reason, this man's personal problems were his own; she had more important things to worry about. "What's in the papers you want me to carry this time?"

"Sorry, but I can't tell you. . . . For your own safety, it's better you don't know. All I want is for you to agree to carry them."

"Do you have them with you now?"

"I did bring them, but they will remain hidden until I know you can be trusted."

"Trusted? I've already told you I was the one responsible for transporting them the last time."

"Ah, but you still haven't said you'll take them this time. . . . Will you?"

Freedom fell silent. The moment of decision had arrived, and she still hadn't made up her mind. "I don't really want to do this," she murmured. "I despise this war so much that I'm no longer sure which side I'm on."

"Come now, you can't be serious. You're a Northerner, the same as I. What will become of the Union if each state is permitted to do whatever it pleases, including withdrawing? And what about slavery? Do you want that boil on the body of humanity to continue forever?"

"Don't preach to me, sir! You can't say anything I haven't already said or thought. I've lain awake nights debating these issues, but nothing seems as clear to me now as it once did."

"My dear, I understand what you're suffering. . . . I, too, have friends and family in the South. If any of them ever discover what I've been doing, they'll shoot or hang me. . . . I never asked for this war, but now that I've got it, I'll fight until I die to assure a Northern victory."

"Against others who are doing the same to assure a Southern one," Freedom sighed, remembering Ty. "All right . . . give me the papers. Somehow, I'll deliver them."

"Wonderful! But you must do it as soon as possible. By tomorrow night, at the very latest . . . The papers must reach the checkpoint before the morning of the day after."

"I assume it's the same place as before—that hollow tree beside the river near the Owen place."

329

"Yes . . . If you've been there, you shouldn't have any trouble finding it. Wait here . . . I'll get you the packet."

Freedom paced up and down beneath the trees until the man returned, packet in hand. Holding it out to her, he said, " 'Don't worry; you're doing the right thing. Nothing is more important than victory."

Freedom grimaced. "Nothing? I wonder. . . ."

"You must be strong, Miss Walker. In wartime, there's no room for tenderness. Harden your heart and do your duty. Don't think too much about it; thinking only weakens your resolve."

"Do all good spies believe that, sir?"

He laughed. "If they don't, they should! Good luck, Miss Walker." He turned and started walking down the dock toward the river and his waiting boat.

"Wait a minute!" she cried. "Will I see or hear from you again?"

He paused and glanced back at her through the slits in his hood. "Miss Walker, if that packet reaches the right person, there won't be a need for you and I to meet again."

"Oh . . ."

"Courage, Miss Walker . . . courage and strength. Don't think, just do it."

"I — I'll try."

"Trying isn't good enough, Miss Walker. . . . Succeed and this war will soon be over."

Back in her room, Freedom undressed and climbed into bed, but her thoughts were not on sleeping. She had stuffed the packet beneath the mattress, and the bed now seemed lumpy and uncomfortable. She could never sleep, knowing the packet was there, brimming with information that might cause more death and suffering . . . no, *victory,* she reminded herself. The hooded spy had said that her mission might result in victory for the North, and wasn't that exactly what she wanted?

Yes! . . . *No.* Not if more soldiers would be killed, more women and children raped, more homes burnt down, more animals stolen, more land laid waste, more crops destroyed . . . *She mustn't think about it.* . . . Oh, yes, she *must.* Too much was at stake. Blind obedience could open the door for William T. Sherman to come marching into Cypress Hall, burning and looting, never once stopping to ask himself if his cruelty was justified.

Where, really, did her duty lie? She had never asked for her present responsibilities, but now that she had them, she couldn't turn her back on them. With Tiger gone, there was no one except her to look after his ancestral home, all his workers, and the refugees he had sent to shelter here. Her first loyalty was to the people who depended upon her for their survival, and the packet of information beneath her mattress possessed the capability of destroying them all.

Getting out of bed, Freedom lit a gas jet, retrieved the packet, and perched on the end of the bed, weighing the missive in her hand. It wasn't heavy, but whatever it contained was certainly weighty. The spy had told her not to open it. By opening the packet and reading its contents, she'd be crossing an invisible line, switching her allegiance from the North to the South, whose code of ethics disgusted her and whose future was growing more uncertain with each day. She'd also be protecting the man she loved and guarding all that he held most dear.

Was there really any choice? No, the choice had been made long ago, the first time she reveled in Ty Carrington's kisses. Hands shaking, she broke open the seal and withdrew three sheets of parchment paper covered with a fine, flowing script. At first, examining the top sheet, she did not understand what she was seeing. Rereading the caption, it all came clear. *Fort Fisher's Defenses,* the caption said, and below was a list of guns, armaments, weaponry, and manpower. The second sheet was a map of the fort, detailing the position of the largest guns, the batteries, the telegraph office, the hospital bombproof, and other places of importance.

The third was an equally detailed map of the North Carolina shoreline and Cape Fear River entrances, showing the locations of Fort Fisher and the smaller Fort Caswell, identifying shoals and wrecks, describing currents, and giving directions for approaching Fort Fisher from sea or land.

For a long time, Freedom stared at the documents, recognizing their importance and realizing what they meant. If the last port open to the blockaders could be shut down, as Charleston had been, then armaments and supplies could no longer reach Lee's troops. Food and medicine couldn't reach civilians either, resulting in tremendous deprivation and suffering, which would culminate in the complete collapse of the Confederacy. The maps and the description of Fort Fisher, Wilmington's main defense, were obviously meant to provide the Union Army and Navy with the advantage they had so long sought: the hammer that would finally break the South.

So it has come down to me, Freedom thought. I must decide the outcome of this war.

Now that she knew for certain what she had only suspected, she felt less fear. A kind of numbness set in. She thought of the protective guns of Fort Fisher that had rescued so many blockade runners from the patrolling Federalists. They had saved her and Tiger, and the soldiers from the fort had then saved the *Sea Whisper.* She thought of the starving inhabitants of so many of the South's cities, now dependent upon the blockade-runners to keep them alive. She thought of Peonie and Mary, Omoroh, Tillie, and Billy Bob . . . of everyone at Cypress Hall.

When Fort Fisher fell, Wilmington would fall, and with it, the plantations up and down the river, not just those where slaves still worked the land, but all the rest. Would the invading Unionists feed and shelter the very people they had come to free? Freedom doubted it. She remembered reading that one of the Northern leaders, General Benjamin "The Beast" Butler, had decreed that runaway slaves were legitimate prizes of war because they were "contraband." That same general, the dictator of New Orleans, was sometimes also called "Spoons" Butler, for having stolen fine old Southern silver-ware during his occupation.

I'm a coward, Freedom condemned herself. I'm a traitor to everything in which I've ever believed, but—God help me!—I *cannot* deliver these documents as I said I would.

She clutched them to her breast. Whether she delivered the papers or not, Fort Fisher was still in danger. Did the commander there realize it? Was he prepared for a massive joint attack by land and sea? Freedom lowered the papers and scanned them a second time. She turned them over. On the last sheet, there was a single cryptic message: *"Support December invasion. Christmas Eve ideal. Fort staffing will be at minimum. Security lax. Proceed as planned."*

There it was in black and white. The war had finally arrived in Wilmington. On Christmas Eve, barely a month away, an attack would be mounted on Fort Fisher. Now what? It wasn't enough to merely destroy the papers, to refuse to deliver them to the checkpoint; the officers of the fort must be warned.

Freedom wanted to weep — or to scream. This was too much to ask! Must she sacrifice everything? If she went to the fort to warn them, would they even believe her? As soon as she opened her mouth, they'd know she was a Northerner and become suspicious. What if they locked her up, discounting everything she told them!

Freedom flopped back on the bed and stared up at the ceiling. She didn't have to decide until morning. Maybe there was another solution, one she hadn't thought of yet. She'd think some more. She'd rack her brains. She'd consider the dilemma from every possible angle. . . . There had to be a way out . . . *had* to be. She was a Northern abolitionist. How on earth could she live with herself after deliberately aiding the Southern cause?

Upon completing his tour of Fort Fisher's battlements, Tiger followed Colonel William Lamb into his main headquarters. They passed through an outer room and did not stop until they reached the inner chamber, where the colonel kept a table and several chairs for private conferences with his officers. Motioning for Ty to sit down, Colonel Lamb headed for a cupboard, opened it, and withdrew a bottle of brandy.

"Join me, Captain Carrin'ton?" he said, holding up the bottle and two glasses. "It's the last of mah private store, but ah'll gladly share it with you since you are the one who supplied it in the first place."

Tiger nodded. "I could use something to warm my insides. . . . The wind off the sea feels unusually cold this afternoon. Guess I haven't yet adjusted to leaving Nassau."

"You need a coat like mine," Colonel Lamb said, pouring the brandy. When he had finished, he handed a glass to Ty, then shrugged out of the heavy gray coat under discussion. "So tell me what you think, Ty. . . . It's been a long time since you've seen Fort Fisher up close."

Tiger sipped his brandy before answering. "You've accomplished wonders here in the past four years, Colonel. I understand now why everyone's calling it the Gibraltar of the South."

The pleasant-faced colonel beamed. He was a congenial man, with a wife and two small children whom he adored and kept close by in a cottage set back in the sand dunes. Tiger liked and respected him, all the more so now that he'd seen what the man had done with little more than earth and sand.

"Ah admit ah'm proud as a fightin' cock over what we've accomplished heah," the colonel said. "You know what I used as a model? The Malakoff Tower, a Crimean War fortification in Sevastopol, Russia. In those days, they really knew how to build a fort to withstand anything the enemy might throw at it."

"Those twelve-foot-high batteries on the sea face should be able to withstand heavy shelling," Ty agreed.

"And don't forget the two batteries on the south," the colonel reminded him. "The largest is sixty feet high and the other forty-five. If we're attacked by land, ah've got us well protected there, too."

"Fifteen mounds, isn't it?" Ty asked.

"Yes, sir . . . each one thirty-two feet high with interior rooms serving as bombproofs or powder magazines, and all of them connected by an underground passageway. When we started, we only had two dozen cannon. Now we've got twice that many, all safe and secure behind a nine-foot-high palisade fence. Took more than five hundred Nigras—both slave and free—to build this place. Our sea defense extends a full mile, and on the land side, one third of a mile. Ah believe we're the largest—and certainly, the most important—earthwork fortification in the South."

"I won't argue with you, Colonel. . . . If the rumors we've been hearing are true, you'll soon have a chance to test the fort's strengths."

The colonel grinned. "Ah only know what ah read in those Northern newspapers you smuggle past the blockade, Ty. Never could understand why they print what they're gonna do ahead of time"

"Freedom of the press," Ty snorted. "Abe Lincoln can't wipe his nose without some journalist printing a story about it. . . . When the Union does get around to attacking the fort, it'll probably make front-page headlines the week before."

Colonel Lamb tossed back his brandy, then cleared his throat. "Don't understand why they haven't been after us sooner, Ty. We're the most important defense in the entire Confederacy, but attention mostly focuses on the cat and mouse game around Richmond and Petersburg, or on Sherman laying waste to Georgia on his way to Savannah."

Ty finished his brandy in a single gulp. "Don't know why either, Colonel. Well, we won't have to worry about an attack until spring. With gale season almost upon us, I don't look for the Federalists to do much more than harass us as usual until the weather clears."

"Will you be spendin' the holidays at home then, Ty?"

"Me?" Tiger toyed with his glass. "I doubt it. Probably spend them in Nassau. The *Sea Whisper's* being loaded with cotton right now. In a day or two, I'll be shipping out again."

Colonel Lamb shook his head. "Mah word, you're a glutton for punishment. What you do is no less impressive or important than what ah've done," he said, refilling his glass and raising it in a toast to Ty. "By God, you work harder for the Confederacy than anyone. Men like you have kept us goin'."

"The Confederacy is my life," Ty said quietly.

"But what about Cypress Hall? Who's been runnin' things there? You haven't married, have you?"

"No, marriage isn't for me . . . and probably never will be."

Ty gloomily studied his empty glass. After nearly a year, the pain was still as sharp as a knife thrust to his belly. He wondered if he'd ever get over it. The mere thought of Freedom Walker lacerated his insides; he ached with missing her, dreamed of her constantly, helplessly relived and reexamined every moment they had spent together. He couldn't stop torturing himself with vivid imaginings of what might have been and could never be—Freedom Walker becoming his wife, bearing his children, lying in his arms night after night for the rest of their lives.

"You're too young to be so embittered," the colonel scolded. "Whoever's broken your heart should be ashamed of herself. She'll be hard put to find a man your like again. . . . Hand me your glass. We might as well kill this bottle and be done with it."

"No more for me, thanks," Tiger said, rising. "I ought to be going. Thanks for the tour."

"Thanks for the newspapers, the foodstuffs, and the winter coats. Ah don't know what we'd do without 'em. . . . Ah just wish you could get your hands on some gunpowder and ammunition. If the Federalists do attack in the spring, we're gonna need more than ah have on hand right now."

"I'll see what I can do," Ty promised. "Though you'd be better off to ask one of the runners who have more contacts in that area than I do."

"Ah *have* asked them! They say they can't deliver. What they do get all goes directly to Lee so he can keep fightin' Grant."

"But if Fort Fisher isn't properly defended, Lee won't get anymore, either."

"You know that, and ah know it, and the North undoubtedly knows it, too, but no one else seems to. Mah guns are useless without powder. Ah also need more men to man 'em."

"I'll try and get more powder," Ty repeated. The way things now stood with Freedom, he no longer

338

had a reason for refusing to ship arms and ammunition.

As he moved toward the door, it suddenly burst open, and a uniformed youth raced into the room, awkwardly saluted, then spilled out his news. " 'Scuse me, Colonel! A young lady is here to see you, sir. Says she cain't talk to nobody but you, sir."

Colonel Lamb cocked an eyebrow at Tiger. "A young lady . . . to see me? Wonder what she wants . . . Look out there, Ty, and tell me if she's pretty. If she is, ah'll see her. If not, she'll have to make do with a junior officer."

Ty glanced past the guard's shoulder. Outside in the anteroom stood a familiar figure, nervously straightening her skirt and distractedly studying her shoes. She was wearing a plain, drab gown, almost the same color as her shiny brown hair, but without its vibrant highlights. Her eyes, Tiger knew, were also brown, giving her the appearance of a pert brown mouse.

He drew in a wrenching breath that seared his lungs. "She's beautiful," he murmured, stepping back from her line of vision so she wouldn't see him if she happened to look his way. "She's absolutely beautiful."

The colonel brightened. "In that case, ah'd better invite her in and find out what she wants."

"Wait," Tiger said. "Couldn't you go out to her instead?"

Colonel Lamb gave him a puzzled look. "Ah could, but why? Is something wrong, Ty? You know this gal?"

"You could say we've met before. Actually, we're well acquainted, but as for *knowing* her—knowing

339

what's going on inside her lovely head — your guess is as good as mine."

"Why don't you wait here?" the colonel suggested. "I'll leave the door ajar so you can listen to what she has to say. Somethin' tells me this ain't a social call, and ah'd appreciate hearin' your reactions."

"I don't normally eavesdrop," Ty said. "But in this case, I'll make an exception. My curiosity is greatly aroused."

And that isn't all that's aroused, he thought. Being this close to Freedom, breathing the same air, made him break out into a sweat, when moments before he'd been chilled. He reached for the brandy and poured himself the glass he had earlier refused. It was ridiculous to feel this way over a woman he hadn't seen — had been avoiding — for almost a year. For months he'd been telling himself that all he had to do to forget her was stay away. But the minute she reappeared, he fell apart.

Brandy sloshed over the rim of the glass as he lifted it to his lips. Damn her, anyway! What was Freedom doing here? What did she want?

Chapter Twenty-four

While she waited to see the colonel, Freedom slipped the string of her brown fringed reticule off her arm and clutched the bag tightly in her damp hands. The papers were inside, and within moments, she'd be handing them over to Colonel Lamb. This was her last chance to change her mind. She wasn't even certain she'd brought them to the right place or the right man. Tiger had always talked about General Whiting in Wilmington; maybe she should have taken the papers to him or to whoever else was now in command. Lately, the Wilmington newspaper had made frequent mention of General Braxton Bragg, a new arrival, as if he were more important than Whiting. Bragg was, she recalled, a hero of sorts.

It certainly would have been easier to go to Wilmington, but also more dangerous. Someone might recognize her from Hattie Draper's and remember her Northern background, or she might run into the spy who had given her the papers. Worse yet, she might encounter Tiger. Worrying about these things, she had decided to board the little steamer that still ran up and down the river, bypass Wilmington altogether, and go directly to the fort overlooking New Inlet. What she had seen of it so far had greatly impressed her. Fort Fisher looked impregnable, so maybe this trip was all for naught. No matter what the Federalists did, the fort could probably withstand it.

Freedom was surprised when a man in uniform came through the door to the next room, smiled at her, and introduced himself as Colonel Lamb. "What can ah do for you, Miss?" he politely inquired.

"Colonel Lamb, I'm pleased to meet you," she responded, flustered, glancing uneasily around the room. "I thought we'd be meeting in private. . . . What I have to say cannot be shared with others."

Instead of inviting her into the room behind him, the colonel made a gesture of dismissal to the young soldier who had announced her arrival. "Leave us for a few moments, lad."

As the boy departed, looking disappointed, the colonel nodded to a chair in front of the desk. "Won't you sit down? It's a long walk from the landin' by the river. . . . You must be tired."

"No," Freedom denied. "I'm not tired. And I'm far too nervous to sit down."

"But you don't mind if ah do," the colonel said pleasantly, perching on the edge of the desk rather than sitting in the chair behind it. "Now, then, to whom do ah have the honor of speakin'?"

"Who I am is not important, sir. I only came here to bring you this." Freedom plunged her hand into her reticule, withdrew the papers, and handed them to the startled colonel.

He looked them over in silence, his eyes widening at first, then his brows dipping downward in a deep frown. "Where did these maps an' descriptions come from, li'l lady? This is privileged information. Civilians have no access to it."

"Look on the back of the third sheet, Colonel. Then I'll tell you where I got it."

He did so, and his eyes nearly popped out of his head. Rising, he regarded her with a stunned, disbelieving expression. "Ah presume you know what you've given me."

"I know precisely, Colonel. That's why I'm here. A man I've never met before approached me with these papers and asked me to carry them to a place near Fayetteville. . . . I said I would. But after he left, I opened and read them. When I saw what they were, I couldn't do it. So I came here instead."

"Where is this man?" the colonel demanded. "Ah'll have him arrested at once."

"I don't know, sir. Nor would I recognize him. He wore a hood when I spoke to him, and it was a dark night. He only risked contacting me in the first place because he'd heard that I was a Northerner, and he hoped to find me amenable to helping the Northern cause."

"Mah God, Miss, you have done a fine service to the Confederacy!" The colonel whirled toward the half-open door behind him. "Ty!" he shouted. "Did you heah this? Come see what this li'l lady has brought."

As Tiger stepped into the room, Freedom's heart took a downward plunge. "Ty!" she gasped.

His face was carved in granite. His eyes burned holes in her. "Whatever this devious little mouse has brought you, Colonel, don't believe a word of it. . . . There's no one in the entire Confederacy — indeed, in the entire world — more loyal to the Northern cause than she is."

"Ty . . . no! This isn't what you think. Every word I said is the truth. A man came to me one night and said he was a spy. He wore a black hood. . . . He gave me these papers, then told me to take them where I took them the last time." She bit her lower lip, not having meant to mention *that*.

"You have carried such papers before?" the colonel interrupted. "What kind of papers? What was in them?"

"I haven't the least idea!" Freedom wailed. "And I only did it *once*."

"She *claims*. . . . " Tiger snarled. "Colonel, I know this woman well. I've offered her my name, my fortune, my love . . . my future. . . . But her loyalty to the North has stood between us, robbing us of all chance of happiness. I've sheltered her in my house, hoping I could change her mind. I've protected and guarded her, when I should have handed her over as a spy. . . . That's what she is, what she's always been. This last is the worst . . . for her to come here with some phony papers, spouting lies that will probably get us all killed. . . ."

"I'm not trying to kill you; I'm trying to save your lives!"

Tiger snorted. His eyes flashed contempt. "Do you honestly expect me to believe that? How can I, when you stab me in the back every damn time I turn around?"

"Ty, please! Be reasonable. Listen to me. . . . When I saw what these papers were, I felt I had to tell someone. That's why I came—to *warn* the colonel, not to lead him into a trap."

But Tiger wouldn't listen, wouldn't believe. He was still angry, suspicious, and resentful. A year had passed, but he hadn't forgiven her. He stood in the center of the room, glaring at her, clenching and unclenching his fists, ready to wring her neck. It was more than she could bear.

"If you don't want to believe me, then don't. You're right, Ty! I still want the North to win. I want the slaves to be freed. I want Sherman to make all you arrogant Southerners crawl on your bellies and lick his boots. . . . I don't know why I ever came here. It was a mistake, a horrible, stupid mistake that I'll regret for the rest of my life!"

As Ty lunged for her, eyes gleaming with malice, the colonel stepped between them. Ty almost knocked him down, then lurched backward, muttering an apology. "Sorry, Colonel, but you see what she is. An abolitionist spy . . . a rabid little Northern patriot who'll stop at nothing to see us ground into dust . . . I was fool enough to fall in love with her, to think I could change her. I thought all she needed was the opportunity to see for herself that most Southerners aren't the depraved monsters the North has portrayed them as. But she hasn't changed; she'll *never* change. Once a Yank, always a Yank."

"Why was *I* the one who had to change," Freedom shouted, "when *you're* the one who's so bloody wrong?" She stepped back, fighting tears and a choking bitterness. "Your world is doomed, gentlemen. It's a world built on greed, outmoded feudalism, and the despicable evil of slavery. It has to fall, and it will. . . . I underestimated what it would take to topple it. I mourned the suffering and loss of life. I actually felt sorry for you and, in my pity, hoped to avert more bloodshed. Well, tear up those papers and forget I ever came here, Colo-

345

nel. If you have to bleed to learn your lesson, then go ahead and bleed. Apparently, I'm as doomed as you are, because I'll have to stand here and watch."

Her words filled the room with raw hurt and defiance. Freedom could not call them back, nor did she feel inclined to do so. She had only said what she felt . . . what Tiger had forced her to say. She didn't care any longer; the colonel could hang her right now if he pleased.

"Ah think," he finally said, clearing his throat. "that we'll have to confine you to the fort, Miss . . . ah . . ."

"Walker," Tiger supplied. "Freedom Walker."

"Miss Walker . . . At the very least, ah must hold you for questionin'."

"Question all you want. I have nothing more to say."

"Don't worry, Colonel. I can tell you all about her." Tiger's angry eyes never left her face. "Miss Walker has a long history of breaking the law, beginning with the Fugitive Slave Law."

Freedom held his gaze fearlessly, daring him to mention Omoroh. "As long as you're going to tell him everything," she goaded, "don't forget to mention how you aided and abetted me in helping a certain runaway slave escape the slave catchers."

He glowered even harder. "Fool that I am, I'd have continued aiding and abetting you — but not anymore, Mouse. This time, you've gone too damn far."

"Ah don't know, Ty . . . These documents look genu-ine to me," Colonel Lamb said after Freedom had been taken away and locked in a one-room cell

346

in one of the mounds. "An' they do corroborate the rumors we been hearin'. The piece in that New York paper that urged an attack on us has apparently won some followers."

"I'm not advising you to ignore the papers; I'm just telling you she can't be trusted," Ty flatly stated. "The whole thing could be a monumental trap. If General Bragg diverts troops from Wilmington to strengthen the fort, then the city itself will be left vulnerable to attack from the north or the south. Grant could be planning to swoop down on the city from Virginia and Sherman's already headed for Savannah, after which there's nothing to stop him from coming here."

"Ah'm aware of all that, but ah can't afford to sit and do nothin', Ty. Besides bein' short on powder, the fort is seriously undermanned. As good as our defenses are, ah haven't enough men to withstand a combined attack from sea and land. Ah *must* request that Bragg divert his troops."

"You think he will? He won't want to weaken the city's defenses, either."

"All ah can do is try."

"Why don't you wait and see if this is some kind of hoax first? You can always telegraph for more men the moment an attack seems imminent."

Colonel Lamb sighed and tilted back his chair, then propped his feet on the table. "That's very risky. . . . They mightn't get here in time. Or else Bragg might figure on sendin' some of his troops to help Lee hold Richmond and Petersburg. . . . Things are so bad up north, ah wouldn't be surprised if Lee orders every man who can still hold a gun to join him there. If ah don't send for troops immediately, ah might not get 'em in time."

"Guess I won't go to Nassau after all," Tiger decided. "The least I can do is stay here and help. . . . Besides, I want to check on Cypress Hall."

"Don't worry about Cypress Hall, Ty. Ah can send someone out there to see how things are goin'. . . . Couldn't you leave an' still be back in time for Christmas? Ah need that gunpowder worse than ever now."

"I suppose if I left immediately I could get back here in time, but of course, I couldn't honor the quarantine."

"We'll waive the quarantine. Too cold now for an outbreak of yellah fevah anyway . . . Get as much powder an' ammunition as you can."

"All right," Tiger said. "My ship should be loaded by late tonight, so I'll leave before first light in the morning."

When Tiger steamed out of New Inlet the following morning, a cold wind was blowing out of the north, and the seas were gray and choppy. He could just make out the outlines of the Federal cruisers studding the eastern horizon. They were riding at anchor, tugging on their chains, and did not appear to notice him. He steamed past without incident and made excellent time on the journey to Nassau, his progress favored by the northern winds and north-running seas.

In cloudy, rainy Nassau, however, he could find no one willing to unload his cotton until the weather cleared; the freethinking workers on the island saw rain as an excuse to loaf. For three full days it rained, causing Tiger to lose the advantage of his quick passage. He spent the time trying to purchase the items Colonel Lamb needed at Fort Fisher, and herein, he encountered further delays.

Never having cultivated the right contacts for dealing in the sale of arms and ammunition, Tiger couldn't readily purchase what he wanted. What was available was already sold, and those who had contracted to buy it did not intend to run the blockade again until after the holidays. Burning with frustration, Ty blamed Freedom. Because of her, he hadn't wooed these merchants. Because of her, he wouldn't make it back in time. Because of her, he was more miserable than he had ever been in his life. The tortures of the past year without her paled in comparison to now; all his worst fears and suspicions had come true. Freedom had chosen victory for the North over him.

He didn't believe her good intentions for a single moment. She was lying and he knew it . . . knew it from the moment he had heard her voice in the outer room of Colonel Lamb's headquarters. Knew it from the look on her face as he stepped into the room and confronted her. If she hadn't been able to resist the temptation to spy for the North the first time, how could she have resisted it a year later, a year during which he hadn't seen her, held her, made passionate love to her, or exerted his own tenuous hold upon her reluctant affections?

He had left that first time with no promise or assurances that he would ever return, unless it was in victory. Apparently, she had decided to make certain he suffered defeat, by whatever devious means possible. Lying awake in the rain and flower-scented darkness of his third night in port, Tiger felt sick with frustration and ready to explode. He'd been

349

celibate—faithful to Freedom—for over a year. And for what? Because he still hoped that somehow, once this was over, they'd find their way back to each other. . . . What utter nonsense!

Swinging his long legs off the bed, he tugged into his clothes and boots, determined to ease his suffering in the only way he knew how—by losing himself in the physical charms of another female. Someone had to pay for the contempt he felt for Freedom and all the members of her deceitful, lying sex! He couldn't recall a single woman of his acquaintance whom he could trust or safely cherish without getting hurt in the bargain. Every last one had let him down—his mother, Stephanie, and now, Freedom.

At least, with whores, a man knew where he stood. Tiger promised himself to find the lustiest whore in Nassau, then to spend the rest of the night relieving his frustrations between her thighs. He finally found his choice in a waterfront grogshop where the dim light made all the girls look young and pretty. Tiger seized upon a buxom redhead who was the furthest possible thing from Freedom's slender beauty. The redhead was spilling out of the bodice of her gown and her hips swayed provocatively with each step, advertising her blowsy femininity.

Tiger picked her because she looked and smelled like what she was. She had none of Freedom's enticing shyness or innocence, none of that rare, soft beauty that almost escaped a man at first glance but grew upon him without his knowing it, until he was completely besotted. No, this girl sported herself with a knowing smile, revealing her cleavage every chance she got and drenching Tiger in a musky perfume that reeked of invitation.

She wasn't the least coy about agreeing to accompany him back to the hotel. Once there, she stripped with enthusiasm and jumped into bed before he got off his breeches. "Gor, but yer a handsome bloke," she purred in a coarse cockney accent. "If yer as good as ya look, maybe I'll agree to waive me usual fee."

Tiger doused the light, climbed into bed beside her, and took her in his arms. He began kissing and caressing her. She responded with hearty delight. He filled his hands with her abundant bosom, willing himself to forget the delicate curves his hands still itched to caress. She stuck her tongue in his mouth, squirmed against him, and clasped him intimately. . . . Nothing happened. He couldn't make himself react.

She drew back in astonishment. "What is it, lovey? 'Ere now, don't I please ya?"

"Of course, you do. . . ." he lied. "You're exactly what I want."

"Then let's git on with it."

For several more moments, they fumbled awkwardly in the dark. Then Tiger rolled away in disgust. "I'm sorry. . . . I don't know what's wrong; this has never happened to me before."

She sat up beside him in the rumpled bedcovers. "It's another woman, ain't it?" she shrewdly demanded.

"I thought you could make me forget her, but it seems you can't."

"Lovey, I can do anything 'cept make a man forget another bitch, if he's bound an' determined to remember her."

"I'm bound and determined to forget her."

"Then let's 'ave another go at it."

"No," said Tiger. "I know it won't work. Sorry, but I'll pay you anyhow."

"Poor bloke . . ." the woman sympathized. She named her fee. "That's what I usually get, but I'll take half since nothin' happened."

Tiger rose, relit the light, and got the full amount for her, including an ample tip.

"Gor!" the woman exclaimed, pleased with his generosity. "Whoever she is, ya better marry the gal, unless she's already married. . . ."

"She's not married. She just . . . doesn't want me and never will."

"A bleedin' fool, then . . . Well, I best be goin'." The woman hopped out of bed and dressed, then blew a kiss at Tiger and departed.

The next day, Ty found a blockade-runner willing to transfer his cargo of ammunition to the *Sea Whisper*—for an unheard-of price. Tiger agreed to pay it, but only because he was growing frantic. If he didn't leave soon, he'd never make it back in time for Christmas. It took several days to load the *Sea Whisper*, but before Tiger could set sail, another spate of bad weather set in, with gale-force winds and high seas.

"We can't set out in this weather, Cap'n," Pete Gambol said, glancing worriedly at the leaden sky.

"If it doesn't clear soon, we'll have to," Tiger told his worried helmsman and the rest of his assembled crew.

"We'd be fools to risk this," Stoker Harris argued. "Mah engines can't fight seas as high as these."

"He's right, Cap'n," Matt Berringer agreed. "If it don't clear, we'll have to give it up and spend Christmas in Nassau."

"We aren't spending it here," Tiger snapped. "I'll give this weather two days to blow itself out, but if it doesn't, we're leaving anyway. . . . That will give us an extra day if we need it at sea, and bring us into port at Wilmington on the twenty-second of December."

The morning of December twenty-third found Tiger still out at sea fighting huge swells, the aftermath of the northeaster that had plagued them all the way from Nassau. It was frigid and gloomy, and a biting wind caught the tops of the waves and blew them in slanting sheets of spray across the bridge. Toward afternoon, the wind died down and darkness descended, a darkness so impenetrable that Ty felt as if he could reach out and grab great handfuls of the stuff.

Despite the crew's complaints and warnings, the *Sea Whisper* breasted the long rollers like a well-trained thoroughbred jumping hurdles at a fox hunt. Tiger still thought he might make it in time, providing he could slip past the blockade with the same ease he'd managed it going in the opposite direction. He and Pete stood on the port wing of the bridge, straining their eyes to see through the murky gloom.

Suddenly, the lookout called down, "Cap'n, I see lights! A whole string of 'em off the starboard bow."

Ty scanned the horizon and saw what the lookout had spotted. "Good God! What do you make of that, Pete?"

Pete was momentarily too stunned to speak. "It—it *can't* be the Federal squadron; there's too many vessels, and the blockaders *never* show their lights, no more'n we do."

353

"I don't know who else it can be, Pete. . . . Looks to me like the whole damn Union Navy has decided to join the blockaders."

"But what does it mean?" Pete cried, aghast.

Tiger hadn't told his men all of his reasons for being so anxious to get home before Christmas; he had only said that Colonel Lamb was growing short of supplies, and let the men assume that he himself wanted to spend the holidays at Cypress Hall. Freedom's claim of a pending attack had not been mentioned, though he was never free of the thought of her or it, night or day.

"It means the North is finally getting around to shutting down our last open port — or trying to," Tiger quietly explained. *It also means Freedom isn't lying.*

His heart did a sudden handspring in his chest. Maybe she really *had* come to the fort to warn Colonel Lamb. Maybe everything she claimed was true. Maybe he had misjudged her, wrongly accused her, treated her capitulation as a hostile act, a cruel betrayal, when in fact, it was an act of love!

Oh, God, he thought. Let me get there in time to help . . . and let Freedom forgive me when I say I'm sorry.

Chapter Twenty-five

I'll never forgive Ty Carrington—never, never, Freedom promised herself as she followed the soldier assigned to guard her. The gray-uniformed young man, lantern in hand, led her across the wind-lashed sand dunes toward a small cottage nestled in a stand of whipping beach grass.

When he got there, he knocked on the door and called out, "Mrs. Lamb? Sorry to bother you, Ma'am, but ah've brought the prisoner—ah mean, the guest."

The door opened a crack, and a small, vivacious woman peeked out, then threw the door wide open. "Oh, come in, chile. It's so very cold t'night. . . . Come in, come in. . . . Thank you for bringin' her, Private. You can tell mah husband ah'll take good care of her."

"Yes, Ma'am," the young man said, stepping aside to permit Freedom to enter.

Teeth chattering, Freedom passed through the doorway and eyed the cozy, warm cottage appreciatively. Comfortably furnished, it boasted a large fireplace where two big logs were merrily burning to ward off the sharp night air. There were curtains at the windows and gleaming wood furniture, the most impressive of which was a long table, surrounded by eight chairs with needle-pointed seat cushions and backs. A modest effort had been made to decorate for the holidays. A tiny pine tree was hung with gaily colored bits of ribbon, and beneath it were several plainly wrapped packages and a bowl of shiny red apples. It was apparent that the colonel entertained here in this charming cottage and tried to maintain his family in some semblance of normalcy, despite the privations of war.

Mrs. Lamb shut the door and turned to her. "Now relax, mah dear. . . . There's no one here but the two of us. The children have already gone to bed, an' ah'm dyin' to hear all about you an' how you ever got branded as a spy."

Freedom was taken aback by the pert woman's candor. "You know that I'm suspected of being a spy?"

"Of course . . . an' exonerated, now that the Union fleet's been spotted steamin' towards us, jus' like you said."

"So that's why I was brought here," Freedom mused aloud. "I thought they'd never let me leave that cold, dank little room in the battery. . . . Are these *your* clothes I'm wearing?"

Freedom glanced down at the dark green gown, one of several that had been made available to her in her captivity. It had been fashioned for a shorter, plumper woman, someone about the size of Mrs. Lamb.

"Yes, dear . . . but ah see now that mah gowns aren't a good fit. Ah'm so sorry about that. Assumin' we survive this comin' siege, you can probably go home to Cypress Hall soon an' get your own clothes."

356

"I'm *never* going back to Cypress Hall," Freedom bitterly asserted. "It's Tiger Carrington's fault that my motives were ever doubted. He convinced your husband that I was up to no good . . . told him I was lying and he shouldn't believe a word I said."

"Now, now, come sit down an' take tea with me. . . ." Mrs. Lamb moved gracefully toward two chairs and a small table drawn up in front of the cheery fire. "With that No'the'n accent, you must expect to arouse suspicion when you come bearin' terrible tidin's and knowin' things you ought not to be knowin'."

Freedom hesitated before sitting down. "Mrs. Lamb . . . please don't think me rude, for I do appreciate your hospitality, but I really shouldn't be taking tea with you as if nothing has happened."

"Why ever not, chile? As ah said, you have been exonerated. T'morrow's Christmas Eve, and we're likely goin' to spend it dodgin' cannonballs an' the like. So sure is mah husband of attack, that in the mornin' the children an' ah have to leave and take shelter on the other side of the river. . . . Thanks to you, he's been able to make a few preparations that'll enable us to better withstand the trial before us."

"Mrs. Lamb, I have to be honest with you. When I first came here, my intentions were good. I really wanted to warn your husband, so he could strengthen the fort and keep men from being killed, so he could send you and the children away to safety. . . . But during these past few weeks while I've had nothing to do but stare at the walls of a bare little room, I've done plenty of thinking. My loyalty to the North is now stronger than ever. Not that I want anyone to die or suffer! But I only came in the first place because I let my emotions cloud my common sense. You see I love—*loved*— Ty Carrington, and I wanted to—to—"

"Protect what he loves? Win his approval?" Mrs. Lamb graciously inquired. "Mah dear, you don't have to apologize or explain things to me. Ah'm the wife of a colonel, an' ah understand these things. . . . Ah don't always approve of what's bein' done in the military, but ah *do* try an' support mah man. We don't always see eye to eye, but ah know he's tryin' to do the right thing. Ah expect it's the same for you. It went against your own conscience, but you was still tryin' to support an' protect your man. Isn't that so?"

"Yes, Mrs. Lamb, that's it exactly. In my heart, I'm a Northerner through and through. Ty knows that, which is why he didn't believe me and thought the worst. . . . Now you must think the worst of me, too. You can't possibly want to take tea with a woman who hopes your enemies prove victorious."

Mrs. Lamb regarded her silently for a moment. "When you put it that way, ah suppose ah don't. . . . But when ah consider that you're a brave, courageous, lovin' woman who's only tryin' to do what *she* thinks is right, ah'd be honored to take tea with you."

"You would?" Freedom could scarcely believe her ears.

"Sit down, an' let's talk woman things, mah dear, not politics. Truth to tell, ah get more than enough politics when mah dear colonel walks through that door. . . . Let's jus' pretend we're two lonely females starved for the company of another female, shall we? . . . Now then, tell me about Cypress

358

Hall. . . . How many rooms does it have? How many flower gardens?"

So Freedom told her, and in the telling, she found herself missing the place as if it were indeed her home. But it wasn't. It was Tiger's. And she no longer had the tiniest flicker of hope that it would ever be his *and* hers, a lovely, sheltered haven like this cottage where they could live, love, and raise their children. If it hadn't been over between them before, it was certainly over now.

Ty found not a single Federal cruiser guarding the entrance to the Cape Fear River. It was almost eerie. All the hounds had joined the rendezvous of lights bobbing approximately twenty-five miles east of Fort Fisher. By telescope, he tried to count the number of ships. There were more than forty, and he was almost certain that the big Union ironclads were there—the *Ironsides, Monadnock, Canonicus,* and *Mahopac.* This fleet must be the largest, most well-equipped the world had yet seen.

As he steamed toward New Inlet, he passed another vessel with its lights out, probably a runner like himself, going slowly, awed by the display of warships bearing down on the fort. Abandoning caution in his haste to get there, Ty poured on the steam and was soon tying up at the landing below the fort. Once there, he debarked and lost no time in contacting Colonel Lamb at his headquarters. Bursting in upon him, he cried, "Sorry to interrupt, Colonel, but have you seen the ships?"

Colonel Lamb detached himself from a conference with two of his officers and came toward Ty with hands outstretched. "Ah could hardly miss them, Ty. . . . Lord, am ah glad to see you. Did you bring back what we need?"

"My crew has already started unloading. . . . It's not as much powder and shot as I'd hoped for, but it's better than nothing. I passed another ship on the way in; maybe she's got some aboard, too."

"Yes, but maybe what's in her hold is meant to blow *us* up, instead of the other way aroun'."

"What do you mean?" Ty asked.

"Looky here," the colonel said. "This clippin' from the *Philadelphia Press* arrived a short time ago, forwarded by one of our own couriers workin' behind enemy lines."

Ty plucked the newspaper from the colonel's fingers and quickly read it. It said that the Federal armada had set sail for Wilmington on December 13, and that the Union plan of attack included the explosion of a ship so crammed with powder that the resultant concussion would completely destroy the fort.

"You think that's what that other ship might be . . . a powder ship?"

"It's possible, though the idea seems mighty farfetched. . . . Did you spot any other runners out there t'night?"

"No, but inasmuch as it's almost Christmas Eve and the weather's been miserable, I'm not surprised. In Nassau, I had a hard time getting anyone to unload or reload my ship."

The colonel consulted a pocket watch. "It *is* Christmas Eve, son, not almost. . . . Them bastards are gonna try an' blow us up on the eve of the good Lord's birthday."

"What can I do, Colonel? I'd like to speak with Miss Walker, if I may, and then my crew and I are yours to command."

"Oh, we're all ready for the attack, Captain, as ready as we'll ever be. Bragg hasn't sent any troops yet, but the men ah've got are standin' by. Your crew can help mah soldiers get that powder safely to the magazines. . . . Go an' see Miss Walker if you like. She's visitin' with mah wife in our love nest by the sea. Don't know if we'll see any action t'night, but the cottage is far enough away from the fort to be relatively safe, an' t'morrow, ah'm sendin' the womenfolk an' children across the river 'til this is over."

"Thanks, Colonel . . . Wish me luck with Miss Walker. I misjudged her terribly, and now I've got to apologize. That armada out there is proof of it; she really did try to warn us."

"She didn't jus' *try,* son. She succeeded. We may not have believed her story, but we acted as if we did. . . . 'Course, we coulda got the same news jus' by readin' the *Philadelphia Press.* . . . You need any help findin' the cottage?"

"No, Colonel . . . If you remember, I had dinner there once with you and your lovely wife."

"That's right . . . ah did forget. Well, good luck, son. 'Ah've a feelin' you're gonna need it."

Mrs. Lamb had gone to bed, and Freedom was curled up in a big wooden rocker in front of the dying fire, dozing, when a knock came at the door. She blinked awake, listening, wondering if she'd been dreaming. . . . No, there it was again. Quickly, Freedom rose and wrapped the blanket Mrs. Lamb had given her more tightly about her shoulders. She rushed to the door, hoping to open

361

it before the noise awoke Mrs. Lamb or the children. She and the colonel's wife had talked long and late, and the pert little woman had appeared weary when she finally retired after failing to convince Freedom to share the bed with her, since the colonel hadn't yet come home.

"No, really, the rocker will be fine," Freedom had insisted. "Besides, your husband may arrive at any moment, and he'll be looking forward to his own bed."

Maybe the colonel had come, though why he didn't just enter instead of knocking puzzled Freedom. Mrs. Lamb hadn't barred the door; she felt safe in the little cottage. No one would *dare* molest the wife of Colonel Lamb, she had assured Freedom.

Yanking open the door, Freedom was startled to find Tiger standing in the cold outside. For a full minute, she gaped at him, her pulse racing as she registered his wind-tossed blond hair, sturdy winter clothing, and bemused expression.

"Aren't you going to ask me in, Mouse?"

"No!" she hissed, coming to life all at once. "Mrs. Lamb and the children are sleeping. This is no time for a social call."

"Then you come out. . . . I'm not here for a social call, and you damned well know it."

"I don't want to come out. I don't want to speak to you. Go away and leave me alone."

His response was to thrust his foot inside the door before she could close it on him, then grasp her wrist and drag her outside. "I came to apologize, and whether you want to or not, you're going to listen."

"I'm not!" she cried, struggling, losing her

blanket in the process.

"You are!"

He shut the door, seized the blanket, and threw it around her too fast for her to argue. When she continued to resist, he picked her up bodily and tossed her over one massive shoulder.

"Where do you think you're taking me?" she demanded, outraged.

"Somewhere we can talk. So you might as well quit fighting me. . . . This conversation is long overdue."

"There's nothing you can say to me, Ty Carrington," she gasped as her midsection jounced against his shoulder. "I won't believe it, anyway. You never believe me; why should I believe you?"

"Words aren't the only way to get through to a stubborn female. . . . If I have to, I'll beat you to make you listen."

"More threats, Ty? More growls and flashing of claws? No wonder they call you Tiger. . . . You think you can get what you want by being violent and nasty."

"I don't think it, I *know* it." Ty whacked her smartly on the bottom. "Don't rile me, Mouse. I'm warning you, don't rile me."

He carried her a long way across the dunes. The wind whipped her hair and clothing. Blowing sand stung her face and eyes. She was acutely uncomfortable slung over his shoulder and feared she might become violently ill. When finally he set her down, she swayed against him, unable to stand for the pins and needles pricking her legs.

"This is far enough," he growled. "From here, I can keep an eye on that flotilla of gunboats while I talk to you."

Inhaling deeply, she glanced around and saw that he had carried her up a small dune overlooking the ocean. The surf was pounding on the shore, and in the distance, a long string of lights resembled a row of street lamps. Filling her lungs with the cold, invigorating sea air, she expelled it slowly. Anger vibrated in every nerve ending, frosting her tone with sarcasm.

"Yes, there they are, Ty, just as I predicted. The Union fleet in all its glory has come to shut down the port of Wilmington, severing the last supply line to the Confederate Army."

"You needn't sound so pleased about it. . . . After all, you *did* try and warn us. That's why I want to apologize . . . for not believing you. Not trusting you enough."

"Your apology comes too late, Ty." Freedom turned her back on him and gazed out at the ominous lights. "I only came to warn the colonel because I suffered a momentary madness, caused no doubt by an excess of love. . . . But I've quite recovered now and am able to see that this attack is undoubtedly for the best. I hope the fort is taken quickly, with small loss of life, but I *do* hope it's taken."

Tiger came up behind her and slipped his arms around her waist beneath the blanket. "You're bitter and angry, Mouse, with good reason, but don't say things you don't really mean."

She tried to jerk free of his grasp. "You know nothing of what I mean! You have no idea what I'm thinking."

He held her tightly about the waist, his lips close to her ear. "No, but I can imagine. You went against everything you believe in order to come here and warn the colonel. Instead of understanding and appreciating that, I behaved abominably, accusing you of setting us up for some further disaster. Forgive me, Mouse. I don't deserve a brave, loyal, courageous woman like you, but I'm asking you to give me a second chance. . . . Say you forgive me, and I'll spend the rest of my life making it up to you."

His warm breath tickled her ear. His hands gripping her waist seared through her gown. The hardness of his body pressing against her back and legs conjured images of sweet, never-to-be-forgotten intimacies, breathless moments of hard conquering soft, flesh yielding to flesh, mouths opening to each other. . . . Lord, how she still wanted him, even after all that had happened!

"Don't think you can seduce me with polite apologies and compliments, Ty. We're no good for each other. . . . I'm not at all what you just said — brave, loyal, or courageous. I may have been those things *before* we met, but afterwards, I became weak, spineless, and a traitor to my own beliefs."

"Sweetheart, don't even think such things, let alone say them. Loving me doesn't make you a traitor to your own beliefs. . . . You can still believe slavery is wrong — hell, *I* think it's wrong! If the Confederacy survives, I'll do everything in my power to free the slaves. I'll make speeches. I'll appeal to my friends and neighbors. I'll court politicians. . . ."

"It won't do any good, Ty. You won't be successful . . . no more successful than you and I will ever be trying to make this relationship work."

"It *can* work, Mouse." He turned her around to face him. "If we believe in it, we can make it work."

She shook her head violently. "No! You're only deluding yourself. I've had lots of time to think, Ty. I've thought and thought. . . ."

"Then think about *this*."

Dragging her to him, he clamped his mouth down upon hers. He bent her backward with the force of his kiss, assaulting her senses with the taste and feel of him. One hard hand cupped her breast. An impudent thumb flicked across her nipple. Starved for such sensations, her body clamored for more. Winding her arms about his neck, she kissed him back. It was madness to let him do this to her . . . madness to respond. But she couldn't help herself. For one last time, she wanted his mouth, his lips, his arms, his body pressed to hers.

In the weeks of captivity she had spent at the fort, she had dreamed of him holding her like this, kissing her with hungry abandon . . . had dreamed and despaired that she'd ever experience his kisses again. Their lives could never mesh. It was impossible. She must find a way to end it . . . must flee him *and* the South. But not now. Not yet. First, she'd love him, one last time.

They clung together, kissing and touching, unable to get close enough to satisfy their yearning for each other. Ty stopped kissing her just long enough to spread out the fallen blanket, then he dragged her down on top of it and covered her with his body. It was easy to ignore the cold, the wind, the fine grit blowing over both of them. Freedom felt only the primal, savage urge to mate, to become one with Ty, to join their bodies in a fierce declaration of possession.

She and Ty pulled up or tugged down clothing as

needed, but otherwise paid them scant attention. Their urgency was too great. Freedom slid her hands beneath Ty's shirt, seeking the warmth of his hard-muscled chest. He burrowed beneath layers of fabric to explore her curves and stroke her into mindlessness. When he finally entered her, she cried out, and the wind whipped the sound from her mouth. She strained to meet each frantic thrust. A fire burned in her loins; his thrusts simultaneously fueled the blaze and quenched it.

She wept in joy—a joy tinged with grief. "Ty . . . Tiger . . ." was all she could say.

"You're mine, Mouse," he growled in her ear. "I'll never again let you go."

"But the war—" she began.

"—is far away," he said. "Far, far away."

Holding back the final ecstasy, he started kissing her again, this time slowly, savoring each and every one. He pulled down the bodice of her gown, caressed her breasts, and lavished kisses in the valley between them. He began to thrust with long, slow strokes that drove her to a frenzy. She arched her back and squeezed him between her thighs. She drew him into her, wanting more of him, all that he had to give. With a deep groan, he gave it. Her name exploded from his lips, then he repeated it softly in a whispered sigh.

Waves of pleasure pounded over her, receding only when an enormous concussion shook the ground beneath. Her eyes flew open. Ty rose up on his elbows. Another concussion followed. Then another and another. The sky erupted in a sheet of flame. Ty tore away from her. She sat up, yanking down her skirt to cover her nakedness; Ty tugged on his trousers.

In the blackness of the ocean, a fire burned, illuminating the skeletal outline of a ship. There was another explosion, greater than what had gone before. The ship blew apart. Great sections of deck planking hurtled into the air and spun into the sea like pinwheels of fire. Barrels and kegs soared in all directions. The ship burned in a pillar of fire and shooting sparks. A cloud of smoke hung over it like a pall.

Freedom went to stand beside Tiger. "Ty, what is it? Did the fort's cannons destroy that ship? Or did her engines explode?"

"You mean, you don't know about it? It's the Union powder ship. According to the Northern newspapers, it's laden with one hundred and fifty tons of explosives. Your Yankee friends are trying to blow up the fort, but they set it off too soon—thank God." He turned to look at her, his face lit by the eerie, reddish glow. "Tell me, Mouse. Does it bother you they weren't successful? If the fort had blown up, this war would soon be over."

His eyes compelled the truth from her. She couldn't lie, not even to hold onto him. He had asked an honest question; she would answer honestly. "Yes," she whispered. "Yes, I'm sorry they weren't successful. I'm sorry they didn't end it all tonight."

Chapter Twenty-six

The attack on Fort Fisher commenced at eleven-thirty the following morning. The Union Navy's big ironclads moved in as close as they could get and initiated a steady rain of shells. Along with the colonel's wife and children, Freedom was sent across the river to safety at dawn, so Tiger did not have to worry about her being in the line of fire. But he did worry about her state of mind: How could she love him so passionately one moment and declare herself still on the opposite side the next?

His own feelings made hardly any more sense. How could he still love a woman who was hoping he and everyone else at the fort would be defeated, possibly even killed? After Freedom's shocking admission, they hadn't had much to say to each other. He had escorted her back to the cottage in silence, then went to the fort to await further developments. After unloading the powder bought in Nassau, he and his men had spent the rest of the night hauling dirt to strengthen the roofs of the magazines in which the powder was stored.

Now, Ty was hunkered down in a battery, attempting to monitor the siege through a spyglass.

Two underground magazines had already been hit and exploded, and some of the outbuildings had caught fire, but all in all, the fort appeared in good shape. Colonel Lamb was conserving the precious ammunition supply, not wanting to waste any while the enemy was still so far off. On Ty's advice, several of the fort's guns had been trained on the old-fashioned wooden frigates among the Federal fleet, and every time a round shot hit them, splinters flew in all directions and fire broke out.

Lacking enough power to destroy the ironclads, the fort's gunners could do no more than harass the fleet and defend the beach so that no landings could be made. Ty had spotted a steamer trying to unload soldiers north of the fort, and by concentrating cannon fire there, Colonel Lamb had forced the soldiers to return to the ship and sail farther north. Thus far, the colonel's careful planning and the excellent design of the fort were proving equal to the Union Navy's best efforts to overpower it, but Ty feared it was only a matter of time. Eventually, the fort's powder supply would be depleted, and then Union soldiers could easily swarm over the batteries and mounds to take the place.

He'd have to return to Nassau as soon as possible—*if* he could manage to get out. While the attack continued, there was no chance, but once it ceased, assuming the invaders were repelled, he'd make the run and hope to God he got through the blockade alive and was able to purchase more ammunition. About two o'clock in the afternoon, the Federal fire worsened. The Rebels hunkered down behind their earthworks, but even so, the relentless

370

hits maimed and mutilated many young men. Occasionally, a spherical shell struck the fort's defenses, nearly spent, then exploded with its base toward the gunners, causing the bottom end of the shell to fall among the soldiers, wounding them with fragments.

Ty saw a young man decapitated by a round shot and another blown to bits while running across the open space between two batteries. All afternoon, the bombardment continued, the enormous detonations deafening. Ty got his fill of blood, dust, and sweat, and he half-wished Freedom was there to witness the destruction being meted out by the Yankees. If he got the chance, he'd go after her and bring her back to the fort to help nurse the poor boys she had so callously forgotten in her desire for a Northern victory.

Toward sunset, one of the Brooke rifles in Ty's battery burst like a thunderclap. The explosion split the huge gun horizontally through its trunnions and sliced it perpendicularly at its chase. Half the breech blew back over the heads of the gun crew, while heavy iron bands around the breech sprang apart and thrashed viciously among the terrified men. Two of the crew were killed outright, and the rest were badly injured. Ty suffered a minor shoulder wound but had no time to see to it, while other men lay moaning in shock and pain.

Worried about additional mishaps, he sent a man to advise Colonel Lamb of the damage and to warn the captain of the fort's remaining Brooke to order a reduction in the charge of powder. Such a reduction would decrease the range of the gun but help prevent another explosion. The colonel then went a step further; he ordered the rigging of an extra lanyard and had the gun crew lie prone in a shallow ditch whenever the piece was fired. Darkness fell on a scene from hell—smoke, blackened faces, and suffering men crying for help. Ty himself desperately craved a sip of cool water.

During the night, he snatched what little sleep he could. Sporadic firing continued, preventing anyone from really resting. Early the next morning, Christmas Day, the Federal men-of-war resumed the bombardment and again initiated landing operations north of the fort. Watching the landing through his spyglass, Ty estimated that at least three thousand blue-jacketed infantrymen were advancing toward the palisade of sharpened logs. On the parapet high above, the Confederates waited with cocked muskets.

Surprisingly, the Union troops halted just out of musket range and reconnoitered. The rest of the day, there were only small skirmishes and exchanges of fire between sharpshooters. Ty spotted the Union General Weitzel, making his own observations about six hundred yards away. Then, as sunset approached, the Federal troops turned their backs on the fort and began marching toward the boats drawn up on the beach. Without even attempting to take the fort, the Unionists reembarked and withdrew.

The ironclads fired throughout the night, but Yankee enthusiasm was strangely lacking. Early the next morning, the menacing-looking warships steamed out of sight. Ty was at a loss to explain the peculiar actions of the Union Army and Navy. Had they pressed the attack, they surely would have won, for the fort did not have enough men or ammunition to resist much longer. The tired Rebels celebrated, but Ty could muster no sense of victory. He knew the Federalists would be back, and the next time, they'd be better organized, better equipped, and better prepared to exploit the fort's vulnerabilities. Soldiers had landed, studied the shore conditions, reconnoitered the fort, and were now aware of what they *should* have done to take it.

With a heavy heart, he made plans to bring Freedom and the colonel's wife back across the river to aid the wounded, after which he himself planned to leave for Nassau.

Returning from the beautiful plantation of Colonel Lamb's friends, the Ortons, to the scars of recent battle was an uncomfortable ordeal for Freedom. Ty did not say two words to her the entire journey, but accusation was in his eyes as he shepherded her and Mrs. Lamb and the children from the wharf to the fort.

"Ah declare, there's so much destruction!" Mrs. Lamb mourned. "But ah'm certainly happy to see that the place is still standin'. Mah husband knew what he was doin' when he built this fort, didn't he, Captain Carrin'ton?" she proudly inquired.

"He did indeed, Ma'am," Ty politely responded.

Freedom felt him watching her the whole time as they entered the palisade, passed through the ruined areas, and approached the makeshift hospital where the wounded were awaiting them.

"Ah want to take the children home first, Freedom, then ah must find someone to look after 'em," Mrs. Lamb said. "Would you mind gettin' started without me?"

Freedom nodded assent. "I don't know much about nursing men afflicted with war wounds, but I'll do anything I'm told, Mrs. Lamb."

"The fort surgeon will advise you what to do. Don't worry. It won't be anything terribly distressin'. We'll help feed the men who can't manage it themselves, an' we'll write letters for 'em, and jus' do the comfortin' things a woman already knows how to do."

"I see," Freedom said, lowering her eyes. She was finding it most difficult to endure Ty's violet-eyed scrutiny, or to glance through the doorway at the young men with the awful wounds and injuries. Not that she was squeamish, but Ty kept looking at her as if those injuries were all her fault. In a way, they were. This was the result of her wanting the North to win. In order for either side to win, men had to bleed, suffer, and die.

"What's wrong, Mouse?" Ty muttered as Mrs. Lamb led her wide-eyed little ones away. "You should be happy. This is what you wanted, isn't it? The South on its knees. Well, we're almost crippled beyond recovery. The next attack on the fort will be worse than this one."

"Stop it!" Freedom gritted, marching resolutely into the hospital. "I *never* wanted this." She gestured angrily to the men on pallets lining the earthen walls of the bombproof shelter, dropping her voice to a soft hiss so she wouldn't be overheard. "These injured soldiers are *your* fault as much as mine. . . . It should be just as hard for you to look at them as it is for me."

Ty responded in an equally restrained tone. "If it's so distressing, why don't you go back to

Cypress Hall? No one will blame you. You can say it's your delicate stomach. . . . I'd rather you weren't in or near the fort, anyway."

"The last place I'll ever set foot again is Cypress Hall," Freedom coldly informed him. "You don't want me to go back there, anyway. . . . I just wish there were somewhere else I could go, somewhere far away from here."

Ty studied her silently for a moment. "I'm leaving for Nassau shortly. You could come with me and stay there until all this is over."

"What would I do in Nassau?"

"What will you do here?" Ty countered. "Except tear yourself apart trying to balance your divided loyalties."

"Leave my loyalties out of this! You've got your own loyalties to worry about."

"Mine don't cause me nearly the worry and anguish that yours cause you, Mouse. . . . Come with me to Nassau. When I was there last time, I saw a sign in a shop window: Milliner wanted. Didn't you used to trim hats? I'm sure you could find employment. I'll give you the wages I owe you, so you'll have plenty to live on with or without a job. You'll have to stay at the hotel, of course, and be very careful to avoid the town riff-raff. I'll get you a pistol to keep with you at all times. You can consider it part of your wages."

"You don't owe me anything, Ty. I won't take your money or your pistol."

"Why? Do you think everything I touch is tainted? You probably do."

"Please stop! . . . I—I won't go with you because I can't trust myself—or you—to be alone together on your ship again. Though I admit that the idea of Nassau right now is most appealing."

Freedom thought of how difficult the last few days had been with Mrs. Lamb, her children, and the inhabitants of the Orton plantation. All anyone had talked about was the siege on the fort and their hope for victory against the North. The Ortons especially had been most critical of "No'the'n greed, cruelty, and aggression." Freedom had had to bite her tongue to keep from defending the much-maligned Abraham Lincoln and to avoid pointing out the weaknesses and failures of Jefferson Davis. She wished she *could* escape to Nassau, where at least she wouldn't have to witness the collapse of the Confederacy or its ultimate victory, neither of which she had any desire to see.

"You wouldn't be alone with me, Mouse," Ty quietly disputed. "My cabin will be yours, and I'll bunk with Pete. Don't worry. . . . You'll be perfectly safe; I've discovered I don't enjoy making love to a woman who's secretly wishing me dead."

"I *don't* wish you dead! How can you say such a dreadful thing? . . . Oh, let's not discuss it anymore. We can't even talk without breaking into an argument."

Tiger's eyes were hard and bleak. "Whose fault is that, Mouse?"

"No one's fault, certainly not yours. You've never made any pretense about what you believe. If anything, the fault is mine. I let you think I had changed. I even half convinced myself I had changed. . . ." Trembling, she looked away from him. "All right, I'll go to Nassau with you, so long as you promise to keep your distance. When are you leaving? I must make my excuses to Mrs. Lamb."

"In a day or two . . . I'll let you know. I'm glad you decided to go, Mouse. It's better than staying here and hating yourself and me for being on different sides."

The journey to Nassau proved a disaster. For three days, Freedom kept to Ty's cabin, afraid he might barge in at any moment and take her in his arms, destroying all her good intentions and melting her resolve to end their relationship once and for all. When he didn't come—when, in fact, he avoided her even at mealtimes—she was devastated and wept silently in her cabin. . . . One week later, she was trimming hats in a respectable millinery shop in Nassau and living at the Royal Victoria, where Ty had insisted upon paying for her room for as long as she stayed on the island. However, she intended to move into the cramped, shuttered room above the hat shop as soon as he left town to go back to Wilmington. As far as she was concerned, he couldn't leave soon enough. Maybe then she could finally forget him and find peace of mind. As it was now, she couldn't keep from running down to the harbor each morning before the shop opened to make sure the *Sea Whisper* was still in port. One day soon it would be gone, and with it, the man she couldn't seem to stop loving, no matter how she tried.

Sick at heart, Freedom devoured every newspaper she could find. The war news was terrible. . . . Rather, it was *wonderful*. The South was headed for sure defeat. Sherman had taken Savannah on December 20, then turned north and invaded South Carolina, just as everyone had feared. The

377

Union cavalryman, Philip Sheridan, astride his famous horse, Winchester, was slowly riding toward a rendezvous with Grant, while Grant himself harassed Richmond and Petersburg. Meanwhile, Lee was struggling to survive the winter, his barefoot troops battling hunger, disease, and despair.

One did not have to be a soldier—or even a man—to guess at the North's strategy: Cut off the South's supply lines, surround and defeat its Army, and starve its inhabitants into submission. Only men like Ty had kept the Rebels going this long; without the supplies he had been risking his life to get through the blockade, the South would have been forced to surrender months ago.

Despite her efforts to think the worst of him, Freedom deeply admired Ty. Loyal, dedicated, and self-sacrificing when it came to his beloved Confederacy, he was also kindhearted, generous, hardworking, and had a strong sense of justice and right and wrong. By comparison, she was weak, vacillating, unable to support her man *or* her political beliefs with strong, decisive action. . . . Instead, she hid in sunny, carefree Nassau, living the good life at the Royal Victoria and engaging in the most useless and frivolous of occupations—trimming hats.

Her self-respect plunged so low that she wondered why anyone had bothered to hire her, and then, quite unexpectedly, she found out. Mrs. Hargreaves, the English lady who owned the shop, let it slip near the beginning of her second full week of employment. "You're certainly a fortunate girl to have caught the eye of so handsome and gallant a gentleman as Captain Ty Carrington. As quiet and mousy as you are, I can't help wondering what he sees in you, Miss Walker."

Freedom's hands hovered over the straw bonnet awaiting the application of a lavender ribbon. "How do you know of Captain Carrington, Mrs. Hargreaves? He hasn't been here inquiring after me, has he?"

Freedom's heart skipped a beat, as she allowed herself to hope. Ty had pointed out the shop to her on her first day in town, but she had made all the arrangements for employment, contacting Mrs. Hargreaves and demonstrating her skills. As far as she knew, Ty had never set foot in the shop. But if he hadn't, how did Mrs. Hargreaves know about him?

"Why, he sent you to me, girl. . . . Said I shouldn't mention it at our first interview, but if I would hire you, he'd see to it that my business doubled. Well, it has, and then some. He bought twenty bonnets from me himself, and lately, several gentlemen from the hotel have come here on his recommendation to purchase bonnets for lady friends."

"Those twenty bonnets are the large order we've been struggling to fill?" Freedom gasped. "The one we've been working on day and night?"

"Yes, your dear captain said my bonnets would be most welcome in Wilmington, North Carolina, where the ladies have been deprived of fashionable attire for quite some time. . . . I sent them to the docks this morning . . . just in time, for the captain has scheduled his departure for tonight. I understand he's made all his purchases now, and everything except my bonnets has already been loaded."

Freedom unintentionally dropped the lavender

ribbon on the floor but didn't bother to pick it up. "Mrs. Hargreaves, you must excuse me, but I have personal business I must attend to at once."

"Personal business! Why, you can't quit in the middle of the afternoon. The shop is still open. . . ."

"I *must!*" Freedom cried, seized with such an urgency she couldn't contain it. Ty was leaving; maybe he'd already left.

"I absolutely forbid it!" Mrs. Hargreaves exclaimed. "I pay you a full day's wages . . . more than the job is actually worth. In exchange, I expect a full day's work."

"Is that why my wages are so generous . . . because Ty Carrington is helping to pay them?"

Mrs. Hargreaves flushed. "That's none of your business, Miss Walker. I should never have mentioned that I even knew the captain."

"Mrs. Hargreaves, if you don't give me permission to leave, I'll just have to quit altogether. And if I do, your success may be very short-lived. . . . I'll tell Ty Carrington about this conversation, and he'll pass the word that no one should buys hats from you at all."

"You *wouldn't!*"

"Oh, yes, I would. . . . All I want is the rest of the afternoon off, Mrs. Hargreaves. I have emergency business that can't wait until later, when the shop finally closes."

By then, Freedom thought, Ty will be gone—gone without ever knowing that I really do love him, that I wish him well, that I hope he doesn't get killed and his home isn't destroyed. . . . Oh, God, we *do* care about the same people and places—Omoroh, Cypress Hall, the refugees,

Colonel Lamb and his family, the soldiers at the fort. I *can't* let him go back to more bloodshed and the certainty of defeat, without knowing of my love, my support . . . my sympathy and understanding. . . .

Without another word to Mrs. Hargreaves, Freedom flew from the shop and went running down Bay Street, headed for the harbor, Ty's ship, and Ty himself.

Chapter Twenty-seven

Tiger was standing on deck giving orders to get under way when he saw a small lighter steaming toward the *Sea Whisper* as fast as it could go. People on deck were waving and urging him to wait. One was the captain of the vessel, identifiable by his battered captain's cap, and the other was a woman— Freedom.

For precisely ten seconds, Ty wrestled with the temptation to ignore her and go about his business as if he hadn't seen her, and in the next ten seconds, he was racing to the railing to give the captain a hand bringing the lighter alongside. He tossed mooring lines and a rope ladder over the rail, and within minutes, Freedom was clambering aboard.

"Oh, Ty! I'm so glad I caught you. . . . I was afraid you would leave before I got here." Freedom was rosy and windblown, her hair streaming about her shoulders, her brown eyes glistening with a liquid warmth.

"What is it? What's wrong?" he warily inquired, remembering that he couldn't have this girl, ought not to love her, ought not to let his heart pound every time he saw her.

She gazed up at him, her face so radiant and beautiful it took his breath away. "Nothing's wrong. . . . It's just that I'm going back with you. I made up my mind on the way out here."

Conscious of Matt and Pete listening intently in the background, along with the captain and deckhands of the lighter, Ty chose his words carefully. "I'm afraid that's impossible, Mouse. . . . You know why I'm going back and what my cargo is. It's safer if you stay here. I insist you remain here."

A teasing grin lit her dark eyes. "I understand you have twenty hats for the ladies of Wilmington in your cargo, among other things. I would personally like to present one to Mrs. Lamb."

Frowning, Ty wondered what she was up to now. "What are you doing here, Freedom?" he bluntly demanded. "You wanted to leave the South, and I got you out. I wasn't planning on ever seeing you again. This is probably my last run."

Freedom stepped toward him and gently laid a hand on his arm. "I've changed my mind, Ty," she whispered. "All I care about is back in Wilmington — or will be very soon. I can't turn my back on my home and the people I love. Everything is clear to me now: Whatever happens, I want to be with you, sharing the same dangers you're facing, enduring whatever you must endure. . . ."

Ty couldn't believe what he was hearing. One part of him wanted to leap and shout for joy, but the other part hung back, fearing betrayal and disappointment. "What will you do when the shells start falling . . . cheer every time they make a hit?"

He couldn't have hurt her more if he'd slapped her across the face. Her mouth trembled; tears clung to her long, brown lashes. "I suppose I deserve that, Ty. . . . It's taken me a long time to — to come to grips with this thing. To figure out how I should feel, what I should do . . . I finally decided that my love for you is bigger than I am, bigger than you, bigger even than this war. It won't let go of me; it won't let go of you. . . . All I care about is being with you, in victory or defeat, no matter which side wins."

A cheer erupted from the onlookers. Pete's voice rang out jubilantly behind Ty. "Well, Cap'n, what are you waitin' for? Kiss the lady an' welcome her aboard!"

But Ty didn't feel like kissing Freedom. He didn't feel like welcoming her, though he'd fantasized this scene a hundred times. It wasn't that he doubted her sincerity; love shone in her eyes and illuminated her delicate features. She bloomed with it, radiated it, sent it forth in pulsating waves. But he doubted it would last. A perfect, sweet rose couldn't last through the winter; neither could her resolution withstand the icy trauma that lay ahead. Once back in the Confederacy, when she again heard the slurs against the North and witnessed the South's bitterness and hatred, she'd reconsider. . . . And he couldn't bear to keep losing her, over and over again.

"What will you do if I refuse to allow you to stay aboard?"

She answered with a fleeting smile. "I stowed away once. I'm sure I could do it again. If not on the *Sea Whisper,* then on some other runner bound for Wilmington . . ." Her voice dropped to a whisper. "Give me a chance, Ty. This time, I won't disappoint you."

Her reassurances only served to recall the last time they'd made love on the beach, after which she'd told him that she wished the fort had been blown up. He didn't think he could forget—or forgive—that.

"I wish I had your sudden certainty that you won't change your mind again," he growled. "But I don't

. . . and you really ought to stay in Nassau. Here, you're safe. Back home, anything can happen and probably will."

She moved closer, so close he could smell the lemon-scented soap with which she had washed that morning. "I don't care, Ty. . . . The future's out of our hands. All we have is the present. Don't send me back to Nassau. I won't go. You'll have to bind me hand and foot to get me off the *Sea Whisper*."

Unable to stop himself, he reached out and pushed back a strand of hair from her eyes. "Brave, stubborn little mouse . . . You never were afraid of the tiger, were you? . . . All right, stay if you must. But don't expect everything to be as it was. I can't handle it. What happened last time mustn't be repeated."

The cheers of Pete, Matt, Stoker, and the crew of the lighter drowned out his warning; the men were delighted to have witnessed a reconciliation, incomplete though it was. Just so Freedom wouldn't misunderstand and count this a victory, he barked at Pete, "Clear my things out of my cabin so Miss Walker can have it. . . . Put them in *your* cabin, Pete. Maybe you won't be so happy about this, knowing you have to bunk with Matt again."

"I don't care, Cap'n," Pete happily responded. "Beats havin' you growlin' an' grumblin' all the time like you been doin'."

Ty blinked in surprise, unaware that his bleakness of spirit had in any way communicated itself to his men.

True to his word, Tiger did not resume intimacies with Freedom or violate the privacy of her cabin on the return journey to Wilmington. He did condescend to share meals with her and speak when spoken to, but Freedom was all too aware of his wariness and reserve. She blamed it on the fact that he knew as well as she did that they were returning to witness the last gasps of the dying Confederacy.

Sometimes, she caught him staring at her, frowning in grim perplexity, but more often than not, he stared at the sea, as if it might hold answers to plaguing questions. The weather was gloomy, echoing Ty's mood, and after their initial enthusiasm to have her among them, the crew members went about their duties with a taut professionalism that was almost unnerving.

We're all waiting for God-alone-knows-what, Freedom thought, and we're scared.

She felt a little foolish for having chosen such a difficult time to declare her undying love for Tiger. It was so ironic. Now, when she had finally done it, had cast her lot with Ty and the South, he was too preoccupied with worry to pay her the attention she craved. He was fighting a lost cause and had no choice but to keep on fighting it until the end came. By the time they arrived at the fort, it might already be too late.

By nightfall of January 12, they were nearing Cape Fear waters. Lookouts had been spelling each other every hour, so that fresh eyes would constantly be scanning the horizon for any sign of the blockaders. Ty himself had scarcely lowered his spyglass in the last two hours. Wearing one of Ty's jackets to ward off the cold, Freedom clung to the railing, braving the stiff breeze and choppy seas to conduct her own watch for the enemy. . . . Odd, how she could now think of the Unionists as "the enemy." But if they meant to harm Ty—and they did—they *were* her enemy.

Suddenly, Matt Berringer called out from the

cross-ties, "Cap'n, ships to the North! Do you see 'em, sir?"

High on the bridge, Ty swung his spyglass around and focused on the far horizon. "I see them, Matt. . . . It's the Federal armada with . . . good God, more ships than she had the last time!"

A commotion broke out on deck, as everyone ran to the railing and peered into the thick gloom of falling darkness. Freedom strained her eyes and could gradually pick out distant lights winking in the blackness. The row of lights seemed endless; it did indeed look like more ships than last time.

Beside her, Pete Gambol sighed and shook his head. "Damn, it's too late now for them torpedoes we got in the hold."

"Torpedoes?" Freedom questioned. "What torpedoes?"

"The ones Colonel Lamb was hopin' we'd bring back. He planned to set 'em out in the harbor where the ironclads anchored the last time. . . . A few marine torpedoes explodin' underwater could stop those ironclads better than all the shells lobbed at 'em from the fort."

"Can't they still be used if we get past the blockade?"

"Don't think we'll get past, Miss Walker. . . . Look at those lights. The way they're linin' up to guard the river entrances, we'd have to fly over their heads to reach safety."

"You mean, we'll be forced to sit out here and watch the attack on the fort?"

"Appears so, Ma'am. . . . I just hope Colonel Lamb got reinforcements since the time we left. They ain't got but eight hundred men from the 36th North Carolina, and of these, a hundred or more are—or were—sick and unfit for duty."

Freedom thought of Mrs. Lamb and her children, and she shuddered. She hoped the colonel had again sent his wife across the river to the Orton plantation. She hoped that reinforcements had arrived from somewhere. Fastening her gaze on the row of lights, she clutched the rail and began to pray for all the men on both sides who would lose their lives in this confrontation. Here, tomorrow or the day after, the eventual outcome of the war would be decided. If Fort Fisher fell, the South must surely fall.

All night long, Ty tried to find a chink in the armada's armor—a tiny, unguarded opening where he could slip through undetected. There was none. He ran north of the fort and the Federal fleet, then tried to double back and come in close to shore, using the favorite tactic of many runners before him, one he himself had often used successfully.

This time, it didn't work. The Federalists knew exactly where to concentrate their ships so there wouldn't be any room between them for a rowboat to slip through undetected. Loaded down as he was with powder, torpedoes, and shells, Ty couldn't risk being fired upon. One hit was all it would take to blow the *Sea Whisper* to smithereens.

Sick with frustration, he cruised up and down, back and forth, wishing he had long guns so he could at least pepper their rear. But he wasn't equipped for fighting, and the Federal armada was. Toward morning, the fleet rearranged itself to find the most advantageous positions for bombarding the fort. The big, ugly ironclads anchored close in, only seven hundred to one thousand yards offshore, from which point they could pour their fire on the salient of the land face, thereby reducing the high parapet to a gentle slope easily scalable by Federal troops.

Thirteen ships moved to within three quarters of a mile of the beach, north of the fort. From this position, they could rake the land face clear to the river, level the traverses, knock out the guns, scatter the palisades, and flatten the twenty-foot embankment. Two powerful frigates, the *Wabash* and the *Minnesota,* claimed an area less than a mile from the sea face, directing their big guns so that the line of fire extended south from the salient. Still farther south lay fourteen more ships, awaiting the signal to move in for the kill, and to the north, the big troop transports got ready to unload blue-clad soldiers once the fort's defenses had been battered down.

Never in the history of mankind had so much firepower been concentrated in one place. Smoke from more than sixty funnels blackened the dawn sky. Ty estimated that the muzzles of more than six hundred guns were trained on Fort Fisher. Even if he could get through with his cargo, it wouldn't be enough. The Union's might was awesome. Ty trembled in fear for the defenders of the fort and wished with all his heart that he could do something to help. Unfortunately, he had arrived too late and brought too little.

As the sky lightened, he passed boldly through the outer line of ships and took a position slightly southeast of the fort, where he could run among the shoals to escape any hounds setting out to pursue him. Knowing these waters as well as he did, he had no doubt he could steam to safety, at the same time luring any vessels foolhardy enough to follow him to their doom on submerged wrecks and sandbars. But none of the Federal fleet paid him any attention; he was small fry now, hardly worth a passing glance.

From his position on the bridge, Ty could see Freedom still standing at the rail. She seemed mesmerized by the unfolding drama. As if she felt his eyes upon her, she turned and glanced up at him. Neither of them smiled or waved. He wondered what her feelings were as she watched the careful orchestration of this wretched, uneven contest. Was she secretly rejoicing that at long last the South would be soundly trounced?

He didn't want to believe it of her, but he'd been disappointed too many times in the past to hope otherwise. She had changed her mind so suddenly. Her capitulation, her proud declaration of love, still seemed incredible. . . . What had she expected? That he would clasp her to him, blithely forgetting all the betrayals of the past? Too bad it wasn't that simple and easy. After today, he couldn't even be sure of having a home to offer her. If the fort fell, the bluecoats would swarm through Wilmington, looting and burning, as Sherman had done in Georgia. The plantations along the river, including Cypress Hall, would undoubtedly be plundered and destroyed. He'd have nothing left except the *Sea Whisper,* a hold full of ammunition, and twenty hats for ladies who could no longer afford to buy them, regardless of how cheap the price.

Gazing down at Freedom, Ty felt such an inner wrenching that he had to clutch his chest to ward off the pain. Her face bore an expression of love and longing that shamed and humiliated him. No matter what she thought or felt, no matter how divided her loyalties, she was here. She had come. She was facing this with him. He didn't have to endure it alone.

Overwhelmed with emotion, he lifted his hand and solemnly saluted her. She broke into a blinding smile that warmed his soul and rattled his self-control. Unable to bear looking at her any longer, he turned away and busied himself with something else.

It seemed to Freedom that she could hear the wash of the surf on the beach near Fort Fisher. Certainly, she could hear the screams of the gulls circling in the air above the fort. Other than that, a strange, tremulous silence hung over everything—the *Sea Whisper,* the vista of land and sky, the fleet of menacing ships with their guns leveled at the fort. Above the palisade of sharpened logs, the Confederate Stars and Bars and the regimental flags of the fort's defenders made bright patches of color against the pale gray sky.

Freedom wanted to shout, "Stop! Don't fire. This is all nonsense. Too many of you are going to die."

She couldn't see the gray-clad soldiers hunched behind their earthen breastworks or the bluejackets waiting to fire their cannons, but she knew that young and old on both sides must be silently saying their prayers and remembering loved ones in the last few moments before the battle was joined. She prayed along with them, prayed especially for the boys who would die this day.

Barely had her lips formed the silent words of a half-remembered prayer from childhood, when sudden activity on one of the long, low monitors caught her attention. From the ironclad's round turret, which reminded her of a cheesebox, protruded the snouts of many guns. Emblazoned on the ship's stern was its name: *New Ironsides.* No sooner had she identified the vessel, when its guns spouted thunder and flame. Spherical shells hurtled toward shore, exploded in midair, and spewed metal fragments, which kicked up lumps of sod on the slopes of the traverses. A moment later, two guns from the fort responded with a deep-throated roar.

As a hundred cannon boomed, Freedom clapped her hands over her ears. Shells whined and exploded. The ship rocked from unseen reverberations. The *Sea Whisper* was anchored out of the line of fire from either side, but each concussion seemed to rattle her timbers. Freedom had never heard such a din; it struck terror in her heart. Dropping to her knees, she cowered behind the railing.

Hour after hour, the bombardment continued. There was scarcely any pause. The wind bore the mingled sounds of splintering wood, men's screams and shouts, thudding earth, and great, shuddering explosions, as one detonation set off another. The Union ships fired unceasingly. Conserving its ammunition, the fort answered sporadically. It was impossible to assess the damage being done. Thick clouds of acrid-smelling smoke engulfed the shoreline. Tongues of flame pierced the smoke, adding to it, whenever the fort's guns were fired.

Freedom lost all track of time as she crouched behind the railing, shivering in fright and dismay. Ty suddenly reached down, seized her arm, and dragged her upright. "Go get something to eat," he shouted at her over the din. "You've been kneeling there for hours."

"What time is it?" she asked, seeing his lips move and understanding what he said though her ears seemed to have gone deaf.

Apparently, he couldn't hear her, either, for he mouthed a response that didn't really answer the question.

"They'll quit soon, when it gets dark. Go get your supper."

Had the attack been going on all day? Her stiff limbs provided the only clue to the passage of time. She could barely move. "Yes, yes, I must eat," she mumbled, abruptly aware of a hollow feeling in the pit of her stomach and a growing nausea.

While she ate—*what* she was eating didn't register—the bombardment continued. Night fell, and even then, it didn't cease. Shells bursting above and beyond the fort's parapet resembled flashes of lightning. The clouds glowed crimson. Toward midnight, the Federal vessels ceased firing, and the sudden silence was more ominous and disturbing than the noise. Ty insisted that Freedom retire to the cabin, but she lay down on the bunk fully clothed, unable to sleep. Fort Fisher had endured one full day of nonstop bombing; how much longer before it fell? What must conditions be like there tonight, in the wake of all that shelling?

Freedom finally slept, but her dreams were tinged with blood, smoke, and gore. Her imagination supplied shocking details of the devastation existing at the fort—men with mangled, shattered limbs, buildings with collapsed roofs, smoke and grit covering everything. . . .

The next morning at sunrise, the Union fleet again steamed into position, and the *New Ironsides* let loose her first broadside. Once again, iron rained from the skies. Freedom counted a hundred shells a minute bursting among the guns and traverses of the fort. Matt Berringer lent her his field glasses, but she spotted not a single man's head showing above the protective mounds of earth. Sand, sod, and timbers erupted as each shell fell; the resultant explosions probably also contained bits and pieces of human beings. She doubted anyone could survive such relentless pounding. Unless each and every soldier in the fort remained hidden in a bombproof shelter, they would die.

They must be dying, Freedom thought. It was inevitable. In order to fire their own guns, they had to come out into the open, braving the heavy shelling.

Gradually, as the day wore on, the responses from Fort Fisher grew fewer in number. One after the other, the Confederate guns fell silent. Sensing victory, the big transports moved in north of the fort and began disgorging men and light pieces of field artillery. Through the field glasses, Freedom watched the blue-clad soldiers struggle in the heavy surf and land safely.

The Confederate guns overlooking the beach area periodically swept it with tongues of fire, but the soldiers kept arriving, hunkered down, and bided their time. As evening fell, the Federal fleet was concentrating all its shelling on those few remaining guns that still guarded the beach. Freedom could imagine what courage it took to man those guns in the midst of whistling shells and deafening concussions. She wept when one of the guns exploded, setting off a series of minor explosions. Such loss of life! Such terrible suffering! Was Colonel Lamb even still alive?

Night brought another surcease, but the brief respite was hardly long enough to enable the fort's defenders to repair the damages caused by two days of hellish destruction. Freedom refused to go below and instead curled up on deck to snatch what sleep she could. Sometime during the night, she felt strong arms pick her up and carry her to the cabin. She knew it must be Ty who laid her on the bunk and gently covered her with a blanket, but fatigue prevented her from thanking him. She was too exhausted to open her eyes.

The sound of booming cannon awakened her the next morning, the third day of the siege. Clutching the field glasses, Freedom rushed on deck. Quickly, she raised the glasses and studied the situation. The

Northeast Bastion, the closest to the beach, had been reduced to a shapeless pile of sand and rubble. Among the debris lay torn bodies in the tattered remnants of gray uniforms. As she watched, a lone gun fired from the bastion in a hopeless effort to stop the long line of Union troops advancing toward it from the beach.

Freedom scanned the waters nearest the area. More boats were bringing soldiers ashore, landing them just out of firing range. A geyser of water spouted between two of the closest boats, and a second thunderclap dropped a dozen or more of the bluejackets. The Rebels were still holding on, fighting to the very last man. Columns of blue began snaking toward the fort, hundreds of men, maybe thousands. Freedom tasted blood in her mouth as she inadvertently chewed her lower lip.

Behind her, Ty said, "This is it. They're getting ready to rush the fort."

Freedom lowered her glasses and glanced over her shoulder at him. Ty's face was ashen, his eyes like two live coals burning holes in their sockets. He had aged ten years. She wanted to comfort him but didn't know what to say. A blast of gunfire drew her attention back to the fort, then all was silent, the brief lull before the final storm. A moment later, a new sound rose from the sea—a cacophony of hoots, shrieks, whistles, and steam blasts from the Federal fleet.

"What on earth are they doing?" Freedom gasped.

"Urging the ground forces to attack, of course. The Navy's work is done. They've reduced the fort to rubble. Now, it's the Army's job to finish them off."

Barely had he finished speaking, when the soldiers surged forward in a solid blue wave. Lightning flashes from the fort cut a swath of death among them, toppling many before they could reach the rifle pits that must have been dug under cover of darkness. Freedom could no longer watch. Handing Ty the field glasses, she fled to his cabin.

Chapter Twenty-eight

By ten o'clock that evening, it was all over. The Union Stars and Stripes flew from Fort Fisher's parapet, made visible by torches and lanterns carried by Federal officers. Ty stood watching on deck as the fleet celebrated the victory by blowing their whistles nonstop and shooting off every remaining rocket they possessed. It was a grand display of pyrotechnics that stirred a reluctant, painful admiration.

Ty swallowed hard against a lump in his throat as big as a cannonball. He felt as if he'd been flayed alive over the past forty-eight hours. Not an inch of covering remained to protect his bleeding emotions. Had he been able to do something other than watch, the pain might not be as bad, but witnessing the ordeal without being able to do a thing to help the fort or stop the attack was an experience he'd never forget. All he could do now was endure the searing agony of defeat.

Freedom came up beside him and gently touched his arm. "Ty, I'm so sorry. I can't tell you how sorry I am. . . ."

She trailed off uncertainly and glanced out at the lights of the Federal fleet. The sounds of rejoicing still echoed across the water. Aboard the ships, men were singing, laughing, joking. Ty hated them for it . . . and hated Freedom for offering empty condolences. Of course, she wasn't sorry. This was the victory she had so much wanted. If anything, she had helped inflict the intense, unbearable pain that clutched at his gut, rendering him half mad with grief and bitterness.

He pried her fingers loose from his arm. "Leave me alone for a bit, will you? I don't think I can talk about this right now."

"I understand, Ty. . . . I'm as upset as you are. I know how you must feel."

Her sympathetic utterances only served to fuel the red rage burning in his stomach. "So you know how I feel, do you? I can't do a damn thing about the soldiers celebrating on those ships, but I can do something about you, the one Yank still at my mercy. I can wring your neck, shoot you between the eyes, or drown you in the sea. . . . That's what I *feel* like doing, Freedom. So why don't you quit mouthing platitudes and go below like a good little girl? At the moment, I can't stand the sight of you."

"Ty, please don't be bitter. . . . Don't shut me out because of this. Haven't I proven how much I love you? This hasn't been easy for me, either, you know."

"Ah, but it's certainly been easier for you than me tonight. Your side won. . . . This was it, Freedom. This was the decisive battle of the war. The Confederacy is stranded, now, cut off from supplies, food, medicines. . . . Cypress Hall is lost to me. They'll either burn it to the ground or turn it into a prison. And sooner or later, Lee will be forced to surrender. What in God's name have I got left?"

"You have me," Freedom said softly. "Ty, *you have me.*"

He didn't say it, but he suddenly didn't want her anymore. Staring at her in the darkness, he needed no light to know the contours of her face and body. He had memorized every detail in preparation for just such a moment as this. Even when denying it, he'd always known that eventually they'd be torn apart by the brutal realities of this damnable war. The time had come. She had always wanted to go home to the North; well, what better opportunity could she have than now? He was surrounded by Union ships. In the dark of night, he had to slip past them and escape . . . but he didn't have to take her with him. He *wouldn't* take her with him. She was a Yank. He was a Rebel. They each belonged with their own kind.

"Pete!" he shouted. "Make ready to lower a longboat."

Freedom's eyes widened, glinting like the eyes of a startled deer. "Why are you lowering a boat? Ty, we mustn't stay here. They'll put you in prison if they catch you. We should leave at once for Nassau."

"I *am* leaving," he said brutally. "But you're not. I'm setting you adrift. In the morning, one of these warships will gladly pick you up. You can tell them I was holding you prisoner. Tell them anything you please. With your Northern accent, they'll believe every word. You might even wind up a heroine."

She clutched at his coat sleeve. "Ty, don't do this! You can't send me away now! I came back with you. I love you. I've stood by you through all of this! Doesn't that mean anything to you?"

"Nothing means much anymore, Freedom. I've got no home, no country, no future. . . . The South died tonight, and I died with it. Don't waste your love on a dead man. . . . I wish you health and good fortune. Find yourself a nice Union officer and give your love to him. It's the only way you'll ever know happiness."

"*You* are my happiness! You're all I want . . . all I'll ever want."

"Pete! Have you got that damn longboat ready?" His mind made up, Ty was determined to get this over with as quickly as possible.

"Aye, aye, Cap'n."

"Then put Miss Walker aboard. She's leaving to rejoin her countrymen."

"Ty! Ty Carrington, you drunken sot . . . Are you in there?"

Ty heard the summons through layers of cotton from a far distance. He rolled over in bed, tried to remember where he was, what day it was, what year. He opened his eyes and blinked at the ceiling. Memory rushed back. Oh, yes, he was still in Nassau, in the same room at the Royal Victoria where he'd been living for the past several months — living until his money ran out or his brains rotted from whiskey, whichever came first.

"Yeah, I'm in here. Who is it? What do you want?"

He sat up, his head pounding, and his glance fell on a pile of newspapers beside the rumpled bed. The top one was dated April 9, 1865. It was more than a month old, but its headline still made Ty's blood run cold. Bold, black print leaped out at him: LEE SURRENDERS TO GRANT AT APPO-MATTOX COURT HOUSE.

The door opened, and a trim, attractive gentleman neatly attired in the uniform of a Confederate Navy captain stepped into the room. "It's me, Ty . . . John Wilkinson. I heard you were here at the hotel, and since I'm leaving today, I wanted to say good-bye before I go."

Ty rolled out of bed, acutely conscious of his disheveled appearance: bleary eyes, two—or was it three?—weeks' growth of beard, uncombed hair, dirty trousers and boots he hadn't removed for days.

"Well, John, this is a surprise. . . ." He cleared his throat, his voice sounding like a rasp. "You've caught me at a bad time. . . . Seems I haven't yet recovered from everything that's happened."

The impeccably groomed officer with the jaunty mustache strode into the darkened room, brushed some rumpled clothing from a chair, started to sit down, then appeared to think better of it. "Ty Carrington, how can you stand it in here? It smells like a distillery set up in a pigsty."

Like Ty, John had been educated in the North. His unaccented speech was as perfect as his appearance. Crossing to the shuttered windows, he flung them wide open. Warm, sweet air rushed into the room, carrying with it a flood of sunlight. Ty had to close his eyes against the glare and sit back down on the bed, before he fell down.

"Did you have to open the shutters?" he growled. "I like the way it smells in here. Suits me fine. I enjoy wallowing in my own stinking misery."

John planted himself in a shaft of sunlight and

regarded Ty disapprovingly. "Is this really Tiger Carrington, the heroic, dashing blockade-runner who fears nothing and no one . . . who's made more successful runs than any other man in the Confederacy . . . who enabled the South to hold out for as long as she did . . . who should be *proud* of his record and accomplishments, instead of holing up in the dark drinking himself to death?"

"You're vastly exaggerating, John. Your own record puts mine to shame, and if I want to drink myself to death, that's *my* business, not yours. . . . Drinking isn't all I do," he added defensively. "Every once in a while, I also swim in the sea, dally with whores, play cards on the veranda, and reminisce over the lost paradise that once was our beloved South."

"What in hell's wrong with you, Ty? This is no way to take defeat. You ought to be winding up your affairs in Nassau, then steaming back to Wilmington to protect your interests there."

"What interests? It's all gone, John. The South is finished. Cypress Hall has probably been burned to the ground, the stables and storage buildings destroyed. What would I be rushing back to?"

"My God, man, you've still got the land! And you must have money put by to get started again. . . . That's more than I've got. As a fellow blockade-runner, I had a hundred opportunities to make my fortune, but I was too patriotic to take advantage of the situation. Being in the Navy, I didn't think I should."

"Well, I wasn't in the damn Navy, but I was a bloody fool, too. The money I've got left in Nassau should last me just long enough to slowly drink myself to death . . . which reminds me. Where's that bottle I opened last night?"

Ty started rummaging around on the floor at his feet, but John beat him to it. "Do you mean this bottle?" He bent down and picked up an empty whiskey bottle. "You've already drained it."

"Damn. I'll have to order another."

"Don't you dare!" John strode over to Ty and sat down beside him on the bed. "Pull yourself together, Ty. You're too fine a man to ruin your life and your health like this."

"My life is already ruined," Ty grumbled. "The only thing I've got left is my health."

"Which won't last long at the rate you're going. . . . Listen to me. The latest rumor is that we're all going to be pardoned—everyone except the most outspoken leaders and the wealthiest men. We'll have to take an oath of allegiance to the Union, of course, but we'll get to keep all our property, excepting our slaves, and we'll enjoy the full benefits of citizenry."

"I don't want to be a citizen of the United States of America. I'm a North Carolinian; I'll stand by my state, but I'll swear no allegiance to the Union."

"You'll have to. It's a matter of survival."

"Then I'll refuse to survive."

"This *can't* be Ty Carrington talking. I never took you for a coward, but could be I was wrong. What is it, Ty? There's something more to your despair than mere grief that we lost the war."

Ty wearily passed a hand over his eyes. "I don't want to talk about it."

"It's a female, isn't it?" John shrewdly observed. "Only a woman can drive a man to such depths of utter desolation."

When Ty didn't answer—*couldn't* answer—John continued. "Is it the lady whose bonnet you were wearing that day when I hailed you outside the hotel? . . . Who was she and whatever happened to her? I remember being most amused to see you in such a predicament—Ty Carrington, the confirmed bachelor, being harassed by a cheeky female!"

Ty had no trouble remembering the incident to which John was referring—that day so long ago when Freedom had tossed the clothes he'd given her off the balcony of their hotel room. Her pantalets had almost landed in his brandy, and he'd been torn between laughing and beating her.

"Her name was Freedom Walker, but I always called her Mouse."

"*Was?* Did she die? Was she killed in the war?"

"I don't know what happened to her," Ty muttered. "On my last run, the night Fort Fisher fell, I set her adrift in the ocean near Wilmington, so the Federalists would pick her up."

"You did *what?* Why in God's name would you do a thing like that?"

"She's a Northerner. It would never have worked out between us."

"Oh, she wanted a Yankee victory and threw it up to you every chance she got. . . ."

"Not exactly . . . well, yes, at first, but later, as we came to care for each other, she made a sincere effort to see my side of things. She tried to support me, even returned to Wilmington with me when we knew the fort would soon be under siege."

"Then what's the problem? Sounds to me like she must have loved you deeply to be willing to change her politics and place her life in danger just to be with you."

"She did . . . and I treated her like hell. I was so damned furious with the Yankees that I wanted nothing more to do with her. I forced her into a longboat and set her adrift in the middle of the night. Haven't seen or heard from her since."

John Wilkinson sighed. "You *are* a bloody fool. . . . But that's no reason to destroy yourself. Now that the war's over and things have settled down some, you can go back and look for her."

Ty shook his head. "She'd never have me now. Not after what I did to her . . . how I treated her . . . And without her, nothing matters anymore. I don't even care that I've lost Cypress Hall. I've no desire whatever to go home and try to pick up the pieces. As far as I'm concerned, the Yanks can have it all."

"But what about your people, Ty? I know you didn't have slaves, but your workers were dependent upon you. If you leave now, you might still get a cotton crop planted . . . The land is there. The Yanks can't take the land. A cotton crop will give you a new start. You can begin again . . . eventually rebuild."

Ty snorted his contempt for that idea. "Don't you understand, John? *I don't care*. I'm not going back, and that's that."

John was silent for a moment, his kind blue eyes sad and disappointed. "But what will you do here, Ty? You can't stay in Nassau forever. The place is fast deteriorating into the same sleepy, sluggish little port it was before the war began. The English are pulling out. The blockade-runners are going home. Soon, there will be no one left but the natives. They'll all go back to fishing for conch and waiting for wrecks to occur offshore in the storms . . . I doubt this hotel can stay open when the blockade-runners leave."

"Maybe I'll be dead by then. . . . How long does it take to die of drink and a broken heart?"

"Damn it, man, stop feeling sorry for yourself! Think of what you've already survived. You can get through this, too. . . . Why, I almost died a dozen times playing hare and hounds between here and Wilmington. So did you. You can't give up now."

"John," Ty finally said, tired of arguing, "it's kind of you to take an interest, but really, my life is my own. Thanks for being my friend, but please, let me die in peace."

John stood, glowering down at Ty, his hands rigid at his sides. "If you won't accept my advice, damn you, I'll leave and give the matter no further thought."

"That's exactly what I am," Ty agreed. "Damned . . . But good luck to you, John. You deserve some luck. A better man than you never captained a ship or ran a blockade during the entire war."

"I think of you as my equal," John gritted. "Sometimes even as my superior — or at least I did until today."

"Sorry to disappoint you. Good-bye, John. Godspeed."

Ty extended his hand for a handshake, but John wouldn't take it. Ty merely shrugged; he felt no rancor. John had said nothing that he himself had not thought. But what John didn't understand was that without Freedom, he really did not want to live.

"There, Omoroh, we've finished this field. Tomorrow we can start on the last one."

Grunting, Freedom straightened her back and wiped the perspiration from her eyes. She handed Omoroh the bag of cotton seed and her hoe. Her arms and legs trembled with fatigue and strain, but she looked back at the field with great satisfaction. Given what little seed they had, she'd made it stretch. There would be a cotton crop this year at Cypress Hall. Of course, if Billy Bob and the other workers left, there'd be no one to pick it, but she'd worry about that when the time came.

Omoroh flashed his wide smile. Looking past Freedom, his dark eyes lit up. Freedom knew without turning around who was coming out to meet them—tall, regal Mary, soon to be Omoroh's wife. The wedding was but a week away, having been postponed until after the planting, which was very late this year due to military operations in the area. Union soldiers now occupied Wilmington and, indeed, all of North Carolina.

Fortunately, Freedom's entreaties with Union officials had not gone unheeded. She'd been able to convince them to spare many homes and plantations—Cypress Hall included—that might otherwise have been plundered or destroyed during the first days of Union occupation. The fact that the Carringtons had emancipated their slaves years ago had balanced the scale, when weighed against Ty's activities as a blockade-runner. Freedom had also been careful to point out to Admiral David Porter and anyone else who would listen that Tiger

Carrington mostly shipped food and medicine, not arms.

Life at Cypress Hall since her return had been lean, with barely enough food to go around, but things were better now that the Goffs and the Butler sisters had departed to find their relatives. Of the refugees, only Peonie Harkness and Mary Brown remained. Many of the workers had also left, lured by rumors of ten free acres and a mule that would supposedly be given to each and every freed slave who wanted them. Billy Bob had been tempted but finally decided to remain because Mancie and Tillie refused to go. So now there were only the truly loyal workers left, along with the ones either too old or too young to start over somewhere else.

When Ty returned — if he returned — he'd find his ancestral home in relatively good shape. And he'd find Freedom waiting patiently, prepared to spend her life waiting for him to come to his senses, because she at last knew where she belonged and what she wanted. She had already forgiven him for setting her adrift in that boat; he had not been himself that night, had not been thinking properly. Three days of no sleep, coupled with the strain of the siege and witnessing the fort's defeat, had unhinged him. In time, he'd get over his bitterness. . . . She just wished he would hurry, for she was so lonely, so anxious to see him again, so eager to lavish her love upon him and start building a new life together. . . . He'd *better* hurry, or the child she carried beneath her gently bulging apron would be born out of wedlock. She had conceived it that night on the beach, when their love had proved stronger than all their differences. . . .

And it would prove itself again one day, bringing Ty back to her.

As Mary drew abreast of them, the tall, handsome Negress seemed strangely excited, more than being with Omoroh would have warranted, since she already spent as much time as possible in her future husband's company. "Missy Freedom, you gotta come quick. We got a visitor."

"A visitor?" Freedom's heart fluttered wildly in her breast. "Male or female? Who is it, Mary?"

"Don't know, Missy Freedom. Ah ain't nevah seed her b'fore. But she come askin' Miss Peonie did she know a young woman name of Freedom Walker. Seems she heard in town you was livin' out here, an' she's come to pay her respects."

Hattie Draper, Freedom thought. Who else could it be but her former employer at the shop in Wilmington, where she'd been working when the war broke out?

"Please go back to the house and tell her I'm coming. I'll go in the back way and clean up before I see her."

"Ah'll do that, Missy Freedom, but do you mind if ah tek a moment to talk to Omoroh first? Ah ain't seed him all day."

The two were gazing at each other with unabashed joy and yearning. Freedom had to stifle a smile. When Mary and Omoroh were together, they didn't need words to communicate. They did it all with their eyes and shy touches of their hands. Mary could tell Freedom exactly what Omoroh was thinking; she had become his voice, while Omoroh had become her strength, her protector, and, Freedom suspected, her ardent lover.

"Never mind, Mary. I'll tell the lady myself.

Maybe Peonie can entertain her while I change into something fresh."

"Thanks, Missy Freedom." Mary was already entwining her arm through Omoroh's, so that he dropped two hoes and the bag of seed. "Now, you just bettah come ovah heah an' tell me what you been doin' all day, Omoroh. . . . Ah been missin' you somethin' terrible."

Walking alone across the fields, Freedom decided that Mary and Omoroh's relationship could not be more perfect if angels had fashioned it. She was so happy for them! The only trouble was that she sometimes envied them, too. How had they managed to achieve such rapport when one of them couldn't speak? Maybe that was her and Ty's problem: They spoke too much. Once something was said, it could be retracted but never quite forgotten. And Ty had obviously chosen to remember every bad thing she'd ever uttered about the South. But someday—oh, yes, someday—he'd remember those perfect moments of love and tenderness, passion and communion, and he'd come back.

Spreading her hands across her swollen belly, Freedom slowly and ponderously made her way back to the house. In the meantime, she must endure the best she could. . . . What, she wondered, was she going to tell Hattie Draper about her obviously pregnant state?

Chapter Twenty-nine

"Freedom, darlin' girl! Ah *knew* it had to be you out here!" A roly-poly little dumpling of a woman waddled toward Freedom, pudgy arms outstretched, gray-streaked yellow curls bouncing.

"Hattie!" Freedom flew into the woman's lilac water-scented embrace. "How did you know I was here?"

After an enormous hug, Hattie drew back and held Freedom at arm's length. In the background, Peonie was smiling and nodding, pleased to discover that Freedom had a friend from town; Peonie was always bemoaning the fact that Freedom went nowhere and entertained not at all.

"Why, ah was talkin' to one o' them handsome Union officers the other day, an' he mentioned meetin' you. Seems you made quite an impression on Admiral Porter an', after him, the Army gen'rals. Well, ah thought to mahself, who else can this girl be but mah own long-lost friend an' employee? There can't be *two* Freedom Walkers on God's green earth, now, can there? . . . Ah see you gonna become a proud mama one o' these days. Ah trust you've up and married . . . how grand an' wonderful! Chile, you must tell me everything

411

that's happened to you since you stole away with that big Nigra runaway—what was his name, Omoroh?"

Hattie blundered on, so that Freedom could hardly get a word in edgewise. But she finally managed, steering Hattie toward a handy sofa in the front parlor and urging her to sit down. "Hattie, do stop! I can't tell you anything while you're chattering like a magpie. . . . By the way, you're looking marvelous. You seem to have weathered the war in fine fettle."

"Oh, mah, yes . . . Ah had to close the shop an' take in laundry to make ends meet, but ah hope to open it again soon an' lure some o' the Union soldiers inta buyin' presents to take home to their womenfolk."

"If the Union soldiers ever do go home," Peonie interjected. "Freedom, honey, can ah bring you somethin' to drink? You look plumb tuckered out after workin' in them fields all day."

"Workin' in the fields!" Hattie cried. "Why, what kind of husband let's his wife work in the fields when she's in the fam'ly way?"

Freedom shot a pleading glance at Peonie. "I'd love something to drink, Peonie. . . . While you get it, I'll tell Hattie all my personal news—things you already know."

Peonie nodded understandingly. "You go ahead. Ah'll jus' leave y'all alone a few minutes, then."

"Thanks, Peonie . . . Now, then, Hattie," Freedom said, easing herself down on the sofa. "First, I'll tell you about the father of my baby. And then I'll tell you everything else."

Twenty minutes later, Hattie Draper was shaking her curly gray-blond head and clucking sympathetically. "Oh, darlin', you have surely been through hell an' back since last ah saw you."

"It wasn't all terrible, Hattie," Freedom assured the old woman. "I love Ty Carrington very much, and his baby and I will be here if and when he decides to come home."

"Well, don't you worry nothin' 'bout Omoroh. . . . Ah won't mention to a livin' soul that he's out here."

"I'm really not worried about him anymore, Hattie. All the slaves are free now. And considering the devastation that occurred in Georgia during the war, I don't expect anyone to come looking for him."

"You're probably right, darlin', but a body can't be too careful. There's still a powerful lot of feelin' against the poor Nigras. Folks are wond'rin' what's gonna happen now that all the coloreds are free. Who's gonna feed an' take care of 'em? They might take to stealin' from their former masters, folks say, or doin' worse. Omoroh better stay hidden out here, jus' in case somebody recognizes 'im in town. There's bound to be a lot of folks from all ovah comin' and goin' through Wilmin'ton; it's one o' the few towns in the South to escape some degree o' ruination."

"Don't worry, Hattie. . . . Omoroh's getting married soon, and he never goes into town. He'll be safe. . . . It's just wonderful to talk with someone who feels the same delight I do in seeing that the Negroes are finally free."

Hattie patted Freedom's hand. "Darlin', ah hope your man soon comes to his senses, comes home, an' marries you, so your joy can be complete. . . . It ain't right that a sweet little gal like you should

413

hafta endure the shame of bearin' a chile with no daddy. . . . Why, it sorely grieves me. You deserve bettah than that, Freedom, darlin'."

"I agree," a male voice suddenly said. "She does deserve better."

Freedom flew off the sofa and whirled about as fast as her ungainly shape would allow. Standing inside the open French doors leading to the veranda was Ty—a very lean and sober-faced Ty, whose violet eyes stabbed Freedom to the bone.

"Ty! Dear God, when did you come?"

"I followed Mrs. Draper here," Ty said quietly. "Only she didn't know it. Nor did I expect to find *you* here, Mouse. By now, I thought you'd be back up North."

This wasn't the way Freedom had fantasized Tiger's homecoming—in front of Hattie Draper, with Peonie coming through the door carrying a tray of refreshments, and Ty himself looking so cool and detached in a charcoal-gray jacket, white shirt, gray breeches, and black boots. Somehow, she had thought she might be alone, able to fling herself into his arms and sob out a welcome.

"I . . . I've been here all this time . . . waiting for you," she stammered. "Surely, you knew I'd be here, Ty."

"Well, I can certainly see why now. . . ." Ty glanced pointedly at her rounded stomach. "You didn't have much choice, did you, with a mousling on the way?"

"I did so have a choice! I stayed because of *you,* Ty, not because of the baby. Don't you dare think I stayed only because I needed a father for my child. What I *need* is a husband. And that husband is you."

414

Ty's mouth quirked at the corners in the old rakish grin she knew so well. "Ladies," he said gravely, nodding to Peonie and Hattie, "would you mind leaving us alone? Miss Walker and I have a great deal to discuss."

Hattie Draper moved with commendable speed for a lady of her ample proportions. Peonie was no less prompt. "We'll just have our refreshments on the veranda at the back of the house, Captain. . . . Ah'll only say, welcome home, an' then Mrs. Draper an' ah will leave you in peace."

When Peonie had closed the door behind the two of them, Freedom found herself glowering at Ty, angry that he hadn't sent word of his pending arrival, hadn't expected her to be there, had taken so long to come home . . . had misinterpreted her motives for being at Cypress Hall.

"All right, Ty Carrington, *talk,*" she commanded frostily, keeping the sofa between them. "Where have you been all these months?"

His grin widened. It was confident but at the same time rueful. "Do we really have to waste time discussing what an ass I've been?"

"Yes," she challenged. "I want an explanation. . . . You could at least have come back to check on your house and the people who care about you."

"I was afraid to come back. I thought everything was gone—especially you. . . . Is the mousling going to be a boy or a girl?"

"Don't change the subject. . . . It was irresponsible of you not to come home sooner. The cotton fields had to be worked, the seed planted, the livestock looked after. . . . You might have guessed I'd be here waiting for you, baby or no baby."

"I hope it's a little girl with big brown eyes, shiny brown hair, and a twitchy little nose like yours."

"My nose is *not* twitchy!"

"Yes, it is. . . . I think that's why you remind me of a mouse. When you get angry—which is quite often—your nose twitches."

"You're trying to change the subject again!"

He regarded her somberly, his blond hair falling in an irresistible tangle of curls across his smoky eyes. "No, I'm trying to avoid controversy between us. From now on, we won't discuss sensitive subjects. That way, we can't fight. We can't get angry and toss away everything that means so much to both of us."

"I didn't toss anything away; *you* did."

"Maybe you didn't the last time. . . . But the time before was your fault."

"It was not!"

"It was. You said you hoped the fort was blown up, as good as saying you hoped I'd get killed."

"That wasn't what I meant and you know it. . . . Are you still angry because it finally fell?"

"Are you still angry that I'm such a mutton headed, mule-stubborn, hopelessly patriotic tar-heel?"

"I'm trying hard not to be," she admitted. "But I still think you should have come home weeks ago, even months ago."

"And I still haven't come to terms with the South's defeat, Mouse. . . . Maybe I never will. Can you love me in spite of that?"

She tossed her head. "I suppose I can try."

"Well, I've come to the conclusion I can certainly try and love a Yankee. . . . So let's get married."

"Do you really mean it?"

"I'll marry you today."

"Oh, Ty, that's way too soon! How about next week? There's a wedding already planned—Mary and Omoroh's. We can say our vows at the same time."

"Mary? Who the hell is Mary?"

"Oh, you remember her. She came here with Peonie. They were refugees from Georgia."

"There seems to be a lot I've forgotten. . . . But one thing I clearly recall: how wonderful it feels to hold you. . . . Now that our wedding date is settled, do you think I could savor that too-long-denied pleasure?"

"Yes, oh, yes!" Freedom hurried around the sofa and launched herself into his arms.

They hugged and kissed. Tears dampened their cheeks. Freedom didn't know if they were his or her tears. What did it matter? Nothing mattered but their reunion. The long, breathless kiss deepened into a passionate clutch, and the clutch accelerated into a tugging at clothes. Freedom was desperate to get skin to skin with Ty. His breath was hot on her ear, his voice vibrating with need.

"Mouse, can we do this? Won't it hurt the mousling?"

"He won't mind," Freedom gasped, arching against his hand as he cupped her naked breast.

"You mean *she* . . ."

"No, *he* . . . He'll be a blond-haired boy with eyes the color of violets."

"God help him if he is. . . . We'll have to give him an exceedingly masculine name and teach him early how to defend himself."

"We'll call him Little Ty. . . . The cub will be

just like his father, a tiger in every sense."

"The one thing we *won't* do is name him after me. Children should never be saddled with either of their parent's names, except for the last name."

"We'll argue about it later," Freedom murmured, moaning deep in her throat. "Oh, Ty, love me, love me, love me. . . . I want you so much. I've missed you so terribly."

"And I love you, Mouse. . . . God, how I love you!"

Those were the last words either of them spoke for an hour. The only sounds in the room were the creak and groan of the sofa as they fell down upon it together, their frenzied breathing, and the gasps, moans, and whisperings of longing and pleasure. Ty took his time rediscovering Freedom's body. He spent an eternity, it seemed to Freedom, stroking her breasts and belly, wordlessly marveling at the changes in them. When he pressed his lips to her navel, she thought she would die of the sweet burning fire consuming her from within. Her heart was bursting; her love overflowed. Ty had finally come home, and the future stretched ahead of them, bright and glorious, shimmering with promise, just as she had imagined it would during all those dark, lonely nights.

When their passion had spent itself. Ty enfolded her in his arms and nuzzled her ear. They were lying side by side, half atop each other on the narrow sofa, satiated and replete. "I suppose we should dress," she murmured reluctantly. "It's scandalous to be lying here naked in broad daylight, while two ladies are having refreshments out on the veranda."

"At the back of the house," Ty reminded her.

"And I'm sure they've got sense enough not to disturb us. . . . Don't move yet. There's so much I want to say to you," he sighed in her ear. "Mouse, I'm truly sorry. I should have come home sooner. I shouldn't have behaved the way I did that night Fort Fisher fell. I shouldn't have spent all that time in Nassau, hating myself, hating you, feeling bitter and depressed. . . ."

She shifted slightly and almost fell off the sofa. "It's over now, Ty. We have a wonderful life ahead of us."

"Wonderful," he snorted. "That's all well and good for you to say, Mouse. Not that I'm not grateful to find the house still standing — and to find you waiting for me, the most wonderful surprise a man could ever have — but I still have my doubts about the future. Life is going to be very different — very difficult — from now on in North Carolina. It won't be the same life I've known and cherished since boyhood."

She squirmed a bit, the better to look up into his brooding face. "Maybe it will be better, Ty. You're expecting the worst, and that's unfair. North Carolina will be admitted back into the Union, and in time, hostilities will lessen. The South will grow strong again. Plantations will be rebuilt. God knows, the world still needs cotton. . . ."

He gently squeezed her thickening waist. "My little optimist . . . Without slaves, who's going to do all the work? Our economy has collapsed. Our money is gone, but our debts are enormous. . . . There must be three or four hundred thousand Negroes — now free — in the state, but they can't read or write. They've never made decisions regarding their own welfare. We're too broke to pay them to

419

work even if they do have skills, which many don't. It's a terrible muddle and makes me wonder if slavery wasn't a grim necessity after all."

"Don't say that, Ty. You yourself have proven that slavery isn't necessary to the economic well-being of the South. You're a living example of how things *ought* to be. . . . And *your* people *can* read and write. They're doing wonderfully well now, even the children. They read as well as you or I."

He nuzzled her hair and exhaled long and slowly. "I'm not going to argue with you, sweetheart. I'm determined not to argue anymore. But forgive me if I can't share your vision of a rosy future. . . . All the fight seems to have gone out of me. I want to run and hide from our problems, not try and solve them. Don't expect me to charge to the forefront of this new battle—the reconstruction of the South. I haven't the heart for it. Someone else will have to provide the leadership and show the way."

She twisted around and took his face between her hands. "But you're exactly the sort of man who *should* seek a position of leadership. I said as much to Admiral Porter when he rescued me the morning after you set me adrift. If not you, Ty, then who? Do you want Northerners to make all of the decisions for the South? Or worse yet, men like the ones who tore out Omoroh's tongue? You can't sit back and do nothing. . . ."

He took her hands and kissed her open palms, first one, then the other. "Cease badgering me, Mouse. . . . I can't do more than I'm able. You don't know how difficult it was to gather myself together and come home at long last."

"I'm sorry, Ty," she whispered, half afraid he might disappear again. She sensed that if she pushed him too far too fast, he might just vanish before her very eyes. . . . She'd have to be patient and give him a chance. Once his wounds had healed, he'd be more willing to listen. Until then, all she could do was love and hold him, easing the pain of defeat as best she could with soft kisses and caresses. "Oh, I'm so glad to have you home. . . . I've imagined this moment more times than I can count!"

"Sweet, tender Mouse . . . I can't wait to make you my wife. Do we really have to delay until next week?"

"You must curb your impatience, my darling. . . . I doubt we could get a preacher out here any sooner. Besides, I want a proper wedding. We *need* some gaiety and joy in this house. We may not have a wedding feast as grand as we might wish, but we can certainly celebrate for all we're worth. I want a wedding I can tell our children about, though I won't tell our eldest that he was already on the way when we married."

"How about if we celebrate our wedding next week and our first anniversary the week after? He'll never know that we counted a week as a whole year."

"That's a splendid idea! Ty, I'm so happy!" She hugged him fiercely. "Let's get dressed and tell Peonie, Hattie, Mary, and Omoroh, shall we? With two weddings only a week away, there's quite a lot to do."

He pulled her back onto the sofa, not allowing her to rise. "Not so fast, Mouse. I applaud your enthusiasm, but I'm not ready to relinquish you yet. It's been so long—so damn, terribly long—since we've been alone together. Can't you spare me a few more moments?"

"Hattie and Peonie will be scandalized if we don't come out in time for supper," Freedom demurred.

"Let them be scandalized," Ty suggested with a wicked grin. "Let the whole household be scandalized. I can't let you go yet."

"All right," she sighed, snuggling close again. "We do have a great deal of lost time to make up."

"We've let politics divide us for the last time, Mouse. From now on, we put *our* union ahead of everything."

"A house divided against itself cannot stand," Freedom said ruefully, voicing a sentiment from another time and place, eons ago it seemed, yet as true today as it had been when first spoken. She thought of Abraham Lincoln, dead of an assassin's bullet this April past, and grieved anew for all the lives that had been lost, the families torn apart, the friendships sundered, the estrangement that had separated her and Ty for so long. Thank God, it was over.

As if echoing her thoughts, Ty whispered, "Never again . . . I swear to you, Freedom. Never again will our unity be broken."

"Oh, Ty, if you and I can do it, maybe the country—the nation—can do it, too."

"I doubt it," Ty said gloomily. "You and I love each other, and look what we've had to go through to get this point."

"I can dream. . . . I can hope. I prayed you would finally come home to me, and you did. We have to believe it, Ty. And we have to be willing to fight for it. We can build a better nation now; I know we can if we really want to."

"Not me, Mouse . . . I'll fight for you, our family, and Cypress Hall. But that's it. That's all I can do. The nation will have to take care of itself. It's not *my* nation, anyway."

Freedom bit down on any further comments she might have made. If he was never able to share her dreams, she wouldn't bully him. She'd be satisfied with what she had — but, oh, how she wished he could see his own potential for leadership in these dark, trying times! She could envision him serving in some sort of office, inspiring men to tackle the state's problems with courage and intelligence. Already, there was talk of a convention being called to reorganize the state government and repeal the 1861 ordinance that took North Carolina out of the Union. A provisional governor was soon to be appointed, and rumors were flying about who that might be. The front-runner was a man named William W. Holden, a native North Carolinian and strong spokesman for Southern rights, but one who had also been a stern critic of Jefferson Davis's presidency in the ill-fated Confederacy. Whoever the new governor was, he would need men like Ty Carrington to help and advise him.

"Like it or not, it is your nation, Ty. . . . It's *our* nation. But that's all I'll say about it for now."

"Good . . . Because I can think of far more interesting things to do with our time alone together, Mouse."

He started doing them — the interesting things — and she soon forgot everything but the miracle of being locked in his arms, trading kisses and caresses, sharing a love that had proven itself stronger than war, separation, betrayal, misunderstanding, doubt, and grief. It was a love, she was sure, that could last a lifetime. Only later, after the sweet loving ended and the child stirred in her womb, did she think about the future again . . . and prayed Ty would find a way to help shape it. Their children, after all, would be living in North Carolina in the United States of America for a long time to come.

Chapter Thirty

Freedom's wedding day dawned hot and humid, and didn't get any better as it moved toward three o'clock in the afternoon, the time set for the ceremony. Hattie and Peonie helped Freedom to dress upstairs in the bedroom she would soon be relegating to a nursery. Hattie—bless her heart!—had found an old ivory satin ball gown for Freedom to wear and had helped alter it to accommodate her pregnancy. Not to be outdone, Peonie had seen to it that the house was sparkling, a modest feast had been prepared by Mancie and Tillie, and the parlor had been cleared of furniture in case it rained and the dancing had to be held inside.

A similar room had been cleared in Omoroh's house, for the plantation workers were bent on having their own celebration, separate from the more staid doings of the white folks. Mancie and Tillie were even now helping Mary to dress, and Omoroh and Tiger were God-knew-where, making their own preparations.

Gazing into a mirror at herself, Freedom could not believe the transformation. She looked radiant

425

and lovely, with no hint of her usual mousiness. Her hair was piled on top of her head, where Hattie had tucked flowers from the garden in among the shiny brown curls. The ivory satin made her skin glow and flattered her rounded figure, and for once, she didn't mind her resemblance to a Southern belle. Soon, she'd be a wife and mother; that was all she cared about.

Over her protests, Ty had insisted upon inviting half the county, eliminating only his mother's friends for whom he'd never cared much, anyway. He had assured her that there *were* some North Carolinians she would enjoy meeting and with whom she'd have something in common. He had also invited all his crew members.

Before going downstairs to meet her bridegroom, Freedom gave herself one last perusal, while Hattie and Peonie adjusted the white lace veil atop her gleaming curls.

"Ah declare, darlin', you are the loveliest bride ah've evah seen," Hattie gushed.

Peonie hugged her and kissed her cheek. "Deah girl, be happy. . . . Ah'm so happy for you. Nobody deserves this day more'n you."

"Thank you both for helping to make this day so special!" Freedom cried, near tears. "I couldn't have done it all by myself. . . . You both seem to have a knack for organizing things and making them turn out wonderfully. And you compliment each other so well."

Peonie and Hattie smiled and exchanged glances with each other. "Why, we think so, too, darlin'," Hattie said. "In fact, we've been discussin' goin' into business togethah, puttin' on weddin's and parties and funerals an' such. Ah could take care of the clothin' aspect, and Peonie could help folks plan an' organize the rest—the food, drink, an' entertainment, where appropriate."

"What a fine idea!" Freedom enthused. "Though Peonie mustn't think we want her to leave Cypress Hall. . . . You're welcome here always, Peonie. I know you have no home to go back to in Georgia."

Peonie smiled, shaking her silvery head. "Why, bless you, Freedom, deah, but ah can't stay here forevah. . . . Ah gotta do something with what's left of mah life, an' runnin' a business enterprise might jus' be a heap o' fun. We weren't gonna tell you 'til later, but Hattie's invited me to stay with her an' help out at the shop when it reopens."

"But you'll visit often, won't you? Mary and I will be most upset if you don't. *Both* of you must come to visit as often as you can."

"Don't worry, darlin', we will." Hattie patted her arm reassuringly.

To forestall more tears, Freedom inquired brightly, "Is it time to go downstairs now? Has Miss Eulie and her harp arrived?"

Miss Eulie was the area's foremost musician. She played a huge gold harp, and Tiger had sent for it via a wagon driven by Billy Bob. Later, there'd be fiddlers for dancing, but for the ceremony itself, harp music was scheduled to transport them all to paradise.

"Ah believe she's already set up, deah, an' waitin' for the doin's to commence," Peonie informed her. "Mary's here, too, bidin' her time in the pantry 'til you make your appearance, then she'll come in and join Omoroh."

"Mary's arrived? Then I best go downstairs

427

immediately. . . . Will you signal that I'm ready, Hattie?"

"O' course, darlin' . . . Jus' don't you go trippin' down them stairs now."

"I won't, I promise." Freedom smiled. Hattie and Peonie reminded her of two mother hens clucking over the same chick, but apparently, there was no real jealousy between them. She was delighted they were going into business together; their plans would surely meet with success.

While Hattie hurried away, Peonie took her arm and led her to the wide staircase. "Oh, mah, with you and Mary both gettin' married, ah'm nervous as can be."

"Now, Peonie, there won't be a single mishap. You and Hattie have thought of everything."

"Well, ah do wish ah knew more of the guests. Most of 'em are strangers to me."

"Me, too," Freedom reminded her, whispering as they approached the stairs.

The strains of harp music drifted up the stairwell, along with the sweet scent of roses. A wave of excitement flowed through Freedom. The moment had arrived. She exchanged another embrace with Peonie, then slowly began descending the stairs. People overflowed the drawing room and front parlor, spilling into the hallway. All eyes turned to look at her. With a start, Freedom realized that a huge bear of a man looking uncomfortable in a black suit and stiff white cravat was Stoker Harris, Ty's chief engineer.

Glancing at the sea of strange faces, she recognized Pete Gambol, Matt Berringer, and several other men from the *Sea Whisper*. And there was Colonel and Mrs. Lamb, smiling widely and nodding at her, the colonel quite recovered from the injuries he'd suffered during the bombardment of Fort Fisher. Beside the Lambs stood the Ortons, also smiling, as if neither minded that one of their own tarheels was marrying a Northern girl. Then she saw the face she loved above all others — Ty's face, turned up to her with a broad grin and a twinkle in his violet-colored eyes.

As she reached the last step, he extended his hand to her, and she felt as if she were moving in a daze, conscious only of Ty's presence flooding her senses. He was resplendent in buff and chocolate brown, which set off his sun-bronzed skin and white-blond hair to perfection. The crowd parted, and she walked beside Ty, coming to stand before the preacher — a different fellow than the one who had performed the burial service for Ty's mother. Mary, looking incredibly lovely in a plain white gown sparingly trimmed with lace, joined Omoroh, and they both came to stand beside Freedom and Ty.

Freedom heard a slight murmuring behind her at the inclusion of a Negro couple in the ceremony, but she paid it no heed. Mary and Omoroh would have a second ceremony among their own people — something involving jumping over a broomstick — but Ty had joined her in adamantly insisting that their two dear friends be joined in marriage in the traditional manner of free people everywhere. Despite his pessimism regarding the future, Ty was at least no longer hiding the fact of his liberal beliefs.

The preacher began speaking, but Freedom scarcely heard a word he said. She recited her vows in a calm, unruffled manner, her commitment having long ago been made and the vows only reaffirming it. Ty's voice vibrated with deep emotion when he spoke his, and Freedom blinked back tears as she listened. After they were finished, it was Mary's and Omoroh's turn. Omoroh indicated his intentions with firm nods, which Mary obliging translated. "Yes, he says, Omoroh says yes, he teks me to be his wife."

Titters of laughter ran through the assembly, to which Mary responded with a regal straightening of her shoulders that silenced everyone. Afterwards, as Freedom returned Tiger's kiss, her joy brimmed to overflowing. The day was perfect. Their wedding was perfect. Their love was perfect . . . and their life together would be perfect, too.

As the ceremony ended, well-wishers swamped Freedom and Ty. Freedom had only a moment to hug Mary and Omoroh, then she was being kissed and hugged by people she didn't even know. For the next two hours, she barely had time to catch her breath. Feasting and dancing followed the wedding ceremony. At some point, Mary and Omoroh slipped out to join their own people, and when Freedom noticed they were missing, she grabbed Ty's hand.

"Ty, let's go see what's happening at Omoroh's house. . . . It isn't right we can't celebrate together, with guests of both weddings mingling. This is a good chance to show everyone that here at Cypress Hall, we don't make distinctions between black and white; we're committed to equality for everyone."

Ty raised his eyebrows at the suggestion, then leaned forward and kissed the tip of her nose. "I have a feeling," he said, "That life with you is going to be very interesting. . . . All right, let's join them, and if our guests want to come along, too, they can. If not, they can stay here and celebrate our wedding without us."

Hand in hand, Freedom and Ty left their guests and strolled behind the big house toward the sounds of laughter and merrymaking coming from the workers' quarters. When they arrived, everyone applauded, then applauded even harder when Ty seized Mary's hand and danced a reel to the fiddler's tune. Grinning, he handed Mary over to Omoroh, then grabbed Freedom and whirled her around until she was breathless and laughing.

"That's enough for you, my dear," he finally growled. "We wouldn't want to harm the mousling."

"Oh, Mousling loves to dance. . . . Feel how hard he's kicking me." Freedom placed Ty's hands on her swollen belly, inside which their baby was kicking up his heels.

Tiger never seemed to tire of feeling her stomach, and a look of wonder always came over his face as he did so. While he was thus absorbed in the miracle of new life growing inside her, she raised her head, glanced over his shoulder, and saw three black-clad, stern-faced gentlemen riding dusty horses down the back road that led to Wilmington. Something about the men—they weren't dressed as if for a wedding—made her frown. She did not recognize any of them, though that wasn't so strange in itself, since she didn't know half the people at Cypress Hall this afternoon.

"Ty, who are those men? Do you know them?"

"What men?" Ty's hand was still on her belly, his expression tender and possessive.

All around them, the Negroes were laughing, joking, and dancing. Some of their white guests

431

were en route down the cobblestoned path to join them, Peonie and Hattie among them. Omoroh and Mary were dancing together, too wrapped in each other to pay anyone else any mind.

"Those men riding up . . . Those men with muskets."

Even as she said it, the man in the lead slowed his horse to a standstill, picked up his gun, and aimed it at the crowd of celebrating Negroes. The other two men drew rein beside him and leveled their own muskets at the throng. The faces of all three were furious, as if what they were seeing somehow enraged them.

"Om'roh!" the lead man shouted. "Om'roh, you bastard, ah knew ah'd find you one day."

At the same moment, Ty spun around to see what was causing the commotion. Quickly, he stepped in front of Freedom, putting his own body between her and the intruders. "Stay back," he whispered urgently. "I'll handle these trouble-makers."

Freedom stood on tiptoe to see past him. Omoroh and Mary had stopped dancing, and Omoroh had instinctively moved to shield Mary from the man with the gun. The man abruptly raised it, and sighted down the barrel at Omoroh.

"Might have known ah'd discover a runaway livin' the good life as if he didn't have no sense. Ah been on your tail for more'n three years now, and ah've finally caught up with you. . . . Say your prayers, Om'roh, 'cause today's your last day on earth."

"Wait, stop!" Mary shrieked, throwing herself in front of her new husband.

"Hold it!" Ty shouted, striding forward. "Whoever you are, you can't ride onto my property and shoot one of my people, even if he is a black man . . . or a runaway slave. Haven't you heard? The war's over, and the slaves are all freed."

Ty approached the mounted trio confidently, and Freedom hurried after him, fearing for his safety as well as Omoroh's. These were not the type of men to respect anyone, not even an authoritative figure like Ty. They had a look of ruthlessness about them, and Ty was unarmed. As she drew nearer, she could detect the odor of whiskey mixed with the stench of sweat and leather. The intruders were half drunk and, despite the heat, hadn't bathed for days.

"We can shoot or hang a murderer," the lead man sneered. "An' that's whut this nigger is. He killed a white man down in Georgia. The dead man's brother hired us to bring 'im to justice."

"You're bounty hunters," Ty clipped. "You've never seen the man you want. How do you know my friend is the one you're looking for?"

The lead man shifted a wad of chewing tobacco from one bulging cheek to another. Then he spat on the ground near Ty's feet. Never looking away from Ty, he reached into a pocket and withdrew a wrinkled sheet of paper. "Shore looks like 'im, don't it?"

He handed Ty the paper. Freedom stood on tiptoe to read it over Ty's shoulder. She had seen the circular before; it contained an excellent likeness of Omoroh, and the description matched perfectly. "That's not Samson," she denied. "Not *our* Samson, whose wedding we're celebrating today."

"It sure as hell is," the man disputed. "And his name ain't Samson. It's Om'roh. Fool claims he's a

African prince."

"That old circular doesn't constitute proof," Freedom started to argue, but Ty stopped her with an upraised hand.

"How did you happen to come here looking for him?" he asked the tobacco-chewing man.

The man grinned, revealing chipped brown teeth. "A pretty lady over to Clairmont Gardens sent us. Seems she was mighty put out she didn't get no invitation to these here doin's. . . . We been ridin' up and down the river askin' folks did they know him, an' she jus' happen to say yes."

"Miss Stephanie Clairmont is mistaken," Ty drawled with a calm Freedom knew was deceptive. "This man grew up here. . . . He's my overseer. I admit to a distant resemblance, but you know Negroes; they all look alike."

"Then why don't he defend hisself? Why's he jus' standin' there like the cat's got his tongue?" The man chuckled and turned to his comrades, who broke into loud guffaws. "You like that li'l joke, boys? The cat's got his tongue all right, don't it?"

Ty turned to Omoroh and Mary. Omoroh was standing stiff and straight, nostrils flared, his dark face filled with fear and fury. Mary was clinging to him and sobbing under her breath. "Oh, no, Lawd . . . not now. Not aftah all this time."

"Don't open your mouth, Samson," Ty cautioned. "There's no need for you to defend yourself to this riffraff. You're a free man who's got witnesses to the truth. We'll speak on your behalf."

"Listen to Captain Carrington, gentlemen," Freedom cried. "This isn't the man you're looking for. He's been here for years and years, running this plantation while the captain was away at war."

"What proof you got, lady? It ain't us, but *you* that needs the proof."

"I *can* prove it," Freedom asserted, amazing even herself. Spying Peonie at the edge of the gathering crowd of guests, Freedom beckoned to her. "Peonie, go back to the house and bring the inkpot, a pen, and some paper, will you?"

Peonie nodded, her eyes wide, and hurried away, with Hattie close at her heels.

"Whut you need with that stuff? We ain't gonna pen no letters," the tobacco-lover sneered.

"Is the man you're looking for literate? Can he write his name . . . do sums . . . write even *your* name, assuming you have one?"

"Naw . . . 'course not. He's jus' a poor dumb nigger. He cain't even speak English. That's why his old master—the one he killed—cut out his tongue. He'd only speak the gibberish of where he come from."

"This man not only speaks English, he writes it—a rather unusual feat for a 'poor dumb nigger,' wouldn't you say?"

The tobacco-lover narrowed his eyes suspiciously. "Niggers cain't write."

"Can you, sir?" Freedom boldly inquired, while Ty stood listening incredulously, allowing her to pursue this farfetched possibility for convincing these men that Omoroh was someone else entirely.

The man scowled. "Ah can read mah own name well enough."

"What is your name?"

"Clem . . . Clem Stoddard."

"Is that spelled C-l-e-m? And the Stoddard has two *d*'s?"

"Ah reckon so," Clem said.

Freedom glanced significantly at Omoroh, warning him with her eyes to remain calm and play along, as if he really were innocent.

"What's the name of the plantation this slave escaped?" Ty asked Clem.

"Rosemont," Clem answered. "It's down in Central Georgia."

"I'm amazed there's a Rosemont left, after what Sherman did to Georgia."

"Part of it is still standin'," Clem confirmed. "Lucky fer us, the war didn't affect none of what we do. The man who hired us still wants Om'roh dead, war or no war. Cain't let coloreds, even a prime buck like this 'un, get away with killin' white men. . . . You're a Southern gen'leman; you oughta know that."

"Oh, I do," Ty smoothly agreed. "But I won't allow a friend of mine to be killed because of a case of mistaken identity."

"We ain't mistaken," Clem growled. "He looks jus' like the drawin' on that circular ah give you. Ah'd stake mah life that he's the same man."

"Can't be. . . . Samson's been in my family for as long as I can remember. He almost *is* family. That's why we're celebrating his wedding along with my own . . . Would I lie about a thing like that, gentlemen?"

"Clem," one of the other men whined. "whut we waitin' for? If you need proof, jus' make the man open his mouth. If he ain't got a tongue, then he's the man we're lookin' for."

"I'm afraid that wouldn't prove anything, gentlemen," Ty said. "You see, Samson hasn't got a tongue, either. I cut it off myself when we were both lads and he stuck it out at me once too often.

436

Swiped at him with a bread knife. Didn't mean to really hurt him. Been sorry about it ever since. It's damned inconvenient always having to wait for Samson to write down what he wants to say."

Clem's face grew livid. "You tek me fer a fool? You're lyin' to me, sir!"

"No, I'm not," Ty insisted. Just then, Peonie came hurrying through the crowd of Negroes and whites who had pressed closer to watch the spectacle.

From the corner of her eye, Freedom saw Colonel Lamb and his wife approaching in Peonie's wake. The colonel's presence gave her confidence that somehow things might work out.

"Heah ah am, Freedom! Heah's the writin' materials you wanted!"

Freedom hurried to take them from Peonie's hands. "Now, Samson, come over to the table. We'll show these three gentlemen that we're not lying."

With Mary clinging tightly to her new husband's arm, Omoroh walked slowly to one of the long tables bearing remnants from the wedding feast.

"Watch closely, gentlemen!" Freedom called. "Samson is about to demonstrate that he can't be the man you're looking for."

His face impassive, regal as a king's, Omoroh picked up the pen, dipped it into the inkpot, and bent over the paper. When he had finished, he lifted the paper and placed it in Freedom's slightly trembling hand. She bore it carefully back to the hard-eyed trio on horseback.

"There!" she exclaimed triumphantly. "Mr. Stoddard, isn't that your name?"

Clem took the paper and stared hard at it. From

his expression, Freedom could tell he was dumb-struck. Behind him, his men muttered their displeasure. "Hell, Clem, you cain't read. How'd you know if that was even your name?"

"Shaddup!" Clem roared, still squinting at what Omoroh had written.

"That *is* your name, isn't it, Mr. Stoddard?" Freedom prompted.

"Damn uppity nigger. Where'd you l'arn to write like that?" Clem exploded.

"Is there a problem heah, Ty?" Colonel Lamb inquired, stepping forward. "Anythin' ah can help with?"

"Not really," Tiger said. "These gentlemen are on the trail of a murderer, but he's not to be found at Cypress Hall."

"Well, then, ah suggest they move along and not cause you any trouble. . . . Ah'm Colonel William Lamb, boys, a close friend of Cap'n Carrin'ton. If he says y'all made a mistake, ah'm sure he's right. An' there's plenty of men heah who'll back 'im up."

Freedom glanced in the direction of the big house and saw that all of the guests had gathered, and the men of the group were walking slowly toward them. Several had guns from the gun case in the library in their hands. Peonie and Hattie must have warned them of pending trouble.

"Y'all won't get away with this!" one of the mounted men cried. "We know that's the nigger whut killed a man in Georgia, an' we aim to collect the reward for 'im."

"Now, boys, don't get riled an' do somethin' foolish," Colonel Lamb placated.

Clem was still looking down at his name written

on the paper. "This is mah name, Ezra. . . . Ah know mah own name when ah see it. How can a nigger whut cain't even speak English write mah name as clear as this?"

"So whut if it ain't the right nigger? He *looks* enough like 'im to be his brother. Nobody'll know in Georgia. They'll string him up an' feel right good about it."

"You'd take a man back to Georgia and hang him, knowing he's not the man you want?" Ty demanded in a voice that raised goose bumps on Freedom's flesh.

"He's only a nigger, Cap'n."

"Get off my land!" Ty shouted. "You miserable, godforsaken scum-butts! Get off my land before I tear you apart. . . . Do you think you're better than all these fine people here, just because your skins are white?"

Ty gestured to the wide-eyed Negroes behind him. They were, Freedom realized, the people who had served him well all his life, laboring long and hard while he was gone, so he'd have something to come back to after the war ended. They were the ones who had been his friends and stood by him, while others had turned away. They were his family—more his family than his own mother had been.

"Your day is done, gentlemen," Ty continued furiously. "Your day is gone. No longer can you strut and swagger, thinking yourself better than others because an accident of creation made you spring forth from the wombs of white women instead of black women. . . . There's a new day coming. In fact, it's already here. Now a man will be judged by his deeds, not by the color of his skin. Now the whole world will discover what it should have known long ago: A black man is as good as a white man. The two are equal. The only thing that separates and sets them apart are circumstances—how much education they receive, who goes to school and who doesn't, who's taught to use his head, not just his hands. . . . You can't hide your ugliness behind your white skins any longer, you miserable little gutter rats. Now all men will know and judge you for what you are—the scum of the South, a plague on all of us, the cause of half the problems we've ever had. . . ."

As Ty paused to catch his breath, Colonel Lamb spoke into the shocked silence, "Ah think you boys best move on, b'foh mah friend here starts foamin' at the mouth or grabbin' for a gun. . . . Y'all have to excuse him, but he feels mighty strongly on the subject of his Nigras."

"He's a plain, ravin' madman," Clem opined. "An' him a cotton planter whut should know better."

"You're the one who should know better," Ty grated. "Get off my land."

"Ty . . ." Freedom laid a restraining hand on Tiger's arm. She agreed with everything he said but didn't want him to get shot for saying it. The opinions he had just expressed weren't shared by everyone; she feared his own white guests might turn on him.

As the three sullen men turned their horses and retreated back down the dusty road, Ty's guests—both black and white—surged forward to clap him on the back or shake his hand. Freedom was stunned, then thrilled, by their response to Ty's inflammatory speech.

440

"You told 'em, Cap'n, an' you're right. It's the white trash who cause most of the trouble, not the coloreds or the decent white folks," one man said.

To Freedom's surprise, the speaker was one of the Ortons. Colonel Lamb then steered Ty away from her, talking as he did so.

"Ty, you oughta give some thought to runnin' for the legislature or takin' ovah that new Freedman's Bureau bein' set up to help the Nigras. We're gonna need schools for 'em, food an' clothin' 'til they find payin' jobs, an' all sorts of help. . . . You're the sorta man we want to make the decisions that need to be made. There's tryin' times ahead, make no mistake, but with the right kind of leadership, we'll survive 'em. An' we'll get back on our feet."

"I wasn't planning on getting involved," Freedom heard Ty say, but his objections only met with stronger encouragement.

"We need men like you to help rebuild the South, Ty. You cain't say no."

Freedom smiled to herself. She noticed Mary was smiling, too, and so was Omoroh. "My goodness," she said, hugging them both. "Didn't you think, just for a few moments, there, that my new husband almost sounded like me . . . a rabid Northern abolitionist?"

"Yes, Ma'am, he did," Mary agreed. "That's exactly what he sounded like."

"Ah do declare," Freedom said, affecting the thickest Southern drawl she could manage. "Ah think there's hope for that man yet, darlin's. Yes, ah surely do."

Epilogue

January 1, 1866

Freedom bent over the huge cradle holding her
five-month-old son and gently kissed his plump
pink cheek. He was already asleep and didn't stir
as she tucked the quilt more closely around his
sturdy body.

"Good night, my little tiger cub. . . . What a
name . . . Cub Carrington. You'll probably hate it
as you grow up. Oh, you're so beautiful, the most
beautiful thing I've ever seen."

With a long sigh, she drew back and stood staring down at the baby for several moments, admir-
ing his wispy blond curls and pink and white
perfection. He was the image of his father, except
for his big brown eyes, closed now until the morning. "Yes, you're every bit as lovely as your father,"
she whispered dreamily.

"You really think I'm *lovely?*" growled a male
voice behind her.

"Ty! Must you always sneak up on me when I
least expect you? I thought you'd gone to bed al-

442

ready. Last night's New Year's celebration did rob us of a whole night's sleep."

"I was lonesome for you," Ty murmured, slipping his arms around her waist. "I can't sleep without you in bed beside me."

"Hush . . . Talk softer or you'll awaken Cub."

"No, I won't. That kid sleeps like a drunken sailor." His grip on her waist tightened. "Come to bed, now, Mouse. . . . I mean it. The bed feels empty when I'm in it all by myself."

"Poor boy," Freedom mocked. "We can't do anything when I get there, anyway. You need your sleep. Don't you have to leave tomorrow for an important meeting with the other members of the legislature?"

Ty had been elected to state office in the fall and was already being bombarded with problems. She was just glad he hadn't won a seat in Congress; on the national level, the House of Representatives was refusing to admit the newly elected members of the Southern states. And she knew precisely how Ty would respond to a situation as unfair as *that*.

"Yes, I have to leave tomorrow. . . . That's why I want to make love to you tonight. I might be gone for quite some time. We're trying to adopt a Black Code, based on the report of the commission appointed to study the Negro problem. Unfortunately, the issues are extremely sensitive: Should freedmen be allowed to vote? To serve on juries? To testify in court against white men? To ride in the same railway cars, eat in the same places, go to the same schools? My head is spinning from all these questions."

"You'll find the right answers," Freedom soothed.

"That's not what's worrying me. I already know the right answers. What I *don't* know is if I can persuade others to accept them. I think, to do what I want, we're going to need another amendment to the Constitution of the United States."

Freedom pulled away from Ty's grasp. "Come to bed, then. . . . You need your rest. I foresee another long, hard battle ahead of you."

"No more battles . . . I'm sick of battles," Ty complained, following her out of the room. "They keep me away from you for too long a time."

Freedom led him into their darkened room, then turned and went into his arms. "But that's what life is, my darling, a series of battles. We must stand and fight bravely, one battle after another."

"You're the fighter in the family, not me." Ty nuzzled her hair. "I'm more the lover."

Freedom pressed her body to his. "Then what are you waiting for?" she whispered huskily. "If you're the lover, you had better prove it."

He tilted her face to meet his kiss. It was a long, wonderful kiss that made her tingle right down to her toes. When he was finished, he said, "As long as you're beside me, Mouse, I can fight any battle that comes along."

"I am beside you—today and always, Ty. We're fighting on the same side now."

"The same side, today and always," he echoed. "The tiger and the mouse."

"And the cub . . ." she added, drawing his face down again, so their mouths could meet. "I love you, Ty. . . . Now, will you please stop talking?"

"Gladly," he murmured. "There's nothing more to say."

"Oh, yes, there is," she contradicted. "Say I love

you back."

"I love your back," he muttered wickedly, stroking her through her nightgown. "And your front, too. It's . . . *lovely*," he mocked.

"Honestly, Ty . . ."

"Honestly, Mouse . . ."

And suddenly there *wasn't* anything more to say — not with words, anyway. The language spoken by their hands, mouths, and bodies was much more powerful, much more fufilling. . . . So they talked far into the night, saying the precious, private things that only lovers say . . . and loving every minute of it.

Afterword From The Author

The blockade-runners of the Civil War were larger-than-life romantic figures who enabled the Confederacy to keep fighting far longer than anyone thought possible. Tiger and Freedom are fictional characters, but they are true to the spirit of the times, when good people on both sides of the conflict could find no common ground of agreement. Omoroh, the African slave-prince, was derived from a real person, though I changed the details of his life, and the siege of Fort Fisher is as true and accurate as I could make it.

If you ever visit Nassau in the Bahamas, be sure and stop by the ruins of the Royal Victoria Hotel. The ghosts of the dashing blockade-runners haunt its wide verandas. You have only to close your eyes and listen; they will whisper their stories on the soft island breezes . . . and one of those stories might well involve a handsome blond tarheel and a little mouse of a girl from Boston, who wanted all men to be free. . . .

Dear Reader,
Zebra Books welcomes your comments about this book or any other Zebra historical romance you have read recently. Please address your comments to:

Zebra Books, Dept. WM
475 Park Avenue South
New York, NY 10016

Thank you for your interest.

Sincerely,
The Editorial Department
Zebra Books